THE DRIFTER

and Other Unusual Tales

EDITED BY

DIANA KATHRYN PLOPA

For reprint permissions, write to:
Pages Promotions, LLC
Birmingham, MI 48009
Info@PagesPromotions.com

© 2022 Pages Promotions, LLC
Edited by Diana Kathryn Plopa

Paperback ISBN: 978-1628282702
E-book ISBN: 978-1628282719
Hardcover ISBN: 978-1628282757
Library of Congress Control Number: 2022919143

TABLE OF CONTENTS

THE POWER OF THE PEN

We believe a more harmonious and supportive society begins with literacy. We believe that a successful life begins with, and is enhanced by, the written word. We believe that not everyone is able or inclined to pick up trash by the side of the road, give blood or donate financially to contribute to their community's well-being. We know there must be an alternative. We believe that alternative is the Power of The Pen!

To support the needs of the world's illiterate population and to give writers a place to share their talent and creativity, we have created a Community Service Anthology Project Program. Two or three times per year, we offer enticing prompts that, when multiple authors contribute, result in a stunning book created from our combined creative energies. Writers of Every Age, Stage, and (nearly) Every Genre Are Welcome To Submit! We offer novice and experienced writers alike the opportunity to join together to create a force to be reckoned with... shared experience through the written word. In addition, student contributors are offered community service certificates to help them achieve their graduation requirements while investigating the potential of their imagination.

One of the things that gives the pursuit of writing meaning is the impact our words have on the lives of others. Whether real or imagined, what we write can, and often does, spark tremendous connectivity with our readers. Words give others permission to feel, learn, and understand points of view or concepts that perhaps they would not have encountered had they not picked up a book.

Works of charity, we believe, are essential to the empathetic, evolutionary path humanity must travel if it is going to sustain and prevail throughout the next seven generations and beyond.

Without the goal of improving literacy standards worldwide, our society is doomed to fail. An illiterate population hinders every aspect of a country's development... it's economy, agriculture, industry and manufacturing, arts, sciences, technology, and most importantly, governing. A society that lacks basic literacy skills is threatened by terrorists, despots, and, most tragically, apathy.

We hope you enjoy reading these stories as much as we enjoyed writing them.

THE HALEY SUE FOUNDATION

Out of everything, there can still be a positive, no matter how negative that thing may be. In 2020 Haley Sue Pearson was a vibrant and alive teacher, singer, friend, coach, wife, daughter, niece, and cousin and was working toward changing the world. She wasn't necessarily changing the world by some grandiose gesture, but instead, she was doing it in an intelligent and concise manner, one person at a time.

Her patient way and adaptable mindset made her everyone's best friend. Some people would say the very idea of her being everyone's best friend was difficult, but Haley honestly was everyone's best friend. She listened, and more importantly, she heard. She wanted to consistently make a difference with every person she came in contact with. She was not in any way shallow or fake but instead was highly adaptable and quickly understood the needs of others.

As a teacher, Haley quickly found the lowest common denominator and showed others what was necessary to succeed. As a friend, Haley paid attention to who you were and made you the center of her universe. In each thing Haley did, she pushed for excellence and pressed to be the best she could be.

It is with that thought of excellence, achievement, and willingness to sacrifice to change the world even a little that the **Haley Sue Foundation** was built. Each year the Haley Sue Foundation will make a difference in a young person's life by giving a scholarship to help with college expenses. The foundation will also be involved in changing the world every day. Whether it is a small gesture or a massive movement, the Foundation will inspire the passions of both young and old and keep the light of Haley Sue shining.

If you believe that everyone who wants to make a difference deserves a chance, then please visit **thehaleysuefoundation.org** and consider helping to change the world, one person at a time.

~Andrew Allen Smith
The Haley Sue Foundation

Contributing Authors

- Amy Klco
- Andrew Allen Smith
- Anonymous
- Ariana Beemer
- Chelsea Gouin
- Chris Nardone
- Christian Collison
- Colleen Alles
- Craig Brockman
- Danielle Ice
- Diana Kathryn Plopa
- D.J. Matthews
- E.M. Reed
- Gabriel Mero
- H.G. Evans
- Jase Riemersma-Cote
- J.L. Royce
- John Bronwen
- Johnny Steven Zawacki
- Ken MacGregor
- Leslie Cieplechowicz
- Lindsey Russell
- Marianne Wieland
- Mary Beth Magee
- Mary-Jane Belko
- Mary Ring
- Matt Lubbers-Moore
- Michael Simpson
- Nicole e. Castle
- R.L. Fink
- Siete 16
- Taysia Lucas
- Veronica Sanchez

25 MARSDEN AVENUE

John Bronwen

Marsden Avenue was an unassuming place in an equally anonymous town of Jensen in Colorado. The neighbors knew each other and were very polite.

All except one house.

25.

It didn't look very different from any of the houses on the street, just a practical little house with a white picket fence – perfect for starting a family.

But no one had lived at 25 Marsden Avenue since the 1950s.

Patrick and Jennifer had long heard the ghost and horror stories behind 25 Marsden Avenue. How the basement whispered in the ear of one Joe Hardy, a supposed owner of the house, and ordered him to kill his family. That was the favorite story of ghosts and ghouls for Patrick and Jennifer, although there were more garish stories to be had – each more Stephen King-esque by the second.

It was why they'd broken in the day before Halloween, to scope the house and search for any signs of paranormal activities for TikTok.

After sneaking out of Jennifer's grandmother's home and climbing a tree to break in through the window, the two had spent the better part of half of an hour looking around.

Apart from one screech owl that had given them both a heart attack, they'd had no poltergeist, werewolf, or even an evil clown creep through. It would be something to say on the school bus on Monday – just how boring it was.

"Maybe it'll be better downstairs?" suggested Patrick, trying to shrug off his disappointment.

"What is that smell?" Jennifer huffed as she walked downstairs. A beam flashed in, and she quickly jumped to the floor. "Get down; someone's outside."

Patrick had already ducked down behind a banister, hoping his shadow didn't show from the light cast from the beam. There were a few moments of studious light moving before the light vanished. "Let's get out of here."

"Don't be such a chicken," scolded Jennifer, waiting a few moments before pointing. "Look, that's where my gran's basement is. We can go down that way; check it out."

"Everything else has been a dud," muttered Patrick, standing and following her.

They headed down the stairs, two steps at a time, unafraid due to their recent disappointments. This was only compounded by a look around the basement. Just an average basement. No rocking chair in the corner, no crazed witch. Empty bar two living souls.

"Well, this was crap," huffed Patrick. "Could've spent the night watching *The Silver Bullet,* not hanging around this dump."

Jennifer didn't answer, content to watch the shivering shadows on the old brick wall, rueful that the house was merely a ghost story.

It was almost a shame that they both realized it at exactly same time that they had turned out their beams.

It was a blatant disappointment in their haste to stay exactly where they were that they comprehended that the light was shining behind them to cast their shadows.

It was pure devastation when they turned around and met a nightmare come true.

A Promise is a Promise

Nicole e. Castle

Travis stands on my porch as I look him up and down, stopping at the bulge in his muddy, blue shorts. I point a long finger at him, "Ya ain't got nothin' I want."

"I promise, Lou, you're gonna wanna see this!"

He steps closer and stares hard at my tits. I don't mind.

"Comin'?"

I take hold of his sweaty hand.

****

Travis has no car, so we have to walk out to the lake.

"Damn, am I stupid," I mutter to myself.

I kick at the dirt. There's been no rain for months, and the dust blows up into my face. Travis laughs his real dumb ignorant laugh.

"Shut up, asshole!" He doesn't like that. "Travis, you know you ain't gettin' none, right?"

"Come on, Miss Louise. I know you're a lady."

I shoot him the eye and stop dead. "Is that what this is about?"

"Naw, honest. I gotta show you somethin'. Somethin' you ain't never seen before."

By now, we've been walking about half an hour, and it's the hottest part of the day. I'm getting ornery. But it's real hard to be mad at Travis. He looks so much like a little boy, his blonde hair stuck up in front and back and the sides. Real cute, in that dumb boy kind of way.

"What're you thinkin' 'bout Travis? Why you so quiet?" He looks at me a real long time.

"I got lots on my mind. I come out here to think, you know. I'm a thinker."

I snicker.

"There ain't nobody I wanted to show it to but you."

"Really? You're just messin' with me, Travis."

"Believe whatchya want to," he pouts.

I pull on his arm. It's sticky. He's breathing heavy. I kiss him, the sweat on my lips mixing with his. He grabs onto my ass and pulls me into him. We stay that way, grinding together in the heat. He forces my mouth open, his slimy tongue pushing down my throat. Then we split and start walking again.

"Let's get to the lake. We can do more there," I tell him.

"Really?"

He smiles. I smile back, licking my lips.

****

I smell the lake before we get there. I don't say anything; no need to spoil his surprise.

"Okay, here we go. Better let me hold your hand."

The lake is below us, straight down the hill.

"What a gentleman you are, Travis." He looks at me cross-eyed, and I giggle. "What's wrong with the trees, Travis?"

"It's been the drought. They's all dryin' up." All around us, the trees are shriveled. The flowers, too. Things all around us, dying.

"This is an ugly place, Travis. 'Specially for thinkin'.'"

"Follow me; this ain't it."

I follow him. We go along a dried-up stream, and the smell of something foul grows.

He runs ahead, and I run after him, tripping our way through briars, blackberry bushes, and brown shrubs.

I almost crash into him as he shouts, "Ta da! Here it is!"

I look at the silent, murky water behind him.

"What's so great about this stinkin' pond, Travis?"

He points out to the water, and I follow his tobacco-stained finger.

"See it?"

I look harder. There in the inky water, on a pile of mud and grass, I see something. "What's that?"

"I saw it a couple days ago. My guess it's lived here for some time, but the drought's forced it up top. Crazy, ain't it?"

And yes, it's crazy. "Is it still alive?"

"I think so. Every so often it'll move, just a hair."

"Gator?"

"Maybe, but a real big one."

And it's huge. Bigger than any I'd ever seen in life or on TV.

"Should we call somebody? Maybe they can help it."

"Naw, this here's its home. Leave it be. Anyways, the sun's cookin' its innards. It don't have long to live anyhow."

I look at him and shrug. I can see his cock is hard. I touch it. It twitches.

"Travis..."

He grabs my arms and pulls me closer.

"Hold it there a minute, lover boy. I gotta see if you're a boy or a man."

He looks at me, this weird glimmer in his eyes.

"Huh?"

"I dare you to swim out halfway and swim back. Then you can do whatever you want to me."

Travis looks at the water, then at me.

"Damn girl, you're crazy! That thing'll eat me up."

"Come on, Travis. I triple-dog-dare you. 'Sides it's half dead. The sun's killin' it for sure. You said so's yourself."

The sun is still high in the sky. The gnats are busy, but we hardly notice. There are bigger things at stake here.

"So?"

He eyes the water, and then he looks at the critter. It hasn't moved since we got there. He sticks one crusty toe in.

"It's warm."

"Then jump in. Get some of the stank off you!"

I grin. And sure as shit, he jumps right in and swims for his life toward the middle of the pond.

I keep an eye on the critter. It still hasn't moved. Travis is fast. He waves to me as he reaches the middle, then heads back. The boy sure can swim.

"Lose those shorts, girl! Your man's a comin'!"

With a quiet grace, it slides from its spot. It makes no sound moving through the shallow water.

"Better hurry up, boy. I'm waitin'." I sit on the bank and watch. It's almost upon him.

I feel bad for a minute.

"You might wanna hurry, Travis."

But it's too late. I see Travis' blonde head one second, smiling at me, and then with a mighty tug, under he goes.

I shiver.

Sorry, Travis. I was up here last week. He spoke to me first, and a promise is a promise.

I keep my eyes on the black water. A pink-tinged foam washes up, swirling around my bare feet.

I wait. Out of the pond, it lands at my feet with a thud.

I pick it up as rain clouds move in. It's the size of an apple, heavy and round. The gold ball shines like a miniature sun in the palm of my hand.

I press it to my cheek. It's cold.

ALICE'S WONDER LAND

Chelsea Gouin

Alice smoothed out her blue gown; she despised wrinkles. Not that her appearance mattered here, anyway. She never knew who she would bump into in this Wonder Land. She had already met a number of colorful characters that had sent her on many odd adventures. She feared she'd never understand this strange land.

"Oh, where is that silly cat?" she asked impatiently. It was almost tea time, and the Cat had promised to escort her to the party. Alice didn't particularly like tea but didn't want to appear rude and miss the party. Besides, the Mad Hatter was looking pretty dashing these days.

Growing impatient, Alice decided to find her own way. The Cat could make his own excuses when he arrived. With a happy skip, she started down the road. Perhaps she would find the kindly Field Mouse along the way. Or those silly Tweedles.

Alice's stroll was cut short, however, when she was knocked over by a rather solid and smoky mass. "Who are you?" the being asked.

She squinted, trying to see the figure through the smoky barrier. "I'm Alice."

"Who?"

"Just Alice," she clarified. Through the haze, she could just make out his eyes, his stare both cold and calculating. She felt uncomfortable underneath his stare and tried to appear confident. However, as his figure became clear, she noticed multiple arms protruding from his form. Now she understood, he was a large caterpillar! Alice was a proper lady, and she certainly did not discuss matters with giant bugs. Politely, she explained she was late for tea and left his presence promptly.

"Allllice..." She had only walked a few paces before she heard the eerie whisper. "Oh, Aliiiiice..." She must have taken a wrong turn, for the alley she was traveling was dark. A cold chill trickled down her spine. "You're late, Alice."

"Cat? Cheshire Cat? Is that you?" she questioned, her voice a strangled octave.

"She's coming for you, Alice. The Queen. She's coming for you." He sounded so close, and yet Alice still could not see him through the thick darkness. "And if she finds you... she'll take your head. No one escapes the Queen of Hearts."

Alice began to run. A cry of fear ripped from her throat as eyes began to peer through the blackness at her. She was a fool to think that Cat would help her out. He was never helpful before, sending her on a mad chase about the Wonder Land. And now, he left her to fend for her life alone.

"There she is! Alice, stop!"

It was her, the Queen! The Queen had found her, and all Alice could do was keep running; keep running past the eyes, so many eyes! Why wouldn't they help her?

"Off with her head!"

The footsteps were catching up to her, so loud, pounding in her ears. The Queen's guards were closing in... they were going to cut off her head for the entertainment of the eyes.

"Off with her head!"

Hands gripped her upper arms in a vice grip. She screamed until her throat was raw, fought them with all her strength, and still, it was not enough. They dragged her back down the alley, back toward the Queen. Fear seized Alice, and the world began to shimmer before her.

"There you are, Alice. You've been a very bad girl."

She gave in and let the blackness take her.

****

"She's out of her bed again! And she missed her medication." Doctor Heart tutted pityingly as the two men situated Alice on a gurney. Knowing Alice's obsession with cleanliness, Doctor Heart was surprised to see just how ragged Alice's blue hospital gown was. After three months of being admitted into The Wonder's Psychiatric Hospital, Alice showed decreasing mental health. She frequently slipped away from reality and lived in a world of pure fantasy to such a degree that even Doctor Heart had not seen.

"Back to your rooms; the show is over!" she barked at the patients who still lingered at their doors. Turning, she faced her other patient, who was still grinning. "Oh, Chester. What am I to do with you? Always stirring up trouble, you are." Chester was stuck in a state of delirium and often fed into Alice's fantasies.

"I'll escort him back to his room, ma'am." Carter, one of her most trusted attendants, offered. He had been the one to report Alice's wandering after she ran into him on his smoke break.

Doctor Heart shook her head. It was always an "adventure" in Wonder Hospital.

ATTACK OF THE KARENS

Siete 16

He threw himself into an alley and crouched down. As he was trying to hide in the shadows, he worked on slowing his breathing. He had to catch his breath if he was going to run and escape, back into the shadows and into the night.

They never hunted their prey during the evening hours. Just during the daylight hours, from noon to sunset.

As he was trying to relax and focus on what he was to do next, he began to wonder if he would make it home and see his family again.

As he was about to take comfort that he would make it and he would lose his pursuers, he started to feel that he would be home and safe again. This night would be over.

Just as he was about to stand and start heading home, Miguel used caution when he looked out and checked both ways. Just like when he was taught by his father when crossing the street at four years old; and when he was fifteen, and he was learning to drive.

Miguel was about to get himself ready to run, but he paused; Miguel thought he heard them coming.

Their sound was not hard to distinguish from the usual sounds that the city made at this hour; over the sounds of cars driving by, tires treading on the road, dogs barking at intruders, and traffic lights clicking to signal who stops and goes.

Miguel had never heard their sound before, but today it would stay with him and haunt his memory. The Karens screeching.

During the day, The Karen is in perfect calmness in their world. The Karen would appear as an average soccer mom that you would know and possibly be friends with or related to.

They are polite, calm, friendly, and appear as a normal woman. As long as they are happy with what's around them. They are nothing to be feared, nor would you have to be wary of them.

But once something goes wrong or awry, or if they see something that they don't like, usually someone that does not look like them. If they see a person being somewhere they don't belong or where they shouldn't be, that's when they begin to change into something terrible. The change turns them from regular soccer moms or your favorite aunt or your best friend's mom; it changes them into something terrifying.

Their faces go through a horrid transformation. It turns them into scary monsters.

It starts with their faces turning flush from the bottom to their foreheads. The red color blotches their cheeks and nose and makes them bright red.

Then, their eyes change from normal and widen and twist shape. The corneas become riddled with blood veins that make them bloodshot, and their irises turn sanguine. The color shifts and swirls within their irises.

Next, their mouths began to shift and extend into a maniacal snarl, and their mandible extends to make their mouths larger. The transformation of their mouths makes it possible for an extra set of teeth to grow while their regular teeth turn into canine fangs.

Also, their hands shift and twist and turn into claws. Their fingers extend an extra inch in length, and their nails become razor-sharp claws. As wicked as the claws are, they are rarely used as weapons. They are used to be menacing instruments of judgment. The Karens use their claws to pass judgment by shaking their wicked first and second fingers at their intended target(s).

Finally, their voices screech in timorous tones that cause one's head to pound and are annoying as nails to a chalkboard to their victims. Their screech not only causes pain to the victim but also gives them a sense of fear and disgust that chills them to the core of their souls. It is not just the sound alone, but a victim can hear hateful rhetoric or derogatory words whispered... shouted... spoken at them that it re-vibrates in their ears and infects their hearts. So much that it brings out an anger that one would rather fight than run from The Karen.

For one to turn and fight a Karen would be a mistake. The Karens have some strange power to shift their appearance to others to look weak and helpless while their victim fights back. This usually makes the victim look more like the aggressor than The Karen attacking them first.

Miguel was about to let fear take over him, but he knew he couldn't. He had to keep his head. He was getting agitated because he wanted to be home, and he wanted to put this horror behind him.

Miguel listened. It sounded like the three Karens that were chasing him had left the area. He took in a deep breath and readied himself to run.

Miguel stepped out of the alley and began his run for home. He had not gotten further than four blocks, and he heard The Karens again.

"Wetback." "Spic." "Illegal." "Go back to Mexico."

Those words they had said earlier triggered their transformation and their need to hunt him. The Karens sounded like they were getting closer.

"Call Immigration." "Wetback." "Not an American." "Taco-Bender."

He was about to continue running, but his heart was getting infected. The anger was building up. Miguel felt the searing white heat from the anger build inside; the weight from the words, the infection, and the anger boiling in him was piling up in so many layers that he could not move one more step.

Miguel had no other choice. He could not run anymore. He had to turn to face them and stand his ground. This was exactly what The Karens usually wanted.

"Spic." "Fence-Jumper." "Narco-Mule." "Wetback." "Beaner."

Miguel was about to fight The Karens, but he was stopped. Red and Blue Lights flashed, and a siren wailed. Miguel felt a bit relieved. The police had arrived.

Miguel had taken a breath and exhaled to release the infection and relieve himself of the weight that The Karens had placed on him.

The Karens focused their vocal power on the police officers. The officers, under The Karens' spell, acted as their arms to punish Miguel.

Unsuspecting of this, Miguel was about to greet the police. Not returning his greeting, Miguel was thrown to the ground and handcuffed. The police arrested Miguel, read him his rights, and placed him in the back of their car.

As the door was closed after Miguel was placed in the back, the officers turned to ask the three women what had happened. Once the officers had taken their statements, they got in their car and took off with Miguel.

After the car left, The Karens looked at each other and began cackling in absolute delight. And as they laughed as their latest victim was taken away, they had shifted and transitioned from their everyday appearance to their Karen Persona.

"Success sisters," the brunette had a beaming smile on her face, "Our tenth one this week."

"Soon, sisters," the blonde added while wiping tears of joy from her eyes, "Soon all of those Beaners will be gone."

"Yes, sisters," the redhead continued, "America will be great again."

The three continued their laughing. Tomorrow there would be more for them to find and hunt. They would continue their twisted Karen fun.

AUNT JULIA

Mary-Jane Belko

Two sets of tire tracks in the mud marked the arrival and departure of the sheriff and the undertaker. Matthew Walker leaned forward and peered through the windshield until the mist blurred the scene before him. The sudden swipe of the wiper blades pushed him back in his seat, his arms rigid in front of him. His breath finally staggered from his lungs, and his hands dropped to his lap.

Was a box of old comic books worth going back there? It was the only happy memory he had from his childhood. *Yes, it was worth going back. Besides, she was dead. What harm could she do now?* Matthew put his truck into four-wheel drive and began the half-mile trip along the bumps and furrows of the dirt road.

Matthew had come to live in Aunt Julia's old farmhouse deep in the woods after his parents died in a house fire. Ten-year-old Matt was spending that night with a friend, pouring through his comic book collection. It would be the only thing left from his old life that he would bring with him to Aunt Julia's. He had left the box behind after he graduated high school, tucked away behind a loose board in his closet where Aunt Julia wouldn't find it. In his hurry to be free of her, he had forgotten it. He hadn't been back to the farm since.

Aunt Julia finally had the decency to die. Matthew got the call from Sheriff Bauer a week ago. Aunt Julia hadn't picked up her mail for days, by the looks of it, and the sheriff had reluctantly made the trip back to the farmhouse to check on her. He found her cold in her bed.

Matthew was relieved by the news. She was finally gone. He'd had no contact with her since he left, but he never escaped the memory of her. She lurked in a dark corner of his mind and sometimes burst in on his nightmares. He thought he'd never be rid of her.

Aunt Julia was his closest living relative. She was born and raised on the farm, as were her parents and grandparents before her—generations of Walkers. She never married, and as the rest of her family died off, she was left alone on the farm. With no husband or children to help her, the forest gradually overtook the plowed fields. She kept just enough land cleared to provide her with most of the food she needed—corn, beans, cabbage. The rest she walked a mile into town for, dragging a rusty grocery wagon behind her. Grocery aisles cleared at the sight of her, and she never had to wait in line for a cashier. Aunt Julia wanted to be left alone, and alone was what she got.

****

Escorted by his social worker, Ms. Snelling, young Matt had arrived at the farmhouse on a rainy autumn day just like this, two weeks after his world burned down. The clapboard house before him had never tasted paint, and the weathered lumber was as gray as the autumn forest around it. Aunt Julia, dressed in her signature gray dress, waited on the front porch. Neither she nor the house gave any sign of welcome. There were no flowers or even pots to put them in—not even an inviting rocking chair on the porch. Lace curtains clung like frost to the windows. Matt shivered.

Aunt Julia didn't meet with his approval, either. She was tall, her gray dress stretched tight over her barrel-shaped torso. Beneath it was the scrawniest pair of legs Matt had ever seen. He was going to live with a fat, gray chicken. *Aunt Chicken,* he thought. He might have snickered just a little if she hadn't taken him by the collar and almost lifted him onto the porch.

Aunt Julia steered them into the kitchen. A single bulb burned overhead. The house had been wired for power since the county finally ran the lines past the farm in the sixties, but Aunt Julia was determined to use it as little as possible. The shadows suited her.

No one was invited to sit. Aunt Julia pointed a long chicken finger at the social worker.

"I assume that folder is for me," she said.

"Yes," Ms. Snelling said, her eyes scanning the spotless room. "I have Matt's birth certificate, vaccination card, school records, and the court order giving you full custody."

Ms. Snelling gave Aunt Julia the folder. Without looking at the contents, she tottered on her chicken legs to a rolltop desk in the parlor and flung the folder into a drawer.

Matthew didn't remember much of the days that followed, only that he was happy on his first day in his new school. Being the new kid was worth it if it meant being away from Aunt Julia most of the day. The school bus couldn't make the trip along the dirt road to the farmhouse, so Matt had to walk the half-mile to the main road. The bus lurched to a stop, and the driver beeped the horn to hurry him along.

After school, he was dropped off by the mailbox, the hot exhaust from the bus blowing his hair back and the tires spitting gravel as the bus raced away. Matt walked with his eyes fixed on the dirt road, kicking loose rocks. He hadn't made any friends that first day. A boy named Chris had introduced himself during recess, but on finding out where Matt lived, he quickly got up.

"Don't you know that house is cursed?" he asked, running away without waiting for an answer.

Matt had to endure the furtive glances and whispers of the other kids until the final bell rang and he could go home. He wondered if Aunt Julia would be waiting for him on the porch, the way his mother always did, but when he finally reached the farmhouse, the porch was empty.

Matt wondered what it meant for a house to be cursed. *Did that mean haunted?* The only scary thing in the house was Aunt Julia, and she was alive enough. Animals didn't like the place, though. Not even birds.

Matt turned the worn doorknob and slowly opened the door. The house was quiet. He had never been alone in the house before. A sudden shiver sent him up the creaky stairs to his room at the back of the house. He closed the door behind him, hoping it would keep the curse away. Still no sign of Aunt Julia. It wasn't grocery day. Flinging his backpack onto his bed, Matt walked to the window and looked out.

Beyond the row of cornstalks on the far side of the house was a small footbridge over a creek than ran along that side of the property. On the other side of the creek, he watched as a gray figure with chicken legs walked among the uncut fieldstones that stood upright from the ground at regular intervals.

Aunt Julia.

Matt had never explored that side of the creek. Aunt Julia had forbidden him to cross the footbridge, and he was only too happy to obey. It was dark over there, the kind of place you just knew to stay away from.

He watched as she paced back and forth, occasionally nodding her head as if she were listening to someone. Matt squinted his eyes but could see no one else in the gloom that always hung over that side of the creek. Turning his attention back to Aunt Julia, he was startled to see her staring back at him. Her white face seemed to float on a disembodied head, her gray dress now indistinguishable from her surroundings in the waning afternoon light.

Matt jumped back and tried to hide behind the lace curtains, but it was too late. Aunt Julia was already across the footbridge and approaching the side of the house, her eyes on his bedroom window.

There was no use trying to hide. Aunt Julia would expect him to present himself for whatever punishment was coming. Matt reached the bottom of the stairs just as the front door flew open.

Aunt Julia bent down to meet his wide eyes. She tilted her head to one side and her lips reluctantly parted in an awful smile.

"Where you spying on me, boy?" she asked.

"No, ma'am!" Matt lied. "I came home from school, and I couldn't find you, so..."

Aunt Julia placed one long icy finger over his lips.

"You know what they say about curiosity, boy? Curiosity kills things, boy. You are a Walker, though..."

Aunt Julia stopped and looked in the direction of the creek. Matt was certain she could see it through the wall.

"Come on, boy," she said, grabbing Matt by the collar.

They moved quickly around the side of the house and past the cornfield. The creek. *Was she going to drown him? No. It was worse than that.* In a moment, they were crossing the footbridge. *She was going to leave him in that dark place.* Matt struggled to free himself, but Aunt Julia's grip was firm.

Once on the other side, Aunt Julia finally let go of Matt's collar. Reverently drawing her gray shawl over her head, she stepped toward the rows of uncut field stones. Matt reluctantly followed.

"Do you know what this is, boy?" Aunt Julia asked.

Matt shook his head. Whatever it was, he was scared of it.

"This is the Walker family resting place. Generations of Walkers lived and died on this farm. Each stone marks a grave. The last two I dug by myself."

Matt's eyes grew wide. The only time he'd been in a cemetery was when his mom and dad were buried. There were beautiful flowers and lots of crosses. Everyone cried.

Aunt Julia wasn't crying. Her pale blue eyes shone with pride as she looked over the rows of fieldstones.

"There are no crosses," Matt said.

"And there never will be!" Aunt Julia yelled.

Matt jumped and tried to run, but Aunt Julia's fingers dug into his arm.

"When I die, boy, you'd better see to it that nobody puts a cross on my grave. I'll have a stone just like theirs," she said, pointing at the cemetery with her free hand. "We Walkers aren't cross people. We commune with the Horned One. Always have. Put a cross on my grave, boy, and I'll come for you. I'll tap on your window in the night and drag you across that creek. They'll find you, boy, pinned to the ground with that cross through your chest. Do you understand?"

Matt didn't know who the Horned One was. He didn't think he wanted to know. He nodded, and Aunt Julia released her grip. He stumbled back across the footbridge to the house and raced up the creaky stairs and into his room. He wanted to slam the door but stopped and closed it softly. He didn't want to make Aunt Julia angry again.

They ate their dinner in silence that night, and Matt went straight to his room after. He waited until Aunt Julia turned on the old radio in the parlor before he took his box of comic books out of a hiding place in his closet. He read until sleep overtook him...

****

Matthew finally reached the end of the dirt road and pulled up in front of the old farmhouse. You could miss it if you didn't know it was there. It was still the color of the bare trees around it. Dim light glowed in one of the upstairs windows. Aunt Julia's room. Matthew felt a shiver crawl the length of his spine. His mind searched frantically for a logical explanation and seized on the idea that the undertaker must have left it on when he and the sheriff took the dead Aunt Julia to the funeral home.

Matthew glanced at his watch. It was only three o'clock, but the heavy clouds would bring the day to a close early. He took a deep breath and opened the truck's door, his feet sinking into the mud. He felt like a small, frightened little kid again, holding tight to the social worker's hand.

He reached into his pocket and drew out the housekey. Matthew shook off a chill and walked briskly to the front door. He had rehearsed this moment over and over again as he drove into town, forcing himself to recall every detail of the house he had tried so hard to forget. *Run upstairs, open the closet, pull the loose panel aside, and grab the box of comic books. That's it. Easy, right?*

He turned the key in the rusty lock and shoved the door open. Flicking light switches on as he moved through the kitchen and into the parlor, he stopped at the bottom of the stairs and looked up into the darkness. Overhead, a floorboard creaked. Matthew froze. His mind began to race again.

It's an old house. Old houses make noise.

He'd heard those creaks before on windy nights, he reminded himself. *It was nothing.* He reached for the switch at the bottom of the stairs, praying the light wouldn't reveal the image of Aunt Julia staring down at him with her cold, dead eyes.

Nothing. Just the wall. To the right was his bedroom. To the left was Aunt Julia's.

Matthew took the steps two at a time. Reaching the top, he turned and saw the faint glow at the bottom of Aunt Julia's bedroom door.

Damn undertaker.

Matthew wanted to go in and turn off the light, but he couldn't force his feet in that direction. Instead, he spun right and lunged for his bedroom door. He threw the door open and fumbled for the switch.

The room was as he had left it. A bed, a few meager sticks of secondhand furniture. No toys. Aunt Julia didn't allow them. "Boys need chores, not toys," she said. Those damn white lace curtains on the window overlooking the cemetery were still there, too. As a kid, he would have given anything for heavy drapes to block that view, but Aunt Julia wouldn't hear of it. "The dead want to see *in* just as much as the living want to see *out*," Aunt Julia always said.

Matthew walked around the bed, staring at the floor as he passed the window. He pulled open the closet door and found the light chain. Dropping to his knees, he placed his hand on the wall and slid a loose board to the side.

It was still there. His box of comic books. A quick peek inside told him they were all there. She hadn't found them.

Matthew tucked the box under his arm and slammed the closet door. He froze, waiting for the shriek that always came from the other room.

Get it together! She's dead and buried right out there!

He found himself looking out the window and across the creek at the Walker family cemetery. There was one fresh mound of dirt at the end of a long row of uncut fieldstones. A wooden cross marked the new grave.

"Put a cross on my grave, boy, and I'll come for you."

No, no, no! That isn't supposed to be there! Aunt Julia is gonna be so angry!

Matthew bolted from the room and stumbled down the stairs.

"It wasn't me! IT WASN'T ME!" he screamed as he fled the house.

Throwing the box onto the passenger seat, he jammed the key into the ignition and spun the truck around, bouncing over the ruts in the mud and out to the main road...

As Matthew's truck disappeared around a curve, a black SUV with *Carson Family Funeral Home* in delicate cursive letters printed on the side door turned off the main road and began the half-mile trek to the Walker house. Paul Carson had noticed a light far back in the woods when he drove past this spot the night before. He muttered a curse under his breath. He'd forgotten to turn out the lights when he took Julia Walker's corpse from the house. Sheriff Bauer had promised to meet him out there just in case some local kids had broken in, which wasn't very likely. Everyone in town was afraid of the Walker place. You couldn't double-dog-dare anyone to go up there. He just wanted the sheriff with him for company.

When Paul arrived at the old farmhouse, a light fog was beginning to collect among the trees. His headlights swept across the front of the house.

Son of a bitch. I forgot to close the front door, too!

There was no sign of the sheriff. Paul stepped from the vehicle and shivered in the cold. This place gave him the creeps. He didn't want to be there when it got dark. He would go in without the sheriff, button the place up, and get the hell out of there.

He trotted to the front door and up the stairs. Turning to his left, he dashed to Aunt Julia's room and flung open the door. A single bulb burned on the nightstand on the opposite side of the bed. He reached down and turned it off. As he turned to go, he found himself facing the window. Through the white lace curtains, he could just make out the little cemetery where he had buried Julia a few days before. There had been no funeral. The local minister had politely declined to say a few words over her grave, and nobody bothered to send flowers. Paul had brought a couple of day laborers with him to dig the grave and put her in the ground. The makeshift cross was an afterthought, just two rotten pieces of fence he nailed together to mark the spot.

It seemed like the decent thing to do.

Paul closed the bedroom door behind him and headed for the stairs. He was halfway down when he heard the stairs creak behind him. Dread overwhelmed him, and he ran for the front door, slamming it behind him as he dropped the house key on the porch. He jumped into the front seat of his SUV just as the rain began to fall. By the time his trembling hand found the ignition, the rain was coming down in sheets. He could barely make out the movement of someone approaching the driver's side of the SUV. A long white finger tapped at his window. Paul sighed with relief. Sheriff Bauer had made it after all.

Paul lowered the window to greet his friend but found himself staring into the cold dead eyes and white face of Julia Walker, a makeshift cross clutched in her hand.

****

Sheriff Bauer found him half an hour later, pinned to the ground. Sweeping his flashlight over the property, the beam came to rest on a gray figure with long white legs slowly making its way to Julia Walker's freshly-dug grave.

The sheriff jumped into his cruiser and fled.

It rained heavily throughout the night, hard enough to obliterate the multiple sets of tire tracks in the dirt. Sheriff Bauer had asked the State Police to investigate the homicide, citing his friendship with the victim as a conflict of interest. The day laborers were questioned, but they had airtight alibis.

Paul Carson's murder would go unsolved.

The people in town knew better and continued to give the Walker farm a wide berth. The story of what happened out there became a part of local lore, the tale becoming more gruesome with each telling.

Eventually, the old farmhouse collapsed in a storm, and weeds claimed the cemetery. The dead could no longer peer in the windows through the lace curtains, but they could walk with Aunt Julia among the fieldstones.

BARTENDER

Andrew Allen Smith

I'd never quite seen anything like this. The two customers at my bar were locked in a verbal battle over politics. The politics I had seen before. Most bar fights start with women, politics, sports, and religion. These two men had taken it to a new level, and although occasionally I asked them to close it down, they kept making it more and more personal. I honestly didn't know what to do. As they started screaming, people either got involved on one side or the other or just left. After about an hour of screaming at each other, I went to them and told them, "Either you two keep it down, or I'll call the police on you."

One of the men quickly said, "Yeah, call the police but don't worry, we'll defund them soon. I know my rights better than you do."

The second man started laughing, "Yeah, let's defund the police, and then the only people that will be protecting you are the ones like me willing to stand up for freedom."

"Guys, I don't care." I was pretty livid at this point. "I don't care if you're liberal, I don't care if you're conservative, all I care about is whether people are buying drinks and having a good time. You're making both of those difficult."

The two men nodded but were obviously not very happy about my display of passion towards neutrality. The good part was I went back to tending bar, and nobody was paying attention to them anymore. Every once in a while, one or the other would tap on the bar a little more complicated, trying to make a point. People ignored them, and eventually, so did I. The crowd started slowly waning as we got closer and closer to last call.

Eventually, I sent the staff home. It was me, a man sitting in the corner in a blue denim jacket with a Cincinnati Reds baseball cap, and the two men still discussing the right and the left of the political arena.

"Aren't you two done yet," I said as I cleared their empties and wiped the bar down. "Bar's gonna close shortly. You two need to sober up. How in the hell could you keep talking for that long?"

"This moron wouldn't listen to anything I had to say," the gruff man in the red flannel shirt said; "all he wants to do is give the world a free ride so that people like me can work their butts off and support the losers."

"Yeah, this moron thinks that he's the center of the universe and that anything he makes is for himself and not to be shared with the world." The second man had a fuzzy beard and a series of bracelets on his well-tattooed arms.

Neither man was big nor small, so I wasn't worried about them. Both of them were normal, except that one was extremely liberal, and one was extremely conservative. With the bar almost empty, they began talking louder and louder again until finally, I looked at them and shook my head.

The third man walked up to the bar and stood behind both men. "Can I get a bill?" he asked.

The man in the red flannel looked back at him. "Hey, buddy, you look like a reasonable person. Do you think the world should be free?"

"There is nothing free about the world," the newcomer said to the two of them. "Everything we do has a price, and those not willing to pay the price should be eliminated. It is the law of the jungle and the way the world should be."

The liberal broke in very quickly. "So if somebody doesn't have a purpose, they should just be gone? So, no Social Security or welfare? Should children just be put to death? Are we going to go back to the dark ages?"

The Cincinnati Reds ball cap looked lightly to the side at the more liberal man. "There are obvious exceptions to each rule. Children are the world's future and should be cultivated if they are taught to make a difference, but they should not be given a free ride because if that free ride is taken away, they cannot survive on their own. At the same time, the children and the elderly each give us wisdom and the future. Our responsibility is to ensure that they are comfortable as it was their responsibility before us."

"But if they can work or make a difference, they should be working or making a difference," the more conservative man said. "We don't need deadbeats running the world."

"That is not for you to decide," the Cincinnati Reds cap said again. "I have heard much of what you had to say this evening, and neither of you is correct about much. One of you wants to eliminate people who disagree with them. The other one of you wants to stop people who disagree with them and who might disagree with them later. Neither of you made a reasonable argument; instead, you just wasted your time and the time of the people around you. I didn't think it was possible, but the two of you are more of a waste than all of the discussions on social media."

The liberal man started laughing. "Just another conservative. If I were on social media, I would block you."

"But you're not on social media."

I was listening to three people talk, and the man in the Cincinnati Reds cap pulled a screwdriver from his pocket, grabbed the back of the liberal's head, and slammed the screwdriver through his eye socket. There was surprisingly little blood. It was somewhat grisly but less than I had seen in movies. The conservative and I sat dumbfounded as the man in the Cincinnati Reds cap held on to the liberal's ponytail, wiped his hands on the man's shirt, then slammed his face into the bar. Again, I was surprised as I saw the screwdriver protrude from the back of his skull, but there was only a tiny drop of blood around the man's hair.

Neither the conservative nor I had moved. We were both wide-eyed and wondering what was going to happen next.

"I don't think we'll be hearing from that side anymore," the man in the Cincinnati Reds cap said. "Can I get my bill, please?"

I reached into my pocket and went through a folder with the remaining tabs. The man had ordered three cokes for the night. I would have thought that odd if it hadn't been so busy. "Is this you?" I slowly handed him the receipt, my hand shaking. "Just three cokes?" I asked with a quaver in my voice.

"That's all I had," the man in the Cincinnati Reds caps said.

I was finding it hard to focus, I knew I needed to remember this man, but for the life of me, all I could focus on was that Cincinnati Reds cap and the denim jacket he wore. For the life of me, I couldn't tell if he was black or white or somewhere in between.

The conservative spoke up. "I'm not sure I agree with you but thanks for what you did."

At the same time, I said, "That'll be $3.50."

The man on the Cincinnati Reds cap took out a five and a ten and handed it to me. "Keep the change. I know this will be a little bit of a hassle, and I'm sorry, but I can't abide by this type of stupidity. You probably shouldn't allow people to talk about things like this in your bar. It irritates the honest people just trying to relax for a minute."

"Yeah, thank you." I didn't know what to say to that.

The conservative spoke again. "I'm not sure I agree with you but thanks for what you did."

"Oh yeah," the man in the Cincinnati Reds cap said, "You're a blusterous buffoon that couldn't protect yourself if you were inside a tank. You vote for violence and destruction, but you have no idea what violence and destruction are, and I heard you talking about eliminating people. You couldn't possibly know what taking another person's life is like. Nor do you know what it's like to protect an innocent person and still watch them die. The other guy will be the death of the world with his high seeming morals that our void of morality. He fights for things he doesn't understand, but you will be the weapon he will use to destroy it all. His narrow-minded vision coupled with your narrow-minded need for violence will be the end of us all."

The conservative went to say something, but before he could speak, there was a screwdriver in his eye as he gasped his last breath. The man looked straight at me as he slammed the second man onto the bar, and the screwdriver's tip punched out the back of his skull.

"You might think I'm a little crazy," the man in the Cincinnati Reds cap said, "but I didn't tell either one of them anything they needed to hear. They wouldn't have listened, nor would they have heard. Everything I said was for you. You were the person that listened to them both and did nothing. You were the person that allowed their influence to seep over into your bar. At the end of the day, you will tell this story. Please make sure you get it right so that people will start to realize that no one wants to hear the rantings of the far left or far right. Then maybe it's time to stop. I know you're sitting there trying to process all of this, and probably the biggest thing you'll remember from this night is the Cincinnati Reds cap on my head. They're a good team. You should see them play in person."

The man turned and walked out of the bar. The bell over the door rang as he left. I was left with two corpses and many questions. When the police arrived, they asked me question after question, and the man was right. I was focused on the Cincinnati Reds cap. I had no idea about anything else. The news crews came, and I told them what the man said to the liberal and the conservative and then to me. I saw it on the news the next day, and on one channel, I heard only the liberal side while the other channel played only the conservative side, and it made me question why I bothered saying anything at all. Then I thought about the man in the Cincinnati Reds hat and knew what he told me was exactly what he expected to get out. I don't know that I'll ever allow politics in my bar again, but I'll be watching for those people in the background who are listening and ready to act.

THE BIBLIOMANIACAL VAMPIRE

Matt Lubbers-Moore

"Successful, sir?" Edgar, the butler, asked as Samuel came in. As Samuel began pacing the foyer, Edgar stood out of the way, stock still, as his master explained the auction bid by bid. With Samuel finally winded, Edgar could slip off Samuel's jacket and hang it neatly in the foyer closet. Samuel headed straight for the study, off the main hall, where he fell into his favorite chocolate brown leather armchair with his feet propped up on the matching ottoman. Edgar took the opportunity to slip off Samuel's shoes as Samuel continued his adventurous tale of how and what he won; four books for over five million dollars. "Shall I fetch the items from your car, sir, so you can examine them in your own home?"

"My car?!?! I wouldn't trust myself driving home such works of art! More importantly, I wouldn't trust other drivers not to damage my precious winnings! No, no, no. A car wouldn't do. I'm having them delivered by an armored truck tomorrow." Having rested for a full minute, he jumped to his feet. He bounded to the library across the hall, where he cleared space in his curiosities cabinet. Although curiosity cabinets ran out of vogue in the early twentieth century, Samuel was a man who loved the old ways, and having a curiosity cabinet in his library suited his sensibilities. It was the same as having two suits of armor in the hall and two marble lions in front of the estate, of which he had both. The curiosity cabinet, however quaint it sounded, was forty-eight feet long, covering the entire east wall where his most prized

The Drifter and Other Unusual Tales

and valuable possessions rested behind plexiglass doors. It was tied into the library alarm system in the event any foolish persons should think to rob him. "Edgar!"

"Sir?" Edgar appeared in the doorway, a glass of sherry in his hand.

"Invite the usual suspects for a party tomorrow!" Samuel grabbed the glass and downed the sherry, "I want to show off my new acquisitions. Tell them champagne at eight and the unveiling at nine SHARP!"

"Sir," Edgar replied, taking the sherry glass from Samuel and disappearing from sight.

Still exuberant, Samuel worked tirelessly rearranging books, establishing a display area on the middle shelf in the center for prime viewing and hooking a white curtain over the shelves for the big reveal. Having done this many times before, he finished the work in only a few hours and crashed into bed at two in the morning.

Samuel was up with the sun the next morning as he counted down the hours to the arrival of the armored truck. His insurance agent would be there shortly to meet the truck's arrival, as well as the auctioneer from last night to guarantee that the books were the same as the books Samuel purchased with the receipts as proof. He devoured a traditional English breakfast and a great deal of coffee. Soon enough, the auctioneer, the insurance agent, and the truck arrived. Samuel and the auctioneer signed off that these were indeed the same books.

The auctioneer questioned his acquisition of the small pamphlet, "I can easily contact the other bidder and take his high bid for the pamphlet. I know how some people can be excited about a big win and keep bidding to win."

"Sure, it was an impulsive buy, but I plan to keep it. Thanks all the same."

With a worried backward glance, the auctioneer soon followed the armored truck down the drive and disappeared around the corner. Samuel carried the books into the library, where the insurance agent took pictures and quoted an amount to insure the four books completely. Samuel always insured the books to the maximum.

Edgar began preparing for the night's festivities as Samuel prepared the books in the library. With twenty confirmed guests arriving that evening, champagne and hors d'oeuvres were chilled and prepared. The oak shelving in the library was usually left open, but when guests with drinks and food were allowed to come into the library, Samuel installed temporary glass doors to prevent any accidental damage to the books.

As the guests began filing in, small groups of two or three, Edgar, attired in his best tux, offered each guest a flute of champagne and explained where they could find the hors d'oeuvres in the library. A little after eight, the last guest sauntered in, grabbed a flute of champagne, and wandered into the library in search of food.

At quarter after eight, Samuel strode into the library looking like G. K. Chesterton, carrying a cane and wearing a cape. The guests had become used to his eccentricities by now, but they eagerly applauded his arrival. The men outnumbered the women in this typical Biblio atmosphere of tenured English professors, antiquarian booksellers, and fellow collectors with their tweed jackets and long beards for the men, hair buns, and cardigans for the women. He mingled with the guests and avoided their curious questions as Edgar wandered the room, passing out fresh glasses of champagne and removing the empty flutes to the kitchen.

At nine sharp, Samuel gained the attention of the crowd with a light tapping on the side of his champagne flute with the end of his cane. The room quieted as they turned to gaze upon the white curtain.

"Ladies and gentlemen, I present my newest acquisitions," he pulled aside the sheet revealing two of the books, both of which were presented facing the crowd. "*Alice in Wonderland* illustrated by Salvador Dali. This is one of only twenty-five hundred that were beautifully illustrated by the famed Dali." Samuel opened the book to reveal several illustrations to the crowd as they *oohed* and *ahhed*.

"The second book is the *Diaries of Samuel Pepys* published in 1899 for private subscription and is only one of fifty-three published. This book has a special place in my heart as my dear mother named me after Pepys as she was a historian of the English Restoration. As this diary covers the date between 1660-1669 she delved herself fully into reading it several times over the course of her career." The crowd *oohed*, *ahhed*, and *awwed*.

"The third book, the pièce de résistance," he said, as he flung aside the curtain once more to reveal the third book. "A first edition of *Don Quixote de la Mancha* by Cervantes and published around 1605 to 1615. The book is in near-perfect condition which is why I paid twice the amount that the last copy went for at auction." Samuel began to choke up a little as he reminisced. "I used to read this as a little child, hiding under the sheets with a flashlight, as I imagined myself as the great Don Quixote, surrounded by his books, longing for a day to return to the era of chivalry and knights, riding off on grand adventures, and battling dragons, witches, bandits, and of course, windmills." The crowd *oohed*, *ahhed*, *awwed*, and chuckled.

"When Edgar called me this morning, he mentioned four books?" a book dealer of some repute asked. The rest of the crowd looked upon Samuel with a mixture of glee and anticipation of what could surpass the *Don Quixote*.

"Ah yes, I bought it on a whim. The auctioneer had actually forgotten about it as the *Don Quixote* was supposed to be the last item to be brought out and close the show with a bang. As the auctioneer thanked everyone for coming, this little guy in the front row, who I had noticed had not bid on anything else, called up to the auctioneer and asked about it." Samuel looked at the little yellowing pamphlet to read the title, "*Vampires of Boston, 1820*. I was still ebullient about my victory over *Don Quixote* that I made a few small bids for this pamphlet. Unfortunately, the other bidder had been unprepared to be bid against and bowed out quickly, so I ended up with the pamphlet for a whistle."

The crowd was not too enthused with what appeared to be a self-published pamphlet that was yellowing and in rough condition. Samuel slipped it back onto the shelf and reclosed the door before being engulfed by the crowd congratulating him on his purchases.

Edgar cautiously approached Samuel, swerving and ducking graciously through the crowd. Upon reaching Samuel, he handed him an introduction card. Samuel excused himself from his guests to move into the hall to speak with Edgar. "Who is this?"

"I do not know, sir. He only asked to meet with you in private. I told him you were occupied with a gathering, but he insisted. I put him in the study to wait." Edgar turned to look at the study door on the other side of the hall with what appeared to Samuel as fear.

Samuel looked at the card again. The front was a raised gold embossed name and what appeared to be a title or occupation as it only read "Patrick O'More: Bibliophile." Samuel turned the card over to see a family crest of sorts; three severed heads impaled on a sword atop a shield with a blood-red clawed lion. Beneath this was a handwritten note,

You have something of mine.

"I'll meet with him. Look after the guests, and I shouldn't be gone long. It's probably a misunderstanding." He walked to the study door as Edgar disappeared back into the library with more fresh glasses of champagne.

As is the custom with uninvited guests, Edgar left the study door partially open so that Samuel could get a measure of them before entering, to be prepared for whatever awaited him. It was a business trick he learned from his father to always be one step ahead of his competition and to always have the upper hand. This was a lesson Samuel had learned well, and it had paid off several times in his career.

Samuel looked in to see O'More with his back to the door. Another lesson that his father had instilled in him was to never have his back to the door when left alone so as to never be surprised. Samuel smiled, thinking this would be an easy discussion and he would be able to get back to his guests shortly. He took in O'More's outdated black suit with tails. He was obviously poor and wearing hand-me-downs, or perhaps this young man shopped in boutique thrift stores that specialized in old-fashioned clothing. O'More was about six feet tall and holding a black top hat with red trim hung at his side.

Slowly, O'More turned to the door as if he knew he was being watched. The hairs on Samuel's arms stood up as he realized he was not the hunter, but the prey as O'More's eyes found his own through the crack of the door. They stared at one another. Samuel felt as if he couldn't move. He couldn't break free from the piercing green eyes on a pale face framed by wild, unkempt orangish-red hair above a black suit with a blood-red vest and bowtie with a red rose in his lapel. Samuel felt as if O'More was boring his way into his brain, reading all his secrets, and leaving him empty. But what seemed like an eternity was only a moment as O'More turned to look at something to his right.

Samuel had to take a deep breath as he began to doubt what had just happened. Straightening up, he walked into the study to confront this uninvited guest. As he entered, O'More set his hat down on the desk, broke out into a huge smile, and offered his hand, which Samuel shook, noting the cold.

"I do apologize for taking you away from your party, but you and I have some business to discuss, and I don't like too much time to pass."

"What business do we have to discuss?" Samuel asked as he gestured for O'More to sit, which he did. Samuel noticed O'More moved gracefully, no movement wasted.

"The item you bought last night was mine." O'More had his hands in his lap, his legs crossed, his voice measured, yet Samuel could hear the anger.

"I bought several books last night. You'll have to be more specific."

"You know what book I am talking about." As Samuel raised his shoulders, O'More sighed. "The pamphlet. The book you told your guests was purchased on a whim."

"You want the pamphlet?" surprise filled Samuel's tone. "I was sure you were talking about the *Don Quixote* or the Dali."

"I already have my fair share of each. The pamphlet, however, is mine."

"I know the auctioneer pretty well, and he would never sell anything without the proper provenance. I won the pamphlet in the auction fair and square. It is mine."

"Yes, I know that my agent who was there to acquire the pamphlet had failed me in my attempt to buy the pamphlet. However, I am willing to pay you double what you paid for it."

Samuel debated with himself as he considered making double what he paid for it, but on the other hand, it might be worth a lot more than he knew, and his father raised no fool. "No deal. I have money. This book is obviously worth something, and I intend to keep it."

"I think you will change your mind," O'More said, his face growing red with anger, leaning towards Samuel, his hands digging into the arms of the chair, sinking into the soft leather. Then as quickly as he had grown angry, he calmed, his face returned to the pale white, his hands once more clasped in his lap, and he was comfortably seated in the chair. The only indication Samuel had that this uninvited guest had been angry were the rips in the leather where O'More's fingers had dug. "Think about it. I will return in two nights." O'More stood, grabbed his top hat, and moved to the door. As he exited the house, he turned, put his top hat on, and growled, "Enjoy the rest of your party," and was gone.

Samuel stood in the doorway, waiting to hear a car start and pull out, yet the night was eerily calm. He stood there for several minutes before Edgar came and brought him back to the party, which he could no longer enjoy.

By midnight the last of his guests had left. Edgar began the process of putting the library back to order as Samuel slumped into his armchair back in the study. The same chair he had faced O'More. He would not sell the pamphlet. He had worked hard all of his life, retired early from a tech company he helped found, and made a fortune selling the stock. He had never married, never had children. His work had been his spouse, and the books were his children.

Yet, something about O'More seemed dangerous. How dangerous could he be if he was just a book collector? Bibliophiles aren't dangerous. Maybe a shove here or there to get into a really good sale but nothing more serious than that. Oh, sure, there had been plenty of book collectors that were also thieves. History was ripe with thieving book collectors. The *Don Quixote* is worth millions though, and people were willing to kill over less. Yet O'More wasn't concerned about the *Don Quixote*. He wanted the pamphlet. "Why?" he pondered to himself.

Edgar woke him around three to walk him upstairs to his bedroom and help him to bed. Samuel's sleep was fitful, disturbed by nightmares of creatures with bright green eyes, blood-red teeth, and claws.

When he woke around noon, he had the urge to look at the vampire pamphlet again. He had to know why O'More insisted on having this particular item. On his way to the dining room, he grabbed it off the library shelf. Edgar had just put out a light brunch when he heard Samuel moving around upstairs.

On principle, Samuel never allowed any of his books in the dining room. Even he never broke this rule. Today was different. He started eating with the pamphlet propped open in front of him. It was an impressive manuscript. If he had been thinking clearly the other night, he would never have bid on this. O'More's agent would have gotten this for cheap, and this whole mess would never have happened. He had attended dozens of auctions at that auction house before, and the auctioneer had never missed a sale. Even last night prior to his meeting with O'More, he had dismissed this pamphlet when with his guests. Yet now that he knew someone else wanted it badly, he had to know more about it, and his desire to own it increased.

As he turned the pages, he noted that the pages were cheap and the ink was second-rate. Published by an anti-vampire league in Boston in 1820. Probably some religious nuts who had moved on from the Salem witches to vampires. Obviously, very poor religious nuts considering the materials they used. He then flipped through the pages and read about all the suspected vampires; bankers, politicians, writers, artists, and even one newspaperman. *These would be the targets of religious nuts,* Samuel mused. The anonymous author speculated about the dangerousness of each; wealth, actual vs. perceived age, power, and hobbies, as well as daytime and nighttime activities. Not surprisingly, most of the suspected vampires were out and about at night.

It wasn't until he returned to his study and reclined in his favorite chair that he came upon Patrick O'More. The ink was faded and hard to read, but from what he could understand, O'More had emigrated to America in 1815 from Ireland and possessed a large fortune allowing him to buy a mansion in Beacon Hill, a region that this group felt was already a vampire hub of activity. "Although vampires hunt alone," the pamphlet read, "they are often social creatures preferring to surround themselves with other vampires and beautiful, wealthy humans." O'More, on the other hand, apparently was different. He was a loner, attending vampire gatherings very rarely and even more rarely socializing with humans. According to the pamphlet, O'More is a collector of books, possibly a sufferer of bibliomania. He is an addict, and nothing gets in his way when he wants a particular item.

Reading on, Samuel discovered that O'More used book stall owners to attend auctions or sales on his behalf. The more successful the book stall owner was at acquiring the books for O'More, the wealthier they became. O'More does not tolerate failure, and if the book agent failed to acquire the book, they were often never seen again. Their shops were torn apart as if by a beast of enormous strength. There was one warning at the end of the section; "Although he may not be the oldest or the strongest, he will kill without provocation for a book." Samuel put the pamphlet down and sat staring off into space for some time.

He then called the stodgy, unkept, but well-informed bookseller from the previous night.

"The vampire pamphlet? I wasn't very interested in that. After you put it away, I didn't see too many people even glance at it. I flipped through it to see if there was anything special, but it looked like a cheap religious pamphlet about the evils of the world. Why do you ask? Think there's more to it than that?"

"I'm not sure. I had a visitor stop by and inquire about it and thought it might be worth more than I initially thought.

"Hmmm, doubtful but I'll look into it."

They hung up just as Edgar appeared in the doorway of the study, informing him that the police had arrived and needed to speak with him.

"Regarding?"

"They said there has been a death and would like to speak with you."

"Show them in then." Terrible thoughts raced through Samuel's mind as he considered what the pamphlet had said about O'More. Two officers walked in and introduced themselves as Detectives Brown and Wilkinson. Samuel offered them a seat, but they remained standing. Samuel did as well. "What's this about a death?"

"A Mr. Geoffrey Washington was killed last night. We believe you may have been one of the last people to see him. Can we ask what he was doing here and when he arrived and left?"

"Oh my. He was the auctioneer at an auction I went to the other night. He stopped by yesterday early afternoon around one and double-checked to make sure the books I won were the same as the ones being delivered. The truck showed up roughly the same time as he did, and he left at the same time as they did, around one-thirty."

"Did he seem worried about anything? Did he say anything about meeting with anyone else?"

"No, he came by, verified the books, asked about one of the pamphlets I purchased, and then left. He didn't say anything about any other meetings."

"What were you doing between seven and nine last night?"

"I was throwing a party of sorts for some friends to show them my purchases. I was getting ready as guests were arriving, and I came downstairs a little after eight. I was with them until midnight." The police recorded this, thanked him for his time, and left.

Samuel slumped back into his chair. Washington had seemed worried. He even mentioned the pamphlet and whether he was planning on keeping it as it didn't fit with his collection. Washington had even offered to refund his money if he wished to get rid of it. *Had O'More already contacted Washington the night of the auction and then killed Washington when he couldn't deliver the pamphlet? What about the agent who had been at the auction on his behalf? Was he dead too?*

He walked over to his desk, grabbed his phone, and called the auction house. At first, he assumed it would go to an answering machine, but a very emotional voice picked up, sniffled a few times, and then, "hello?"

"Good afternoon. Is this Mrs. Washington?"

"No, no. He wasn't married. I'm his assistant, well was his assistant. I'm sorry sir, if you're looking for Mr. Washington, he was killed last night."

"I'm so sorry. This is Samuel Darnston, and I was calling to ask if he knew of the man I was bidding against the other night."

"Oh, Mr. Darnston. This is terrible. I can get that information for you. One moment." The phone was put down as he heard a rustling of papers. "The office is a mess as the police have been going through everything to see if he had any unhappy customers, which I can assure you he did not."

"Was the motive robbery?" Samuel asked.

"It doesn't look like it, although we keep very few items of value on the premises. There's very little cash, and none of that was taken. Which lot number are you referring to?"

"Oh, I'm, well, to be honest, I'm interested in the vampire pamphlet, the last item of the night."

"That item," she said dourly; "Mr. Washington was very upset with me. I had misplaced the paperwork for that, and the item almost didn't get put in the sale. The man you were bidding against, a Mr. Mason Brown, a book scout that was friends with Mr. Washington, was the one who informed us that we had missed the pamphlet. Mr. Washington was very angry with me."

"Why would he have been angry about that one volume? It made him very little money, and he could've sold it at the next auction."

"It was supposed to be sold to Mr. Brown. It had been planned to be one of the earlier items to be auctioned off before the high bidding started. When you started bidding, Mr. Brown dropped out as his employer was unclear as to how high to bid. Mr. Washington was going to speak with you after the show ended to see if you would reconsider purchasing it and let Mr. Brown have it instead. However, you had already left by the time Mr. Washington managed to step away from the podium and wade through the crowd of bidders who wanted to speak with him."

"I'm surprised he didn't ask outright yesterday when I saw him."

"He said he had mentioned that he had talked to you about the pamphlet but you laughed it off and wanted to keep it."

"That is true." Samuel sighed. This conversation only confirmed what he had already suspected. "Did he meet with Mr. Brown later?"

"No, but I heard later that his employer stopped into the bar that Mr. Washington typically frequents after a successful auction to inquire as to whether Mr. Brown had been successful. He had grown furious when he was told that he was not. Apparently, he was so angry that he put a dent into the bar when he slammed his fist into it. Mr. Washington agreed to meet with him again last night but sent me home early. Oh, I wish I had been in there! I may have been able to do something." She began to wail, and Samuel did what he could to assure her that there had been nothing she could have done. She did manage to give him the phone number for Mason Brown before hanging up.

He called the number she had given him, but it only went to voicemail. He left a message asking him to call him back, but he suspected that Brown was in no condition to call him back. He found the address for Brown's bookstore, surprised he hadn't heard of it before, and decided he would visit the following day.

Samuel decided a trip to *Calvin's Place* was in order. *Calvin's* was an old-timey watering hole that many of the locals went to, but over the last few years had been a part of the gentrification of the city and was now a hipster brewpub with an incredible menu and outrageous prices. Many of the locals stopped going, instead traveling a few blocks over to *Paddy's Bar and Grill*, where they'll go until that too is gentrified, and they begin to go elsewhere. Such is the nature of local watering holes.

Walking in the door he found the place packed for a Sunday evening. Yuppies and hipsters in their polo and flannel, respectively. He made his way to the bar, where he found an empty stool. It had been a few years since he had been here last. It used to consist of a lot of wood surfaces. It was now mostly a sports bar with chrome and televisions in every corner. The place was deafening. The bartender, bearded with a man-bun, came over to take his order. Placing a menu in front of him, he leaned on the counter as close as he could and asked what Samuel would like.

"A glass of merlot and some information." The bartender narrowed his eyes but inquired what Samuel would like to know. "There was an argument in here on Friday night. I was wondering if you were here."

"Yeah, I was. Mr. Washington stopped in to grab a bite to eat and a beer when this creepy-looking guy came in. He was very jovial and pleasant until Washington gave him some bad news, I guess. Suddenly the guy pounds the counter, puts a huge dent in the bar, and storms out."

"Where is the dent?" The bartender pointed down the way towards the middle of the bar, where a fist-sized dent was very visible even from six seats down. "And you say he stormed out?"

"The place is typically this loud, but as soon as his hand hit the bar, everyone stopped to look at what happened. He then glided out. I'm telling you. The guy creeped me out. We had to call the cops because we need our insurance to cover the damage, but Washington was out of here shortly after the other guy left. I have no doubt the guy killed Washington. None."

The bartender walked away to grab Samuel's glass of merlot and tend to his other customers. Samuel sat, considering what he had learned. As he pulled out his wallet to pay for his drink, O'More's business card floated out of his pocket. Picking it up, he stared at it again.

Patrick O'More, Bibliophile. Samuel searched the name O'More on his phone. Apparently, the name originated in Ireland from the word O'Mordha, meaning majestic. The family was deeply hated by the English, and around 1600 the family was leading the "7 Septs of Leix" which fought to keep Ireland free. They failed, and the O'Mores were scattered. He read through more of the family history, but there had been no mention of a bibliomaniacal vampire, so he closed the app again. He headed home, where he grabbed the pamphlet and read it from front to back one more time before wrapping it in Kraft brown paper and tying it with twine. Noticing that it was getting dark, he called for Edgar.

"Sir," Edgar asked, appearing in the doorway.

"I need you to put this in the safe for me, please." Edgar took the parcel and left the room. Samuel decided to get to bed early, knowing he would have a long day ahead of him.

****

After a quick breakfast, he made his way into town. Pulling to a stop in front of one of the most decrepit buildings he had seen in a long time, he now understood why he had never been to this particular bookstore. First, there was no sign or indication it was a bookstore. Huge glass windows covered in bars and plywood made the storefront look vacant. Second, it was in one of the worst neighborhoods in the city. Third, whatever stock may be inside would be of no interest whatsoever to Samuel. "Although, looks can be deceiving. If O'More used him, maybe Brown knew what he was doing?"

He got out of his car, crossed the empty street, and walked up to the building. The door was reinforced steel. He gave a low whistle in appreciation. He turned the knob expecting it to be locked but found it turned with ease. He pushed the door open and walked inside. The space was full of shelves that were, in turn, full of books. Stacks and stacks of books. Covered in dust an inch thick. The stock was ancient, easily from the 50s and 60s. Nothing of value on the shelves, the once beautiful dust jackets lay tattered or were nonexistent, leaving the boring yellow, orange, green, and blue hardcovers bare to the elements. The store looked abandoned. Why would O'More, supposedly a wealthy and powerful bibliophile, use a book scout as his agent for a high-end auction?

Walking further into the store, he found a cash register, also from the 50s, with huge mechanical buttons and a wooden drawer. The business cards stated, "The Thoth Bookstore," with the Egyptian god of wisdom printed on the back.

The building was eerily silent. No sounds from outside could penetrate the thick walls and boarded-up windows, and other than his breathing and steps, there was not a sound from inside, either. The building was stifling between the heat and the dust. He came upon a wooden door in the very back of the shop. Turning the knob and walking through, he found a pristine office. Samuel glanced around, but the papers held little interest other than showing a robust bank balance. Off the office was a stairwell leading up and down. He surmised down would lead him to a basement warehouse full of useless merchandise and junk. Up, on the other hand, might be an apartment where he may find Mr. Brown.

Taking the wooden stairs up the narrow stairwell, he found himself on a small landing with only one door. He called out, asking if anyone was home. No answer. He walked through the doorway to find a small kitchen with eat-in dining space. It was cluttered with books and papers. These he found of interest as they were higher quality than the stock downstairs, yet worth slightly more. As he flipped through the books, he found he was looking at ten to twenty thousand dollars worth of books, easily. "Looks are deceiving," he repeated to himself. The kitchen had two doors leading out of it. He poked his head into an ancient and decrepit bathroom and headed for the other doorway.

A living room made up the vast space. Beautiful windows looked out on the worst of the city, but it wasn't the view that caught him short. It was the body. The mangled human, once a man, was utterly and completely beaten to death. Blood and gore stained the carpet, splattered the walls, and even sprinkled the ceiling. He made the call to 911 on his cell phone. Though he hung up when the operator told him to stay on the line and to get out of the building immediately as he could still be in danger.

He knew there was no danger here. It was out there. Samuel walked to the window. He stared in the direction of his house, knowing that the *creature* that had done this would soon be coming to his own home, that it could do to him what he did to Washington, to Brown, to countless others throughout the centuries, if the pamphlet was to be believed. And at this moment, he certainly believed.

Ignoring the body, Samuel tiptoed through the rest of the rooms. The bedroom had a few bookshelves lined with rare thousand-dollar books.

"Nah," said the police officer when he pointed out it couldn't have been a robbery when there is a fortune in books just a few feet away from the corpse. "Meth addicts and crackheads can't read. They wouldn't be interested in books. Cash and pills are all they want. Robbery gone wrong. Simple as that."

And that was that. Hours after arriving at the Thoth Bookstore Samuel returned home weary and beaten. He answered a hundred questions the police asked about why he was there, what business he was in, how did he know the victim, and what his interest was in Mr. Brown. Weary, he knew what he had to do. To protect himself, to protect Edgar, and to protect his books, he knew exactly what he would need to do.

****

Upon arriving home, the bookseller called him to let him know what he had discovered regarding the pamphlet. "Apparently, every so often, one of these pamphlets goes up for sale. They never get much interest from the sellers and are often sold for a pittance, but they always sell immediately. The last was sold a couple years ago in Nevada. The buyer was another dealer who claimed to be working on behalf of an interested party. The one before that was purchased through eBay seconds after it was listed. What are you thinking?"

"I think this pamphlet is dangerous to their owners." Without explaining, he hung up on his friend. To Edgar, he said, "When Mr. O'More arrives tonight, hand him this note along with the parcel you put in the safe last night. Hopefully, he'll write a check and be on his way."

Samuel handed the parcel to Edgar, who disappeared. Samuel caught his reflection in the window; mid-fifty, greyish brown hair, light brown eyes. A handsome man to most. Tonight, he just felt old.

At ten on the dot, the doorbell rang. Samuel sat in the study where he could see the front door through the work of mirrors. Edgar opened the door and greeted O'More. He passed over the parcel, explaining that Samuel would like him to read the note attached. The parcel was put in an inner pocket, and a check was handed over.

"Nice doing business with you," Edgar said as he closed the door, but not before O'More looked into the mirrors, caught Samuel's eyes, and smiled.

Edgar reappeared in the doorway of the study to inform Samuel that the business had been taken care of and handed him the check for three times what Samuel had paid for the pamphlet.

"Excuse me, sir, I wonder what the card meant, "You win?"

"Just a life or death wager. He won the pamphlet, and I won the satisfaction of making three times what I paid for it," Samuel replied.

Edgar went back to the kitchen to fetch a drink for Samuel.

Samuel sat in the study staring at the check. He thought back to the conversation he had with O'More the other night. True, he didn't need the money; rare books are rare, but he only had one life, and he was damned if he was going to end it all for a pamphlet that a bibliomaniacal vampire wanted; if indeed he was a vampire.

Samuel's father taught him a lot about business, and Patrick O'More held all the power. "Patrick O'More, Bibliophile," was the only information on the check; no address or contact information was given, not that Samuel intended to contact O'More. There in the memo of the check were just two words, "Very Wise."

Birth of a Devil

Chelsea Gouin

Deborah Leeds pulled the hood of her cape over her face, making sure her features were hidden. Keeping to the shadows, she made her way deep into the woods. She went slow in order to push away the branches that were in her way. She needed to see her Sisters; she needed their protection more than ever now. She paused and listened, making sure she wasn't being followed. She couldn't be caught, not now. Definitely not now.

Upon entering the clearing, Deborah saw she was the last of the Sisters to arrive. The other four were huddled around the small fire. They greeted her with enthusiasm. "Sister Deborah! We welcome you to our Circle!"

She took her place on the pentagram drawn into the Earth. After lowering her hood, she glanced at each of her Sisters. "I come to you, my Sisters, seeking your help. I am in grave danger. I am husband-less, burdened with twelve children I cannot take care of, and hardly can produce enough food to feed one. The magistrate came to me and told me he would tolerate me no longer. I was to be barren or be cast from the Village."

The Sisters bowed their heads solemnly. They new Sister Deborah had no interest in ever finding herself a husband. She loved her children, all of them, but her struggles were great. She put her Craft above all else and had suffered the consequences.

Deborah felt tears prick her eyes. "I am afraid, my Sisters, that I am with Child." There were startled gazes, collective gasps, and a thick curiosity around the pentagram. "I have not been with a man, I swear it! And yet... I find myself carrying another. Help me, Sisters. Rid me of this burden!"

"No!" Natalie stepped closer to the flames and stared at Deborah with hard eyes. "You mustn't lose this child. He must be a gift! A gift from the Goddess. She's granted you this babe to do her bidding upon the Earth."

"Yes," Deborah agreed. Her face started to show a glimmer of hope. "Yes, that must be it! Sisters, chant with me. Thank the Goddess for her Blessing to us!" They raised their hands and chanted their ancient words.

~Nine Months Later~

The pounding on the door startled Deborah out of her heavy sleep. She'd stuck to her home on the edge of town, leaving only to travel in the woods for her supplies. Her children were provided for by the Villagers as they always had. Water was fetched from her younger children, and the eldest paid for their meager food rations.

She rose from her bedroll, rubbing her aching lower back. This pregnancy was a lot harder than any of her previous births. She peeked out her window and saw the sun was high in the sky. It must have been midday, and the children should have been at the schoolhouse. She dragged her groggy body to the front door and opened it to an official-looking man.

"Mistress Leeds?" She nodded her head in acknowledgment. "It is my deepest regret to inform you that you are no longer welcome in this Village. It has been decided that you may stay here in order to give birth to your child, but then you must leave immediately. The agreement made by you and Simon has been broken, and orders must be followed. I am sorry." He handed her a rolled bit of parchment, bearing Simon the Magistrate's wax seal.

She sunk to the floor as despair filled her. She tried to choke back her sobs as desperation filled her. Pack up her belongings? What belongings did she have? Three bedrolls and an old tea kettle. Deborah knew she needed her Sisters; they would know what to do. She chanted underneath her breath as pain wracked her body.

Not now! She thought. Her whole body seemed to be convulsing. She felt like she was being ripped in half. She planted her feet firmly on the wooden floor and attempted to push the baby from her body. "I am protected by your might, O gracious Goddess, day and night." She hoped the simple spell would be enough.

****

"Deborah?!?" Natalie cried out. She was the first to arrive at her Sister's home, drawn from the spell her Sister had no doubt used to call them. She could see a trail of blood leading deeper into the small cottage. She followed the red stains to the back of the home to find Deborah lying dead in a pool of her own blood. Her eyes were rolled up into her head, and in her hands, she clutched...

Natalie dropped to her knees and pried the dead Sister's hands off the squirming mass. A small baby boy was cradled in her arms. She hugged the baby to her chest and sobbed. "No... this Village will pay. They will not get away with murdering Deborah!"

The four sisters stood on their points of the pentagram. The child of their dead Sister lay in the center. The Sisters set down their lit candles at their feet. Each wore a black cloak in order to show their mourning for their Sister.

"This child was given to Deborah with a purpose," Natalie declared. Her voice was raw from her constant crying. "Our Sister has fallen before her time, and it is up to us to discover this child's destiny. Sisters! It's time!"

Natalie had studied the book for days. Memorizing the spell of Black Magyck. It had to be done. Then the Book could be buried for all she cared. But first, she needed revenge.

The Sisters raised their hands to the sky.

No peace find; No friend keep
No lover bind; No harvest reap
No repose take; No hunger feed
No thirst slake; No sorrow speed
No debt paid; No fear flee
Rue the day you wronged me

Natalie pulled a knife from the folds of her cloak. "Spirits of Darkness, Spirits of Chaos! I offer you the blood of me in order to use this Child as your will to seek revenge on the Village that Damned our Sister."

The other three repeated her offer and dropped their blood within the circle around the baby. "So mote it be!" they yelled. Their candles flared to life, blinding the Sisters temporarily. The baby began to scream as if in agony until the forest was filled with silence.

Natalie stared in horror. "What have we done?"

Right before her eyes was no baby. Instead, a hideous creature had taken its place. It unfolded it's large black leather wings and took flight, leaving Natalie shaking with fear.

A Taste for Bitter Things

J. L. Royce

In every marriage, there comes a moment when one partner (or both) looks around and wonders, *How did it come to this?*

It's nearly dusk, and I watch our house from the shelter of the woods. I can imagine it consumed by encroaching nature and night, by the comforting darkness. Surrounded by woodlands, it's already halfway there: gutters overflowing with the autumn leaves, pine needles blanketing the patio, lichen devouring the shingles, moss carpeting the steppingstones leading across the lawn.

She hasn't been keeping up with the chores. Too busy scheming.

Let it go, something whispers. Give up the endless sweeping, cleaning, struggling... lying.

Better this place should sink into the earth than someday become an attraction for the curious and bored: *The Murder House.*

I stand at the edge of the autumn-fragrant woods crowding the backyard. The nearest neighbor's lights are distant, barely visible. From a slight elevation, I can see into the bedroom: candlelit—how romantic. I sip a strong black coffee and watch through the naked window.

Her slim white backside: cheeks sunken like a youth's—too much yoga, or yogurt, or whatever. But you're not supposed to notice these things. Why, I wonder? I notice other women; why not my own wife?

You'd rather I bulged over my waistband? she would ask. No, that's not it; I just want...

She's riding someone, I can't tell who, male or female, younger or older. She may well have seduced someone older just to break the stereotype. Older than me: *See, it isn't* youth *I'm seeking...*

The coffee has grown stale in my mouth, but I swallow anyway.

What do *I* want?

She bounces hard, leaning down, breasts pendulous, swaying. I glimpse her face through a shifting curtain of golden hair. Her eyes are closed, imagining something I don't want to think about.

I could walk away and not return but remain transfixed. I feel the agitation growing, the need to act. The coffee drained, I crush the paper cup. I'm tempted to chuck it into the carpet of leaves but don't. Is it paranoia? Possible evidence?

Just another shadow amongst the deepening shadows, I make my way around the back of the house. The yard is empty—always empty. We never had children—no doubt the best for everyone, particularly them. I dart across the open space to the kitchen door and find it unlocked.

No one will be paying attention. I ease it open, and I wince at the click as I close it behind me. Wavering light escapes from the bedroom down the hall. Speakers are playing some wordless music with a Latin beat: workout music.

Oh, yes.

In the gloaming, I search for and find a cold granite edge, and follow it down the counter to the humming bulk of the refrigerator. I set down the crushed cup and open the door. A shaft of chilly light emerges to reveal the counter and the wooden block with its array of knives. I consider my choices.

The bread knife is my favorite of the lot, but scalloped and serrated: quite unsuitable. I pass over the broader carving knives and withdraw the fillet knife: long and thin and wickedly pointed.

I add a paring knife, short but nimble. Two knives: doesn't hurt to be prepared.

It's a short walk down the hall. I stop at the half-bath. The knives go on the toilet seat, and I yank off my shoes, fumble in the dark at my pants and underwear, drop them on the floor. I retrieve the knives and turn to leave, then pause at a glimpse of myself in the mirror: face shadowed, knives clenched, aroused.

****

We were content at first. She was the sail; I was the rudder to keep her course; she was the climber; I was the rope to halt her fall. When the novelty of our marriage wore off, she didn't leave me; but she made it clear she wanted... more.

My heart pounds as I listen to the sounds from the glowing doorway. So close; part of me wants to delay, but I fear I'll lose my nerve. I creep towards the flickering candlelight, pause in the shadows at the threshold, watching.

She faces away, blocking her partner's view of the doorway. Their groans are synchronous, insistent. I stare at the familiar planes of her back, the shoulders jutting like wings, the relentless motion at her narrow waist. I creep into the shadows behind her and reach the foot of the bed undetected.

Lust drifts from them, rich as grapes left to rot on their vines. Her straight blonde hair is bobbed but bias-cut, long in front, enshrouding her face. She's pounding up and down, reaching for something, about to step off a ledge, a moment away from free-fall.

I can help her take that final step. The time has come.

One soft footfall, another, and I'm standing almost alongside her. I raise the knife. At the top of its arc, it emerges from shadows and catches the candlelight, and she gasps, wordless, crimson lips pleading for release.

Do it.

The blade falls true, all my strength behind it, and penetrates its target: his heart pierced, my fist rests upon her lover's chest.

His eyes and mouth open wide in comic surprise. Releasing the knife, I clamp my hand over his face. He reaches out for her, for me. He flails, but she is elsewhere: falling, eyes closed, falling free, shoulders thrown back in flight: a thing of beauty wild.

The paring knife is ready, but it proves unnecessary; after a few ragged breaths, his struggles cease. Releasing the knife embedded in his chest, I climb atop the bed, over him, and face her.

Her movement slows; I slip a hand between them, urging, but she shakes her head—*All done*—and opens lovesick eyes to gaze at me: those eyes, eyes of ice and sky, the final color one might see, drowning in a frozen lake.

"I thought you weren't…" she pauses to catch her breath. "And then…"

The moment replays across her face. "That was the best yet—*you* are the best," she murmurs and smiles; and we are in each other's arms and kiss, her passion still simmering.

"What about you, did you—" She pulls away and searches my face.

She doesn't wait for an answer. She lifts herself from the corpse, backs away on her knees, gripping me, drawing me along, her smile sly and promising until at last, I sit perched at the foot of the bed, and she descends to kneel before me.

I still hold the paring knife. She's relentless, recklessly beckoning me to know the freedom of falling. One hand clasping her head, I stab the mattress with the other, groaning, and stab, and stab.

****

Cheek on my thigh, her breath is warm. Her lips move like a dreaming infant's. I want to lie back, relax, but of course, cannot.

I stroke her fine hair. "Can you do one thing for me?"

The icy eyes open, inquiring. She would do anything now.

"The gutters—you know how frightened I am of heights—"

Her eyes roll. She rises, waggling a finger, and scutters (legs-bent, thighs-clamped) to the master bath.

Spit-rinse, squat-drain: she flushes the toilet and reappears in the doorway, wiping her mouth with the back of a manicured hand.

Her expression: *Men.*

"Of course, baby," she promises and flips on a lamp. She stares into space and says, "Alexa: play my favorite pop."

The driving beat ceases abruptly. I pull the blinds. Anyone could have seen us from the woods, but that is part of the thrill. She pads from candle to candle, holding back her hair as she blows them out.

She ignores the sprawled corpse, sorting out discarded clothes, hers and the dead man's.

I wonder at her calm: too young to be this old, too innocent to be this—

"I'm for coffee." She gestures at the bed without looking at the carnage. "You'll clean up?"

"Of course." My voice sounds hollow to me.

She strolls into the hallway, hips moving to some bubbly melody. "Want some?" she calls back.

"Yeah, sure—strong and black!"

Unnecessary; she knows just what I like, as I know her tastes.

I circle the bed and study the body: neither fit nor fat, about my age. She wasn't looking for younger *or* older.

He could have been me. Who would have thought?

I withdraw the fillet knife with some difficulty—why it always pays to have a spare, in case you need a second thrust. I wipe the knife on the bed, set it aside, then loosen the fitted sheet, fold it over the body, and draw up the plastic drop cloth beneath it.

"Think you'll need to use the Sawzall?" she asks over the music.

Little domestic sounds escape from the kitchen: water running, cabinets opening, mugs descending to soft-land on the stone counter.

"No." I heft the limp body. "No, I think he'll fit."

Cleanup is easy: nothing much spilled—not like some of our earlier encounters. As I struggle with my burden, I imagine her petite form stretching naked on tip-toe. I long to touch her again, tenderly. But she isn't made for tenderness.

Disposal is simple since we installed the Beast in the Basement: an alkaline hydrolyser. No more tense, corpse-laden midnight drives.

The smell of coffee wafts in. She's singing to herself, an old pop tune:

When the night falls down, I wait for you… as you come around…

I stiffen with a pain so real I glance at my chest. No, this is no heart attack, nor a knife blade—a far deadlier weapon.

The song comes so easily; her voice is clear and bright:

…heaven is a place on earth.

I squeeze my eyes shut tight and pray: *For what I have done, and what I shall do...* I descend the basement stairs.

I love my wife—God forgive me; I do.

CHALLENGED

Marianne Wieland

I am not strong. I am not weak. I am nothing, and I am no one. I cannot see. I cannot hear. I can talk, but I have no language. I have thought, but I cannot think. Someone once said, "I think; therefore I am." If I believe that, I am not here. I am at the end, yet I am only at the beginning.

As I sit on this chair that has been chosen for me, outside, among nature, I hear the sound of breath. I feel the heaviness of rain. I smell electricity in the air from the coming storm many miles away. There is something else that I can't identify yet, but that makes it no less tangible than anything else I am aware of.

I look right. I see nothing. I look left. I see nothing. It is just out of my reach. I feel the change that is coming silently. So silent that I am the only one to know of its existence. There it is. Right there... so close... so close now. I stretch, but to no avail; I can't reach it.

I am not allowed to move. I am not allowed to do many things. My lot in life has been different from that of others. My choices, not my own. My life, not my own. Are there others like me? I don't know. I know nothing, just like they want.

Wait! There it is again. Like before. Creeping closer. Growing stronger. Inching along in a cloud or a mist. I can't tell, but I feel like my skin is crawling. Electricity is what I feel, but not like the storm. This is different. Too different. It is almost upon me, and I can't stop it or explain it, even in my own mind. I try to call out for help, but I can't make a sound. I open my mouth as it descends upon me. I want to scream. I am alive with the feeling of breaking out of my own skin. I can do nothing. Nothing at all.

I hold my breath. I close my eyes tight to keep out the fear trying to swallow me whole, for I do not know what is happening. I feel as if my skin has opened. I feel my blood rushing forth in an effort to escape my body. I feel my bones crushing; and the pain. I cannot begin to describe the horror that has descended upon me. I feel another sensation that I cannot describe, only feel. It slides in and out and through me. It cannot be stopped. Why is this happening? Did I cause this? What have I done?

I feel wetness on my face. I don't understand the source. I feel the pain subsiding quickly, and the wetness spreads. Darkness is all I can see now. Am I blind? Where am I? I am no longer in my chair. I am floating or flying high above the earth. I feel the wetness more fully now, and I know it is the atmosphere around me. Everything is so clear. I see through renewed strength and energy. Through the heavens. The stars are so close. I can almost touch them. I reach, but the sensation of touch eludes me once again.

My body is not my own. It belongs to this energy field that is flowing through me. I continue to fly deeper and deeper into the darkness with the sprinkling of lights here and there. As I fly by, they move out of my way. One at a time, like they have been choreographed to do this dance only for me. I gain energy from each one I pass. I see visions of other places and times that I am not sure belong to me. I feel that familiarity and that discord all at the same time. I don't think I own these visions. They belong to another, but as I gain speed, I cannot say with any real conviction if that is true.

I want to see my destination. I want to feel it. I want to live it. I am vibrant. I am free. Free of my body and mind. As I realize that, I see the darkness turning to light. Closer and closer. But I am not as light now. I feel a heaviness in my limbs. In my mind. The lights no longer move out of my way. But I can push them away with just a touch. Just enough to get through. It is as if they do not want me to pass. What are they trying to keep me from?

Closer. Closer. The closer I get, the heavier I become. The lights look almost angry at me. I don't know why. I feel the electricity start to crawl on my skin again but not like before. This is just a tingle. Almost like I am anticipating something that I cannot see. Cannot know. I cannot stop as I propel forward into pale blue light.

I see others there. Moving all around. Transparent beings move through each other without shape or substance. The light goes on forever in its pale blue abyss of what appears to be tranquility. I would believe that if not for the faces of the unknown. As they move, they seem to grow. And as they grow, they appear to be in anguish. Their transparent faces in silent screams. Their hands reach to grab what is not there. I can feel the cold flowing through them.

I look up. There is someone coming from up above the activity, of which I am in the midst. There is more substance to this being than to those with me. His descent is slow. Painfully so. Literally, painfully so. The closer he gets, the more silent screams I see in those around me. They reach to get away but only grow taller and more solid. I am transfixed on the faces that are clearly in so much torment in such a peaceful, cool, pale blue atmosphere.

The one above continues his slow descent, and I notice a change in myself. The tingling becomes more electrified. I can see through myself. I am becoming one of them. I begin to move to escape the crawling of my skin. The feeling of movement going through me. I think it is those around me, but it is within myself. The wetness is upon me. The cold, the heaviness. He is almost here, and the electricity hits me like a branding iron. I open my mouth to scream, but no sound emerges. Where am I? Why does it look so peaceful? Why does it embrace me with so much torment?

He is by me now, and I feel only misery. He is beautiful. He is light. He has a glowing smile for me, but his eyes are hollow. The more pain I am in, the more he smiles. I can't endure anymore. *Please!* I try to speak. Nothing but silent screams come out. The others are backing away. Growing smaller as they depart. More transparent. I cannot move as he rests his hand on my shoulder. The pain is like freezing fire at its zenith. I feel myself being hurled out of the pale blue light as he laughs at my misery. I don't understand. The pain decreases the farther I move back into the black void. And the lights that tried to block my path step away as I grow smaller and smaller, speeding through the atmosphere, the same as I ascended.

I feel short of breath. I feel the rapid beat of my heart. I have returned from my mobile prison. I am dry. I am in my chair again, just as they want. I hear someone approach. I stare straight ahead.

"Still where we left her. She never moves. She never speaks. She is less trouble out here. Leave her alone."

I don't know how long this can go on. They are right. I stare, but that is all. I am still in shock from where I was taken. My body is tired from the activity I had not been expecting. I long to change positions, but I do not want to move. Fear has descended, and I cannot wake from it.

I grow cold. My hands and feet grow numb from the cold. I feel like I cannot breathe. Something is happening again. More frightening than before. I feel a sense of movement below me. The ground is moving. Crawling. I can see the grass-like waves moving. The ground is flat, but it now appears like rolling hills.

I try to block the images from the brain I am not sure I still have. I have not recovered from the pale blue place. I cannot go where I feel the hills want me to go. They want me to go forward. I cannot move. I cannot move of my own accord, but I feel myself moving, still in my chair, forward toward the first hill. I am propelled up the side until I get to the top. Here is where time stands still. There is no past. There is no future. There is no present.

I start to sweat despite my frozen hands and feet. There is a smell I cannot identify. It is the culmination of the dust I see rising from the ground. I see it swirl around my head where it tries to gag me. I choke with the strength of the putrid smell. I watch the dust rise into the sky, and as it rises, it mocks me. I hear voices but see no one. Just the hills that continue to move like waves.

I have been sitting still at the top of the first hill waiting for what might come next. I have the chill of fear all over me. Something is about to happen again. I don't feel pain like before. This is much worse. My skin crawls like the hills. It rolls like waves, and I can see the dust rising from within my body. The smell is like death. I retch, and the dust crawls out of my mouth. *I cannot breathe. I cannot breathe! Someone, help me!*

I feel the dust circling my neck, cutting off the circulation of blood to my brain. Stopping the flow of air to my lungs. My frozen feet and hands are unable to help me to help myself. I feel the blackness moving in. The tiny pin points of light closing in just before I become unconscious. And as the dust around my neck increases in pressure, I feel, more than see, the ground opens like a canyon before me, and I am falling over the edge. The dust squeezes my neck in one last attempt to stop all air flow and end my life for good.

I know I am falling. It feels faster than when I was flying into the sky. As I fall, the dust swirls in and around me like a cushion. No longer is it around my neck, but breathing is still too hard. When I inhale, I suck in dust and choke again. Falling into blackness. Into doom, I am sure. I don't know how I know. I just do. Again, I wonder what I have done to deserve this.

How long I was in the motion of falling, I could not say. I begin to bounce off an invisible wall, and as I do, a flash lights up my darkness for a second. As the bouncing continues, I feel like I am part of a game. With each bounce, I lose a patch of skin. I can see muscle and tendon. In some spots, I can see bone. But there is no blood. Just the dust circling through the torn spots of my body. Down, down into the abyss, I continue to travel. The dust carrying me along, as I somehow knew it should.

I begin to feel pain again. In my hands and feet first and then moving up my body. The dust begins to move faster through me, leaving holes as it weaves its way through me. Sharp, stabbing pains that draw blood as it lacerates me. I try to scream, but the dust invades my vocal cords. I want this to end, but I feel like this is what the dust wants to hear. I will not voice what is in my mind. But how can I not?

I see and feel the dust leave me as I hit something solid. The ground? I am not sure that is what you would call it. It looks like a swamp, but it has a sticky, salty smell like old blood. I realize my chair is gone and I am freezing. I have open holes in my flesh where the skin and muscles have been torn. It is then I realize I am standing in my own blood. It is leaving my body and flowing onto the ground. Moving in waves like a river. How can I have that much blood within me? The more blood that flows, the colder I become. The colder I become, the less the pain.

The atmosphere in this place has an orange glow, and I can see things flying high overhead. I cannot make out the shapes, but I do not feel fear at this time. I realize they are moving closer to me and as they come, the colder, what was left of my skin, becomes. I am unable to move. I am stuck to the ground by my own blood. By my own fear and weakness. By all the wrongs I have done in my life to others and to myself. Then I realize something. The holes torn in my body are my fault. The blood escaping from my body is not all my own but the blood of those I have wronged.

I am encircled now by those who are flying around me. They are putting thoughts in my head that should not be there. Thoughts of things that I could never even let myself think. Unspeakable things. The pain increases as the thoughts increase. My skin is frozen, and pieces are falling to the ground, swept away into the blood stream. The memories and thoughts increase until I am tormented into screaming for my life to end. As I continue to scream over and over for the end to be swift, I can feel the dust return. Swirling around me as I now understand what a horror of a human being I had been in my life. Faster, they circle as I scream until sound will no longer come out. I fall to my knees and feel remorse so great that I know I cannot endure it any longer.

"Please, let it end. Take my life. I deserve it." This comes out in a whisper and as soon as I utter it, everything stops. I know the dust is inside me. Waiting for those words to be said aloud. I feel intense heat as flames shoot up all around me. I feel the flames inside me just as the dust wants. I burst into flames before blackness descends on me once again.

I have a great sense of time having passed. Many hours, weeks, months, years. I do not know where I was. Where I had been. Where I am going. I open eyes that should not be there. I feel with my hand that should be gone. I am in my chair where I had been left. I am afraid. I am afraid of fear. Of my mind and where it has taken me. Or am I really gone? I can feel my sore throat. I had been screaming. The hairs on my arms have been scorched. I have been near intense heat. There are red spots on my feet and a layer of dust on my lap. The hill that has never been there is now a permanent fixture. This has been real. As real as my other experiences have been.

The sun is setting. It is still light yet, but I know they will come for me soon, and this time I almost welcome it. I can take no more today. I cannot do this. I cannot. I must leave. I utter as loud as my voice will allow. *Why me? Have I not paid enough? Is there nothing good left inside of me?* I repeat this over and over again in my hoarse whisper. I beg until I can beg no more.

I look to the sky. For what, I do not know. For comfort. For sanity. For reality, although I have some sense that my reality is not the reality of others. I do not know why this is. Why am I here? Why do I exist? I have some sense that I have asked these questions most of my life, if I had a life, and answers have always eluded me.

I feel something on my shoulder. I have a flash of fear, but I realize it is just a bird that has chosen to land there. I cannot see it, but I hear the song. I feel it leave and land on the ground, but when I look, I see it is a child. About ten years old. She is smiling at me. She is smiling through her tears. She touches me, and I feel peace. I feel wanted, and I realize I feel what she feels. By her touch, I am giving her what she needs. She touches my hair. She touches my hand. She touches my heart. I feel her hand massaging my heart into life. Her life. My life. As she touches my head, I feel her in my brain, and I know that she is me. I am in another time. Another dimension. I cannot explain or understand it, but I feel alive for the first time.

She takes my hand, and I hesitate for a few seconds. I see she hesitates too, but with my smile on her face. She nods once, and I know why I hesitated. I was waiting for the mist or the dust to come after me once again. She places my hand on her heart, and as she does, I feel myself shrinking into her. I am becoming her even though I know I am her. We are one, and I know for sure I am going to leave here once again, and somehow, I am aware that it is for the last time.

I step forward into the future. The past. The present. I feel my bare feet on the soft grass. I am walking and lifting my hands to the beautiful sunset sky. The evening birds are winging their way to their homes for the night. The beauty all around me is bowing to my presence. I gain strength from it, and although I am only a child in body and spirit, I feel myself grow in height and body mass. I am looking down at the trees and the life all around me. I feel them watching me, but it is a good feeling. I feel the evening sun on my skin warming me. No mist to make me feel like I am in a cold sweat. I breathe deeply, and there is no dust to choke me. I am really free this time.

I take giant steps because, with my size, it is normal. Normal is something I have never known. I reach to feel the tree tops. The wildlife embraces me, and in my heart, I bow to them. I know they understand. They move with me as I go toward my destination. In my brain, I do not know where I am going, but my feet know exactly where I need to be. I am a willing participant this time.

The grass gives way to soft sand. I feel it between my toes, and I am lifted to a height of exhilaration that I have never known but have always wanted. I reach down and run my hands through it. As the sand runs through my fingers, I know that it signifies the time that has passed in my life. Way too fast. Aided by my many failures and wrongs. But I know those no longer exist in my life. They have been exorcised by the mist and the dust, and I now know why I was taken to those places of horror. I have been cleansed so that I can live. So that I can know why I exist. So I can enjoy what it feels like to be happy and loved. For once, I understand the motive and something greater than myself.

I see the ocean before me. I have never seen it before but have heard of it. It has been a longing I have forgotten in the dark recesses of my mind. My childhood dream. The realization hits me as to why I am now a child. I am having thoughts and remembrances of that time in my life before the darkness descended upon me. Consumed me. But why that happened is being kept from me, and I know in my heart that it is for the best. I also know I have already paid for those wrongs and they are no longer mine to keep.

I step into the warm water of this clear turquoise ocean. The surface is like glass. I can see the ocean floor. I walk farther into the deep, and the water surrounds me, filling me with joy and peace for the first time in my life. I sink down under the water, and I open my eyes. I see beauty like I could not have imagined. Fish of all kinds and shapes. Plants of the sea. I have no knowledge of other creatures, but I know they are here only for my good.

I float on my back. My hair fans out around my face. I feel the warmth in the dimming light of the sun. The sun is standing still for me. For this moment in time. It is warm, and I am one with the universe. I know this is where I am supposed to be for all time. Because of my size, I am very far out in the ocean, but I can still feel the ocean floor on my feet. I stand and walk through the water. Farther and farther away from the shore. The creatures of the sea and air are with me. Time continues to stand still for me. I have become the joy I have been seeking for a lifetime.

I look to the shore. It is closer than I thought. I realize I am moving not of my own accord once again. I see someone there waving at me to come back. I realize it is me. It is time to go. I am no longer joined to myself as a child. I feel different inside, and although I still feel peace, there is an underlying sense of the unknown again. Just enough to make me reluctant to leave my sanctuary of the ocean. I turn to look behind me, and the creatures are gone. But in my rational self, I realize they cannot leave the water as I can. The birds are still overhead.

I step onto the warm sand and take my hand in hers. She smiles at me, and I know that I am no longer able to touch the tree tops. I am my normal size again. I still feel good. Freedom is earned. It is not a right. That thought runs through my brain as we make our way back to my chair, where my life is spent. I know this has all been a lesson for me. I have that knowledge and understanding. I have paid a price for my life, and I have been rewarded as well. Now the balance has returned. I know for once in my life, I matter.

I sit, and as I do, I see my child self backing away, and her smile leaves as she does. I feel part of me is gone. I stare into space just as they come for me.

"Time to come in for the night." I hear one of them say this. She puts her arms under mine and pulls me up in my seat. She is not kind.

"Be careful," another says.

"No reason to. She can't feel. There is nothing left of her brain. The experimental drugs have had no effect on her. She is just another ward of the prison system given to us for experimental testing. Sometimes there is an improvement, but not with this one. She was a vicious criminal. She does not deserve any kindness. She is just a shell now. Her brain has been dead for years. No thoughts. No reaction. No hope for any improvement. She will be terminated in the morning."

"That is really too bad," said the other one. "She is still young."

"Not so young that she could willingly take the lives of so many others. Tried to take her own life so many times without success. Now we will take it for her. She would not care anyway. She has no heart. Never did. She had many small strokes from abusing her body with recreational drugs. She lost the ability to speak, hear, or think. The new laws allow the system to take her life when we are done with her body. We are done. It is documented that her brain is dead. She is too much work to keep playing these games."

I feel the terror come back. I try to speak or move, but I cannot. I stare into space. My brain is very much alive. Why can't they see? As they put me roughly into the uncomfortable bed, I understand. I am not strong. I am not weak. I am nothing, and I am no one. I cannot see. I cannot hear. I can talk, but I have no language. I have thought, but I cannot think. Someone once said, "I think; therefore I am." If I believe that, I am not here. I am at the end...

COLD MOON

Nicole e. Castle

Cold moon
shines through our window
right into my eyes.

Eyes that watch my brother slide out of his warm bed
and tiptoe, oh so softly,
across our bedroom floor.

I can hear him,
shut our door, oh so softly.

I can hear him,
Slink down the stairs, somehow missing
the loose boards, into the kitchen.

At the backdoor, it opens, and closes, oh, so softly.

I lie still, my breathing heavy.

I can hear, the crackle of the blades of grass
as he walks upon the lawn

I rise and step to our window.

Bright moon
shines down upon my brother

Naked and silent
he blends with the snow, his pale skin gleams
with the breath of winter.

It licks him and he quivers.

I stare at his small feet that dangle in the air.
He stares at the sky and
plucks a star from the void.

The moon
shines into our room,
sniffing for me.

DESIRE

Mary Ring

White knuckles wrapped around the cord, William rapidly pulled the plug. He held his breath, keeping his eyes closed, and waited for the beeping to stop. *Unplugging it had to work,* he thought to himself. *There was no way unplugging it would not work.* However, within a few seconds, the beep noise resumed. Cautiously he opened his eyes, just long enough to reveal the bright green trio of sixes continuing to flash on the display. Closing his eyes, William slowly let out the stale air he had been holding in. He called out for his wife, Rachel. *She always knows what to do,* he thought. After waiting for her response and hearing nothing, he shuddered. The hair on the back of his neck stood up.

He felt sick. Only a few hours prior, he had eaten an abnormally large meal. All of the food settling in his stomach was suddenly creeping back up into his esophagus. Quickly taking a deep breath, he swallowed to keep the food down. Planting his cold, wet feet firmly on the ground, he reopened his eyes. Glancing at the unplugged cord on the floor and back around again, he surveyed his surroundings. Unsure of what was really happening and what was not, William carefully lifted his feet from their firm position and started to move. As he worked his way around the room, he steadied himself by keeping one hand on the countertop. The smooth surface felt refreshing to his sweaty palm. Suddenly, he found himself at the kitchen table.

William sighed, taking another glance at the microwave as he sat down. *Unplugging it had to work,* he repeated this statement to himself. He kept his eyes on the microwave as he heard the beep continue. Slamming his eyes closed and his fist against the wooden table simultaneously, he took another deep breath. The realization that this sound was, matter-of-fact, only in his mind became clear. He continued to keep his eyes closed as he sat at the table, pondering what else he could do to make the noise stop. He knew he would have to eat more.

William stood up and slowly maneuvered his way back toward the microwave. The beeping was deafening, the sound was unbearable, and he needed to end the noise. Grasping the cord, he plugged the machine back into the outlet and watched as it powered on. The microwave was black, mostly shiny, and with a quick glance, it could pass as brand new. The bright numbers flashing on the display showed the wrong time of day due to the repetitive unplugging and plugging in. William pressed his index finger three times against the worn-down number six on the touchpad, then he pressed start.

Waiting for his leftovers to reheat, he paced the floor. The beeping noise in his mind had finally stopped and was replaced with the peaceful sound of the microwave humming. William started to grow excited about his meal, despite still being full from eating earlier. Clearing his throat as it finished reheating, he called out to his wife Rachel to let her know that the food was ready.

Hearing the beep to signal the food was done gave him an adrenaline rush; this time, the noise was real. William paused for what felt like hours, taking in the moment. Hesitating, he carefully opened the door and took out the bloody plate. He stared at the warm mush and licked his lips; it was too delicious to resist any longer.

Using his bare hand, he began to eat the bloody slop, shoving it into his mouth.

"Sorry, Rachel," William whispered to the empty room. He couldn't stop eating her.

Diary of a Vampyre Slayer

R.L. *Fink*

There's one thing about Vampyres I really hate. Actually, scratch that. There are two things that I really hate about them. The first is before they turn, they are normal, with jobs, homes, pets, and families. Then, some other Vampyre bites them, and they turn into a monster, which I have to kill.

The second is because they have turned, they are a problem I have to deal with, even on weekend mornings. There was a time when I didn't have to wake up until noon, and only then because I was hungry and needed to eat Frosted Flakes on the couch while watching cartoons. Now I'm up as soon as the sun is up, and there are no cartoons to watch, even if I decided to take a day off because most of the network has probably been turned already. Or I killed them.

If they had promised to balance being a walking corpse and broadcasting the latest *Tom and Jerry* on Saturdays, I might have reconsidered. The only movies I have left are the ones I salvaged before this whole mess started, and I've got them memorized.

But I digress. My name is Alex. That's it. Just Alex. I used to have a last name. I used to have a family too. Well, I had my dad, who took me to baseball games, intimidated any boyfriend I brought home, and taught me how to drive. Now he's in hiding with a few select families who have managed to avoid the bite. One day, when this is all over, I'll be able to see him again. Until then, I have to keep fighting.

It's morning at the abandoned mall. I stepped over a body with my leather boot, trying not to slide in the blood on the floor. I'm trying not to make any noise to bring out the rest of the cavalry. I have been watching this place for weeks, and there were about a hundred Vampyres sleeping inside. There was a time when going up against those numbers would have been suicide, but I've gotten pretty good over the past two years.

Before entering, I threw a couple of my homemade garlic stink bombs in the air vents. They hate it; they absolutely hate the smell. It drives them completely bonkers. It also puts them to sleep for a couple of hours, so all I have to do is walk in, preferably when there's still a little sunshine, and then stake them through the heart.

Now it sounds easy, but here's the catch. Some Vampyres have started building an immunity to the stuff, and they're the ones I really have to watch out for. They are not newly-dead Vampyres either. They have actually been around for a while, and they want to kill me just as much as I want to kill them. Don't get me wrong, the stink bombs are useful, but it mostly helps me get rid of the foot soldiers, the grunts. If I could stop the generals, I might actually have a chance at cleaning up this world. But since I haven't figured out a solution yet, I'm here hunting in this abandoned strip mall and getting Vampyre ick on my new leather boots.

One of the Vampyres lying on the ground stirred, and I went over, stake held ready. She looked like someone's granny, with white hair in tidy little curls around her head, wearing a pink pantsuit, rather worse for wear. Even her sneakers were those orthopedic ones for people with bad arches. She looked so peaceful lying there. I bet she used to clip coupons and bake cookies for her grandkids. I hesitate for a second, and then her body tenses, her nostrils flaring.

She's on her feet, her eyes open in half a second, and the sweet, wrinkled little face turns into a feral snarl. I plunge the stake home before she has time to tear my eyes out with her little granny nails, and she vanishes into a pile of slippery ooze.

It's a side effect of being a Vampyre. The way it works is once someone is bitten, a virus enters the body through the saliva and into the bloodstream. It enhances certain qualities about them; gives them speed, strength, and the need to kill anyone who doesn't smell like them, who isn't like them. All the extra takes a toll on the body, rots them from the inside. If they're newly-dead, sometimes I can stake them, and nothing happens.

Except, of course, they give off the smell of a Thanksgiving turkey my dad once accidentally left in the car for an afternoon. If they have been Vampyre for at least a few months, their bodies resemble a gooier texture, like a smashed pop tart or cafeteria pudding. Then there are those who have been Vampyre for a REALLY long time, ones who have been like that for two years or more. Those will turn to dust; like Colin. When I finally catch him, he'll look like the powder on the bottom of a bag of Cheerios.

I walked around the mall twice, and no one else stirred. Then I noticed a blood trail on the floor. Something has dragged one of the bodies into the shadows and is feeding. My heart sped up a notch in fear—could it be him? Then a pang of disappointment hit me as I realized he wouldn't do something this stupid. Like me, Colin has gotten smarter over the years and more experienced.

By nature, Vampyres prefer the sweet tang of normal, human, *Homo sapien* blood. Considering that it is harder to come by now, Homo vampyrus works just as well. It's like the difference between a fresh loaf of bread just out of the oven, versus something that has been pushed to the back shelf for a few months. Fresh is best, but if you're starving, who cares if there's a little mold growing on the crust?

The noises were coming from a darkened shop, something that used to be an old Kids Gap. Man, I miss those days. Every year, a week before school started, I'd drag my dad in there and leave him standing uncomfortably by the neon couches with pop music blaring from the speakers and pick out some new outfits for school. Afterward, we'd go to the batting cages and work on my swing. Dad would buy us hot dogs from the street vendor, and we'd stay there until the manager yelled at us that it was closing time.

In those days, all I had to worry about was making the softball varsity team in the spring, passing a math test, or getting a date to the fall dance. Now here I am, wide awake on a Saturday morning, busting my butt to stay alive. The sucking noises continued, and I crept closer, picking up a mannequin's arm lying on the floor as I went. Here comes the tricky part because if this goes wrong, I'm going to look like hamburger meat.

Pricking my finger, I rub a thin line of blood along the plastic arm and wave it around like a piece of steak. I can hardly smell the coppery aroma, but I know the Vampyre can because the feeding stopped.

Remember that bread simile I used a while back? That brief prick of my finger—to the sucker in the corner—is like opening the bakery door to a starving person. Except, in that case, a beggar wouldn't go charging for my jugular vein. Well, maybe, if my neck was made of fresh bread.

Some of the clothes racks were thrown out of the way as a dark shape hurtled toward me, fangs bared in a snarl. I swung the arm, timing it, so I hit it in the throat and tipped it over onto its back. I drove the stake into the male Vampyre's chest before it had time to react and the body dissolved into a pile of stinking ooze.

I have done this so many times now, and it's still disgusting. Poor sucker. He was probably some normal guy who had a family and dog before he was bitten. Now he looks like a large pile of frozen chocolate custard on a hot day.

I know at that moment I thought I should probably knock on wood or something because I heard the sound of slow clapping approaching my position. I yanked my sunglasses out of my pocket and put them on. I know who it is, but unlike a stupid grunt, I actually need to see this jerk.

"Glasses look good on you, Lexy," said a familiar voice. Nathan Horgan, former captain of my high school football team, stepped into view just outside the pool of light. At six-foot-two, with blond hair and the body of a swimsuit model, he still looked like Glendale High's favorite heartbreaker, complete with a raggedy letterman jacket. Except for his eyes. They were the eyes of a monster, blood-red and hungry for the kill.

"Wish I could say the same thing about you, Nate," I said, scanning the darkness behind him. "Maybe you should try and get some sun."

Nate smirked. "That's funny. How long have you been waiting to use that line?"

"Oh, a couple weeks," I said casually, still scanning the empty mall. I didn't like how quiet it was. Alive or dead, Nate never traveled far without a posse of obedient followers. "I don't see your boss around. I'm only important enough for his right-hand thug?"

"Annoyances like you are only dealt with by number one men like me."

I forced myself to laugh, daring him to step into the light. "Get any closer, and I'll make you look like number two."

Nate snarled, and I caught a flash of fangs, but he didn't move forward. I had to make him even angrier.

"So, what's the plan, Nate? We going to fight? Or were you hoping to catch a movie with me?"

"Not today," Nate smiled and licked his lips. "You're going to die."

I yawned, trying to look bored. "You've been saying that for two years. Maybe I should get you a card. I'm sentimental that way."

"Not sentimental enough to stop killing my children."

"You call those victims your children?" I felt my temper rise. "They were regular people before you turned them into bloodthirsty monsters."

"They were special. Chosen. To help carry out the master's great plan."

"Actually, they're practice, for me," I goaded him. "Until I can hunt Colin down and put a stake in his heart."

"Don't you dare say the great master's name!" Nate stepped forward with a hiss, and I steeled myself to hold my ground. "You are not worthy of that honor."

"Colin, Colin, legs like ramen." The words didn't rhyme, but it still got Nate mad enough because, without warning, he stepped into the light, his hood pulled low, protecting his face from incineration. I took a step back and grabbed another stake.

Nate lunged, swinging at me with fists protected by leather gloves, trying to chase me into the shadows. I fended off the blows, and we circled in the light, looking for an opening in each other's defense.

"I like the gloves Nate," I panted, "You borrow those from Gucci?"

"The owner is a friend of mine," Nate said, "makes it easier to go outside."

"Gotta love Vampyre discounts, I suppose." I dodged a blow to my head and got a punch in the stomach that had me almost bending over.

"You should try it some time. Join us," Nate said.

I shook my head, fighting for breath. "Tell Colin he can jump on a stake."

Nate dove at me with fangs bared, and I stepped sideways, letting his own momentum carry him into the shadows again. Then he turned, unexpectedly calm, a smile on his face, and shrugged. "Well, I tried."

Raising his gloved hands, he clapped twice. I felt the hair on my neck stand up as I heard the sound of approaching boots and the sound of marching ringing through the abandoned mall.

I could see the figures of Vampyres approaching, their red eyes glowing like the embers of a fire. Within a few seconds, they surrounded the ring of sunlight I was standing in.

"Let me guess!" I tried to keep my voice casual as I let my hand stray into my jacket pocket, feeling for the circular object among the other items. "You gave me a little warm-up, so now it's time to send in your muscle to do the dirty work."

Nate shrugged again. "Or you could save us all the time and just give up."

I had fought too long to stay alive to give up now. "Keep dreaming, jerk," I snapped and flipped open the make-up compact I'd been holding in my hand, catching him full in the face, the reflected sunlight burned a fist-sized hole in his cheek.

Nate screamed in outrage and pain as the smell of burning flesh filled the air. The sucky thing is, given time, his wound will heal, courtesy of the virus. But it still pissed him off.

"Almost hit your eye that time, Nate," I taunted him. "Would you like me to try again?"

"Joke while you can," Nate rasped, clutching his face. "My children will rip you to shreds." He turned to the waiting Vampyres. "Finish her off! No mistakes this time."

There were hungry snarls from the watching Vampyres. They circled the light like jackals, held back by the sunlight. I called out to Nate, trying to delay the inevitable.

"What, that's it? Just going to go slinking back to your master and hope they kill me?"

"Goodbye, Alex."

"Whatever you say, sweetheart," I shouted, struggling to remain calm. "What is it? Twentieth time is the charm?"

Nate did not reply, he merely pointed to me with a gloved hand. The Vampyres surged past him, licking fangs eagerly. The fight to the death had begun. Again. One or three of the stupid ones jumped at me and tried to knock me out of the sunlight. I dodged and two actually collided with each other in a ray of sunlight. They fried instantly, scorched flesh turning to ooze. The others hissed and circled like a pack of hyenas.

I tried not to look like I was shaking in my boots and give them my best smile. I'd faced overwhelming odds before, but it looked like Nate had recruited an army—and then some.

"Now, boys and girls," I said, raising my voice to be heard over the snarling undead. "I just want to go over a few ground rules with you. No cheating, no biting, and above all, no tattling to daddy. And if *any* of you get ooze all over my new shoes, I am going to be very, very annoyed.

All I got in response was more hissing. "Why do I even try?" I sighed. "I'm wasting perfectly good comeback lines on you blood addicts!" I had four stink bombs stuffed in my back pocket, and I took them, lit and threw them into opposite ends of the pack. The ranks thinned considerably as, one by one, the Vampyres succumbed to the smell.

I switched my stake back to my right hand just in case any of them got too close and searched through my jacket pocket with my left until I found what I was looking for. I had another surprise for those who were still standing. Something I learned back when I was in Pre-K. I pulled out my magnifying glass and focused a beam of reflected sunshine on an unsuspecting Vampyre. He let out a scream as first his hair, then his head caught on fire.

I hit a female standing next to him with particularly long locks. Her head and torso went up in flames as well.

I learned this by accident a few weeks ago; Vampyre hair is extremely flammable. Probably due to their lack of decent hair conditioner, though it could also be the fact that they're, well, undead. I hit another, and another. It was like burning ants again, except on a much larger scale. There was mass panic in the room as the Vampyres ran around, trying their best to beat out the flames. Some got too close to others, and they caught on fire as well. The smell of burned hair and decomposed skin makes me want to puke. Vampyre killing isn't tea and cookies with the Queen. If it was, maybe there would be more of us. Or maybe not. Colin has been doing a spanking-good job of killing off everyone except... well, me.

More Vampyres were howling for my blood, and I kept the mirror in my left hand and my stake in my right, alternating between stabbing and frying. I tried to keep up a steady rhythm, but wouldn't you know, the other team tends to cheat; some coming all at once, others sneaking up behind. But I still managed to get them all. The mall now smells like the time the grill exploded during Dad's barbeque birthday party a few years ago. No one was hurt except for the rack of pork ribs roasting on the fire. This is worse, though. The pork ribs didn't scream in agony.

I fought the bile rising up in my throat. Some of the Vampyres were hobbling around on charred limbs, stumbling and slipping in the ooze of their defeated companions. A few fell over, twitching, and lay still as they, too, began to decompose into organic matter. The rest were sleeping off the effects of my stink bombs. If I didn't step out of the light soon and stake them, they would rejoin the masses trying to attack me.

I'm tired; so tired. My adrenaline rush waned, and my arms and legs felt leaden. I wish I could stop fighting. I wish I could rest. I was dripping with sweat, and I raised my arm, frying another Vampyre as I wiped my sweat with my less sweaty shirt. Just when I thought it couldn't get any worse... I heard the sound of more boots approaching in the distance. That bastard, Nate, sent reinforcements.

There was no way I could stake them all. I had only one thing left to try, and I'd never tested it before. I took two bottles out of my pouch, testing the weight as I scanned the approaching army.

I had only a few things in my favor. Firstly, they were hungry. I knew from experience, Colin purposefully starved them in order to make them more eager for blood—my blood in this case. Their senses were on high alert, especially their sense of smell. They were seeking the scent of fresh human blood like sharks in the water. While there are ample bodies lying around they can snack on, I am a tastier morsel than the charred lumps of Vamp flesh languishing on the dirty marble floor. All this self-preservation exercise was, unfortunately, making me smell better and better with every minute.

Secondly, the cremated Vampyre creates a smoke that is very disorienting for the newbies who are relying on their olfactory systems. The bottles in my hands came with smoke too, but the added aroma to the rest of the smells in the room would make it extremely confusing. However, the bottles also contained an ingredient that could be my salvation or death, depending on my timing. My blood.

I squinted, looking to the back of the mall; the reinforcements were getting closer. If I waited any longer, I could be stuck in a mass blood bath of no return. I lit and tossed the bottles, aiming for the doors where the new Vampyres were coming in. The little objects exploded, releasing a cloud of vaporized human blood scent over them all.

There was a crumbling stair railing to my left, and I leapt for it, managing to grasp a bar with a couple fingers, pulling myself up and out of the way. If the Vampyres were hypothetical sharks, the bottle was a hypothetical dummy dropped in the water and covered with bloody steaks. Or, in their case, another bleeding shark.

The mall became total chaos as Vampyre turned on Vampyre, totally consumed in bloodlust. It didn't matter what they tasted like now. The scent of my blood overwhelmed it all. Ordinarily, the two parties *might* have been smart enough to realize the room didn't suddenly fill with humans, but they were hungry. Their primal super sniffers had been awakened. Neighbor turned on neighbor, neither realizing they were one and the same species.

Using the distraction below to make my escape, I followed the railing as far as I could and then dropped the ten feet to the ground and sprinted for the open doors. Very few Vampyres were in the area. Most had converged to the back of the mall where the feeding frenzy was. Those that tried to stop me, I staked, staying to the sunlight as much as possible. I was exhausted, my heart was pounding, and my legs were seizing up from exertion. The door was just a few more steps away...

I was almost there. I could see the blue sky outside the open door when a pair of hands fastened unexpectedly around my ankle. I stumbled and fell, helpless as fangs latched onto my pant leg... and bit down.

FRANCIS

Andrew Allen Smith

Jimmy has always been a little odd. He's been my next-door neighbor since we were six, and as we entered high school, we just drifted apart. I went with the more mainstream group and became a cheerleader, just like every all-American girl would want to do, and Jimmy became that kid that sat at the back of the room and gazed out into the sky while the rest of us were lost in this world.

If you think about it, Jimmy probably had it easy. He was so brilliant that he didn't have to study or sit around and do homework. He was funny to the people around him, but he only engaged when they engaged him and spent far more time daydreaming and drawing on his 'filled with graffiti' notebook. From the outside, he was an average person, and although I didn't think of him as a friend anymore, we were friendly, and he always spoke highly of me to others.

This afternoon as I was walking home from school, he joined me. I usually never saw him on my walk from school, as he usually was at school late studying in one of the labs or talking to the biology teacher. As we walked together, it was awkward at first. I asked how he was doing, and he said, "fine." I would ask questions about how his parents were, and again he would say, "fine." There appeared to be no rhyme or reason to it, and the more we interacted, the more I wondered why we were walking together at all.

"What are you doing for your science project this year?" I was honestly curious as I hadn't started on mine.

"I've been working on an interface where I can talk to insects," this was obviously of interest to him. "I've spent a significant amount of time developing a pheromone and micromagnetic pulse interpreter that should give me the ability to talk to higher orders of insects."

"That sounds awesome," I wondered about all the ants and being able to tell them to leave the house. "Have you tested it yet?"

"I began testing it last week and was super stoked with success. I was working with a Polistes Dominulus, and I couldn't believe how well things translated. I was able to have her navigate a maze for some honey just by teaching her left and right. It was one of the most awesome things I have ever dealt with."

I could imagine him sitting in his room playing with his wasp, and of course, my mind wandered, and I almost giggled to myself but kept it in. "That sounds awesome," I lied. "How do you think you're going to do?"

"I'm not sure it's gonna matter," he looked distraught for a moment and then said, "I already have my next two years planned out, and the science project won't give me much of an advantage. What are you going to do?"

I was on the spot now since I had brought it up. "To be perfectly honest, I don't have anything. My parents don't have any time to help, and I know it's my responsibility, but I think I've over-committed to everything and never seem to have enough time."

"There's always the stand-by baking soda volcano." I know he was being sweet, but it was almost like a slap in the face. How could he be so bright and me so not clever?

"I think I can come up with something better than that." I was a bit irritated at his smugness. "I was just curious after last year with your rocket engine. Did you ever find it?"

"Well, kinda." He was a little awkward about the whole situation. His rocket engine had gone up so fast that everyone lost sight of it in a second. "It appears that my rocket is in geosynchronous orbit. Every day at 4:00 AM, I am in range of the tracker for about an hour. There's a tiny solar panel on it, so it may run for a few years or more and let me know that it's out there, but as of yesterday, the orbit is exactly the same as when I launched the rocket last year."

"Oh my God." No one was ever told this about his last project.

"Yeah, I say that too." Jimmy pulled out his phone. "This is the picture from this morning as it passed the International Space Station. NASA has called a few times when they pick up the signals."

The picture was very clear, and you could easily see the space station's solar panels. "That's a really clear picture."

"Remember, I launched it with a disassembled Android phone as the brains. I had put the cameras from the phone on the front and sides of the rocket. The whole insertion period is on video."

I was irritated that he had gotten so bright while I had gotten popular. That's not how it's supposed to work.

I was supposed to be the center of attention and the brain.

"If you would like to come to see the project, I would love to show it to you." It seemed that Jimmy was in earnest, and I felt a little bad about my negativity towards him.

"I would like that." I again lied, but in the back of my mind, I thought if I could get something out of Jimmy's intelligence, I wouldn't have to work so hard.

The house wasn't that far away, and we soon walked up to his porch. The last time I had been in his house could have been as much as four years ago when I scraped my knee, and his mother bandaged it for me since both my parents worked. The house was a large Victorian kept in near perfect condition by Jimmy's father, a contractor in the area. We used to play in the house when we were young as it had eight large rooms on the first floor and six bedrooms on the second floor. Jimmy's two older siblings moved out, leaving him the entire house to stretch out. He took off his shoes at the door, and so did I. We walked upstairs to where his bedroom used to be, and he walked past it to what used to be a playroom. Inside was what could only be described as a mad scientist's lab. The room was filled with everything from plasma globes to numerous computers with flashy screen savers or actual running programs doing something I could not discern. There was a kitchenette and a small couch in the room as well. A worn blanket was on the couch that I recognized from years ago when Jimmy and I played in the house.

"This has certainly changed a lot," I said.

"Yeah, when Mom and Dad saw how interested I was in science and technology, they gave me free rein." Jimmy was walking to a corner where several glass cases covered the wall. "This is what I've been working on."

A computer with a strange screen had numerous wires going to open circuit boards on the side of an aquarium. Inside the aquarium, a hundred or so wasps wandered about as wasps do in the wild. On the screen, there were words that were short. I saw food, water, and prey, to name a few. The words scrolled by reasonably rapidly. Jimmy pressed a few keys on the computer, and the wasps seemed to perk up. I looked around Jimmy to see the word he had typed was "honey." Then he pressed a button, and a small dropper extruded a single drop of golden liquid into the center of the aquarium.

The wasps immediately went to the center and competed for the single drop, all except one. That one seemed to be watching Jimmy or me and was not as interested in the antics of the larger group. Jimmy put a small container to the side and slid a small door open, and that one wasp walked into the container. Jimmy then closed the small door and moved the container to another workstation. He put the container on the side, slid open a door, and the wasp buzzed a little, walked into the large area, then turned and looked at us both again.

"This is Francis," Jimmy smiled. "Francis is the one I have worked with the most. Watch this."

Jimmy typed into a computer connected to this particular aquarium, "Hello Francis."

The screen sat for a second, and then the wasp began moving, and a small second screen could see a close-up of Francis as the computer typed out, "Hello, keeper."

"Keeper?" I was slightly surprised that the words seemed to come from a wasp and that they made sense.

"Francis knows she's a prisoner," Jimmy was typing. "I'm not sure if I should release her because she may not return. The lifespan of a wasp is not very long, but they appear to have a significant amount of information they can pass down generation after generation by DNA. Francis is a queen and can live up to a year, but most wasps die within a few weeks. I have only been working with them for about six months, and her children in the other area pick up rudimentary commands from birth. She is far smarter than they are and can command them very easily. She works like a translator when I am talking to them."

I was a little freaked out. Bug boy here was talking to a bunch of wasps and giving them names. "Why Francis?"

"Mainly because she likes to sing. Hang on, let me show you." Jimmy fiddled with a speaker, and it clicked on. He then typed, "Can you sing for Audrey?"

The answer was actually kind of funny, "No."

"Can you sing for me?" Jimmy had a funny look on his face.

Francis began vibrating, her wings in different directions, and suddenly I heard the sound from the speakers. It sounded like something out of a lousy opera, but there were noticeable note changes as Francis sang. In the end, it lasted maybe a minute.

"Thank you," Jimmy typed.

"But how can she do that?" I was freaked out about the singing more than anything else, "I mean, she's not a musician. She's a bug."

"There was a study a few years ago in Michigan about how intelligent wasps are. I think that study didn't go into enough detail. I was playing with cell phones and found there was a certain frequency that a wasp reacted to. I spent six months here starting to translate simple pictures into words and actions that could be interpreted and sent from this console. I rebuilt it for the larger group, and it wasn't until I got a queen, Francis, that I didn't have to start over all the time. Like I said, most wasps only live a few weeks, meaning I had to start over with new ones that I would capture, but Francis has had two advantages. First, she will live much longer; second, she is laying eggs in the nest in the other aquarium, and I no longer have to catch wasps. This makes it easier for me to manage."

"Is Audrey, mate?" the screen flashed. "You are changed."

"What does she mean by that?" I asked.

Jimmy typed, "No," and then looked at me. "She knows who my mom and dad are, and wasps are very good at differentiating people. She knows the difference between objects very well too. If you left the room and returned, she would know you were Audrey. If she didn't see you for days, she would still know you were Audrey. For her, though, she applies wasp logic: females are in charge and mate with males. I have explained to her that it is different for humans. She understands, but I suppose it is a difficult concept for a wasp."

"Audrey is lie," the screen said.

"And what does that mean," I was feeling a little concerned.

"I'm not sure." Jimmy typed back to the screen, "Audrey is friend." Then he looked over at Francis staring at me.

"No," the screen said, "Audrey is lie."

"What does she mean by lie?" The silly bug was starting to make me nervous.

"She understands a lie, but I've never seen her interpret a person as a lie. At the start, all she ever asked for was to be free, and when she asked, I would say soon, and eventually, she said I was lying. It is a pretty straightforward concept in the animal Kingdom, I suppose. I said something, and I didn't deliver. Since then, she has come to terms with being captive but still doesn't like it."

"Are you going to let her go?" I asked.

"I'm not sure that would be a good idea," Jimmy was a little worked up. He typed honey on the screen, and a dropper placed honey in the aquarium as he turned to me. "She's no super wasp, but she understands a lot more than most wasps do. When I removed the need for her to hunt, kill, and took away all of her natural predators, she became like an information sponge. If I'm right and this information is passed downstream genetically, it might not be a good thing to let her loose in the wild. On the other hand, it would control itself relatively quickly because she no longer fears predators and can actually identify many different types of animals as predators."

"You know this is a little overboard for a high school science project," I laughed.

"Yeah, but it got you to talk to me." Jimmy moved closer to me. "I've missed you so much, Audrey, over the years."

I stepped back, not sure what to do. I am sure Jimmy thought that maybe there could be something between us, but I was sure not feeling the same. "I'm not sure what you're thinking, Jimmy, but I was just curious. I better go home."

"I just missed my friend." Jimmy lowered his head. "I had hoped for more but knew you had outgrown me."

"I'm sorry, Jimmy," I said as I went to the door and went downstairs. Jimmy came to the top of the stairs and looked down at me. I turned to see him, and it was apparent he had a tear in his eye.

"Do you think we could ever, like, go out?" Jimmy was hopeful in his eyes. "Just as friends?"

"Let me think about it." I wasn't sure why I said that because usually, I wouldn't have even listened, but something today made me feel different.

I let myself out the door and walked next door to my house.

I thought about Jimmy and his fantastic work with the wasps. There was no way my project would be anything near his. I wondered if I would be doing a baking soda volcano again this year.

Our house was nowhere near the size of Jimmy's parent's, but it was a lovely house, and I came inside once again to be alone. My parents both worked, and I was often alone for hours at a time. I usually had practice and dance team, and would not be home until late. But today allowed me to see Jimmy and be home alone. I thought about Jimmy again and realized I had grown into a pretty awful person. Sure, everyone wanted to be me, but I'm not sure if I wanted to be me. Having recently broken up with my boyfriend of six months, I realized that many things I was trying to be weren't meaningful. I set my backpack down and thought about Francis. Maybe Francis could see more than Jimmy was aware.

I left my backpack but grabbed my phone, went back to Jimmy's house, and knocked on the door. It was a few minutes, and Jimmy finally came to the door.

"Did you forget something?" It was apparent he was solemn, and I thought I probably just broke his heart somehow.

"Can we go talk to Frances for a minute?" I asked.

"Why would you want to talk to Francis?" Jimmy was a little guarded.

"I think I know why she said I lie." I slid into the door brushing against Jimmy a little but passed him and walked toward the stairs.

"That's a little forward, isn't it?" Jimmy followed me, and soon we were in his overly advanced lab.

Francis was still in her separate area, and numerous words were on the screen. The funny thing was that most of them were sentences. Jimmy tried to block the screen, and I pushed him out of the way to see a short conversation about how he liked Francis and me telling him that I did not like him.

"This is kind of what I was expecting," I said, "I have to be honest with you. When I came over here, I was looking for an idea. It's been a long time since we've been friends, then somewhere along the way, I found it was a problem to be a friend to you. You just didn't fit in my life anymore. When I sat over at the house, I realized that the wasp probably sees truth and lie a little differently than we do. No, I'm no scientist, but I'm betting I'm right."

"That's a huge assumption." Jimmy was looking at me like a German Shepherd figuring things out. "You're assuming that the wasp can see past all of our truth and lie because her perceptions are much keener."

"Basically, yeah." I sat at the chair in front of Francis. Francis had finished her meal of honey and was paying reasonably close attention to me. It's hard to tell where a wasp's eyes look, but it seemed I was the center of attention, so I typed in, "Audrey likes wasps."

The screen paused, then returned, "Audrey Lie."

I typed into the screen again, "Audrey likes dogs."

The screen paused for a moment, then returned, "Audrey, true."

"That's starting to make sense. I always thought that the reason Frances picked up on things so quickly was simply that she was brilliant. It's more accurate to say that her more complete perceptions of the world allowed her to weed out the things that were unimportant or that were emotional and focus on what was real. Imagine an insect as a perfect lie detector."

"That's exactly what I was thinking." I lowered my head. "When I got back to the house, I thought seriously about how terrible of a person I have been. I considered how nice you were and how much I was not being honest with you or with myself." I looked at Jimmy. "I'm not a very good person anymore."

"I think you are," Jimmy smiled; "somewhere inside of you."

The screen moved, "Audrey, true."

"Isn't that cute." I was laughing a little.

"Jimmy, mate," the screen lit up again.

"I don't think I'm ready for something like that," I said as I looked at Jimmy; "but I think I need to spend a little more time away from the people I've been hanging around with."

My cell phone began ringing, and I saw it was Chad. Chad and I dated for six months until I discovered he had been cheating. He was older than me, nineteen, and unwilling to let me go.

I declined the call, and then I looked over at Jimmy.

"You like me, don't you?" I asked.

"Well, I'm not sure." Jimmy was turning red, and to make matters worse, the screen suddenly said, "Jimmy Lie."

We both began laughing. I looked at Jimmy. "Please forgive me. I will try to be a better friend. I can't believe we both used to chase each other around this house."

My text message ding went off. "I saw you go into the house with that freak."

Chad was texting. I couldn't count the number of times I've blocked him; still, he texted using stupid programs that sent from different numbers every time.

Suddenly, another notification was, "If I can't have you, no one can."

"I had better go," I said to Jimmy. "I'll try to get in touch with you later."

The screen lit up, "Audrey Fear."

"Is that true?" Jimmy asked; "are you afraid?"

"No, I am not afraid." I was hoping I could get out of sight of the damn wasp.

"Audrey Lie," the screen lit up again.

"What's going on?" Jimmy asked.

There was a crash downstairs, and Jimmy moved towards the door.

"Don't," I said; "it's Chad, and he's crazy." I showed Jimmy the text message, "I know he has guns and knives, and he's just a little too crazy. I think he's coming for me and I'm sorry. Are your parent's home?"

"No, I am alone until later. They went out for the day."

"I'm sorry, Jimmy," I said as the door slammed open. Chad was standing there, and it wasn't someone I had ever dated. He was mussed and furious.

"What are you doing here with this freak?" Chad waved a small gun. It was small, but I knew it was more than enough to hurt either of us.

"We were just talking about a science project," I said.

"I like science. Why don't you show me the science project," Chad yelled.

Jimmy walked up to Chad and said, "You need to leave. Get out of my house."

The speakers behind me began buzzing, and I heard the now familiar music, only it was much different.

Something weird was happening. Chad shoved Jimmy to the ground.

"Trying to steal my girl, you little worm?" Chad growled as he pointed the gun at Jimmy. "Maybe it's time you meet your maker."

The buzzing was getting louder, the speakers hadn't turned up, but the buzzing was incessant.

"What the hell is all this buzzing crap?" Chad yelled.

The screen behind me was scrolling at high speed. It kept saying "Keeper Hurt" over and over. Jimmy tried to get up, and Chad kicked him in the face knocking him to the floor again. Chad walked to the more enormous aquariums with the dozens upon dozens of Wasps now covering the glass window.

"Now that's a lot of bugs," Chad rubbed his finger across it, and I saw wasps try to sting glass. I glanced at the screen behind me and saw the screen scrolling with multiple messages, then looked to the screen where Chad was standing, and all I saw was one word repeating over and over from seemingly everywhere.

"Chad, you have to leave. I don't want you to get hurt. You have to leave now," I pleaded.

"Ain't nothing in here gonna hurt me except you. You broke my heart."

"You cheated on me over and over, Chad. You don't want me. You just want to control me," I pleaded as the word scrolled over and over. "You need to go now."

"So," Chad exclaimed; "I didn't love them. I only loved you."

It seemed as though it was getting darker in the room. It was then I saw the window. It was slowly darkening, covered in something I could barely see. The buzzing was intense, almost deafening, where Francis was making her music, and all I could hear was buzzing. There was something else, too. It was almost like wood was crunching. I didn't know what it was, but it too was both subtle yet pounding in my ears.

"No, Chad, you only love you." I started to walk out, wanting to put distance between Chad and Jimmy. Feelings jumped through my mind as I realized this was a situation of my making. I was the evil one here. I knew who Chad was when I started dating him. I just lied to myself about him. Audrey lie.

Jimmy was struggling to get up off the floor, and Chad was grasping at my hair as I tried to get free. The gun was between us, and I needed to get away. I bit down on his hand. He smacked me across the face with the gun barrel. I sprawled across the floor and tasted blood. The buzzing continued to pound in my ears, threatening to burst my eardrums. It was everywhere. I saw Jimmy. He was almost at the window. He seemed to know what was going on. He was limping and hurt badly. Chad grabbed me by the throat and pulled me to my feet. I tried to catch my breath, but he had my throat tight. I choked and gasped, trying to breathe, and through the corner of my eye, I saw the window open and darkness close in on Chad and me.

"What the..." Chad exclaimed.

It was as though the specter of death entered the room. A cloud moved across the room with a purpose that no human could easily understand. Chad fell backward, pulling me on top of him, and I felt a million legs crawling all over my body, touching me, tickling every piece of my skin with tiny legs moving in unison to get off me and to their carefully assigned victim. I was in shock from the mere thought of what was happening and could not move. Still, it was what was before me that made me hold my breath as I watched hundreds of stingers press themselves into Chad's face, his arms, his eyes, so many that he couldn't even scream through the agony of so much venom at once. I watched from far too close the needle-thin stingers enter and exit Chad's skin and saw him open his mouth to scream only to be overwhelmed with even more wasps. His body began to convulse before me, and with the horror unfolding so fast, I simply fainted.

I don't know how long I was unconscious, but I opened my eyes and was on the small couch in Jimmy's lab. Nothing was buzzing, and nothing seemed to be going on. I tried to sit up, but Jimmy held me. "Take your time. The police are on the way."

I was covered in tears. As I sat up, I saw Chad in the corner, gun by his side, covered with a small jacket. The buzzing was gone, and, on the screen, next to Francis, all I saw were the words, "Keeper Safe."

The memory was burned into me of the event. As Francis had played her music, there was only one-word scrolling everywhere on the large aquarium. One single word, "Kill."

THE HEART-EATER

D.J. Matthews

Jake plopped onto a log in front of the campfire with a groan. Shoving carrot-colored hair off his dampened forehead, he tugged off his new hiking boots and rubbed his blistered feet.

Kevin was looking out over the water, "Wow, smell that fresh Hawaiian air!"

Jake scowled, "Kevin, it's hot and sticky," he smashed a mosquito on his arm, "and we're going to get malaria or dengue fever."

Kevin turned, giving him an annoyed look.

Sam poked his black head out of his tent, "Would you two shut up?" the flap flipped closed.

Kevin rolled his eyes, "If you hadn't gotten drunk, you could be enjoying this view and the fresh air."

Sam shoved his middle finger out of the tent.

Within seconds, snores emanated from the thin fabric.

"Why did we have to come all the way to Hawaii and sleep in a tent in the jungle? There are plenty of hotels and hot chicks down there. We could have just hiked up the mountain."

Kevin threw a muscular arm over his shoulder and pointed to the painted evening skies and the crystal blue water licking at them. His long, bleached locks tickled

Jack's bare shoulder where his tank-top ended.

"Adventure, my friend. Look at that view. We can't see the island from a hotel."

Jake shrugged off Kevin's arm, smashed another mosquito, and pushed up his glasses, "I'd rather not see the jungle unless it's in a book or a movie, and we shouldn't have left the state park."

"For once, get your nose out of the books and live a little. I'm doing this for you, buddy. You need a little adventure in your life. We've camped a million times. We don't need a dedicated campsite with a cute little fire ring and an electrical outlet. I want to experience the real Oahu."

Jake's brows pierced his hairline, "No, you're doing this for you, but I'm here to make sure you don't do something stupid."

Kevin laughed, "Do I ever?"

Jake narrowed his gaze and stared at his friend for long minutes, then picked up his bottle of water and took several large gulps. They sat in silence, listening to the sounds of the crackling fire and the shuffle of nocturnal animals around them.

Jake turned to say something and paused. "Hey, did you hear that?"

Kevin looked around, "Hear what?"

"It sounded like drums."

"Oh yeah, they do a show on the beach for all the tourists. Guys dress up in little grass skirts and pound giant drums while the girls dance around, and a man breathes fire. The tourists eat it up."

"This sounded close." He glanced over his shoulder, then at Kevin, "You know, there's a legend about these jungles."

"Oh, yeah?" Kevin settled on the ground, his back against a log, ankles crossed in front of the fire. "Do tell."

The scent of the fire and heat-filled vegetation filled Jake's nostrils. He shifted to the ground, leaning his back against the log, elbows resting on his drawn knees. "I read it in a book."

Kevin smirked, "Funny. What's the legend?"

"He was called Chief man-eater, a real-life cannibal, an inhabitant of the mist lands," Jake waved his hand, "These lands."

Kevin grinned. "You're making this up."

The fire crackled, and bits of timber floated up to disappear into the night. Stars twinkled overhead.

Jake took off his glasses, twirling them between his fingers. "No. No, the legend is true. Led by Ke-alii-ai Kanaka (The-chief-who-eats-men.) His followers were called 'heart-eaters.' After a battle between two warriors, the victor, whose strength was almost gone, would tear out the heart of the dying opponent and eat it to steal their strength for themselves. It's said that those who the chief and his followers partook of their flesh still roam the misty mountaintops looking to replace what was stolen from them."

Kevin laughed, "That's great. Trying to scare me, so I agree to go to a hotel tomorrow?"

Jake slipped on his glasses and shook his head, "Nope." He grabbed his boots and hobbled toward his tent, "I'm turning in, and yeah, I want to stay in a comfortable bed tomorrow."

Kevin waved him away, with a reference to the female anatomy.

Jake flipped his friend the middle finger and laughed as he crawled into his tent.

****

His body felt water-logged. A faint *thump, thump, thump* sounded, and he rolled his eyes. The saturated sleeping bag felt heavy. Jake rolled over, his heart pounding with the heat. Sweat slid down his cheek. He unzipped the bag and tossed it off. *God, it's hot!* Leaning on one elbow, he yawned and glanced around. The walls of his green tent glowed, and flames wavered in the shadows. *Shit, Kevin forgot to put out the fire.*

Rising to his knees, he reached for his pants. The ground under his fingers shuddered. Sucking in a breath, Jake unzipped his tent and poked his head out. A plume of black smoke billowed just above the tree line, and fire licked the branches of trees and brush nearby.

"Shit!"

He bolted from the confines of the tent and wobbled as the ground shuttered once again. He slapped the flimsy cloth, "Get up!"

A warbled, "Shut up!" came from Sam's tent.

"Fire!"

Kevin poked his head out of his tent a moment later, "What?"

Jake pointed, "Fire."

Kevin gasped and scrambled out. He shook Sam's tent, "Get up! There's a forest fire."

Sam crawled out and glared at Jake. "What did you do, nerd?"

"Run!" Jake said.

Sam's gaze swung to Kevin, and his eyes rounded, the inferno surrounding them, edging closer.

Stumbling from his tent, he took off running through the jungle, darting this way and that to avoid trees and swaths of fire.

Heat so intense it singed his nostrils blew toward Jake. Snagging his backpack and glasses, he started off. His latest read, *Dante's Inferno*, fell out of the side pocket of his backpack, and he snatched the book just as flames licked the side of Sam's tent a few feet away.

Kevin sprinted past, glancing back, "C'mon, Jake."

The ground trembled again. Soft thumps echoed through the surrounding wood. Jake stumbled, dropping his book a second time. Snatching the book out of the dirt, he tucked it under his arm, adjusted his backpack, and darted into the jungle. Legs pumping. Heart racing, he sprinted in the direction he'd last seen Kevin and Sam.

He tripped over a downed tree, his chin bouncing off terra firma hard enough for him to taste copper. Dazed, he pushed himself upright and straightened his frames. *Thump, thump, thump.* He blinked. *It must be after midnight, and they're still doing a show?* He glanced back. Flames reached toward him. Trees crashed to the ground, sending fireflies of embers into the night sky. Jake screamed; the roar of the fire inching closer swallowed the noise.

He darted left and came to a wall of flames and changed course, only to run into another mount of fire. Lava slid toward his feet. Heat singed his bare toes. In his haste, he'd left his shoes.

"Shit, shit, shit!" Choking on the sulfur and smoke-laden air, he fell into a coughing fit. Using his elbow, he tried to block the smoke.

Aimlessly, he wandered, searching for a way out and his friends. Fire reached toward him at every turn. Shielding his face with his elbow and holding his backpack with his other hand, he pushed forward. *Where are Kevin and Sam? They wouldn't just leave me. Well, Sam might,* he amended.

A twig snapped. Jake spun, his eyes scanning the smokey wood, "Kevin! Sam!"

A voice whispered in the dark, but he couldn't tell where it came from. *Thump, thump, thump.* A sudden flurry of movement surrounded him before a scream stilled the night. Something darted past his leg, and he stumbled, landing on one knee, hissing with the blow to his kneecap. Jake coughed hard as the acrid scent of sulfuric fumes, burning wood, and vegetation filled his mouth and lungs. He slipped his pack off, shoved his book inside, and reached for his phone. Pressing a finger to the sensor, the phone winked to life. Jake lowered and tried to shield himself with the surrounding brush. Quickly, he dialed and pressed it to his ear using his opposite a hand to help conceal the light. Silence filled the space. Frowning, he jerked it away from his ear and glared at the screen.

"Crap, no signal."

Probably knocked out by the eruption. He had no idea how close they were to the mouth of the volcano, but they were on it, and that was too close for him. Shoving the useless electronic back into his pack, he zipped it and slipped the straps over his shoulders. Snatching at the hem of his shirt, Jake covered his mouth and nose. He started moving again, in what he hoped was the way down. It felt like he was going down. He'd never had a sense of direction.

The ground shivered beneath his feet. *Thump, thump, thump.* Lava eased toward him like a serpent, and he changed course. The molten rock sizzled and burned through the foliage, eager to consume all within its path. He stepped on something sharp and went to his knees. Heat kissed the sole of his foot, and Jake scrabbled up, hobbling back toward what he hoped was safety. *We need to get off the mountain before that volcano blows. Why did I ever agree to this!*

"Kevin! Sam!"

This time there were no voices, only the *thump, thump, thump* of the drum. Smoke billowed and pulsed all around him. Coughing, Jake limped forward, a bruise already forming on his heel. Why hadn't he grabbed his shoes instead of his book? *Stupid, stupid, stupid.* Tugging at his back, he darted through the dense, smoke-laden wood looking for his friends and praying he was headed in the right direction to get off this God-forsaken volcanic mountain. Of course, it didn't matter what mountain you were on in Hawaii; they were all volcanos. Kohala was considered extinct. *Why couldn't Kevin have chosen that mountain to climb?* Jake cursed, stumbled, and crashed through the jungled forest with abandon.

"Kevin! Sam! Where are you?" Air whooshed behind him. Prickles of fear skated up his spine. Darting a quick glance over his shoulder, Jake sprinted till his lungs burned. He wasn't certain what made him need to flee. Something just felt off. A hidden log caught his foot, then another, and he crumpled onto the ground face-first.

Seconds passed. Breathing hard to stymie the panic threatening to consume him, he nearly screeched when a hand touched his shoulder.

"Sam, Kevin? That you?" Relief filled him.

"Man, am I glad—"

He rolled to a sitting position and stopped short. The figure loomed. Jake felt his mouth open. The man staring down at him with a broad smile was neither Kevin nor Sam. *Thump, thump, thump.* The large-bladed knife gleaming in the glowing embers of the fire rapidly raced toward them, dripping with a mysterious dark liquid. Sucking in, Jake floundered backward. *Heart-eater.* Leaves crunched, and twigs snapped under his retreat. The thumping was nearly deafening. *Or was that his heartbeat? Am I close to the luau?* He'd never wanted to be at a party so badly in his life. His feet finally found purchase as the man inched closer, raising the blade overhead. Jake found his voice. He screamed and darted into the wood, praying the knife-man wouldn't follow. *Thump, thump, thump. God, I wish they'd stop pounding those stupid drums.*

His lungs burned. The stitch in his side was so painful he nearly collapsed, but he kept going. Pushing his body to its breaking point. Fear of the stranger and the volcano pushed him forward until he could no longer breath or move. He placed a sweaty palm on a tree trunk and dragged in a deep lungful of air. The muscles in his unfit legs jiggled in spasms of protest. Blood rushed to his face, pounding with every hammering heartbeat.

"Jake!"

Kevin's voice was a welcomed relief.

"Kevin? Kevin. Thank God. Where's Sam?"

"Don't know. We gotta get outta here."

"Just let me catch my breath."

"No, no, we gotta go now. He's coming."

Jake felt his blood turn to icy, "Who?' But he knew; he'd just seen who.

"Don't know; he had a knife."

"You saw him too?"

Kevin gripped his arm and yanked, "C'mon."

"No, we have to go this way," Jake said.

"Are you crazy? That's where the knife man is."

"No, I just ran away from him in this direction."

"Okay, okay, so we go this way," Kevin said.

Together, they bumbled through the woods, unconcerned with how much noise they made.

The fire raged, sending up charred bits of wood. The sound of falling timber echoed through the vast expanse around them.

Jake caught sight of something on the ground.

"Kevin, wait!"

"What? Do you see the knife-man?"

"I think it's Sam." The two hurried over.

"He's passed out."

Jake rolled him over and gagged. His chest looked like it exploded from the inside. Blood bubbled. His unseeing gaze caught in a scream. Jagged flesh encompassed his upper torso.

Kevin turned and vomited, "Shit! That's messed up, man."

"What did this?"

"Who knows? Bobcat or mountain lion."

Jake frowned, "His chest. It's like something ripped out—"

Kevin sucked in, "His heart," he made a gagging sound and covered his mouth. "Heart-eater."

"What?" Jake turned, "That's ridiculous!"

"It's like the legend. Look, man, we gotta get out of here."

Jake eyed him, "That was just a myth."

"Until..."

Jake placed his hands under Sam's shoulders, "Help me."

"He's gone, man. Look at what's left of him."

"Grab his feet."

"No. Leave'em."

A loud *pop* sounded seconds before a limb fell onto Jake's head. Something began to writhe. A large brown serpent hissed.

"Ah, get it off, get it off."

He scrambled out from under the animal. Jake jumped back, lost his footing, and landed hard on his backside. And the snake darted toward the dense jungle, "What the hell? There're no snakes in Hawaii."

Kevin tugged Jake's arm, "C'mon, we have to get out of here before we end up like Sam."

Jake scowled, "We can't just leave him. We've gotta call someone."

"Who? The forest service? Look around, man. He's dead. His chest looks like a tank rammed through it. And the whole mountain is on fire." Kevin retched, placing a hand over his mouth. "Nothing we can do."

He sucked in shaky gulps of air.

"Wha—"

Kevin slapped a hand over Jake's mouth and pointed. They dropped to the ground, breathing hard through singed nostrils.

Jake felt his heart bounce in time with the roar in his ears. *We're gonna die out here. So stupid. I should have stayed home.*

Through the vegetation, they saw a figure move silently in their direction. Heat blasted their faces like a dragon's breath, steeling the oxygen as the fire and the man eased closer. *Thump, thump, thump.* Jake swallowed hard. His belly quivered. A cough threatened to spew out. He pinched his throat and tried to swallow it back.

Kevin eased backward into the vegetation. Jake gave Sam's mutilated corpse one last look and backed away as quietly as he could. The crackle and snap of trees succumbing to the fire blended with the roaring between his ears, and Jake felt like he might pass out.

Each knee and hand placed carefully to avoid a twig or branch lest it snap and give away their location. Jake crawled slowly in Kevin's wake. He put his hand in something slimy and fought the urge to fling the goo and shout. A shudder passed through him. He glanced up and saw Kevin a few feet ahead. He crawled a few more feet. *Thump, thump, thump.* He glanced back. Sam's remains were no longer visible. A sense of dread washed over him. *If we don't get out of here, that'll be us.*

****

The ground vibrated beneath his palms. A sense of urgency filled Jake to his core. Through the inky undergrowth, he followed his friend. *Thump, thump, thump.* The distant sound of the drumbeat had his nerves standing on end. Smoke and mist surrounded them. A noise sounded behind Jake, and he paused. His heart tittered. *Thump, thump, thump.* The drum slid closer. Taking a deep breath, he glanced over a vibrating shoulder and swallowed the scream that lurked there. *Thump, thump, thump.* Movement mere feet from them sent a wave of nausea barreling through his body. *The heart-eater?* He turned back to warn Kevin, but his friend was gone. He swallowed.

"Kevin."

The softly whispered words went unanswered.

"Kevin?"

Tendrils of fear slid up his backbone. "Hey..."

Crackling and hissing broke the dark silence. The fire and lava inched ever closer. He wanted to stand and run. Animals scurried by, sending tingles up his spine. Crouching, Jake twisted this way and that, looking for Kevin, but he couldn't see anything through the heavy smoke and mist settling in around him. His throat burned with the need to cough. *Shit, where is he?* A rustle nearby garnered his attention. Heart thumping wildly, Jake stilled. *Thump, thump, thump.* He fought the urge to call out to his friend again. *Maybe he sees the heart-eater.* Footsteps on soft earth sent his nerves skittering out of control. *Heart-eater.* Eyes darting around in the darkness, he looked for a place to hide. *Thump, thump, thump.* A large palm with broad leaves was to his left.

Shifting at a snail's pace, Jake backed into the foliage. Seconds passed. The world stilled as a figure emerged. *Thump, thump, thump.* A few feet from him, the whites of the knife-wielder's eyes glowed against the dull surroundings. Jake swallowed against the lump in his throat. A chatter of spasms filled his chest and slid into his extremities. He fought his muscles to remain still. Flames gleamed off the blade of his knife as it edged closer to his hiding position. A scream split the night. His blood congealed. Jake felt the blood drain from his face and his limbs go rigid. *Was that Kevin or an animal? It sounded human.* Wide-eyed, he watched. A smile split the stranger's face, his teeth flashing. Jake pressed a hand to his mouth to keep from crying out. He could feel his body tremble and forced himself still. *How am I ever going to escape? What happened to Kevin? I don't want to die.*

The stranger turned, the long shank glistening in front of him. He edged closer. *Thump, thump, thump.* Jake wanted to close his eyes but couldn't look away. Like a moth to a flame, he watched. One step, two steps, the dripping blade moved like a psychic through the forest straight for him. *Thump, thump, thump.* Something pinged against the tree to his left. The thud was loud against the silence. The whites of the heart-eater's eyes shifted. He gave Jake's hiding spot one last look and moved off. Ears pricked; Jake listened. The soft footsteps moved away. Releasing a long, shaky breath, Jake eased his bare back against the rough bark of the tree. He couldn't move. After what seemed like hours, Jake got control and shifted. His muscles screamed. *I need to find Kevin and get out of here.* Picking his way through the wood on all fours, he tried to put as much distance as he could between him and the heart-eater.

Another scream split the night. Jake paused. His heart hammered. The terror of another living being made the hair on the back of his neck stand on end. It was close, very close. *Was that Kevin, or could there be others out here? Thump, thump, thump.* He swallowed and felt air whoosh from his lungs, sending a wave of dizziness through him. They hadn't seen a sole on the hike up, but the area was dense, and Kevin had led them off-trail to a part of the state park not regulated or monitored. *Stupid. I should have dissuaded him.*

A rustle sounded close by, and he held his breath, listening. *How many are there? I wish we'd never come.*

With no idea where he was or where the heart-eater was, he tried to keep moving. Heat and the acrid scent of burning wafted toward him, letting Jake know he was close to the fire once more. Cursing his terrible sense of direction, he stopped. *Am I going the wrong way?* He couldn't tell. The ground felt like it had sloped. Either he'd doubled back, or the fire was getting closer. *If only I could see.* The air suddenly shifted. He wasn't alone. Pinpricks of warning had his arm hairs standing on end. Rubbing a hand over the tingles at the nape of his neck. *Thump, thump, thump.* The coppery scent of blood filled his nostrils. Jake tried to still the erratic beat of his heart, certain the predator could hear every thud. I'm trapped.

The footsteps stopped. Straining to hear, Jake breathed slowly in through his mouth, tasting the fire and blood filling the small space. A loud screech and a squeal sounded so close it could have been beside him. Jake jumped. A wild boar bounded past, nearly knocking him off his feet. A relieved gasp whooshed from his lungs. Not the heart-eater. Heavy footsteps sounded. Thump, thump, thump. This time, he was certain of whom those footsteps belonged. The heart-eater. The pounding steps on soft earth followed the boar. Now's my chance. Jumping to his feet, Jake lumbered through the wood, determined to find Kevin and a way down the mountain to safety.

He darted blindly, trying to stay quiet. Several times he tripped on an unseen root or log but somehow managed to stay vertical. Jake darted through the brush, fighting his way toward freedom; he couldn't pinpoint the direction.

A shout split the night and his fear. He paused. Kevin? Heaving, he pushed onward and prayed his friend had not suffered the same fate as Sam.

Glancing over his shoulder when he thought he heard soft footfalls behind him, he turned, and suddenly the ground was coming toward his face. Landing in a heap, Jake groaned. His ankle hurt, his lungs burned, and his head felt like it would split open like a melon. Heavy breaths stirred the loose dirt, and he sucked in a mouthful of earth. Reaching for his ankle, he felt his fingers sink deep into something warm and moist. Twisting, he stared. Kevin stared unseeing at the sky. His mouth was open in a soundless scream. He scrubbed his hand on his shorts, trying to wipe away the horror. Jake's mind went back to the sounds he'd heard. One of those had been his friend. Retching, he turned away and then vomited in the bushes.

"No, no, no. Kevin. Oh, God no. Kevin."

Curling into a ball, freckled fingers covered his face to muffle the sobs racking his narrow shoulders. The scent of his friend's warm blood invaded his nostrils, and he jerked his hands from his face. He could feel the stickiness on his cheeks and gagged. *Why, oh why, did we ever come here?*

Thump, thump, thump. Jake slapped a hand on the ground. He was sick of that drum. He wanted to go home.

Shifting onto his knees, he wiped his face and nose on the front of his shirt and scrambled to find his backpack in the dark. He located the strap and hefted it onto his shoulders. The buzz of the fire was close. Smoke wafted toward him. *Thump, thump, thump. I've gotta get out of here.*

He kneeled beside his friend, "I'm sorry."

The shark tooth Kevin never took off caught his attention. He remembered when Kevin caught the shark off the coast of Florida last year. He said it was his lucky charm. Closing bloody fingers around the tooth, he yanked. *Some lucky charm.* Jake closed his palm over the tooth, then tucked it away in his pocket. He rubbed his palms in the dirt to get rid of the stickiness left by his friends' blood. Easing back on his heels, his eyes searched for movement. His breaths came in short bursts. All around him, the world was on edge, chittering and snapping as he waited and watched. When he was certain the heart-eater was nowhere near, he moved.

This time, he knew he was alone. *I gotta find a way out.*

Hurrying through the jungle, Jake wanted to put as much distance between him and the heart-eater as he could. Something dropped on the ground behind him. Fear slid into his throat, choking him. He glanced back. *Crack.* The sound of his eyeglass lenses shattering against a tree broke the silence.

"Unh."

Dazed, Jake blinked up at the trees closing in around him like hands. His back arched over his backpack. He could feel something poking into his shoulder. Gingerly, he touched his face and withdrew muddy fingers. He could feel his upper lip swelling and his nose throbbed. Gulping, he lay on his back, eyes closed, letting his somersaulting stomach and dizziness settle. A hiss close made him jerk. Flames licked at the bark of a tree a few feet away. Jake scrambled to his feet and doubled over. Dizziness so strong he nearly fainted, washed over him. He wobbled and slid to his knees, placing his hands on the ground. His backpack flopped to the ground with a thud. Heat warmed his back. *Need to move.* Dizziness swirled through him. His face pounded out of his thrashing heartbeats. Taking several deep breaths, he placed a hand on one knee. Taking several deep breaths, he made it to an upright position. Wavering from tree to tree, he made his way toward what he hoped was the downside of the mountain. His eyes watered, blurring his already impaired vision. Smoke filled his lungs, and the sulfuric scent made his chest ache with the need to cough. Fear of the heart-eater kept the cough at bay.

Jake forced himself to open his swollen, watery eyes. Glancing up, he saw the beginnings of dawn. Blinking through the smoke and pain, he searched the horizon and eased forward. The once light backpack felt as though boulders had been added to it. He would either run into the road that they had veered off or land in the ocean, he reasoned.

Nearly blind now, Jake swallowed his terror. Stretching his hand out in front of him, he took a tentative step, then another. With his foot, he felt for the next step. He needed to get off the mountain before the heart-eaters found him or the volcano blew, but how? He couldn't see. Looking up, he tried to find the moon; but saw only blackness and the glow of fire. Going down the mountain wasn't working. Down seemed like up, and the fire was everywhere. Eyes stinging from either the smoke or his fear, he couldn't be certain. He wiped his eyes with his shirttail and rubbed his upper lip, feeling sick. His face pulsed. *Thump, thump, thump.* Swelling in his nose meant he had to breathe through his mouth. Breathing through his mouth meant he choked on the smokey air. Defeated, Jake sank to his knees. Alone, lost, and blind, he wished for morning or death.

****

Every few minutes, Jake slid to the ground and hid in the undergrowth, and listened. Guilt ate at him. Shame for leaving his friend behind settled like a yoke on his shoulders. Mist and smoke wafted through as if searching for something. *Gotta keep moving.* Sliding to his knees, he crawled forward.

Thump, thump, thump. The beat sent fear skittering through him. He'd heard the sound all night. Now, in the pre-dawn, Jake realized what it truly was. *Thump, thump, thump.* The beat inched closer. Jake held his breath, and crouched under what he hoped was a large palm.

He emerged from the mist, blade shimmering. A scream caught in Jake's throat. He needed to run, but he was all but blind. Vulnerable without glasses, the world was fuzzy. A smoky mist swirled around him. He cleared his dry throat, feeling the sting down to his toes. *I have to try again.* His legs felt like jelly. Jake rose to his knees and sucked in a breath when he saw the fuzzy outline of a person. Easing in the opposite direction, the imposing figures jumped in his path, then brushed their limbs along his thighs and chest.

Thump, thump, thump. He jumped to his feet and ran. Lungs burning, feet bruised and bleeding, he ran harder. He wanted to live. His shoulder banged into something solid, throwing his body sideways. Stumbling, Jake tried to sidestep the object. *Thump, thump, thump.* The sound of flesh slapping flesh made him freeze. Suddenly, pain ripped across his chest. *Thump, thump, thump.* Landing on the ground in a heap of agony and terror, he felt the stranger straddle his middle. Jake let out a terrified screech that sent birds scattering overhead, and animals went still as if afraid for him. *Thump, thump, thump.* The knife plunged. Jake swatted at the blade. He opened his eyes. Salty tears streamed down his temples to soak the ground. He ripped the knife from Jake's chest, sending a wave of agony through him. The blade glinted with fire as the heart-eater raised it over his head. *Thump, thump, thump.* His toothy smile was menacing. Jake rolled. The taste of the dusty earth filled his mouth. Darkness descended like night. The coppery taste of his blood filled his mouth. He licked dry lips. *Thump, thump, thump.*

****

Voices drifted toward him. Images of the heart-eater over him filled his mind. Then there was nothing. Something warmed his face. The fire. *I'm going to die.*

Blackness swallowed him.

The sound pulled at him. His eyes darted behind closed lids. He was tired. So tired. There was a metallic scrape. *What is that?*

He tried to open his eyes, but they felt like lead.

A hand touched his arm, and Jake jerked. His scream sounded ragged and warbled. Something slid over his mouth, and he swatted a hand at it with limp hands.

"Relax, it's oxygen."

"Who?"

"You're in a hospital."

Hospital? No. I died. Didn't I? Was it all a dream? No, that isn't right. Kevin and Sam. He'd seen them. Had gotten Kevin's blood on him.

Thump, thump, thump. His eyes flew open. He blinked. His eyes felt thick, his limbs heavy. The walls were a pale shade of mint. Light peeked around the edge of cheap plastic blinds covering a narrow window.

"Where," he licked his dry lips and swallowed, "am I?"

"You're at Queen's hospital."

Jake frowned. "How?" His cough was raspy.

"Firefighters found you and brought you in. You're lucky to be alive."

The faint thump sent his nerves skittering. Tears filled his eyes; he didn't feel lucky. He was alive, and Kevin and Sam were lying somewhere on the mountain with their hearts ripped out of their chests.

"I'm going to get the doctor."

Jake nodded and closed his eyes. He felt as though he hadn't slept in weeks. The door closed with a soft click. A series of faint thumps sounded again, and he felt his blood run cold.

Suddenly claustrophobic, Jake opened his eyes. His gaze darted around the room.

He needed to talk to the police and find his friends' bodies. They deserved a proper burial. He was ready to get out of this hospital and off this island. *Once I get back to the mainland, I'm never leaving terra firma again.* He sat up. *Where are my clothes?* Swinging his legs over the edge of the bed, he found a bag with his clothes under the bed. He tugged on his jeans and shoved his hand in his pocket. His fingers closed around Kevin's shark tooth necklace.

The door creaked open. *Thump, thump, thump.* Jake felt his pulse thrum. He turned. A tall man dressed in scrubs entered. *Thump, thump, thump. Good, now I can get out of here.*

The doctor stepped closer. He pulled his mask down and smiled. *Thump, thump, thump.*

Jake opened his mouth in a silent scream, the shark tooth slipping from his palm.

The heart-eater raised his knife. Jake stared up at the ceiling with dead eyes.

THE HOUSE ON THE HILL

Chelsea Gouin

Based on the New Baltimore Legend

I stared in excitement at the dilapidated house in front of me. The yard was littered with garbage, the windows were cracked and dirty, and the orange bricks were crumbling. Despite all of this, the house was strangely beautiful.

Ryan slid beside me and slipped his arm around my shoulders. "Noel, I don't know how you managed it, but it's so awesome that we're investigating here tonight!" He walked up the moldy front porch, grinning in anticipation.

The Hathaway House or the House on the Hill, was the one thing New Baltimore had to brag about. The ancient home was one of the most haunted spots in Eastern Michigan. I had got permission for our high school's Paranormal Club to do a ghost-hunting expedition for an entire night.

I was president of the Paranormal Club, and this was the last hunt for us seniors. To have scored a local location was twice as thrilling.

I glanced up at the window's peak, thinking I had seen a shadow in the window. Perhaps it was just wishful thinking. I followed the group inside the building, noticing Mike and Ryan were already splitting the club in order to give individual tours of the house.

"Hi!"

I jumped and let out a small shriek at the greeting. "Uhm, hello," I mumbled, adjusting my glasses.

The girl grinned. She cocked her head and began to twirl one of her brown curls. "The other two have already started the tour. Do you mind if I tag along with you?"

I checked my clipboard of notes and scanned the list of participants for this trip. There were ten, which meant we shouldn't have an odd one out. "What's your name?"

The girl blushed. "Mary. I was a last-minute add. Ghost hunting just seems so scary!"

"I'm Noel. Welcome to the team, Mary." She seemed relieved. "I'm assuming you know some information about the house?"

She shrugged. "Just a bit."

I extended my arm to show off the property. "Well, this house is hundreds of years old. Originally owned by the Hathaways in the early 1800s, it's been an asylum, a bed and breakfast, and just an estate. However, it's believed that the original owner's spirits still haunt these walls."

Mary's eyes grew wide. "Really? Why?"

I felt my adrenaline rush. I had spent the past year researching this house just for this purpose. "Well, the Hathaways have a very interesting history. James and Evaligne had one daughter, Maybel. James was known to be cruel, especially after he became paralyzed and stuck in a wheelchair. A few people who've investigated have caught pictures of mist bodies in the shape of his chair in the basement."

Mary shivered and crossed her arms. "People have pictures of the ghosts?"

"Yes!" I plucked a few print-outs from my folder of research. "These are pictures from Oakwood Cemetery, right next to this property. The Hathaway plot is right up front. As you can see, there are always a few orbs and the occasional mist body around the graves."

Mary glanced at the photos I held. "You said they had a daughter?"

"Maybel," I nodded. "She was their only child. She fell in love and was engaged in her early 20s. Her father disproved of the engagement. From what I read, it is believed he pushed his daughter down the stairs, snapping her neck and ending her life."

"That's terrible!" She glanced over her shoulder. "Are *those* the stairs?"

"Yes," I eyed the dusty staircase. A prickling sensation inched up my neck. I dug my digital voice recorder from the depths of my pocket. "Let's check it out."

Mary's eyes grew wide, but she slowly nodded in agreement.

I winced as the stair groaned under my weight. I sent a sheepish smile to Mary. "Noel and Mary, investigating the staircase," I spoke into the recorder. We paused on the landing and were overcome with an uneasy feeling. I pushed it aside and said clearly, "Maybel, I'm not here to hurt you. I want to help you. Please, give me a sign you're here."

A cold wave overcame me. I swore I felt a hand on my back. I shot a glance at Mary, but she was only staring intently at me.

"Are you mad, Maybel?" I called out. "Are you mad that your father killed you?"

There was a definite blow between my shoulder blades that caused me to stumble. I felt my feet leave the floor, and I found myself tumbling down the steps, landing with a sickening crack at the bottom.

My glasses fell off in the tumble, leaving my vision blurry and out of focus. I struggled to fill my lungs with air. Mary seemed to vanish from the landing. Suddenly, her voice filled my ear.

"I'm not going to move on, Noel. I had my life stolen from me when I was only twenty. I plan on getting those years back. I just need a body." A tittering laugh filled my head as the world faded to black.

IN ALL MY DREAMS I DROWN

Chelsea Gouin

Tamara gripped the shriveled board, desperately praying that it would be enough to keep her from going under. "Eddie!" she screeched, trying to desperately search for her lover amongst the chaos around her. Icy rain pelted her and clouded her vision. A heavy wave crashed over her, dragging her into its depths. The saltwater burned her throat, and she could only manage to croak out, "Eddie..."

Her eyes stung from tears and salt, leaving her vision fuzzy. Through the haze, she thought she saw the shadowy outline of a ship. "Help..." she whispered. "Help... Eddie..."

****

Tamara gasped and rolled out of a cot. She groped around the dark room, and her hand found a lantern. She turned the key, and a bright flame shone from inside the cage. Using the light, she peered around the room and discovered it was just an empty cabin with a small cot. The slight sway was all she needed to know that she was aboard a ship.

"Ah, I see you are awake," a deep voice rumbled from behind her.

Startled, Tamara spun around and collided against a solid form. Strong hands gripped her arms and prevented her from falling. "Steady," a voice whispered in her ear, sending a chill down her spine. The hands guided her back to the cot, where she shakily sat down.

She lifted the lantern once more, trying to take in the man's face, but he firmly pushed her hand away. "No light!" he commanded.

Tamara stared at the floor, heat rising to her cheeks. "Thank you... for rescuing me. If not for you, I would have drowned."

Though he was hidden in shadow, Tamara could feel her visitor's smile. It made her heart beat faster. "It was my pleasure, love." Another shiver snaked down her spine. "I brought you a nightgown. You must be aching to change out of those garments."

Tamara glanced down and noticed her gown was soaked through and clinging to her body. She wondered if the stranger noticed. "Thank you, sir." She reached for the gown, and her fingers brushed his. The man's hand was hot to the touch, and she drew back quickly.

The stranger gently removed the lantern from Tamara's grasp and set it on the bedside table. "It's time you go to sleep. You went through quite a lot already. You must be very tired."

"Oh no, sir!" Tamara stood from the cot, panic setting in. "I mustn't sleep! I... I have night terrors. I am sure once I am on shore, I can rest easy again." There was a low chuckle from the man, and Tamara felt her breath leave her in a rush. She felt a stirring within her and wanted nothing more than to be embraced by the stranger.

The hands were upon her again, guiding her to recline on the cot. Wherever his fingers touched, a burning trail existed. Through the shadows, Tamara sought out his eyes but saw only glittering black pools. Her eyes grew heavy as a foreign desire bubbled inside her.

A crash of thunder was heard outside, and the ship lurched from the force of the storm, waking Tamara from her haze. "Surely there is something I can do for you, sir. As the Captain, you must be fairly busy. I can mop the floors or... or..." she broke off, sitting upright again. "Please, sir, I will do anything. Just... please, don't make me go to sleep."

His hands reaccessed her face, brushing back her long dark locks. He offered no soothing words or any suggestions of comfort. Tamara sensed that he was not the type of man to do this for anyone. It sent another thrill through her body.

"Eddie!" she gasped. "When you... did you... Eddie..." she felt tears sting her eyes. Eddie had always teased that he'd lose his life to the sea, and she knew he had met that very fate. She was lying against the cot again, clinging to the jacket of the man above her. "Sometimes I feel as if the ocean will swallow us whole... leaving only our bones..." she whispered.

Her eyes fluttered shut as his hands once again trailed down the side of her face. "Hush now, hush love, it's time to go to sleep."

"Captain..."

His hands encircled her wrists, holding them away from her body. He was leaning over her, his weight pressing against her breasts as he whispered in her ear. "Yes, Tamara..."

She tilted her head; the lantern's glow was enough for her to get a glimpse of his face. She could make out a painted face, dark, fathomless eyes, and curled horns. She was on a ship that was manned by Lucifer himself, and she willingly offered herself to him. His lips found her neck, burning the flesh it touched. A small moan escaped her lips. She could hardly open her eyes. As she felt her body descend, she whispered, "Please, wake me up. In all my dreams I..."

INVESTIGATION: GRAND PACIFIC HOUSE MUSEUM

Chelsea Gouin

Jessica gasped and spun around on the narrow staircase, pointing her flashlight into the face of whatever had snuck up behind her.

"Dammit!" Noel cried, flailing her arms in order to simultaneously redirect the bright beam and maintain her balance. "The steps are old! They *creak!*"

Jessica twirled a long lock of her chocolate-colored hair, a light blush creeping over her cheeks. "Mike just has me so nervous!"

Noel rolled her eyes. Mike and Ryan, amateur ghost hunters of Algonquin High, had convinced the girls to join them on their latest haunt. Mike's uncle was the one who "hooked them up" with the location.

The Grand Pacific House Museum was a former hotel located one town over, in New Baltimore. Filled with relics from across the decades, it was a fun and friendly place to visit... during the day. At night, in the dusty darkness, the shadows stretched over barren hallways as each creak and groan of the floorboard magnified the sinister silence.

Jessica shivered as she reached the second floor. Cautiously, she swept her light around the hall, jumping slightly when a mannequin's painted face stared back.

Noel snorted from her spot, leaning against the banister. "Where did you want to begin? I'll warn you, though, the boys will probably try and pull something to scare you. They love this stuff, but they'll still muck up the investigation for a few laughs."

"Which rooms were the active ones again?" Jessica asked, still side-eyeing the mannequin.

Noel pointed her light to the closest room on the left. "The curator's office has the name *Anna* etched on the window; supposedly, her spirit manifests." She pointed to the room directly across from it. "The suite. Emma Losh, the former wife of the original owner, and her oldest son Burt are said to speak to guests. At the other end of the hall," she lazily gestured to the farthest room, "is a 1960's kitchen. Guests feel uneasy in there and just generally don't like it; some claim it feels like they're being watched. Across the hall is a storage closet. Guests aren't allowed in, but docents and volunteers have heard the boxes falling off shelves without anyone near them. Finally," and as she swept her light to the far room, Noel straightened, "The bedroom. Maybe it's all the baby dolls stored in there, but there's an unsettling vibe. The air is definitely thicker as soon as you cross the threshold. Guests have complained about getting nauseous when viewing the room, and children often get too upset to even peek inside."

Jessica shifted away from the open door. "Maybe the suite?"

Noel agreed and led the way to the large room. She settled onto a velvet settee. "Get comfy. We'll try for twenty minutes in here; unless something really compels us to stay." She pulled a small black cube from her bag. "This is a Shadow Box. It emits white noise, making it easier for spirits to get through and speak to us."

Jessica nervously sank into a wooden armchair across from Noel, twirling a strand of her hair. "Now what?"

Noel smirked. "We wait."

"Got it. We're moving rooms," Noel affirmed before silencing her walkie-talkie again. She straightened her ponytail, glancing over at Jessica's progress. She was in the corner, scanning the scarred piano with an EMF reader waiting for it to blip.

The girls had some moderate success in their first twenty minutes. Jessica swore she saw a shadow dart past the doorway right as the lights on their EMF lit up bright. The shadow box had cackled a few times, and Noel thought it sounded like the name "Anna" was croaked through the static in addition to "glass" and a few other less-tangible phrases. A few times, the EMF seemed to light up in response to their questions but not enough to know for sure.

The boys had checked in, saying the barn behind the museum was wielding amazing results, so they were staying out there for another shift.

"Ready to move on?" Noel asked, shoving the equipment back into her messenger bag.

"I think I'd like to try the kitchen," Jessica ventured.

"And I'll be in the bedroom!"

The girls split off in the hall, Noel facing the dreaded bedroom. Her heart thudded heavily in her chest, her hands beginning to quake as she inched toward the threshold. "Knock it off," she muttered to herself, imagining Mike's smug grin when she admitted she was too scared to even go *in* the room. With a deep breath and that asshole's face in her head, she clenched her eyes shut and walked in.

A loud scream had Noel scrambling quickly back out the door only a moment later, though. She spun her flashlight into Jessica's panic-stricken face. "What's wrong? What happened?"

With a shaky finger, Jessica pointed into the kitchen. Noel cautiously crept into the dark room. "What did you see?" she whispered back.

Jessica was fidgeting in the doorway. "There was a spider in the sink!"

Noel stopped in the middle of the room. "A spider? Seriously?" Jessica merely shrugged in response, mumbling about its size. "We're trying to talk to the dead, and you're worried about a *spider*?" She stomped out of the room, pausing at the bedroom's door frame. "Did you want to join me in here? Or are you brave enough to face the *spiders* alone?"

Jessica stubbornly stuck her chin up. "I'll be in the storage closet, thank you very much." She trudged to the next door.

Rolling her eyes, Noel entered the bedroom, too frustrated to remember to be scared. She went about setting up the Shadow Box on the vanity that housed a cracked mirror and gently placed the EMF on the springy bed in the corner. She swept her flashlight over the dark room, not hovering too long over the porcelain dolls nestled in bassinets and toy wagons. With a deep sigh, she asked, "Is anybody in here?"

Silence greeted her, and Noel winced. All the shows aired on TV had the benefit of cutting out the complete awkwardness of talking to an empty room. She almost regretted splitting up with Jessica. At least she'd offered company. Noel ran her hand over the hair brushes and combs decoratively displayed on the vanity. "Were any of these yours?" she asked. Still nothing. Subconsciously, she glanced over her shoulder, seeing only the lace bedspread and the lifeless EMF.

The room definitely felt... different. Noel had only gone on a handful of investigations with the boys, preferring her previous job of researching the locations than actually being the one to explore. The more time she spent with the boys, the more she *wanted* to be into this kind of stuff. While she had experienced some weird things in her investigations, she still had doubts about whether or not she believed in spirits.

Her thoughts were cut short by a loud crackle from the shadow box. Noel eyed the cube, but no other noises or any indication of otherworldly beings manifested. "Is something here?" she called out again. The EMF gave a quick blip, just a short flash of lights. Noel swallowed a lump in her throat, her heart rate picking up. "Tell me your name?" Nothing. "It's okay," she coaxed. "I'm just here to chat... get to know you, possibly help you..." The box cackled again. Noel strained her ears to hear anything more than the ringing silence surrounding her.

"Mirror..."

The voice was faint, barely audible over the white noise emitted from the box. Noel would have missed it had she not been staring so intently at the cube. Startled, she glanced into the glass, seeing her own pale reflection. The mirror was in rough shape, the edges cracked with jagged edges and long since discolored to the point her fiery hair shined dully back. She scanned the room behind her in the reflection. "Uhm, what am I looking for?" No response. "Spirit? I'm looking into the mirror... what is it...?"

"...Anna..."

Noel spun around, feeling as if the word had been whispered against her neck. She scooped up the EMF, scanning the area only to get no results. She moved it to the mirror, and the lights spiked to their full meter. She jumped back suddenly as the Shadow Box crackled loudly once again.

"...anna...Anna...ANNA...." the box cackled, only to go completely silent again.

"Anna?" Noel called out. "I'm Noel... I'm a high school student in Algonac... t-tell me about yourself..." she asked, louder than was necessary. The box merely cackled another, "mirror."

Noel peeked at her reflection again. At first, she saw herself again, alone in the dark room. Slowly, however, her features began to melt away. Her green eyes blinked to a ferocious hazel, her red hair falling from the ponytail she'd thrown into waves of sapphire-black, her rounded cheeks thinning to sharper angles pointing to a sinister smile. "Let me in..." the reflection whispered.

Noel stumbled away from the vanity, falling back onto the bed with a yelp. She fumbled for the walkie-talkie she'd secured to her belt, ready to call for backup or an explanation or just to get the hell out, when a loud crash and shriek resounded from the other side of the wall.

Scrambling out the door, she flung the closet open to see Jessica smashed against a far row of shelves, a cardboard box with various knick-knacks strewn at her feet. Her brown eyes were wild as they met Noel's equally fearful ones. "I *swear* I didn't touch anything!" she whispered.

Noel nodded, still shaking from her own encounter. "You all right?"

Jessica hummed, swinging her light to the top shelf and scanning the empty space the box had occupied. "It was so weird... everything was so quiet and still, and then I *saw* it move!"

Noel hunched over and began piling the items back into the box. "I was getting some... weird stuff next door. I mean, *weird*. I think we should call it a night."

"Agreed," Jessica shivered.

"Here, page the boys. Tell them we're done, and we'll explain it later." Noel handed Jessica the walkie-talkie. "I'll finish up here."

Noel finished replacing all the spilled items and squeezed the box back into its shelf space. Just as she stepped off the footstool, a sharp sting had her crying out. Twisting and craning her neck, Noel could just make out raised red scratches on her shoulder. *Great,* Noel thought, *even the spirits want us out.* Adjusting her glasses, Noel bent to retrieve her messenger bag.

"Jessica?" she called out, noticing the empty hall. The door to the bedroom was closed. Noel jiggled the handle. "Jessica?" she said, a bit more frantic. Noel slammed her hand against the wood. "Jessica! Are you okay? What's happening?"

There was a crack of static on the other side. The Shadow Box Noel had left it on the vanity in front of the...

"Don't! Jessica! Don't look into the mirror! It's *Anna!* I don't know what she's doing, but whatever you do, *don't* look in the mirror!" She continued to pound on the door and scramble with the brass knob in panic. Why wasn't she answering? What had happened? "Please, Jessica!"

A long, low shriek wailed back, cut off by a deafening silence.

"JESSICA!"

A bang down the steps had Noel spinning around wildly to see Mike and Ryan thundering up, flashlights in hand.

"Please!" she screamed. "Jessica's in there!"

Mike leveled his shoulder and rammed into the frame, but the door didn't budge. Ryan joined in, and after a few tries, the door finally gave way, and they stumbled in.

Jessica was on the bed, hugging her knees with a shocked expression. "Oh, *thank* you!" she cried, hugging Mike quickly. "I-I don't know what happened! The door... it got stuck! I thought I was trapped in here forever!"

Mike smirked. "Ah, no worries! We saved you from the big, bad ghosties."

Noel rolled her eyes. "Joke all you want, but I swear I saw something in the mirror. I think it was Anna. I don't remember too much about her from my notes, though?"

Ryan was picking up the equipment left around the room. "I heard a few stories, but they all sounded rather silly to me. Her name is the one carved into the glass in the curator's office. Other paranormal teams that have come through estimate she was anywhere from ten to sixteen, a pretty frequent guest of the hotel, possibly when it was a boarding house. They think she died here from TB or another aggressive illness for the time."

"Yeah, that sounds like pretty typical stuff though... what of her spirit? What claims were made about that?" Noel asked.

Mike shined his flashlight under his chin, casting shadows over his boyish features. "She's looking for a *body*."

Noel shivered. "Knock it off, Mike. I saw what I saw. I'm just looking for some answers."

Ryan shrugged. "I mean, I guess possession isn't off the table. And according to 18th century myths, if mirrors weren't covered up after death, souls could get trapped there."

"Not helping," Noel punched him in the shoulder. "So you left a couple girls to fend for themselves against potential possession?"

Ryan gave a half smile. "I knew you could handle yourself, Noel. You wouldn't be afraid of the silly stories..."

Noel's heart skipped a beat... was Ryan *flirting back*? Any lingering fears of whatever she had seen in the mirror seemed to melt away.

"Yeah, Hannakuah saves the day," Mike mumbled. He slung his arm over Jessica's shoulders. "You guys hungry?"

"Starved!" Ryan agreed, leading the way to the steps.

Noel allowed a small, sad sigh at being left behind. Oh well, small steps. "You okay?" she asked Jessica. "I heard you scream, but it was so eerily quiet."

"Never better! Just a bit frightened... thought I might have seen something in the mirror too..."

Mike gave her shoulders a squeeze. "All I see is a beautiful woman."

As they moved toward the door, Jessica snuck a final glance into the mirror's cracked frame, a smirk snaking over her lips. "Me too."

KRAKEN

Chris Nardone

The ship emerged from the fog like a shadowy sentinel, the ghostly tendrils wafting up resembling something from the deep. Austin St. James felt an icy chill in his gut and wondered for the tenth time why he'd taken this job. His specialty was salvage, but a lot of the time, his clients were the kind who wanted him to fracture a maritime law or three.

The red-headed man with the wiry, muscular build sporting jeans and a flannel shirt ran his hand through his Van Dyke beard as he thought back to the circumstances that led him and his crew to this point. There was a mysterious figure in the underworld St. James had heard about from time to time. He was known as The Admiral, and if he wanted to hire you, you knew it was going to pay well. You probably had to leave your conscience on the gangway, though. The fact was St. James was a little hard-up for cash. There hadn't been much out there for him and his crew, so when the call came from The Admiral, St. James went with it and figured, to hell with the consequences.

As Austin stared across the short expanse of sea at the ghostly ship garnering his attention, the acid in his stomach burned. St. James' ship was the *Hammerhead*, a two hundred and thirty-foot research/salvage vessel that didn't look like much. But Han Solo from *Star Wars* was Austin's hero, so he modeled his ship like the *Millennium Falcon*. It was junky-looking, but St. James had made "special modifications" to the engines and had hidden compartments for weapon placements that had gotten him and his crew out of many a tight spot.

"You gonna tell us what the fuck is up, skipper?"

St. James turned to see his on-again, off-again bed buddy Lila Jansen standing next to him. Lila was a tall, lithe brunette wearing dungarees; she resembled the actress, Geena Davis. She also had a trucker's mouth from being around her father's oil rig roughnecks all her life. St. James looked through the field glasses near the bow of the fog-enshrouded ship and could just make out the name of it through the misty darkness.

"Looks like we found the ship our Admiral wanted us to find," St. James said. "The thing is, how did he know it would be at these coordinates? This whole thing stinks to high heaven."

"I guess the shit-load of money he's paying us makes no never mind to you, douche bag?"

"Well, there is that, Miss Lovey Bumpers." Austin and Lila had their own way of speaking to one another, which made their crew shake their heads. "What does Olly have to say? Are our navigational controls still on the fritz?" Oliver Stanton was St. James' computer hacker extraordinaire, and he looked the part with funny glasses and a pocket protector.

Jansen nodded. "He says the source of the interference is coming from that ship."

"I want all the guys to go with me, even Greek. He knows ships like Troy Aikman knows how to read defenses." Greek was Velios, St. James' captain, he used for the *Hammerhead*. "Looks like we're going to do a little exploring."

"Speaking of which, you still owe me for those pussy Steelers losing to the Cowboys in the Super Bowl, bub."

"I got your money, doll face. We'll discuss terms when we go to bed."

"Dream on, fuck nuts, dream on!"

****

The *Hammerhead* was tied alongside the derelict ship, which St. James discovered was called the *S.S. Kraken*. Lila Jansen, Oliver Stanton, Velios, and two other seamen named Trent and Frewer had joined Austin St. James on the deck of the *Kraken*. Two other members of St. James' crew, Hanover and Fleming, were staying on board the *Hammerhead*, as was the pilot they employed, Joey Mason. A Hughes model 500 chopper sat on the pad on the aft end of the *Hammerhead*.

"Greek, what's your take on this ship? Any ideas?" St. James asked.

Velios was middle-aged and scruffy, with black, curly hair and a weathered face.

"If I'm not mistaken, it resembles a British cargo steamship from the Blue Funnel Line of Alfred Holt and Company. Notice the color of the funnel, although it's quite rusted."

The group could see the single funnel at the center of the ship, and it did have a bluish tint to it. Velios continued. "I'd say about four hundred eighty, eighty-five feet in length. Has a beam close to fifty-eight feet and a draft around forty feet or so."

Oliver Stanton chuckled. "Yep, you sure are a human computer for ships, Greek."

Velios had a very puzzled look upon his grizzled façade. He kept glancing at different parts of the ship, scratching his head and running his hand through his stubble.

"You look like you've seen a ghost, Greek," St. James commented.

"Not far from it, Austin," Velios answered. "These types of ships were launched in the early part of this century. How in the hell did it get here?"

"Let's see what we can find out," St. James said. "Lila, you and Oliver come with me, and we'll start at the bow and work our way amidships. Greek, you take Trent and Frewer and start aft, and we'll meet in the middle. Wear your comm units so we can stay in touch."

Velios nodded. "Right you are, Austin."

Ten minutes later, St. James and his group moved down a decrepit companionway. He held up his fist to signal a stop. They were armed with automatic pistols, although, in all likelihood, this would be a situation where they wouldn't be needed. St. James also carried a Bowie knife sheathed on his belt. A mysterious thumping could be heard coming from the end of the passage.

"You guys hear that?" St. James asked.

"What the fuck is it?" Lila whispered.

"It is an old ship," Stanton replied. "Could be anything rattling around."

Their comm's crackled with comments from the other group. "Frewer, here. Haven't found anything yet, but if I see giant eggs being popped out of an alien queen, I'm asking for a raise!"

Trent piped in using a mock-serious voice. "'Let's go over the bonus situation. Can we just talk about the bonus situation? Yeah, I've got nothing here, either."

St. James couldn't help but chuckle at his resident movie buffs' cinematic allusions. He had just reached the end of the corridor and placed his hand on the rusted hatch handle. The thumping was causing the breath to be trapped in his throat. He looked back to Lila and Oliver and nodded. They signaled they were ready too. Austin turned the handle and pushed open the steel door. An icy hand seemingly reached out and touched his wrist. He gasped in fright and recoiled back into his two companions. The Bowie knife was in his fist in a heartbeat. When Austin St. James peered into the cubicle, he was gaping in open-mouthed horror.

The decomposed hand kept spasming against the bulkhead, which was the obvious source of the thumping noise. The rest of the rotting body seemed to be partly fused against the bulkhead in a horrific display.

"Shit on me," Lila gasped. "How the fuck do you explain bullshit like this?"

Stanton pushed his glasses farther back on his nose. "I know Frewer and Trent would love the reference, but it's almost as if Mr. Scott totally screwed up in beaming this guy. I mean, where is the rest of him? Jesus H. Christ!"

The molded corpse had all three of them breathing heavily, but the reports from Frewer and Trent didn't help.

"Son of a bitch," Frewer cursed. "I just found three decomposing bodies! There goes one year of my life."

"Greek and I just found four more," Trent called out. "Game over, man, game over!"

About ten minutes later, St. James, Lila, and Olly entered what they believed to be the Captain's stateroom and found one of the only things of value... his personal safe. Meanwhile, Trent, Frewer, and Velios discovered an oblong iron container, maybe about six feet long, in one of the cargo holds.

"Let's get back over to the *Hammerhead* and see what we can find out about this ship," St. James said. "We'll take the safe, but leave the container for now."

The mystery of the *S.S. Kraken* would only get deeper from there.

****

A few hours later, after they returned to the *Hammerhead*, Austin St. James met with Oliver Stanton and The Greek in Stanton's computer center, which had state-of-the-art technology the hacker could access with just a tap of the keys. The main terminal was in a half-moon configuration, with just enough room for St. James and Velios to peer over Stanton's shoulders while he worked.

"I'm assuming you have a full database of ships on this contraption?" St. James remarked.

Stanton grinned, pushing his glasses back up on his nose. "No sweat, boss. We should be able to find out all about our little lost ship here."

As Stanton typed commands on his keyboard, the machines whirred and hummed.

Velios spoke up while the computer worked. "You know, that oblong, metal crate seems to be the source of our navigational controls going haywire. I wonder why?"

"Maybe we'll find out," St. James said as the computer screen flashed with information.

"Okay," Stanton sighed, squinting at the screen. "*S.S. Kraken*, built in Glasgow in 1908, a British cargo steamship from the Blue Funnel Line of Alfred Holt and Co., just like Greek said." Stanton perused the data, and squinted a little closer at the screen as he read. His head jerked back slightly in surprise. "What the hell?"

"What is it?" St. James asked.

"Its last departure was in October 1913," Stanton explained. "Departed Liverpool and docked in New York."

"What's so strange about that?" Velios wondered.

"Well, it gets even stranger," Stanton said. "Records say the *Kraken* burned up in a fire at the docks, late October of the same year."

"What is going on here?" St. James asked.

"Maybe we should contact The Admiral and tell him what we've found," Velios suggested.

"That's a good idea," St. James said. "We need to check in anyhow."

"I just had a thought, Olly," Velios said. "I once knew a guy when I was a young seaman. He was extremely odd, but his knowledge of ships was amazing. See if you can dig up where he might be residing. I do believe he's still alive and kicking. The name is Charles Berlitz. He was the one who first told me about the Blue

Funnel ships way back when. Who knows, we may get lucky."

"And if I have to fracture a law or two breaking into secure databases?" Stanton asked with a sly grin.

St. James patted him on the shoulder. "Don't get caught."

It was later in the morning when Oliver Stanton touched base with Austin St. James and had a match for the old sea dog they were looking for. He was now residing in an adult care facility in Norfolk, Virginia.

****

Austin St. James gazed out the window of the Hughes Model 500 helicopter as it raced through the sky towards the mainland. Things were happening now, and the salvager/mercenary was having a hard time digesting it all. He was in the co-pilot's seat next to the *Hammerhead*'s resident pilot, Joey Mason, a clean-cut young man wearing mirrored shades and a ball cap worn backward. In the rear compartment sat Lila Jansen, visibly uncomfortable with the dressy blouse and skirt she was attired in. St. James was also clad in professional-looking garb, a grey suit with a dark tie.

Austin thought back to his call to The Admiral about finding the mysterious ship they'd been tasked to locate. The clipped, aristocratic-sounding Englishman ordered them to keep abreast of the mysterious ship and wait until others arrived, who would take control of the operation. St. James discovered his Swiss bank account had already been credited with the amount agreed upon for finding the *Kraken*. *Something just wasn't right*, St. James kept thinking. He knowingly omitted to The Admiral that he'd sent the gang back to the *Kraken* to do some more digging to find out just where the hell this ship had come from and why their benefactor wanted it. *Didn't The Admiral know that Austin St. James didn't always play by the rules?* He figured they had a good four to five hours before The Admiral's organization located their position off the U.S. coast. And with their navigational equipment on the fritz, it could be longer.

"Berlitz... Berlitz," St. James kept saying the name quietly to himself during the trip to shore. "Why does that name sound so familiar?" He also kept running his hands across the weathered, leather book he now held. It was the Captain's log of one John Finnegan. It was the only thing of value they got out of the safe found aboard the *Kraken*. St. James began to read...

~October 25, 1913, Liverpool, England~

"Looking forward to this trip to New York City. Am proud of how hard my crew has worked to get this ship sea-worthy. It looks to be an interesting voyage."

St. James continued to read on...

~October 28, 1913~

"Where are we? The last thing I remember is we were steaming along at flank speed. Now, we are no longer at sea. We are docked, and being held at gunpoint by people dressed rather strangely. A few of our captors have spoken out of turn, I think. They sound American.

Something about an experiment gone wrong, I don't know. I was able to glance out the porthole and saw the skyline of a city, but it was not New York. I'd know that skyline anywhere. What in God's name is happening to my crew and me?"

There was a tightness in St. James' chest as he continued to pore over Captain Finnegan's log...

~Date Unknown~

"We are back at sea, but I know not where. Our compasses are not working. A crewman seems to have gone missing. It appears as though he found means of escape back when we were docked from what I was told by the other men. But now, a new horror has befallen us. We are now carrying a long, steel box in the hold… a little short of coffin-size with no means of opening it. It was not there when we left Liverpool. And some of our crewmen… how do I explain this? From the time we were mysteriously docked to now, have become trapped inside bulkheads. Their bodies are fused with the steel. Some are crying out in agony. I have no answers for this horrific chain of events."

~3 Days Later, Date Unknown~

"Yet another malady has appeared. Six members of my crew have taken ill. The symptoms are unlike anything I've ever seen. I have sailed these seas for a long time. I'm at a loss to explain."

~6 Days Later, Date Unknown~

"My crew is facing dire times. The original six members who took ill have died. I now have another ten members who have contracted the mystery illness. I have a feeling the source of the sickness is the cargo we were burdened with during our strange captivity. There is an ominous force emanating from the box. I know this deep in my soul. Somehow it is responsible. Worse yet, a massive storm is heading our way."

Austin St. James' heart was beating frantically, willing himself to read the final entry.

~9 Days Later, Date Unknown~

"*All of my crew are dead. I am sick and very weak. Something is alive inside the container. It's trying desperately to get out. The storm will not let up. Don't know how much more the ship can take. This damned box was the death of us all. Where were we? I still have to wonder? Will not write any more. This is the last entry...*"

"What's that, sailor?" Lila asked. "A 'dear diary' with all your lewd escapades?"

"No, doll face," St. James answered, hoping she or Mason didn't notice his obvious discomfort. "It's the Captain's log from the *Kraken.*"

"What are we going to do with the steel container?" Lila asked.

"Frewer was trying to pry it open when we left the *Hammerhead.* It looks to have been sealed pretty tight, though." St. James had half a mind to radio back and tell his men to get the hell off that ship. But, it was much too late for that.

Then Joey Mason spoke up. "Better buckle down, guys. We're making our final approach to Shepherd's Village at Park Avenue."

"Are you setting this thing down on the front lawn, Joey?" Lila asked.

Mason giggled. "Sure am!"

"Don't get a parking ticket," St. James muttered.

The chopper came down outside a two-story, rectangular building with a circular lobby entrance posted at one end of the facility. As Austin and Lila exited the helicopter, a worker from the place dressed in a nurse's smock greeted them. "Hello. I was instructed by a Special Agent Kirk regarding a resident of ours, Mr. Berlitz."

St. James nearly snorted with laughter in reference to Olly Stanton's nerd love of *Star Trek*. "That's correct, ma'am," St. James replied, flashing his counterfeit I.D. "I'm agent Dallas of the FBI. This is my partner, Agent Cartwright. We understand Mr. Berlitz is a recognized expert in the field of nautical vessels. We needed some information regarding a case we're working on. We'd most appreciate your assistance."

"Right this way, agents."

Ten minutes later, they were in a well-kept room that had a kitchenette, space for a cozy E-Z chair, television, and a cubby hole for a single bed. Charles Berlitz looked to be in his late eighties and was wrinkled and frail as he lay in his bed sitting up.

"Mr. Berlitz, I'm Austin St. James. One of my colleagues is a man named Velios, Captain of the *Hammerhead*, a salvage vessel. You may know him as The Greek."

Berlitz seemed to be staring off into space for a few long moments before he realized he had company. Lila let out a long, frustrating breath. "This old fuck isn't going to help us, Austin. How would he remember anything about the *Kraken*?"

Berlitz's head turned slowly like a robot, gazing directly at St. James. "What do you know about the *Kraken*, young man?"

St. James leaned forward. "I know we were hired to find it," Austin said. "We were given specific coordinates and found it dead in the water."

A strange smile turned up the corners of Berlitz's wrinkled mouth. "Blue funneled steamship, correct? It sailed for New York City on October 25, 1913? Is that the one?"

"Yes, it is!" Lila exclaimed. "What do you know about the last voyage?"

What the man said next hit both St. James and Lila Jansen with a massive uppercut of shock and awe. "My dear... I was on that ship."

"Holy fuck!"

"No, it can't be!" St. James stammered. "How is that possible?"

"Three days out of Liverpool, something happened," Berlitz stated.

St. James explained the entries from Finnegan's log. The old man laid back in his bed, eyes closed, smiling and nodding to himself. "What happened to the *Kraken*, Mr. Berlitz?"

"We were transported from the middle of the Atlantic Ocean and ended up in the Philadelphia shipyards. But, from what we were able to discern, it was no longer 1913. It was October 28, 1943. Does that date have any meaning to you, young man?"

Then it hit Austin a few agonizing moments later. "Berlitz... Berlitz. Holy shit! Charles Berlitz was the author of a book called *The Philadelphia Experiment*. But, you're not him!"

It was alleged the experiment involved cloaking ships and teleportation. None of it was ever truly verified and dismissed as a hoax or stuff of legend for the UFO nuts. Some of the reports detailed when the destroyer in question, the *Eldridge*, reappeared, some crew members were fused with bulkheads... *just like the Kraken*, St. James thought.

"Of course, I'm not him," Berlitz answered. "I only took the name. Who knows what the truth is and what's not the truth anymore. What I do know is that I was born in the year of our Lord, 1878. I was a crewman aboard the *S.S. Kraken*. We left Liverpool and three days later found ourselves in Philadelphia. The whitecoats there kept wondering where their destroyer, the *U.S.S. Eldridge* had gotten to. There was some confusion, and I was able to slip away and get off the ship. I watched from the cover of the docks as the *Kraken* became enveloped in a strange light and disappeared from sight. Whether they returned to their own time, I will never know. But, I spent the next thirty years trying to dig deeper into this mystery. I was even hired by the shadow group responsible for the debacle in Philadelphia that day... unbeknownst to them."

"Where did the mysterious steel box come from?" Lila asked.

"This shadow group decided to fix one problem by depositing it on the *Kraken*. Apparently, the scuttlebutt was they had some sort of life form in their possession... um... not of this world, the story goes. They put it into the cargo hold and sent the ship back into the void. While the shadow group had the box in their possession, it did exhibit some sort of defense mechanism. People exposed to it for too long got sick and eventually died. That's why they wanted to be rid of it."

"Jesus fucking Christ, Austin," Lila gasped. "This is totally insane!"

"The last thing I remember before I resigned," Berlitz explained, "is that a theory was being postulated. Ever since 1943, there were sightings at sea of this mysterious steamship with the blue funnel. It would appear in the Pacific, then in the North Sea, then in the Indian Ocean. Then someone else would report seeing it in the Atlantic, the Mediterranean, you name it. Their idea was that because the *Kraken* was caught up in the *Experiment*, it was phasing in and out of our continuum on a regular basis. The whitecoats in the shadow group seemed to narrow down its phasing pattern and radar signature. They've been trying to get their hands on it for the last fifteen years or so. The Admiral wants it very badly."

St. James' head jerked up. "What do you know of The Admiral?"

"His father was one of the original scientists involved in the *Philadelphia Experiment*. You know him?"

"He fucking hired us," Lila growled.

"We have to get back to the ship!" St. James said.

Austin and Lila quickly thanked Berlitz and rushed from the room and back to the chopper.

****

Back on the *Hammerhead*, Frewer was beat after trying all afternoon to pry the box open. He'd had some luck with a pry bar, and circular saw, but the steel was unlike anything Frewer had ever encountered. He eventually made about an eight-inch cut but had to rest a bit. It was probably time to go topside and chow down on some of the MRE's (Meals Ready to Eat) they'd brought over from the *Hammerhead*. Then he'd see where Trent and the others had got to.

The cargo hold was dimly lit and creepy. Frewer moved for the stairwell and had just taken his first step up when he heard a scraping sound come from behind him. He stopped to listen... nothing. Taking two more steps up the metal stairwell, Frewer detected a screech of wrenching steel. Turning sharply, he peered through the shadowy gloom but couldn't see anything. He thought of a line from a movie as a putrid stench invaded his nasal passages and he felt a presence behind him.

"This isn't happenin' man! This isn't happenin!"

A ghostly, yellowed hand with long, tapered fingers gripped his mouth tightly, cutting off any scream. Trent was at the top of the stairwell and heard a scuffle come from below. "Frewer, what the hell are you doing down there?"

Trent made his way down into the cargo hold, his eyes adjusting to the dim light and shadows. "Okay, enough of this shit, man! Quit horsing around!"

It was then Trent felt an ominous presence in the cargo bay with him. He could almost see a hulking shape in the corner, and heard ragged, hissing noises he guessed was someone breathing heavily.

"Frewer?"

Something was growling now, sending chills up and down Trent's spine, turning his legs to jelly. Trent barely had time to react as a soaring figure came toward him. He never had time to scream.

****

Before taking off in the helicopter for the return trip to the *Hammerhead*, Austin St. James and Lila Jansen changed back into their casual clothes. Then, Joey

Mason angled the chopper east over the ocean for the rendezvous with their ship as dusk began to settle.

"Have you been able to contact the ship?" Lila asked.

"It's that damned interference," St. James replied. "We can't get jack shit!"

"Maybe we should call the Coast Guard?" Mason suggested.

"This whole operation is off the books, Joey," St. James said. "Not the best idea."

It was close to a half-hour later when Mason pointed out the Plexiglas windshield. "There they are!"

"If we get close enough, we should be able to hail them for landing clearance," St. James announced.

"Something's not right, Austin," Mason said. "We should at least be able to get static and muffled transmissions. But, I'm getting nothing."

Austin, Lila, and Joey Mason then watched in horror as the *Hammerhead* was engulfed in a thunderous explosion. The blast broke the ship in two, and within minutes, the salvage vessel slipped silently beneath the dark, rolling waves.

"Mary, Mother of fucking God!" Lila gasped.

"Holy shit, Austin, what do we do now?" Mason stammered.

It took St. James a few agonizing moments to realize what he'd just witnessed was real life and not some intense dream. When he came back to his senses, he took in the dark shape of the *Kraken*, the waves gently rocking the steamship. "See if you can land it on the stern," St. James ordered.

He remembered that part of the ship had a row of lifeboats, which might be the best place to put the chopper down. The Hughes was a very compact machine, so St. James hoped it could be done.

"I don't know, Austin," Mason said. "It could be dicey."

"You want me to try it, Joey?" St. James asked. "I've spent a lot of hours training in this thing."

"No, I got it," Mason replied.

The helicopter came down in a small area devoid of lifeboats. The landing skid bumped the lifeboats on either side a few times before Mason settled it in between. St. James dug into his duffel bag and strapped on his SIG-Sauer pistol in a shoulder holster, the one he'd used in his FBI disguise. He then unsheathed a Combat Machete with an eleven-and-a-half-inch blade. In his boot sheath, he slid his Bowie Knife. He also pocketed a small flashlight.

"You both stay here," St. James informed them. "I'm gonna take a quick look around." Both Lila and Mason opened their mouths to protest, but St. James held up his hand. "No arguments. Just stay here and keep your hands near your guns... just in case."

St. James exited the chopper and began to make his way forward amidships. He needed to find the rest of his crew and find out what was going on with the metal container that had been brought aboard the *Kraken*. He could hear the waves lapping up against the side of the *Kraken*'s hull, but other than that, it seemed like an eerie stillness had invaded the derelict ship. St. James, pistol leading the way, hot-footed it towards the hatch for one of the cargo bays. He passed some of his group's supply crates brought over from the *Hammerhead*. A portable computer the size of a briefcase, tool kits and ordinance crates, plus their food stores, were now scattered across the deck.

He pulled open the bulkhead hatch and flashed the light down the stairs. He then took the steps one at a time, gun leading the way, searching for anything out of the ordinary. When he reached the bottom of the steps, St. James almost gagged at what he saw. He held back the dry heaves as he took in the remains of what used to be Trent. Blood was splashed everywhere—on the floor, the walls, and in a thick torrent underneath his corpse. Trent's head was at a grotesquely distorted angle, being held to his neck by only a few bloody strands of tendon.

"Lord in Heaven!"

St. James went to the container and saw the plates had been ripped off. *What the hell?* Whatever had been in the container was now loose. *What had Berlitz said? A 'life form' of 'unknown origin.'* St. James heard a noise behind him. Turning, he saw a shadowy figure at the bottom of the stairwell. Even in the poor light, St. James recognized him. It was..."Frewer! What the hell is happening? Are you alright?"

He began to shuffle lazily towards St. James as if in a trance. "Frewer, we have to..."

Suddenly, Frewer's hands were reaching for St. James, and it was in that heart-stopping moment of terror Austin realized something was horribly wrong. Frewer came into a spill of light, and St. James saw the man was deathly pale, had glowing yellow eyes, and his neck and head were covered with ugly, open sores that oozed pus. St. James was nearly taken flat-footed but recovered to knock the Frewer-thing's outstretched hands aside. Then he planted a boot into Frewer's sternum, knocking him back a few paces. When the lumbering Frewer-thing started for St. James again, the mercenary noticed a crowbar lying on the floor next to the container. As Frewer lunged, St. James palmed the crowbar and rammed it into the thing's neck. As it exited through the side of Frewer's head, St. James was expecting to see a gush of blood and gore. But, only the slightest trickle of crimson exited from the horrible wound. The Frewer-thing growled loudly as he attempted to pull the object from his body. With St. James' heart pounding wildly, he took up his pistol and emptied half the magazine of 9mm slugs into what was left of Frewer's head. It exploded into ghastly chunks, and the thing that used to be Frewer toppled to the deck... unmoving.

****

Joey Mason and Lila Jansen waited impatiently for St. James to return to the chopper. "I can't sit here like this while Austin is out there," Lila grumbled. "This is fucking bullshit!"

"Let's just wait a few more minutes," Mason said. "He'll come back, don't worry."

Just as Lila made a move for the handle on the door latch, they both recoiled as something thumped against the side of the helicopter. "What was that?" Lila asked.

"I don't know," Mason answered. "It's probably Austin."

"We'd better make sure."

As Mason reached for the latch, a hissing noise assaulted his ears. It got louder and louder... and louder.

Mason opened the hatch and peered outside. "There's no one here."

In a split second, Joey Mason was yanked violently from the chopper, Lila heard the breath whoosh from his lungs. She gasped in horror as Mason began to scream but it was replaced with a gurgled yelp. Lila ducked back behind the pilot seats, trying desperately to suppress a scream as blood spurted in thick jets through the open hatch. She heard an awful chorus of flesh ripping and bones snapping as though they were kindling. Lila couldn't hold it back any longer. A strangled scream erupted from her throat.

Then she detected a presence in the hatchway of the chopper.

****

As Austin St. James got topside, his only thoughts were to get back to the chopper and get the hell away from this death ship. Movement out of the corner of his eye arrested his attention. He turned to his left and saw two of his crewmen stumbling and staggering slowly toward him. It was Captain Velios and Oliver Stanton.

"Jesus!" St. James exhaled. "It's only you two. You're never going to believe this but..."

Both men closed in on him, and St. James realized with a cold dread the paleness of their skin, yellowed eyes, and open sores. He palmed his Bowie knife as Velios growled, reaching out to grasp him.

"Aw, come on, Greek, don't make me do this!" St. James pleaded but knew the man was too far gone from hearing and understanding. The Bowie slashed the Velios-thing from forehead to chin. St. James didn't see any blood and received a slapping punch to his face that knocked him back a few steps and drove him to his knees. Quickly composing himself as Velios moved forward, Austin twirled the knife in his hand, and it seemed to puzzle the creature for just a mili-second. The salvager lunged, planting the big blade of the Bowie into the Velios-thing's heart. It roared with pain, but the figure did not go down. St. James stepped back, unsheathed the Combat Machete, and swung with all his might. The long blade sliced through Velios' neck, the head tumbling to the deck and disappearing into the shadows.

St. James had lost track of Olly during his fight with Velios, and the next thing he knew, the paled Stanton-thing was coming at him. Growling and grunting with spittle flying from his lips, the creature slammed into St. James and knocked him to the deck, his machete jarred from his grasp. He only had time to brace his left forearm against the Stanton-thing's neck as it snapped its jaws, desperately wanting to taste flesh.

The thing that used to be Oliver Stanton was much stronger in this form, St. James realized. Fetid breath assaulted him, and he had to hold back the bile that stirred in his throat. The thing was inching closer as St. James reached up with his right arm and jammed a thumb into Stanton's left eye. It just made the creature even angrier. Jaws edged ever closer to St. James' face as he figured he couldn't hold out much longer. Then, he thought of the pistol under his shoulder. Desperately grabbing for the weapon, he snatched it up and thrust the gun forward. St. James triggered a trio of 9mm rounds that exploded the Stanton-thing's head, showering him with bits of gore and tissue. Shoving the corpse from him and wiping his face as best he could with his sleeve, St. James got to his feet, eyes wide with shock and fear as he prepared to make his way back to the chopper, retrieving his machete and knife in the process.

"Enough of this shit!"

Half-staggering and half-running, St. James made it back to where their supplies were scattered around the main deck. That's when it happened. A mysterious ripple slowly moved like a wave from the front of the ship and ensnared Austin St. James in its weird, mind-bending fluctuation. St. James' movements slowed down for a handful of seconds. He thought back to what Berlitz told him about the ship phasing in and out of the space-time continuum. Was it preparing to make another shift? Had it already? St. James had to get to the helicopter and leave this madness behind him. Before moving on, though, he kicked open an ordinance container and palmed a couple of the thermite grenades they always kept on hand. When he came around the corner of a bulkhead with the chopper in sight, St. James stopped dead in his tracks.

There was a short, fireplug of a figure squatting just outside the chopper. St. James heard a surreal chittering and hissing noise emanating from the thing. It was a little over five feet tall and was a sour, puke-yellowish color. The hairs on St. James' neck went stiff. The bi-ped figure was busy slathering up the blood, and gore St. James could see next to the hatchway. Then another of the ripples engulfed the ship, and St. James watched in fascination as the thing turned in slow motion, standing to face the salvager.

Austin St. James figured it was an alien, the one from the container, but it was not like the "grays" in popular culture. It was short, like he first noticed, and he had long, oblong eyes and a pointed skull. Its arms and hands were thin and spindly, with fingers that were long and bone-like. But, it had a long, cylindrical-shaped snout. When St. James stepped closer to the alien, he was chilled to the bone as four tube-like tongues slithered across its snout to lap up the remnants of blood splashed across its malevolent façade. As St. James thought back to the open sores on the crewmen he'd come up against, he now saw the cause of that. The four tongues of the alien tapered to a flat piece with little jaws, like that of a leech.

"Holy fucking shit! It's like an alien vampire!"

St. James could almost see the face of the alien change into annoyance at having been interrupted while feasting on blood and gore. It mewled and hissed, leaping through the air in an instant. St. James had just enough time to quick-draw his pistol and empty the remaining 9mm bullets at the oncoming form. The projectiles did absolutely nothing as a backhand slammed into St. James' chin, sending him hard to the deck. As he tried to regain his feet, a bony foot plowed into his ribs and lifted him off the ground, sprawling him backward.

St. James staggered back to his feet, managing to grasp the Bowie knife from his boot sheath. The alien yanked him to his feet and shoved him hard against a bulkhead. Death was staring Austin St. James directly in the eye. What could he do with his knife? Would it even hurt the other-worldly being? The alien's mouth opened, and the four leech-tongues slithered out, seeking the blood they so desperately needed.

At that moment, a space-time fluctuation happened once again, and everything slowed to a crawl. St. James watched in fascination as the tongues shot forward like a whip cracking. His hand moved like through quicksand, but he managed to swing up his knife and bring it down in a slashing motion. As the ripple ended, the blade of the Bowie cut through the slithering tongues, and a viscous, pus-fluid erupted from the horrible wounds. The alien screeched in mortal agony and staggered back, spindly hands going to his ruined mouth. St. James took hold of a thermite grenade and snapped the pin out with a deft flick of its finger.

"Chew on this, you ugly mother fu...!!"

St. James rammed the canister into the alien's mouth, then back-pedaled, diving for the cover of a bulkhead. Seconds later, the alien vampire exploded into chunks and bits of flesh.

The thermite started to spread quickly throughout the ship as St. James staggered over to the helicopter, seeing the dismembered pieces of what used to be Joey Mason. He burst inside the chopper, expecting to see the grisly remains of his friend, Lila, also.

"Austin, is that you?"

It was dark, and there were shadows of light dancing across the cockpit as St. James spotted Lila Jansen, who appeared shaken and in shock. They embraced warmly for a few long moments, but then St. James broke away. "We have to get out of here. Something strange is happening, and the ship is on fire."

St. James got the chopper revved up in record time and soon pulled away from the Kraken. He happened to glance back and watched another ripple engulf the fiery ship. Only this time, the shimmer lasted much longer, and in another few heartbeats, St. James saw the S.S. Kraken disappear from the ocean.

Behind him in the rear seat, Lila sighed heavily as she sat back. "Is it over?"

"I hope so."

The radio in St. James' headset squawked, and a cultured voice with an accent spoke up. "I see from our radar that you managed to survive, Mr. St. James. Quite a pity, I must say."

"Admiral? You fucking son of a bitch! My whole crew is dead! My ship has been sunk! I wouldn't be surprised if you had everything to do with it! Tell me I'm wrong!?

"Of course, dear boy! We needed you to find that ship, but we didn't tell you to board her and investigate, did we? You apparently witnessed things that were not meant to be seen. That was a mistake."

"Who the hell are you? What interest do you have with the *Kraken* and the *Philadelphia Experiment*?"

"My, my! You have learned a lot, haven't you? My family was part of the program, along with the Americans. We've been trying to locate that ship for a long time. And now, it has shifted once again."

"You listen, here, Admiral. When I find you, I'm going to…"

"Austin," Lila gasped from behind him in the passenger seat. "I'm not feeling so good."

"Lila? Are you feeling sick?"

Suddenly, there was a guttural shriek, then Lila was attacking him from behind, her yellow eyes blazing with raw hunger. She opened her mouth to sink her teeth into his flesh when St. James' elbow rammed into her face twice. The chopper started spiraling out of control as she tumbled into the cramped cockpit area. The Lila-thing snorted and growled as St. James managed to hit the door latch, flinging it open with the cold wind blasting him like an uppercut. The she-thing struggled, but it didn't seem to like the wind, either. St. James slammed her against the frame of the chopper a few more times and then pushed her towards the abyss.

"I'm so sorry, Lila."

She sailed into open space as St. James got the chopper back under control and put the earphones back on his head. The Admiral's voice was there once more. "Are you still there, St. James? Know this. We will hunt you, we will find you... and we will kill you. There is no hiding from us."

"Give it your best shot, asshole!"

Austin St. James cut the connection, taking the chopper down to wave-top level to avoid radar. In the distance, he could see the mainland and wondered what in the world he would do now. He was now a hunted man.

****

Aboard the luxurious Bayliner yacht, the party was in full swing. A clean-cut man clad in evening attire was at the railing sipping a martini when he spotted something in the water.

"Help! Please, someone, help me! I can't swim for much longer!"

Dropping his drink, he raced down to the rear of the yacht and threw a life preserver to what he thought was a young woman, paddling for dear life in the ocean. She slowly made her way to the man's outstretched hand, and he hauled her aboard. The man could see she was a well-built brunette woman but couldn't see her face clearly in the shadows. She coughed up water and sputtered loudly as she tried to catch her breath.

"Thank you so much," a dry, cracked voice gasped. "I thought I was dead."

"Just take it easy, miss. Let me get you some blankets."

"Oh, that's so very kind of you," said the same voice, now more clear and dripping with malice.

As the man turned to walk away, Lila Jansen's eyes glowed yellow, and she opened her mouth wide, baring her teeth.

Flesh ripped. Blood spurted.

LIGHTHOUSE OF SAMSARA

Jase Riemersma-Cote

Howard was not the type of boy people imagined when they thought of a sailor. He was the type of boy who never looked anyone in the eye, and when he talked, he mostly mumbled to the ground. He was orphaned at a young age, but he was adopted by a sea captain around his pre-teen years. He may not have talked about it to anyone, but his skills on a boat have shocked even the Captain himself. It was like he became a different person when the ocean breeze flowed through his hair and the smell of salt filled the air.

However, there came a day when he and the crew ran straight into a storm, one that gave no signs. Never did the clouds blacken, nor did the wind carry the feeling of a storm. Their ship was no match, and it turned into a thousand pieces, ripped apart by wind, waves, and rock. Now, Howard was alone with no help in sight. He drifted on a lone board, and his heart was about to rip through his chest. It was too much for him, and his consciousness slipped away.

Waves. Seagulls. Sand. Pain. Headache. Opening his eyes with great anguish, he looked around at his surroundings. He could see around the entire island, but there was only one thing his eyes were locked on. Lighthouse. Shelter. Food. People. Help.

A smile crossed his face as he ran for the door to the lighthouse. He reached out for the knob, but he paused. A sudden sense of déjà vu washed over his mind, but this feeling made his stomach twist and his head pound with fear. He looked behind himself out of paranoia, but there was nothing there. There were no shadows under the few trees scattered across the island. Swallowing his fear, he turned the knob with a trembling hand.

After opening the door, he quickly looked around the room. It was an average lighthouse. There was a spiral staircase up to the roof and more stairs to the basement, the living quarters. Seeing as someone would have spotted him if they were on the roof, he went down to the basement.

As he was going down, he almost slipped down the stairs. He grabbed the railing as hard as he could, causing him to hit his back hard on the stairs, but he did not fall. When he looked down to see what he had slipped on, he saw that there was a strange sheen on one of the steps. He reached down to touch it, and he felt that it was slimy.

His skin began to crawl as he continued to descend. Maybe it was the silence and the ringing of his footsteps throughout the whole lighthouse, maybe it was just his anxiety and the grief for his crewmates that had yet to fully settle in, or maybe it was the eyes watching him in the shadows that disappeared right before he saw them. Whatever it was, he couldn't stop seeing things, like hands or mouths, out of the corner of his eye.

When he reached the quarters, he didn't feel any safer than he did when he was on the ship during the storm. At least on the ship, he felt like he had control. At least on the ship, he had friends by his side. At least on the ship, there was not an itchy feeling in his chest that made him check behind his back as often as he could. As much as he wanted to close his eyes, he could not stop looking at every corner to try and spot what was watching him from the darkness.

He reached for the door with a trembling hand and twisted it as sweat dripped down his arms. He vomited when he saw what was in the room. Nothing. There was nothing there. It was empty. No monster. No beds. No people. His head was like a boulder, and his stomach felt like it had been pounded like a steak. He started to take deep breaths. After a few seconds, minutes, or hours, he wondered why there was absolutely nothing in the room. Even if it were abandoned, he thought, there would still be beds here.

He heard footsteps. *Thud. Thud. Thud. Thud.* He started by curling up into a ball. *Thud. Thud. Thud. Thud.* Next, he started to taste the tears. *THUD. THUD. THUD. THUD.*

Finally, he heard, "Hello, sonny. Are you okay?" Howard looked up. It was an old man dressed in a yellow rain jacket.

"No. Can you help me, please?" Howard responded. The old man, without a reply, took his hand and pulled Howard off the ground. The old man's hand was wet for some reason, but it was too sticky to be water or sweat. They climbed up the stairs. "I want to... uh, step outside for a second," Howard told the old man. The door's window was strangely dark, but he just wanted some fresh air. When he tried to open the door, it was locked.

"Kid," the old man grumbled in a garbled voice, "There is no outside anymore. There is just you, me, and the lighthouse." At that point, Howard's mind sank into the cold abyss of terror. A beast now stood in place of the old man. It was a mangle of limbs and faces. It shifted colors as it moved. All of the faces were people he knew: The Captain, the old man, his mother, his father, and more. The lighthouse started to melt, too, revealing more faces and arms. The only thing left in Howard's brain was the primal need to run.

His legs carried him over the stairs up to the roof. He could hear it. It sounded like a mix of nails on chalk and the screams of the damned. He could hear every tooth grind against the bones of corpses, every hand tearing a chunk of flesh, and every hungry scream.

He reached the top of the steps. There was nothing. It was just a dome of flesh. When he heard the sound of the monster climbing the stairs, he knew his fate. It was either to be eaten alive or to jump down the middle of the spiral staircase, praying that his neck would snap from the fall. His bones refused to move at first as his mind showed him all the memories he had made, failing to stop him from jumping. It was the most painful experience he had ever had, but he knew it would be better than the other opinion. As he fell to his doom, he heard the creature scream in disappointment. He grimaced as his neck broke in two.

****

Hope was not the type of girl people imagined when they thought of a sailor. She was the type of girl who never looked anyone in the eye, and when she talked, she mostly mumbled to the ground. She was orphaned at a young age, but she was adopted by a sea captain around her pre-teen years. She may not have talked about it to anyone, but her skills on a boat have shocked even the captain himself. It was like she became a different person when the ocean breeze flowed through her hair and the smell of salt filled the air.

However, there came a day when she and the crew ran straight into a storm, one that gave no signs. Never did the clouds blacken, nor did the wind carry the feeling of a storm. Their ship was no match, and it turned into a thousand pieces, ripped apart by wind, waves, and rock. Now, Hope was alone with no help in sight. She drifted on a lone board, and her heart was about to rip through her chest. It was too much for her, and her consciousness slipped away.

Waves. Seagulls. Sand. Pain. Headache. Opening her eyes with great anguish, she looked around at her surroundings. She could see around the entire island, but there was only one thing her eyes were locked on. Lighthouse. Shelter. Food. People. Help.

A smile ran across her face as she ran for the door to the lighthouse. She reached out for the knob, but she paused. A sudden sense of déjà vu washed over her mind, but this made her stomach twist and her head pound with fear. She looked behind herself out of paranoia, but there was nothing there. There were no shadows under the few trees scattered across the island.

Stairs. Empty. Man. Dark. Beast. Fall. Abruptly, she remembered everything. Not just him, but countless others too. Countless incarnations of her soul had gone through the same thing inside that lighthouse. Howard, however, was different. All of the others didn't jump from the top of the lighthouse to the bottom. All of the others were ripped apart by the amalgamation. All of the others cannot face the choice.

At first, she laughed, and tears began to fall down her face. Her stomach hurt, and she fell to the ground.

"This... must be... some kind of... a sick joke to you... huh?" she yelled at the lighthouse through the laughing. After she picked herself up, she walked around back. As she walked, she remembered the rest of her life, but now, they didn't feel like her memories. They felt more like remembering a movie or a dream—like she had never experienced them herself. She giggled.

Around back, there was a shed that was never there before. Inside, it had food and a sailboat. She grabbed both and headed to the beach. At first, her stomach hurt at the thought of leaving. At least she knew what was in the lighthouse, but she had no clue what was in the waters. It could be worse, for all she knew. Those thoughts quickly left, though, as she pushed the boat to sea. She looked back at the lighthouse, which now had its light on with her 'parents' at the top, waving and calling her name.

She looked back to the sea, wondering what adventures she'll have in the freedom of the open ocean.

MILESTONES

Marianne Wieland

Damn! He thought it was later in the day than it actually was. Four o'clock. He still had two more hours to go before he was to arrive at his 'surprise' retirement party. He was working some overtime today to help out a fellow trooper who had been there for him at a time when no one else had bothered to see the distress he was in. This life he had chosen for himself had not been the easiest for his family. The things he had seen and done in the name of the law had made for many a sleepless night for himself and his wife.

Tick, tick, tick. He could hear the sound of his watch, no, his heartbeat. Maybe his watch or... no... yeah... his heartbeat. He was going to go nuts before much longer if this kept up. He started drumming his fingers on the steering wheel. Five minutes had passed. One more week to go, and he would be home every day. He could be there for his kids when they got home from school. He could relieve his wife of some of the household chores and the cooking. He loved to grill. He could do it every day. He could build that deck he had been dreaming about. Maybe put in a swimming pool. The kids would love that. He could have the house where all the neighborhood kids wanted to be. That would keep his kids at home, thus minimizing the trouble they could get into or the harm that could be done out in the real world. He wondered what his wife was doing right now. He knew she was at the station, along with his children, his parents, his grandparents, his friends, and his co-workers. So many people. There was a lot of love in his life.

He wasn't supposed to know about this party, but a new trooper had asked if he would be at 'that old geezer's' party on Saturday. Old geezer. That's what they labeled him after twenty-five years of dedicated service to the public.

Tick. Tick. Tick. It was very quiet out here on this stretch of highway today. The sky was a little overcast, and he hoped the party would be over by the time the rain that had been predicted began. He saw a car coming and became alert. Ten miles under the speed limit. Just as bad in his mind. People tended to leave caution to the wind and pass on wide curves with double yellow lines to get around those who chose to go on a 'Sunday drive' every day of the week. He stretched his neck, first one way and then the other. Then he repeated the move twice again. He might be retiring, but he was still only fifty years old. Best to keep his muscles limbered up. He stretched each finger, one by one. He drummed on the steering wheel again. He looked at his watch. Eight more minutes had passed. He thought about getting out to stretch his legs, but as sure as he did, someone speeding would be upon him, and he would not be able to get back in the car fast enough for a chase to ensue.

He heard a noise coming up on his left. A loud roaring noise with gears grinding. His patrol car was parked next to Mr. Tucker's corn field, and he realized the noise was Mr. Tucker on his old tractor. He gave a half salute-half wave as the tractor passed, heading down the road in the opposite direction. *He needs to get the combine out and harvest his corn instead of playing around on that worthless old tractor,* he thought. He started to hum. It took a minute, but he realized that he was humming that old song... something... something...

Old Dan Tucker, you're too late to have your supper. Supper's over, breakfast's cookin'. Old Dan Tucker standin' there lookin'. Five more minutes had passed. *Would this day ever end?!*

****

She looked at her watch for the hundredth time in the last fifteen minutes. Time was running out. Still, with all the help, she was sure they would not be ready in time for her husband's party to start. He had no idea about the party. She wanted everything to be perfect, the lights out, and all the guests ready to shout 'surprise!' when he came through the door. Everyone was pitching in, from the kids to her grandparents and his. They were lucky. Both his parents and hers, as well as both sets of grandparents, were all alive and well. They were truly blessed.

She looked at the time again, and another half hour had passed. She knew he was working overtime today, but that had been part of the plan to get him out of the way so they could decorate the large conference room at the station house. The kids were stringing crepe paper streamers across the ceiling. Dad was hanging the banner. Grandma was mixing the punch. Grandpa was wiping his false teeth on the white tablecloth... *Shit!* She called for her oldest son, who was supposed to have been keeping Grandpa out of trouble.

"You do know you're supposed to watch him, right? Do you see what he's doing?"

Her son looked at Grandpa. "That's nasty! What an old fart."

She pulled out some latex gloves from her pocket and handed them to her son. "Get the teeth and clean them. Put them back in his mouth and consider yourself lucky he wasn't diaper digging and making fecal artwork on that white tablecloth." Her son grabbed the gloves and went to handle Grandpa, but not without much protesting.

She continued to work on the party and make sure everyone was carrying out the duties to which they had been assigned. She was so happy that her man was going to retire from the police force. It had been a long twenty-five years. Not much sleep on her part, nor his. No matter how hard they tried, the job had always invaded their private lives. She was always proud of the service he had given to those he had sworn to protect, but she would be glad to have him to herself for a while. He could help out around the house, maybe do some grilling, and build that deck. The possibilities were endless. She was sure that he would take on another job at some point, but for a while, they could finally live some of the good life.

Her mother stopped her from making yet another checklist, and reminded her that this party was as much for her as for him. She spoke of many things that had happened over their lives that they both could be proud of. The first home they bought together. The birth of their three children. His promotions through the years. His first motorcycle, you know, the one she had plowed through Mr. Tucker's corn field and sustained a broken femur. Her mother could always make her laugh. It was funny now, but not back then. But he had taken care of her. Had taken leave from the force to make sure she had everything she needed to recover. She loved him, even after all of these years, more than anyone would ever know.

****

"Huh? What?" He shook his head. *My god!* He had dozed off. He looked at his watch... *for fifteen minutes! Damn!* Anything could have happened. He never did that! Too much was at stake. He started drumming on the steering wheel again. He started his mental checklist, the thing that always brought him back to the present.

His keys were in the ignition. The radar was on and working. He had logged all the tickets he had given out for the day. Cell phone, check. Wallet, check. Trooper hat, check. Gun, check. Bullets, check. *Wait!* Gun and bullets before cell phone and wallet. *No.* Cell phone, gun, bullets, wallet, hat, and radio. *Must not forget that.* He hated when things were out of order. That was how mistakes were made. People were killed.

Tick. Tick. Tick. An hour left to go. He was getting hungry. *Crackers.* He always had crackers. *Where the hell were they?* He started to search. No crackers, but a candy bar was wedged between the seat and the console. He didn't think it was his. Should he eat it? Or not? *What to do... what to do.* He took a deep breath and then another. He counted as he continued to breathe deeply. This had a calming effect on him, and he was able to settle back and think about the coming party.

He was sure it would be a big affair. Between his wife and the Captain, they would put together a very nice retirement party. He thought about all the great times in his life. His milestones, if you will. Those things that make a man, well, a man. Passing from one milestone to another and hoping that he was able to teach his sons how important these steps were in a man's life. He hoped he had been and would continue to be a good example. He thought of his wedding day, the birth of his first child, then the second and the third. His promotions, coaching his son's softball teams, and ballroom dancing with his wife. God, he loved her. More now than the day he married her. He was looking forward to being with her every day. Maybe he would take her on a second honeymoon. Better yet, he would ask her to marry him all over again. Renew their vows. *Yes.* He would do it at the end of the party tonight. She would never expect it of him. Especially in front of everyone. He might even sing her 'their song.' *Froggy went a courtin' he did ride... uh huh. Froggy went a courtin' he did ride... uh huh. Froggy went a courtin' he did ride... with his guitar by his side, honey, baby, mine.*

****

"People, people, gather 'round." The captain was calling everyone together for last-minute instructions. The excitement was alive in the room. Everyone came together around the captain while he explained what they would do when he arrived. They would make themselves scarce and yell surprise when he came through the door. Everyone had confetti and would throw it in the air. Balloons would drop from the ceiling. The kids would blow noisemakers. Not too much longer now!

****

He heard his radio come to life with a BOLO alert. The message was garbled, and he couldn't understand what was being said. Something about a shooting... somewhere... or was that a song? *What the hell?* Fifteen minutes left until his shift was over. He grabbed his cell phone, so he could call in to get a clear message.

Beep. Beep. Beep. His radar had picked up a live one. He started his cruiser. Yes, there it was. Twenty over the speed limit. He pulled out behind the green van, lights flashing, sirens blaring. He should make that call. This wouldn't take long. He would call after. He was keeping pace behind the van and calling in the license plates. This guy wasn't slowing down. *Shit, of all days to get involved in a chase.*

****

"Everyone! Quiet down!" The captain had made everyone wear a party hat. What a milestone for her husband, she thought. Maybe the best so far. She was shaking with anticipation.

****

Finally! The van pulled over to the side as he heard the radio give the 'all clear' to any warrants or problems with the license plates. *This should go quickly. Probably a bunch of hopped-up teenagers.* He stepped out of the cruiser, checked his gun, and started to walk toward the van. *Yeah, teenagers,* he thought. He could hear loud music from inside... *Another one bites the dust... and another one's down... and another one's down... another one bites the dust.* He slowed his walk. Something felt wrong. Something was off. He could feel it. He put his hand on his gun as he leaned down to look through the window. A pretty girl was looking back at him. *Strange.* Not what he expected.

"I need your driver's lic..." He felt it. A kick to the back of his legs. He hit the ground, knees first. An arm came around his neck, and a serrated hunting knife sliced his throat from ear to ear. Blood spurted out of his separated arteries. He was thrown aside, bleeding from his fatal wound. The van pulled back onto the road.

****

"Here he comes!" She went to be the first to greet him. As she opened the door, all she heard was music from a radio... *And another one's down... and another one's down... another one bites the dust.* A spray of bullets hit her first before the AR 15 blew the rest of the room to bits.

Mother Knows Best

Chelsea Gouin

Emmaline hummed a cheery tune as she traversed the winding path through the woods behind her manor. The weather had just begun to turn after a fairly warm autumn season, and she was glad for the foresight of wrapping herself in her shawl before setting out earlier in the day. It was a rich sapphire to match her eyes, the only bit of color over her drab black mourning attire. She fondly ran her fingers along the edge of the garment; crude flower designs were stitched there from her young maid's cross-stitch practice.

Emmaline couldn't help the soft smile from forming as she reminisced on the girls. Janine and Clarisse weren't too much younger than Emmaline herself and had been such permanent members of the manor. She often thought of them as sisters instead of her staff. Despite only a few years separating them, Emmaline found herself longing for the carefree innocence the maids exhibited. They had yet to be spurned by the harsh realities of the world as she had, hadn't yet felt the sting of punishment of a bad choice.

No, no, Emmaline admonished herself, shaking her head so roughly a few of her hairpins wiggled loose from her tight bun. She had set out today to relieve herself of dark and gloomy thoughts. Emmaline had ventured just to the edge of the woods, close enough to hear the bustle of town before her nerves got the better of her. She just wasn't ready to face the members of the small community and the whispers of all her past sins.

It had only been a few months since Emmaline's baby boy had gone missing, but his mother ached as if it had been an eternity. Still, she longed to run her fingers through his dark tuft of hair, to hear his soft coos as he shook his rattle, or to feel his pudgy fingers wrapped around hers. The last time Emmaline had dared venture into town, she was mocked for her mourning attire and ridiculed for her anguish at seeing the notice of her missing son gone yellow and buried by other missing notifications on the bulletin. The Constable had been less than sympathetic to her case. After all, her son had been born outside of wedlock. Abandoned by the man she thought was her happily ever after and then, the son of their union was seen as poetic justice, all immediately following her father's tragic passing.

With a much heavier sigh, Emmaline shifted her heavy canvas to her opposite shoulder and finished her walk back to the manor. She called out to the girls and got no response. Checking the kitchen, she noticed a pie cooling in the window and figured the girls must have made their own trip to town to gather missing dinner ingredients. She smiled fondly as she hung up her shawl, noting the girls' aprons thrown hastily aside.

She was alone and knew that Clarisse and Janine tended to stretch their time outside the Manor as long as they possibly could to avoid their least favorite chores. Still, Emmaline hastily climbed the flights of steps and snuck her skeleton key from its hidden location as she tip-toed up to her attic studio. Once securely locked inside, she observed the surroundings. She took inventory of her various paints and tools, and making a note of what would have to be restocked the next time the girls made a shopping trip.

Once Emmaline had tidied the room to her liking, she knelt beside her canvas bag and unzipped it cautiously. Inside, the usual painting supplies and portraits normally stored after an afternoon in the woods were not there. Instead, bound tightly in excess hair ribbon, was a small boy, his round eyes wide and full of tears, his cheeks ruby red and streaked with salty tracks.

"Shh, shh," Emmaline hushed, scooping the toddler up and cradling him close. "You're okay! Mummy is here!" She gently untied the ribbon from his wrists and around his mouth with great care not to tug on the boy's hair.

The boy took a shaking gasp of breath and continued to sob. His little hands curled into fists, and he tried to dislodge himself from her arms while crying out, "No!"

Emmaline began to sing a lullaby that had soothed her son since his birth, but the toddler didn't cease his struggles or his cries. She tightened her grip around his wiggling body. "It's okay, dear. It's okay! I'm going to take care of you! We're going to be a family!"

"I want my mum!" the boy sniffled, wiping his tears away with the back of his hand.

"I'm your mum!" Emmaline said softly. "I'm going to feed you, clothe you, and love you! We'll sing songs and tell stories; we'll be a happy family, I promise!"

The boy struggled in her tight grasp, his sobs growing louder as she cooed at him and bounced him in her arms.

Emmaline tutted. "Now, be a good boy for Mummy!" she pleaded. "I need you to be quiet; we mustn't let the others know you're here... not yet!" She tried to cover his mouth with her hand, but he gave a screech and bent himself backward with such force he pitched himself from her arms and tumbled to the floor.

There was a second of silence as both overcame the shock of the boy's tumble. Emmaline felt as if she'd been doused in cold water, doubting her capability as a mother if she couldn't even calm a distressed child.

The boy began to cry again as the shock wore off. Bruises began their steady throbbing along his body. He tried to crawl to the door, but he was immediately scooped up by Emmaline again, her tears mingling with his.

"Oh, my baby! I'm so sorry; let Mummy kiss it and make it better!" She tried to pull him close to press her lips to his forehead, but the child's small bunched-up fists wailed upon her face, and he continued to scream, "No!"

Emmaline could feel her blood racing in her veins as she was pummeled by baby fists, her ears ringing with continuous screams. This *wasn't* her baby. He wasn't her child. Her baby would never disrespect his mother like this. She was a *good* Mother. Any child would be grateful for her welcoming them into her home. Her fingers curled into the child's soft flesh, her nails sinking into his back as the room was painted red in her gaze.

"I'M A GOOD MOTHER!" She screamed into the boy's crying face, shaking him as she continued the mantra. "I LOVED MY SON, AND HE LOVED ME!" She rattled the boy harder, and his screams proceeded to rise in decibel. Emmaline knew what she had to do. This was a mess she couldn't expect her maids to clean up for her.

So, while tears continued to streak down her face, she covered the child's mouth with her hand to muffle the noise and, with a sharp twist, effectively broke his neck. The body went limp in her arms, and she cradled him close, humming her eerie lullaby once more. Softly she closed the child's eyelids and folded the body up, placing it back into her canvas bag. She took her time lacing her boots and wrapping herself in her shawl once more.

Her trip down the winding dirt path wasn't as hurried as it was this morning. She leisurely followed a trail that had been overgrown with foliage, leaves crunching under her as she continued. Partially hidden by thick trunks, deep off the traveled paths, was a ditch that Emmaline vaguely remembered was, at one point, going to be some sort of a shed her father would have constructed for tinkering. Other than prepping the foundation, he hadn't gone much farther before falling ill. But the ground had remained a steep pit, yet to be discovered by anyone but herself.

With a *tsking* noise, Emmaline unzipped her canvas bag and lifted the limp body of the boy she'd been so pleased to find just hours before. His round cheeks and dark shock of hair had reminded her so much of her son. She'd been sure he'd be the one to fill the hole in her heart, but alas, he was more like the last few. She laid the corpse into the ditch as if tucking the boy into bed, just as she had the previous boy, and the one before. Of course, looking now, her previous "children" were hardly recognizable but for some rotting flesh clinging to bone.

Emmaline sent a quick prayer for a restful journey to heaven for the boy and began picking her way back to the Manor. She wondered if she'd run into her maids once she returned to the main path. *Maybe tomorrow,* she thought, *I could try a little girl...*

MR. JELLYMAN

Johnny Stephen Zawacki

A chill I can feel, the goosebumps they rise
As a darkness envelopes this place
His breath I can feel, though his body it hides
He's there but I can't see his face

But I know there's someone, from my skin as it crawls
More than once I've confirmed that it's true
So, don't close your eyes, it's not safe for your soul
When the Jellyman comes 'round for you

Mr. Jellyman lurks in the shadows of night
He'll prey on the weak and the small
But make no mistake, he's a huge appetite
And he'll go after any and all

So, I'm hiding my vest, as the specter roams 'round
No escape, no comfort to share
As the Jellyman searches I want not be found
Not of this - no, I want it ne'er

So, I'm telling you now, beware and forewarned
That the Jellyman will come for you
Don't let your guard down, when he's taking his form
Cuz there'll be nothing that you can do

Mr. Jellyman lurks in the shadows of night
He'll prey on the weak and the small
But make no mistake, he's a huge appetite
And he'll go after any and all
Oh, make no mistake, he's a huge appetite
And he'll go after any and all
Yes, he'll go after any and all

My Neighbor Is A Vampire

Chelsea Gouin

Kris shook her head, tears welling in her aqua eyes. "Wh-what...? You're a... a *what?*"

Lou held his hands up slowly, inching closer to Kris. "I know how it sounds. But you have to trust me... it's... it's not what you think." When Kris shrank away from his approach, he paused. "I'm still the same person..."

"Yeah, who drinks *blood*." Kris shook her head. This was ridiculous. She and Jez were *joking* when they began Project V. There was no way her next-door neighbor was actually a vampire. Taking a deep breath, she glanced at Mr. Lou through her lashes. "Can I see them?" she whispered.

He quirked a light eyebrow. "See...?"

Kris bit her lip, a blush sneaking over her cheeks. "Can I see... your fangs?" She jumped when a low chuckle emitted from Mr. Lou.

He held his hand to her, which she tentatively grasped. He pulled her closer. His icy eyes bore into her wide ones. Her gaze slipped, however, when the light glinted on two elongated fangs. The feeling of ice water washed over her, and she stumbled back. If it was at all possible, his eyes grew even paler.

"Oh, Lord..." Kris choked out as she continued to back away. "You really *are* a vampire!"

Lou clasped a hand over his mouth. "Shit! I... I didn't mean to frighten you, Kris." He turned away for a moment. When he faced her again, his teeth were normal. He ran a hand through his short spikes with a sheepish expression. "I guess we should talk, huh?"

Kris pulled up a chair from the kitchen table and plopped down. "I have some time."

Lou sat across from her, slowly folding himself into a relaxed pose. "Where to begin...?" He rubbed the stubble on his chin. "You should know that I am four hundred years old. I'm considered of Elite lineage. I'm also tasked with guarding and aiding the future Vampire Princess as she reaches her coronation."

"Whoa, whoa, whoa!" Kris held up her hand. "Slow down there! You're telling me that you're... four hundred years old? But you look..." she gestured.

Lou smiled. "I am rather young for my race." His grin grew to a sly smirk. "Do you find me attractive, Kris? I hear mortals can't resist our aura."

Kris blushed and rolled her eyes. Lou was always so different outside of the classroom and it always caught her off guard. "You wish, Lou. You were saying something about a Princess?"

"Yes. The Vampire race is run by Royalty. The throne is currently vacant after the tragic loss of our King and Queen. Their daughter has recently been discovered but has yet to come of age to succeed to the throne. My... bloodline of Elites has always been the ones to guard the Royalty."

"Excuse me if I don't quite follow what you're explaining," Kris interrupted. Her head was spinning with the news; each new piece of the complicated puzzle only frustrated her more than the previous.

Lou chuckled. "I'm sure you're looking for more... *fun* information, yes?" She blushed again. "Don't fret; it's only natural to be curious. Over the years, vampires have grown stronger, allowing us to tolerate sunlight. However, some of the older lineages are still irritated by it. We possess extraordinary speed and strength as well as longer lives. The other powers vary by class. The Royals have more powers than I could possibly list, whereas an elite possesses no more than three. I have two." He held up a hand to cut off Kris's question before she could even ask it. "I do not like to divulge that information. It is the equivalent in my world of asking someone their social security number." Kris looked slightly put out at the brush aside. Lou leaned in close, his breath brushing her ear. "And yes, we survive off of blood. Human blood."

Kris let out a shiver as his breath tickled her skin. Lou was always teasing her when they were outside of school. She was used to playing the flirtatious game, but it had always felt... innocent. Now there was something darker in his tone, something that frightened her. She shot out of her chair and rushed to the front hall, scooping up her bag in the process. She muttered a goodbye and rushed across the lawn back to the safety of her home, locking the door behind her with shaking hands.

****

When had things turned so complicated? How had a simple English project about an old, gothic novel turned into all this supernatural nonsense? Her neighbor was some fanged royalty? Perhaps she'd hit her head, and this was all some weird, coma-induced dream.

Her phone buzzed, dragging her from her tumbleweed thoughts. Of course, it was her best friend, finally replying hours after she'd texted her about her rendezvous with her neighbor.

Can't sleep. Meet me @ park?

After texting a quick confirmation, Kris slipped on some sweatpants and a hoodie before sliding silently downstairs. Just as she squeezed the front door shut behind her, she saw a figure stumbling along Lou's driveway. It leaned heavily on the wall, dug through pockets, and fumbled with the door. It collapsed as soon as it crossed the threshold.

Kris darted across the lawn, flinging herself through her neighbor's door. Crouching, she uncovered a very pale Lou, a thin trail of blood sliding down his face.

"Lou?!?" Kris called, leaning closer, listening for breath. "Dammit, Lou! Wake up!"

He groaned, his face scrunching in pain. His eyes slowly slid open, revealing irises transformed to a frosty white that chilled Kris to her very core. "Shit!" he slammed his eyes shut and tried to twist away from her.

"What? What can I do to help?" Kris asked, shaking his shoulder. "What happened?"

Lou shoved Kris' hand away. "Get out of here! If you wish to live, get the hell out!"

Kris gasped at the sight of his fangs, but she merely grasped his shoulders tighter. "No! I can help!"

A low growl rumbled deep within his chest. "I'll be fine... I just need blood."

Kris visibly paled. "Blood?!?" she squeaked.

Lou groaned. "I have some in the fridge. But damn... you smell good."

Kris felt her breath leave in a whoosh as that icy stare connected with hers. She pushed her blonde hair back, revealing her neck. "Drink from me..."

"No!" Lou yelled, reluctantly turning away. "Stubborn girl! Don't offer what you don't understand!" He again focused on her neck, eyes zeroing in on the pulse point. "Leave... now. I'll be fine once I drink my fill."

"You're the fool if you think I'm going to leave you." She took a deep breath, attempting to steady her nerves. "Now, please..." She squeezed her eyes tight, no longer able to stand Lou's hungry gaze.

Kris jumped when she felt a slight pressure on her wrist. There was a deep chuckle followed by a whisper as soft as a lover's caress. "Your heart is racing... relax..."

Suddenly there was a sharp sting followed by a long pull. Her blood was on fire. The blaze grew hotter and hotter inside her until she screamed and tried to yank her arm away. But Lou held fast, and his fangs stayed buried deep in her skin.

Tears pricked Kris' eyes as the heat became unbearable. Finally, she peeked at Lou, only to find he was staring at her. Suddenly, the fire dulled to a warmness that almost sang in a sweet pulse. Her tension melted, and she seemed to drown in his twin pools of endless black. So far was she drawn in; she didn't feel him slip out his fangs or lick the wound shut.

"I feel..." she whispered before completely blacking out.

Narrow Escape

Marianne Wieland

Mildred was on her way home after a long day working with school children. She'd been a volunteer at her daughter's school for several years, both on the playground and in the classroom. Today she also volunteered in the lunchroom. She was still picking spaghetti out of her hair.

She loved working with the kids most of the time, but her daughter was getting to that age where 'mom' was more of an embarrassment than a comfort. That's why Mildred had requested to stay in the elementary school for the next term. Her daughter would be in junior high when the next school term started.

So many things to do today. Many errands to run. She began to tick off the places where she needed to make stops. She had to pick up her dry cleaning since she had forgotten it every day for the last two weeks. She had also forgotten to stop at the post office for mail that could not be delivered after someone knocked down her mailbox. Then she had better pick up a new mailbox at the hardware store. Denny worked there.

Her nephew would fix her up with everything she needed for the repair. Probably even come and fix it for her. She was lucky to have so many family members close to home. She'd lost her husband a few years ago, but she had managed by herself and with some help from her daughter. But she had good neighbors and friends she could call if she really needed anything.

"Dry cleaning, hardware, post office," she said out loud to herself. She could remember things easier when she did this. Her head was so full of what she needed to do. Maybe she should just write it down.

"Pharmacy, grocery store. Probably should get some gas if I see a good price," she continued to speak out loud.

"Okay," she said. "Dry cleaning first."

Mildred loved to chat when she had the time and sometimes when she didn't. She had been coming to this dry cleaner for years, and the same couple of people were always working there. *I can afford to be friendly, right?* After a nice chat, she got back in her car and drove away. She happened upon the gas station and filled the car up before moving on.

"There's the post office," she said. "Better stop there while I am in the area."

She had to park around the side of the building, near the jail, and walk to the front. She knew the people in the post office very well too, so she had a nice chat with her friend, Fran, who had worked there ever since she could remember. They caught up with the day-to-day gossip in their neighborhood.

After returning to her car, Mildred turned on the radio to keep her company. She loved the 'oldies' station and sang loudly, off-key, but she didn't care. She didn't have to rush home as her daughter was studying at a friend's house.

The hardware store looked deserted. She was the only car in the lot and considered they might be closed for some reason, but she saw Dewey looking out the door and motioning her to come inside. He'd heard of her mailbox incident and had the supplies at the counter for her.

"I can come over tomorrow afternoon and put it up if that's okay with you," he said.

"That would be wonderful," said Mildred. "I'll make my special chili that you like, and you can have dinner with me for your help."

"I can't wait, Aunt Mildred," said Dewey. "You're the best! I'll just keep the supplies and bring them when I come over."

"Sounds like a plan," Mildred replied as she gave him a hug before she left the store.

It was strange how everything seemed to be deserted. She passed very few cars on the road. She had a bad feeling that she couldn't seem to shake but shook it off anyway and turned the radio back on.

"...Special Bulletin. A man escaped the county jail earlier today and is believed to be hiding in the area. He left the jail on foot after stabbing two guards. The man is of average height and build. White. Mid-thirties and wearing a gray prison jumpsuit. If seen, do not approach. He is dangerous. Leave the area and call for help...."

The announcer went on to give a more detailed account, but Mildred's mind had gone into overdrive, thinking about the town being in danger. This had happened before, and there were discussions at all the town meetings about the lack of security at the jail. The turnover of security guards was ridiculous. No one stayed there for long. Now Mildred was really spooked. She decided to stop at the closest grocery store and make the pharmacy her last stop. She wanted to get home and make sure her daughter was safe.

Of course, at the grocery store, she ran into a couple of neighbors. They discussed the jailbreak at length and what they could do to make their homes safe until this man was found. One of the neighbors had seen a bunch of police officers near the post office and 'crime scene' tape roping off an area behind the feed store. He'd asked the feed store owner what was going on and was told a woman's body had been found. She'd been murdered behind the store, not thirty minutes earlier.

"I was at the post office about an hour ago," said Mildred. "I even parked on that side of the street."

"You were lucky, then," said the neighbor. "That could have easily been you."

Mildred hurried to get the items she needed from the store and nearly ran to her car. She threw the small bag into the passenger side of the front seat and headed to the pharmacy for her daughter's medication. She called her daughter to let her know what was going on and to stay inside her friend's house until she came to pick her up.

Mildred was driving faster than she normally would, but she wouldn't feel safe until she was at home with all the doors and windows locked. She needed to be with her daughter, and she felt she wouldn't rest until this man was caught. What her neighbor said about the murdered woman haunted her. *It could have been me,* she thought.

Mildred was in line at the drive-thru window for the pharmacy pick-up. She was agitated and anxious to get out of there. It should only take a moment to get the medication. She had called it in earlier in the day. Finally, it was her turn at the window. She made eye contact with the pharmacy tech. The young man looked upset.

"I'm here to pick up my daughter's medication," said Mildred.

The tech looked her in the eye, then turned around to speak with the pharmacist.

"I'm afraid there was a problem with the script," said the tech. "You need to come into the store so we can straighten it out."

"I'm in a hurry," said Mildred. "I don't have time for this. Just tell me what the problem is and fix it. I have to pick up my daughter."

"No," said the tech, still looking her in the eye. "You have to come inside to fix this. I can't let you have the medication until you do."

"Oh, for Pete's sake!" Mildred put the car in gear and started to pull away.

"Please park in the handicapped spot by the door," said the tech. "You will be able to leave quicker."

Mildred was so frustrated she almost floored it to get to the front of the pharmacy. She was really pissed now. Her daughter was waiting. A killer was on the loose. If her daughter wasn't out of the medication, she would forget it altogether.

She parked in the space, as she was instructed, and ran in the door. Of course, the pharmacy was in the back of the store, just adding to Mildred's frustration. The tech and pharmacist were waiting for her when she approached the pharmacy counter.

"Something must be really bad," said Mildred.

The tech and pharmacist came out of the enclosed pharmacy area and sat her down in the chairs that were provided for customers.

"What is going on?" Mildred was starting to lose it.

The pharmacy tech spoke first. "I could see into your car since I am located higher up than your vehicle at the drive-thru window. There is a man crouched down on the backseat floorboard and he has a large butcher knife. I had to get you out of that car."

"I called the police," said the pharmacist. "That is why we instructed you to park by the front door."

Mildred almost passed out. She started crying, shocked at how close she had come to death. The man might have killed her and her daughter if not for the tech. The tech put his arm around her and let her cry. After a few minutes, a police officer arrived to speak with them.

The officer informed them that they had apprehended the man and he was indeed the man that had escaped from the jail. The knife still had blood on it so they would be able to prove he had been the one to murder the woman behind the feed store.

Mildred was so grateful that she had not left the pharmacy. They all went to the front entrance and gave their statements. Mildred was given an escort to pick up her daughter and return home. The officer checked her home because she was so frightened, and it was all clear. She and her daughter thanked the officer and together gave thanks for the quick-thinking tech that had given Mildred her narrow escape.

****

Several hours later, Mildred's daughter was asleep, and she was preparing for bed when a knock sounded at the door. She looked out and saw the police officer from earlier standing on her front porch. She opened the door to see him smiling.

"This is just a follow-up to make sure you are okay," he said.

Mildred smiled back and opened the door wider. She never saw the butcher knife he was holding behind his back.

OF BUGBEARS AND GOBLINS

Michael Simpson

I

"I've finally come to the conclusion," Alfred Fitzroy-Maldovar said, "that Seymour is a bugbear."

"Well..." Richard Henry responded in his typically slow and thoughtful manner. They were in Alfred's library in the Moldovan family mansion, Overbrook, on an overcast Thursday afternoon. As always, there was a dark-gray chill in the air that hung there and never turned to rain. As if the whole soaking-the-earth thing just required too much damn effort.

Richard cleared his throat and offered a tentative assessment. "His clumsiness *is* a bit of a nuisance, and your china has suffered, but..."

"I'm not talking about ordinary clumsiness, Rich. I mean, he's literally a bugbear."

Richard sighed deeply—a clear sign he was either thinking or worrying. (For Richard, the two were indistinguishable.) He eyed his half-empty tea cup suspiciously. He was always uneasy around Alfred. As he often told his friends at the club, he never knew when his friend would "get a wild hair." He was sure his tea wasn't spiked (in fact, he suspected the teabags had been reused), but he wondered about Alfred's.

"What do you mean, *literally*?" Richard emphasized the word as if he had never encountered it before and felt it was something you shouldn't say in a library—especially in the tone of voice his high-strung friend used. It seemed an offense to the rows of musty books that filled the floor-to-ceiling shelves. For a moment, he felt he could almost see them all shudder in disgust. Alfie, as he was known by those forced to associate with him because he was of their class, never read a book and barely comprehended newspaper headlines—except for the cricket scores.

Alfie leaned against the mantel above the fireplace. The fire itself was exceedingly small and only warmed the immediate area around it, which was why Alfred didn't sit in the massive leather chair only a few feet away. He gestured high in the air as if he were trying to draw something, his image of Seymour, perhaps.

"I mean, he's one of those goblin creatures."

"But those are just made-up folk tales and myths. They're not real."

"Tell that to the kitchen staff."

"Have they been complaining about him?" Richard asked. Although an educated man (he graduated 12th in his class at Cambridge), Richard was in awe of what he called the "instinctive wisdom of the common man." If fact, he was intimidated by them; not because their opinions were insightful or articulate, but, as he himself admitted, "They're just too damn rough about everything."

When his friend didn't immediately answer, Richard asked the question again in a slightly different way.

"What have they been saying about him?"

"Nothing," Alfie blurted out. "They don't say anything. They're too bloody scared, that's what I think."

"I'll admit he is a rather large man. One does not immediately warm to him, what with his height, and his bulk, and his somewhat sullen manner."

"And don't forget his beard and all the hair, that bristly hair. I swear he's covered all over with it. You might as well call it what it is—fur!"

"So why don't you just fire him. Or maybe suggest you can't afford to keep him on... say you'll give him a good reference."

"I'd want to have some police around, no matter what I tell him."

"I'm sure that won't be necessary. Be fair but firm with him. Be straight. I'm sure he'll understand. I'm always surprised by what good manners the big ones have. It's as if they feel obliged to apologize for how much space they take up."

"It's more complicated than that."

"How so?"

Alfred stared randomly around the high-ceilinged room and made curiously tight mincing motions with his lips as if giving the words he spoke as little room as possible to escape into the world.

"I'm afraid Beatrice has grown rather fond of him."

"Beatrice? Fond of him? My God, Alfred, how do you get into situations like this?"

"Actually, it was Beatrice who suggested I take him on. She took pity on him."

"Next thing I know, you'll tell me it was a dark and stormy night."

"Actually, it was stormy, but it was more like late afternoon. We don't get many storms up here, you know. Not real storms. Still, it was rather dark. He looked very pathetic and somehow not as big when he was wet. I didn't fully register his size until he dried off."

"Have you talked to Beatrice about this?"

"About what?"

"About your suspicions."

Alfred exhibited a sudden and deep interest in a spot on the mantle.

"No," he finally said. "I'm afraid her fondness has gone beyond mere fondness."

"Are you suggesting some kind of intimacy?" Richard gasped.

"I'm afraid so."

"My God, Alfred. She's no bigger than a field mouse. And he's... he's... a bear."

"Exactly my point. How is it even possible?"

"I shudder to think."

II

"I'm afraid her fondness has gone beyond a mere fondness."

That was the last thing Pansy, the housemaid, heard before she dashed off to the kitchen to tell the other household servants. She had been listening by the main door to the library. She had enough gossip to outdo anything either the Master's valet or the senior lady's maid had ever delivered. Of course, everyone knew what was going on, but the big news was that Master Albert now knew what everyone else knew.

Pansy was flushed with the excitement of it. What would Master Albert do, and—more important—what would happen when Mistress Beatrice heard about her husband's suspicions, which everyone agreed were absolutely true. If their master dared to confront her, how would she reply? Would Seymour have to leave? Would he be in disgrace, or would the whole thing be done quietly and discreetly? And what about the changed situation of their master and mistress? Would they continue to give parties? Would they attend parties together? The consensus was that they would *attend parties* but would severely limit *giving parties*, if they gave any at all.

But a fortnight later, the question of giving and attending parties became moot. Here is how the local newspaper, *The Gazetteer*, recounted the events under the headline: "*Local Gentry Dies in Freak Library Accident.*"

Sir Albert Muffington Fitzroy-Maldovar of County Landon, husband of Lady Beatrice Eugenia Fitzwilliam-Compton of County Albert, died last night as the result of a freak accident in Sir Fitzroy-Maldovar's library. The preliminary report of the local constable, Adam Lockley-Elderbeer, concludes that while climbing a ladder in his library, the late Sir Albert fell. The back of his skull felt the full impact of a large volume of the Fitzroy-Maldovar's family chronicles, which go back to 1609 when Sir Edmund Fitzroy first purchased the estate as a wedding present for his wife, Lady Abigail Maldovar. Lady Beatrice did not discover the body until close to midnight when her husband, who often stayed up late in his library, did not return to their bed.

The rest of the article listed Sir Albert's prominent relatives and his more famous associates. Richard Henry's name was not among them, but that did not deter him from still occasionally visiting Albert's officially grieving widow, even though he had obvious suspicions about the extent of her grief. But his curiosity was also piqued. After his last visit with Albert, he wondered about the status of Seymour. Would the large, ungainly man (Richard refused to credit his friend's mad assertion that Seymour was a "bugbear") still maintain his humble position as gardener, or would Beatrice make subtle adjustments to improve his situation?

Richard was not a brave man, and his ideas rarely reached beyond the conventional—two characteristics he shared with his late friend Albert. But Richard, regarding social status, was an immensely curious man. If he had been a cat interested in feline class structure and status, he would have already used up the majority of his nine lives.

Unfortunately, Richard was not a cat, but a man and only had one life.

III

Several weeks after Albert's death, Richard found himself in the dank woods near the Moldavor estate trudging through thick, dripping underbrush with Seymour ahead of him and Beatrice beside him. The overhanging clouds saturating the sky were the color and texture of steel wool. The air had the chill of a well-iced cocktail and a comparably bracing effect but, as Richard observed, not nearly as numbingly pleasant.

A small group of the estate's tenants and one or two of the late Sir Albert's friends were hunting deer. Richard had been asked to join and was not happy. He was not a huntsman; he repeatedly explained to everyone he could collar. But Beatrice, with the prerogative of the recently widowed, had insisted he go. When Richard protested he had no suitable hunting jacket or boots, she brushed it off.

"No, my dear, there is plenty of hunting paraphernalia at hand. And if I'm any judge, you and my dear Albert are the same size. Or, rather (with the hint of a tear at this point), he was your size."

Richard was quick to seize the high ground. "Don't you think that's a trifle morbid?"

Beatrice laughed rather jaggedly, "No, no. You were friends. If you have come to hunt with him, he would have given you one of his jackets—and boots too, for that matter. He was such a generous man. And besides, (a little sniff, a handkerchief applied to her eye) it would bring back fond memories of him. It would make me happy. We used to walk in these woods quite often."

That was a lie, and Richard knew it. But he was in no position to argue. Hence, his trudging through the cold with a sport rifle in his arm. Apparently, Beatrice was quite knowledgeable about the makes and the proper way to handle the rather awkward weapon.

Perhaps it was the cold or her persistent chatter, but for the first time in his long relationship with Albert and his wife, Richard actually developed a strong impression of her. It was as if he saw her for the first time in almost unbearable detail. She was beautiful, of course, in an angular, pinched way. Her eyes were quite striking, almost stark in their roundness and intensity. Yet she was a small woman, barely taller than the rifle she was showing him how to use. And her hair was dark and thick, almost too lush for so small a woman. And the arched forehead, on the verge of being too much. The thick black eyebrows.

As they walked, she clutched his arm. And he was surprised by her strength.

"I'm so very glad you're here," she said. "It feels like I'm being given back a little bit of my Albert. It has been hard for me." At that point, she clutched his arm so tightly that he yelped.

"I'm sorry," she quickly said. "Did I hurt you? I didn't mean to. I get beside myself. So much grief and then the gossip. The ugly gossip. You've heard it, of course. Everyone has."

"I..." Richard felt there was nothing he could say that wouldn't make things worse. If he admitted he had heard the rumors, she would want to know what he had heard. If he denied knowing anything, she would surely tell him—in more detail than he wanted to know—and increase the pain of her own grief. If that is, there was any pain in her grief. If her grief was really grief at all.

He couldn't help but look at Seymour's hulking back as he trudged in front of them. There was something strange about how he walked, about how he held the rifle. He wasn't turning his head from side to side. He wasn't scanning the thick, wet brown-green of the brush they were walking through. He wasn't looking for anything. He was just walking.

"Seymour is a much-misunderstood man," Beatrice suddenly said. It was as if she knew what he was thinking. "Albert's dislike of him—yes, don't try to deny it—Albert was very uncomfortable around Seymour. And that hurt Seymour very much."

"Albert thought he was a bugbear." Richard wasn't sure what made him say that. It was a small act of rebellion.

For a moment she stood stock still; and, because she was holding his arm, he was forced to stand still too. The stillness and silence had an ominous feel to it. He could hear large raindrops hit the broad leaves of the taller trees around. He was also suddenly aware that he couldn't see or hear the others who had come out to hunt.

"People are so cruel," Beatrice said, all the sweetness out of her voice. It was as if she were using her true voice for the first time, not disguising it.

"I'm sorry," he said. He was in a panic. Why was he feeling panicky? He found himself stammering. "I shouldn't have said that. I'm not sure why I blurted it out."

"You blurted that out," Beatrice said, and her voice was flat and deliberate, "because Albert said it during one of your talks. You two were always talking."

"I don't think he really believed it."

"Oh, yes, he did."

Beatrice loosened her grip on his arm. For some reason, he looked down at her hand as she moved it and was struck by how gnarled and thin her finger bones were... like sticks covered with only the slightest film of skin. And her nails... like claws.

She had stepped away from him, and her voice was soft again.

"You were staring at my hand," she said. "What were you thinking?"

"I wasn't thinking anything."

"Yes, you were. A word came to mind. What was it?"

He felt suddenly weak and helpless. He didn't want to say it. He wasn't even sure what the word was... but at the same time, he knew...

"Tell me what you were thinking. You can say it."

He resisted; his mouth trembled, and he was angry with himself for being so weak.

Then he heard her say, "Seymour, we've stopped. You can turn around now."

She addressed him again. "You can say it. You won't hurt our feelings."

He felt the rain starting, getting heavy, and he looked down at the rifle in his arm and felt how heavy and useless it was. Then he looked at Seymour, and he saw, purely and clearly, the rage in his face, the thick tangle of hair so thick it twisted anything human out of his expression.

"Goblins," Richard said.

Then he heard the blast, he felt the sudden spike of icy rain, and the bullet hit him at the same time.

ONE NIGHT AT SKATE LAND

Chelsea Gouin

Lauren swiped on one last layer of lip gloss before giving a final satisfied, flirty pout to her reflection in the mirror. She was only half-listening to Casey moaning about not even wanting to go out in the first place from her spot in the backseat. She needed to lighten up. They were going to Skate Land, and Casey was freshly twenty-one. She had no idea what was in store.

"Shut up!" Chloe groaned, running her fingers through her already perfectly straight hair. "We're going to drink a Four Loko, and skate, and by the end of the night, you'll have long forgotten Tony!"

Casey sniffled, avoiding her friend's eyes in the rearview mirror. Chloe didn't understand, all she had to do was blink, and she had another guy fawning over her. Casey had *worked* to catch Tony's eye. And Tony had made her so *happy* in the few months they had been together.

"Come *on*," Lauren sighed. "We're about to get blackout drunk and probably hook up with ten guys tonight... no moping!"

Chloe smirked across the seat at her best friend. "Try not to make out with the Uber driver this time."

Lauren rolled her eyes. "Only if you promise to keep your hands off the DJ!"

Both girls giggled, but Casey merely picked at the fringe on her ripped jeans. "I don't understand why we're here..."

Lauren twisted in her seat, determined not to let Casey's miserable attitude bring the party down. "Have you ever even *been* to Skate Land?"

"Sure... when I was five."

Chloe's eyes sparkled mischievously. "You're *so* missing out! Just wait until you see Skate Land... after dark!"

When they did enter the rink, Casey wasn't impressed. The same dingy hangout she remembered from when she was a kid greeted her. Loud music was blaring from a set of speakers where a DJ nodded along behind flashing neon lights. A few couples twirled around the rink while others were sipping drinks by the bar, gauging the assembled crowd.

Chloe leaned in close to Casey, practically shouting to be heard over the techno beat. "Skate Land is *the* place to be! It's where people meet up, break up, and *hook* up."

"I'm going to grab us some drinks!" Lauren yelled at them. It wasn't that she didn't empathize with Casey because she did. Breakups suck... but Tony had a reputation. He went through girls like water, and everyone knew it. Besides, Casey was out with her girlfriends to celebrate her birthday. This was not the time to be such a stick in the mud.

As Lauren squeezed in between the crowded bar, she waved down the bartender. He was of the usual Skate Land stock, arms covered completely in tattoos and face freckled with spiky piercings. His mohawk was dyed bright pink, and his guyliner was already smeared from sweat. "What can I get ya?"

"I need three Four Lokos!" she yelled back.

He raised a perfectly manicured eyebrow. "Suicide wish?"

Lauren flirtatiously smiled back. "My friend's 21st birthday. And she's getting over a break-up."

He smirked and pulled the cans from the fridge. "Let me mix up a special birthday shot. On the house."

Casey drummed her fingers in tune with the beat against the vinyl tabletop. The "cafe" next to the bar smelled of pizza grease and regret. The couple making out loudly in the booth next to her was a prime example of exactly why Casey wanted to stay home; maybe cruise YouTube for some cute cat videos... stalk Tony's social media... and eat chocolate ice cream while crying over *The Notebook*.

Chloe dropped a warn pair of skates in front of her, drawing her out of her fantasies of Tony appearing to her rescue tonight. "Strap these on! Lauren is coming over with drinks. We're going to have a good time, I promise!"

Sure enough, Lauren appeared only a moment later, three colorful cans tucked under one arm and three shot glasses balanced in her hands. "Green tea shots, courtesy of the bartender!" She grinned as she slid them to each of her friends.

"Happy birthday!" Chloe cried, slamming back the shot. The other two followed suit, pleased by the choice of alcohol.

"Oh no!" cooed a voice from the other side of the floor. "Looks like they forgot to take the trash out."

Nemesis number one, Dawn, was striding toward them, followed closely by her usual hoes. Dawn had applied self-tanner so thick that she seemed to glow orange under the flashing lights. On each side were her lackeys, with bottle-dyed blonde hair and matching sneers.

Lauren rolled her eyes and loudly cracked the tab on her Four Loko. Even these bitches couldn't ruin a night at Skate Land.

"What are you doing *slumming* with these girls, Casey?" Liz asked, throwing back her long blonde hair with a glare at Lauren.

Casey twirled a loose strand that had fallen from her messy bun. "Well... it's my birthday..."

"Where's Tony?" a tinny voice whined. Annnnnd, there she was.

"I was wondering where the last member of the Mickey Mouse Club was," Chloe mocked as she eyed Dawn's younger sister. Though not nearly to Dawn's level of entitlement, Kaitlyn still tried the princess act with every flutter of her fake eyelashes.

She tugged on a bit of her dark hair, leaning forward in mock sympathy. "He's not... texting someone else, is he?" she pouted her painted-on lips.

Casey glared at Kaitlyn. "He has standards, Kaitlyn. You might want to try batting for the minor leagues instead." With that, she took a long chug of her Four Loko, almost choking on the sugary taste.

The gang snickered. "When you're ready to *really* party, come find us," Dawn offered with a swish of her weave.

Chloe practically growled as they nudged passed her to get to the rink. "I can't *stand* that bitch! After graduating, I thought I'd finally be away from her claws..."

Lauren shrugged. "I heard she was caught hooking up with one of the bandmates in the janitor closet last time she was here."

Chloe snickered. "Sounds about right."

Casey only gave a half-hearted smile. She *liked* Liz and hated that her friends always painted her in a bad light. It was Liz, after all, that had helped Casey win Tony over. He had been talking to someone else... well, a few someone else's actually, but with Liz's guidance and makeover tips, Casey had wormed her way into Tony's heart. Or so she had thought. Clearly, he had found some other girl to amuse him, proving the rumors she had so adamantly fought against to be true. She had been just another conquest.

"Enough!" Lauren sighed, tugging on Casey's arms. "Drink up, and let's go!"

Reluctantly Casey took another swig from the drink, causing her friends to cheer. Sure, she'll show Tony tonight that she was more than just a fling. And if the rumors about Four Loko were true, then she wouldn't even remember her name in a few hours.

****

The girls had skated for a few hours, taking shifts buying drinks, and trying to score as many free shots as possible from the bar flies. Having already downed the first quarter of her can, Casey felt much more relaxed and light-headed. She even took a few turns around the rink with a guy who claimed to be an up-and-coming "big thing" in the local music industry.

Lauren had dipped into a booth with a dark-haired guy and seemed pretty comfortable. Chloe skated up to Casey's spot on the wall, tugging her phone out of her pocket. A small smile tugged at her lips as her fingers flew over the screen, quickly typing back a response.

Casey playfully bumped hips with her, grinning ear to ear. "Who's that?"

Chloe hit the power button, effectively blacking out the screen before Casey could read the name. "Not a big deal... yet." she smirked.

Casey decided not to further tease Chloe, knowing she wouldn't share anything until she was quite ready. "I've got to pee!" Casey screamed over the heavy tune.

Sliding into the women's restroom, Casey was immediately spun around and slammed against the tile wall, her arms held behind her back.

"WAIT!" a familiar voice called out. "Wrong one! Let her go!"

Casey rubbed her wrists, glaring at the tall, muscular girl who continued to glare down at her. "What the hell, Liz?"

Liz sheepishly shrugged. "It's like, commonly known that beef is squashed in the bathroom here. And Dawn wants to personally mess Chloe up... sorry!"

Despite the alcohol-induced haze she was functioning under, Casey had to admit that Skate Land was becoming more and more of an adventure the longer she stayed.

"Wait!" Liz called out again before Casey could push open a stall door. "That's stall *three*." When Casey didn't react, Liz elaborated. "Stall three is the dealer stall, so unless you want... party favors... move on to the stall on the end."

Shaking her head, Casey followed the advice and pushed open the door of the final stall... only to quickly slam it closed again.

"You okay?" Liz trotted over, taking in Casey's suddenly pale face. "You're not gonna puke, are you? Drink the Four Loko too quick?"

Casey shook her head rapidly, tears pricking her eyes. "Don't... look..." she whispered, but Liz ignored her and curiously cracked open the door.

Sprawled on top of the toilet was Dawn's lifeless body. Her eyes were wide, nearly bulging out of her sockets. Her mouth was stuffed with a decorative scarf she had been sporting earlier. Her throat was still trickling blood. And her chest... carved into her chest was a scrawled text, "He was never mine."

Liz gagged, spinning away from the scene. "When did this happen?"

Casey merely choked down the bile that was creeping up her throat. *What the hell happened here?*

****

Lauren joined Chloe, sipping on a fresh cocktail purchased by... she thought he said his name was Mike? The details were fuzzy. Chloe was furiously tapping away on her phone and didn't hear her friend's approach.

"Where's Casey?" Lauren asked, leaning over to ensure she was heard.

Jumping, Chloe shoved her phone back into her pocket. "Bathroom!"

Lauren's head was snapped back from a painful yank to her curly hair. She winced past the sting to focus on Kaitlyn's pretty face, twisted into an angry snarl.

"What's your problem?" Chloe screamed, clawing at Kaitlyn's wrist.

Lauren gripped the fist tangled in her hair, stomping hard on Kaitlyn's boot with her own skate-clad foot. "Let go!"

Kaitlyn released her grip, smacking away Chloe's batting hands. "You had your chance; he's *mine* now!"

A small crowd had edged closer, looking for some Friday night entertainment. Sinking her nails into Kaitlyn's small wrist, Lauren hissed, "We'll take this somewhere private." She dragged her into the dark party room, their features illuminated only by the occasional swoop of the neon lights. Chloe firmly shut the door behind them.

"What the *hell* are you going on about?" Lauren asked, defensively crossing her arms.

Kaitlyn mimicked her pose. Her lips pushed out in a pout. "*Tony*," she whined. "I finally managed to drag him away from your little bitch-friend, and now *you* think you're going to scoop him up?"

Lauren stared blankly at the smaller girl for a moment. "What?"

Chloe's eyes flicked between the two girls, contemplating if it was worth staying or seeing if Casey had survived the Skate Land bathroom. Lauren was a tough girl; she could handle herself.

"I tried calling him earlier tonight," she stamped her foot. "But he said he was talking to someone else. He said he couldn't keep messing around with girls anymore... that he truly fell in love..."

"And?"

Kaitlyn marched closer. "Everyone knows you were hooking up with Tony! Maybe Casey was too blind to see what a backstabber his friend was... but everyone else knew!"

Lauren slapped Kaitlyn across the face. "It was an *accident!*" She shoved her back against one of the tables. "It was at a party; we were drunk... he didn't *tell* me he was seeing her!"

Maybe it was the fact that she actually finished the can of Four Loko, a feat not easily done nor recommended... or maybe it was that Kaitlyn's smug face had smirked at her just one too many times... but Lauren was *not* letting this little hussy make her sound like *she* was the ho. Dawn, Kaitlyn... they thought the whole world revolved around them; that if they just flit their eyelashes or puckered their lips everyone would bend over backwards to accommodate their every petty need... not today. And especially not over an asshole like Tony...

Grabbing a fistful of Kaitlyn's hair, Lauren slammed the girl's head into the table. Every snide comment ever muttered through the years rang over and over as she repeatedly smashed her head down.

"That's enough!" Chloe screamed, practically tackling Lauren. Kaitlyn lay quite still, a pool of blood forming a ring around her head. "We gotta get out of here."

Chloe tugged Lauren, now in a daze, out of the darkened room. She pushed her into the adjacent party room, sitting her down in one of the chairs and instructing her to take deep breaths. "I'm going to find Casey; we've got to get out of here before someone finds Kaitlyn."

****

Casey was wandering the sweaty bodies currently mashed up against one another in a pseudo-mosh pit. She had abandoned her skates in her desperate attempt to find her friends. Liz was still retching in the bathroom and was currently of no use to Casey as she tried to figure out what the hell came next. *Where were Chloe and Lauren?*

She checked her phone again, but there were no missed calls and zero unopened texts. She sent another quick SOS to the girls. This time including the small detail of the dead body in the bathroom. Maybe then they'd be trying a little harder to find her.

Hadn't Chloe finally chugged the last of the Four Loko can, too, though? Maybe they were both passed out somewhere. Or had they found rides home? Casey was shaking, her heart racing as her foggy brain tried to come up with a logical plan.

Her crowd-weaving was halted by nails sinking into the tops of her arms. A soft voice hissed in her ear, "He was right to dump you, bitch." A sharp sting brought attention to the knife now precariously pressed against her throat. "He *loves* me... and once I eliminate all of you, he'll never stray from me again."

Casey's socks were no match for the polished roller rink and slid from her assailant's grasp. Crawling between stamping feet, she managed to get a few feet before a skate-clad foot crushed her pinky. Screaming in agony, she tried to pull her hand back, but the foot refused to budge.

"This somehow seems fitting," The voice was back in her ear.

The knife was plunged into her back, leaving her to bleed out among the party-goers far too drunk to notice her under their feet.

****

Lauren's head was beginning to clear. She should check on Kaitlyn... call 9-1-1... take a shot, anything but sit in the dark room alone. *Where the hell was Chloe and Casey?* Suddenly remembering there were devices called iPhones that told you precisely where your friends were, she tapped her home key to see a long list of missed calls and texts from Casey. Curiously she glanced through them... a *dead body*?

Lauren glanced around the dark room, the flashes of red light casting ominous shapes around the emptiness. She sidled closer to the pinata, rooting around for the bat she knew was tucked away for the game. Just as her fingers closed around the handle, the door behind her clicked open.

Spinning around wildly, Lauren brandished the bat in front of her only to see Chloe standing there, her arms held up in an innocent gesture. "Shit, Chlo!" she sighed. "Did you see Casey's text? Dawn's *dead*?"

"Yeah! As soon as I saw it, I came running back," she shook her head, nervously peeking through the small window on the door. "I couldn't find her out there. Think she finally found someone to take her mind off Tony?"

Lauren rolled her eyes, setting the bat aside. "I honestly *don't* get what the big deal is with him. Sure, he looks like Ryan Gosling, but he's a major dick." She plopped down into the nearest chair to untie her skates, the strings a tangled mess from her earlier drunken attempt to tighten them.

Before Lauren could stand on her now skate-less feet, a sharp blow connected to her abdomen, knocking the wind out of her and causing her to crumple to the floor. Gasping for breath, she rolled over to see Chloe staring down coldly at her, bat clutched in her hands.

"Chloe?!?"

Her friend kicked her in the ribs. "Listen, Lauren... I really wanted to keep you out of this. We're *best friends*... and I was just trying to protect you... but you're so damn stubborn!" She swiftly kicked her again.

Groaning, Lauren attempted to shield herself. "We *are* friends Chloe... just... help me understand what's happening!"

Chloe twirled the bat contemplating the request. "Well, I met Tony back in grade school. We were in the school production of *Cinderella*. He was my Prince in the play and vowed to be there for me *all the time*." She snorted. "We were seven; of course, his promise held no weight... until it did." A soft smile curled on Chloe's lips. "Every summer we spent together even through middle school. He was my first kiss, my first love," A sigh. "And then high school happened. There were so many temptations for Tony... so many girls in such short skirts, how could he resist? So, I let my Prince stray... come summer we were back to being a fling. You see, no matter how many girls there were, I was always the one... the *only* one he came back to. But enough is enough...

time for him to grow up and let pumpkins be pumpkins, right?" She chuckled. "So, I told him I was breaking the news to Casey. He said he'd be more comfortable being 'public' with our relationship if I burned all his old bridges... after all, he really did *care* for Casey; he just didn't *love* her. But," Chloe stepped on Lauren's hair, twisting it under her boot hard enough to make Lauren gasp, "The only bitch you can trust is a dead bitch, am I right?"

Using all her strength, Lauren rolled over and hugged Chloe's knees, causing her to topple over. "Why me, though?" Lauren huffed, grappling with Chloe's flailing arms.

"I've seen the way he looks at you," Chloe spit at her. "I wasn't worried, though. I'd never think my *best friend* would try to steal my man!"

"Honestly!" Lauren screamed, kneeing Chloe in the chest and tossing her into the opposite wall. "Does Tony have some sort of golden dick?" Rolling her eyes, Lauren glanced over at Chloe. Her eyes were glassed over, and a trickle of blood ran down from her forehead. Lauren straightened her clothes and pulled out her phone, intending on calling the cops, and then an Uber to get her the hell out of there.

She never made it to the door. The bat cracked her skull before she could even unlock her screen.

****

Chloe rested her head against the cool glass of the car window. She'd already popped two Tylenol the second she had slid onto the leather seats. "Thanks for picking me up. I hadn't meant to get quite that drunk," she muttered sleepily.

Tony smiled, taking his eyes off the road only to give her a reassuring wink. "I'm glad you were able to clear the air with your friends. And I'm glad you texted me to pick you up. How was your night?"

She sighed, letting her eyes drift close. "Oh, you know... typical night at Skate Land."

Past Back

Leslie Cieplechowicz

The dirty, stringy clouds streaked over the steel sky and sent dripples of rain down onto the muddy, weedy earth, studded with broken concrete strewn across the decaying industrial complex. Hulls of buildings loamed, their rusting, damp girders holding up remnants of crumbling walls and dangling, tinted factory glass. Two figures picked their way over the dead landscape, a tall, slender woman, her dirty blond hair stuffed under the hood of a gray sweatshirt, the cuffs of her faded blue jeans stuffed into EMS-issued boots, scuffed and cracked; and a shorter man, with messy, muddy brown hair and ashy cheeks sunken in from years of drug use and cigarette smoking, sagging camouflage pants, and an unlit cigarette dangling from his lips. Both carried backpacks with tripods strapped to their worn exteriors.

"Just a sec, I gotta light this," Nick stopped and clicked a lighter. He inhaled deeply.

Jillian rested a boot on a flaking drum, her hazel-chipped eyes flicking over the buildings lining the south edge of a dying, poverty-stricken city. She had been on many explorations over the past eight months, but this one today made her slightly ill at ease. The two had come to take pictures of the place, a crazy, weird hobby called urban exploring or "urbex." Jillian never thought she would be one to partake, but an on-the-job shooting that resulted in her untimely retirement from her beloved EMS had changed her mind. After fifteen years on the road, a patient had ambushed her and her partner, resulting in two bullets in her spine. She needed something to stir her blood and give her an adrenaline high like she used to get. Now she wandered the country, taking pictures of decayed, abandoned buildings, forgotten and broken like she was.

Jillian glanced at Nick, who was attempting to text on his phone.

"Fucking A, there is still no signal." He threw his glowing butt onto the ground. "Good?"

She nodded, and they continued their hike. Jillian stared at the back of Nick's head. He was a leftover from her days as a paramedic. Their paths had crossed a few times over the years, with his love of drinking, dappling in drug dealing and use, and not watching his blood sugar, making him a regular to call 911. He gave up his criminal ways and his booze and, like Jillian, needed some excitement to feel alive again. After she left EMS, they reestablished contact at a Coney Island they both frequented as it had the best Philly cheesesteak burgers.

"How long are we gonna look for this medical clinic?" Jillian asked. Nick heard the complex had an emergency clinic to treat its workers. All the antique equipment was supposed to still be there and intact, as he had seen images from another explorer. Jillian had to admit the dusty exam table strewn with empty syringes with an aging, reflecting light glowering over it would probably make for some cool pictures.

"It has to be in the building right up ahead. We hit all the other ones."

The drizzle clumped, and heavier drops splattered down. A loud crack sounding like a gunshot, caused both to stop with a jerk.

For a brief moment, Jillian was back with her EMT partner, Riley, on the dark, hazy street, responding to an innocuous call of "man down," rolling the stretcher to a rumpled figure in the middle of the street. Their eyes met as they saw the dark pool of blood around the fallen man. The left side of his face was a steaming, shredded mass with a dangling eyeball, part of his brain tissue splattered on the pavement. They saw the slow rise of his chest and stooped down to grab vital signs. A dark figure materialized in front of Jillian and Riley, his tattooed left hand gripping a .45 Glock, which was aimed at their patient's head. The gun fired, and the rest of the fallen man's head exploded, spraying Riley and Jillian, who both jumped up. Jillian stared into the shooter's emotionless, metal-grey eyes as he unloaded two bullets into Jillian, then one into Riley, before his gun clicked and jammed. As Jillian crumpled to her knees, gasping for air, she heard police sirens. As she clutched her gut, she saw Riley lying next to her. Jillian smelled the metallic odor of her blood as it leaked from her body, then darkness shrouded her. The vision ended, and she was back, standing next to Nick. She clasped her shaking hands together to hide them from her partner.

Like feral dogs, Jillian and Nick held their breath and perked their ears, trying to locate the source of the noise. All they heard was the hiss of the rain. They looked at each other. Nick shrugged. He motioned with his hand. Both ducked into the crumbling doorway of the factories.

"I don't think it was anyone," Nick whispered.

"Me neither." They had been told they may encounter scrappers, a wild lot who tore apart vacant buildings for the metal to sell. They could be unpredictable and sometimes had unruly dogs with mean attitudes to enforce their owner's unhappiness at seeing other people.

"The clinic has to be in this building."

Jillian nodded, still unable to shake the unsettled feeling she had from being here. *I am just tired from being up the past three nights,* she reasoned. She had been unable to sleep because of vivid nightmares, collateral damage from the shooting, and wondering if, somewhere, the shooter was looking to finish her off just as he did her patient. As they penetrated the hull, she felt her heart rate pick up, and a familiar dose of epinephrine flowed into her vessels. For an adrenaline junkie, it steadied her.

Jillian and Nick stepped into a dim, cavernous room, weak rays of light creeping through a dark ceiling with twisted strips of peeling gray paint dangled down like dusty stalagmites. They yanked out heavy-duty flashlights from their backpacks and flicked them on. Branching off from the room were black corridors, their doorways framed by fallen, rusty steel beams. Littering the floor were remnants of broken, fragmented machinery, corpses lingering from a time long past. Rotting wooden beams hanging from the walls were painted in a white mold that glowed from the explorer's lights. The odor of damp, rotting wood permeated the air.

"How about we start at the two hallways over on the west wall?" Nick flicked his light in that direction.

"Sure."

The two slithered around the machine, avoiding jagged edges from broken window panes and nails rearing up from a decaying wooden floor. When they reached the two corridors, they paused.

"Which one do you want to try first?" Jillian said as she glanced behind her.

"Hmm, I wish I could text that explorer for more info," Nick stuck another cigarette between his lips and began to chew the tip. He looked at his phone. "But still no service."

"Okay, I guess we hit the one on the right, then do the one on the left."

Nick glanced at his watch. "It gets dark in around thirty minutes. I don't want to be messing around here much longer. We don't have much time."

"Hmmm, what's your idea?"

"How about I take the right, and you take the left? Do a quick recon and meet back here in a few."

Jillian gnawed the inside of her cheek as her uneasiness intensified.

Nick's eyes narrowed. "Come on. You aren't backing out on me now? We have been exploring for over three hours, trying to find the place. I want to get the pics and then get some food." Nick began to rock from one foot to another. "Remember my blood sugar?"

Jillian could feel his irritation. The last thing she wanted was a big pissing match between the two of them on the long ride home. "Yeah, sure." She gripped her flashlight with her left hand and grabbed her backpack harness to hide the twitching in her fingers.

"Cool." Nick disappeared down the corridor, his words fading, "See yah in a few."

Jillian exhaled slowly. Nick was a knowledgeable explorer but sure could be an asshole at times. "Easy peasy," she mumbled as the darkness of the hallway swallowed her.

Jillian's boots crunched softly as she walked. A darkened entrance illuminated with her light's beam. She crept into the room and flickered on the lights. Rivets of dirty water drew tortured lines down the walls. A rat squeaked and jumped back into the dark. Jillian jumped and then felt cobwebs wrap her face. "Shit." She rubbed it with the cuff of her shirt. A moment later, she realized the room was empty and headed out.

After a few minutes of traversing the corridor, she came upon another doorway with a faint glow from the interior. She ducked inside.

The dying rays of a bloody sun cast thin shadows across the large room. Black liquid streaked the broken walls, and when Jillian focused her light on it, her eyes detected patterns as if someone had drawn the shapes. Something groaned. Jillian's light flared wildly over the room. On the far wall was a painted handprint. The strong, familiar odor of blood spilled crawled up her nose. She realized what the liquid on the wall was.

A moan of an animal in pain came from behind a small pile of rubble. "Oh my god, oh my god." She stayed rooted to her spot, years in EMS training her not to panic.

"Help." A man's whisper reached her ears.

Her mind clicked through all the people who would be in here. A scrapper? Another explorer? Her rescue nature suppressed her fear for a moment, and she inched toward the pile, then peeked over.

For a moment, her mind froze like a broken computer, unable to process what she was viewing.

"Riley? Oh my god, Riley?" Riley lay on the ground on his back, his bruised eyes gummed with leaking blood. A gashed lip framed a gasping mouth with toothless gums. His fleece jacket was ripped in multiple spots glued to his body. Bare, pant-less legs were contorted into right angles. A collapsed chest rose slightly, the hole between the ribs bubbling frothy, pink foam.

Jillian crouched next to him. "Why are you here? Oh my god? What happened to you?" She touched his cheek as he tried to turn his face toward her voice. "What happened to you? Oh my god, I need help." She threw her flashlight down, grabbed her phone from her backpack, and realized there was still no service. "Oh my god, Riley." Tears welled in her eyes and dropped on his cheek as all her years of training forced her into the horrible reality. His life was draining quickly, and there was nothing she could do to stop it.

She sobbed and hugged him. "Don't leave me. Please don't leave me."

A slight cough startled her. Her gaze shot up as she reached for her light. A shadowy figure hovered in the entrance. "Nick?"

Her flashlight illuminated the familiar metal-gray eyes from her nightmares. Jillian inhaled sharply and scrambled to the depths of the other side of the room. Her hands clawed over the rubble. Her boots slid backward. She spotted a large crack in the wall and plunged for it. Hands grabbed her ankles and dragged her back. Her hands dropped as they broke through the rotting floor.

She screamed and thrashed, breaking free. Two tattooed arms seized her right arm and torqued her around. A fist smashed into her face, and she felt a fragment of bone slice her tongue. Another, then another, then another, until darkness.

****

Light seeped through Jillian's eyelids as she attempted to open them. A piece of cloth filled her mouth, and she coughed, causing a sharp pain to slice her brain. As her eyes focused, she tried to move her hands, then legs, and realized she was bound to a chair, each limb zip tied to its frame, set in a small room with a single heavy door, lit with a flashlight propped on its end, the air heavy with rotting, moldy wood. On a makeshift table near her was a rusty saw, a bent screwdriver, and a hammer caked in debris. *Why? Why?* She thought. But she knew why. She and Riley survived the shooting and gave enough information to identify the shooter, although police never caught him. He was just finishing up business. Her foggy brain didn't understand why the assailant was there. Then she remembered Nick. *Where was he? Bludgeoned in some empty corridor?*

Jillian's eyes rested on the table, and her stomach knotted. She tried yanking her hands free, then her legs. Then she tried rocking the chair back and forth. The door creaked and swung inward.

Nick walked into the room. Jillian wanted to scream. Her eyes pleaded with him to untie her quickly. He paused, then a figure trailed in after him. The shooter smiled slightly when he saw Jillian.

Confusion clouded thoughts. *What?*

"It's nothing personal, love," Nick said softly as he took a large envelope from the shooter. "Just business."

"You will find it is all there. Just as we agreed," the shooter's voice was low and raspy.

Nick nodded. "Pleasure." He turned and strode out the door without looking at Jillian.

Jillian couldn't move. Her limbs were limp, her gaze fixated on a wall. She couldn't process the magnitude of the betrayal.

The shooter slid over to the table and picked up the saw. "I have been on the run these past few months. Because of your helpful information to the police." He stroked the saw and stood behind Jillian. "Do you know how bad it is for my business to have cops snooping around all the time?" He grabbed her hair and yanked her head back. Jillian felt the saw's teeth at her throat. "So many problems." He gripped her hair tighter. "What is the saying? Snitches get, hmm what? Oh yes, dead."

Jillian's animal instinct screamed. She exploded, her body flying against the chair. She felt the tie on her right release as the chair's frame cracked. The shooter roared and pulled her hair harder, and the chair flipped backward.

There was a creak, a groan, then a snap. The decaying floor caved inward, and the shooter and Jillian plummeted twenty feet into the basement. Jillian felt the chair shatter as she and it crushed the shooter against the floor. Stunned, she lay there for a moment, then rolled off the debris, trying to catch her breath.

The shooter lay next to her, his body sprayed with fragmented wood. His eyes fixed upward; a jagged, wet crack traced over his skull. Blood seeped from his ears. Jillian crawled closer, looking for signs of life. She exhaled. Riley, she had to find Riley.

****

Jillian hugged Riley's cold body and shut his eyes. "I will miss you so much." She lay with him for a moment then the room's darkness spurred her to leave. She sniffed and wiped her running nose. "I am sorry I couldn't save you." Crawling to her feet, she hobbled out through the building, stumbling in the dimness until she reached the outside, lit by a cold full moon.

Limping in the moon's haze, Jillian picked her way back to her car. Her head pounded, and she felt numb and empty. Only her fading will to live kept her going. She could make out the outline of her car ahead. As she approached, she saw the glow of a cigarette, Nick's laughter, and the faint glow of his cell phone near his cheek. He leaned against her car. "Yeah, yeah. This is a good place to pick me up. I will send you the coordinates."

Jillian slowed. She fixated on him. A slow rage ignited, burned her heart, and extended its tendrils into her fuzzy brain. Her thoughts sharpened and then focused on just one.

Jillian scanned the ground. She picked up a jagged fragment of concrete. Her breathing slowed as she crept forward toward the vehicle.

With a snarl, she lurched forward from the shadows and struck the back of Nick's head. He screamed, then crumbled onto the ground. As he stared up at her, she kicked his head with all the rage of a crazed animal. His head popped. Her booted foot smashed into his head again. As she hovered over him, her breathing ragged, his pupils grew fixed and dilated.

Dropping the rock, Jillian yanked her car key from her pocket. She slid into the driver's side and, with trembling fingers, dialed 911 on her phone. A familiar, warm voice from her EMS days answered. "911, what is your emergency?" The voice from Monica, the dispatcher, caused sobs to shake Jillian.

"Hey Monica, it's Jillian. I am going to need some help."

PLANTS GROWING IN DARKNESS

Craig A. Brockman

I had nearly forgotten my mother. "She followed a rabbit down a hole" is what my grandma had said.

Everyone called me Kayla. Only my mother called me Kayl, which sounds like that awful leafy vegetable. Online, I still use Kayl as a username on secret accounts.

After her stroke, Grandma tried to talk. She talked too much, but hardly anyone could understand what she said. She would slur and spit, talking mostly to her plants. Sitting at the table and watching her eat, talk, and spew was horrible. *Why try to talk? Just eat. Talk later.* Or she would sit on the porch and yell at the kids next door, her hair all crazy like a handful of dry weeds. That neighbor lady must have had fifteen kids, all under the age of ten. All brats. They would leer and holler back at Grandma, "Blah, blah, blah, ya old witch."

At dinner, Grandma would yammer on and on, gushing food like a small volcano: chunks on her shoulder, globs hitting the table. I would lay down my fork, fold my hands, and listen the best I could. But it was hard. I would usually grab something to eat later in the kitchen when my stomach settled.

When Grandma got around to mentioning my mother and the rabbit down the hole, I knew it was usually a sign that she was ready to trail off and stop trying to talk. She would push her plate away with a quick nod—her signal that she was ready to be wheeled away from the table. She would try to say she missed her daughter—regretted is what she meant. Her thoughts would become sad and internalized whenever my mother was mentioned.

"Living with some junkie in Omaha," was one of the last things Grandma slurred about my mother. But no one had tried to reach my mother anymore. Asking Grandma about my mother was like being two magnets at opposite poles: The closer I came to asking about her, the farther Grandma was repelled.

The year after high school, I stayed with Grandma, cleaning the house and helping her. Grandma had a nursing assistant, but she never came into the rest of the house. She would be there in Grandma's bedroom early in the morning; then, she would return at night to put her to bed. But Grandma still tried to do much of the cooking: wheeling along the kitchen's tiled floor or sometimes crawling to wrench the oven door open and slide in a pan or cooker. It was therapy for her.

I liked her cooking, so long as I didn't have to watch her eat it.

Then there were all her terrible plants. In her incredibly old house, I did what I could to help take care of her forest of plants that sprouted from every nook and cranny. But it was mysterious: Though there were countless plants, none were kept near a window unless the window was covered or curtained. There were windows everywhere in this massive house: leaded glass windows with carefully crafted window seats, a broad landing on the stairs with soaring triple panes of brilliant stained glass, and in the dining room, tall windows hung with ancient lace curtains. Yet, there were no windows graced by plants.

If I tried to move a failing plant closer to the light, Grandma would scold and scoot it back with her foot.

Grandma blathered to her plants incessantly. Insanely. "There's a nice girl. Now you be a good boy and move your limb away from your sister. I see that Sweety needs a drink of water. Aw, now what's with that wilted look?"

It was crazy and mostly hard to understand. But again, I thought it was therapy.

I took care of the plants the best I could. Most of them required only a splash of water every few days. The succulents got drenched every week or two. I learned the whole routine while Grandma would point with a tremulous finger or stutter some indecipherable directive. Eventually, it all got worked out.

Strange things were beginning to happen, though. Yes, I was already skittish living with that old woman in that ancient house, but now I was getting spooked—nervous.

I know it's weird, but it felt as though the plants would grab at me. They would tangle on my sandal or snag my jeans. It was creepy when I watered them. They were delicately brushing against my hands, or somehow a thread of vine would twist onto my ring. I was afraid I was becoming crazy, like Grandma, but they seemed to love my shiny ring. I convinced myself I simply imagined things. I have a way of "blowing things out of proportion," I've been told.

At night, the house would come alive. It was such an old house. "The house is just mumbling as it settles its bones," Grandma explained to me with fractured words after one particularly noisy night. On nights like those, I would never leave my room because it scared me when I heard the clammer. I had been raised in a new apartment with my dad, so I had never lived with noisy walls. But I became more wary on that morning, when I asked her about it.

"Bats," she said, burbling.

"Bats?" I said. "I *hate* bats. They have rabies, Grandma."

She waved her good hand, a side of her mouth turned up in a smile. *End of discussion.* Each night would disturb me more. I hated being trapped in my room, afraid to go to the bathroom or get a glass of water. I would hide under my quilt, scared of the bats' wings—or whatever it was. It sounded like the patter of feet along the hallway and into the other bedrooms or like the slapping of tiny bare feet down the servants' stairs to the kitchen.

****

I had almost grown used to the bustle at night—or I had come to believe it was nothing to be afraid of. Like Grandma said, she had lived in this house for almost half its *lifespan*, so she would know if the house was haunted or dangerous. *It had to be safe. To hell with the bats.*

My own lost mother would have grown up in this home. I realized I could comfort myself at night by pretending the noises were merely the sounds of my mother bustling around the house, caring for me, keeping me from harm. Then I would drift off to sleep.

"Kayl." I awoke at the sound. Not only was it my name, but the name only my mother called me. "Kayl." Hoarse and far away again as I arose from sleep. It was as though my mother was calling to me in a dream. I rubbed my eyes at the brightness of my room filled with sun. Then I heard a crash, far away and downstairs in the direction of the kitchen. Because she could not get upstairs, Grandma slept on the first floor. She was always up before dawn making that big breakfast—way more than she and I could eat.

The crash sounded bad. I ran out of the room in shorts and a T-shirt, down the stairs, sliding into the kitchen in my socks to see Grandma in her wheelchair. Her head swiveled toward me with that almost-creepy half smile. Just as I came through the door, I could have sworn I had seen her brace both hands firmly on the arms of the wheelchair and smoothly plop into the seat. I thought that was impossible for her. She always transferred slowly, with help and great difficulty. If she got out, she had a way of wedging the chair and crawling into the seat.

Two metal bowls were on the floor and another on her lap. Nothing seemed strange except the clamor until I remembered her big metal pans were always stacked on top of the refrigerator where she could not reach them. On at least two occasions, I had to lift them down for her. She did not have a broom handle or a stick nearby she could use to move them. The nursing assistant would not have moved them. She had a separate entrance on Grandma's end of the house and never entered the kitchen. She was long gone before Grandma got around to the breakfast routine. I always did the dishes and cleaned the kitchen.

"Good morning, Kayla," Grandma garbled in a tone unusually pleasant for her.

"Grandma. What happened? Are you okay? How did you get those pans down off the refrigerator? Why didn't you get me to help you?"

"Oh, dear. I just knocked them off the counter. They are always stacked over in the corner, there." She pointed a shaky finger with her good hand.

It was no use arguing with her. She was stubborn and always right.

That was a spirited day. Grandma was feisty, and there was no more pleasantness from her for the rest of the day. She was harsh, scolding me again for not caring for the plants properly.

The weather was riled, blowing a frigid, wet October day against the old bricks and ratty shutters of the house. The windows were hazed with moisture, and every room smelled like a cold, damp basement. Even Grandma's forest of plants seemed unsettled. Every other plant was leaning, or a branch had been bent over. Blossoms had fallen, and one or two plants had toppled under their own weight. I suspected that Grandma had bumbled about, causing the damage as she tried to care for them, not trusting my concern for her precious plants. Throughout that disturbing day, she talked to them, her blubbering speech wavering between scolding and comforting.

To each one, she blabbered something. "That's okay, Sweetie. Why were you such a bad boy? Aren't you the pretty girl? No worries, little one;" and other word-sausages that only her plants would understand.

By evening, it seemed the house had settled. Spooky quiet. I woke up at midnight, expecting the usual creaking and scurrying, but it was silent. I fell into a deep sleep.

"Kayl. Kayl, help me." I was dreaming something about my mom. I no longer remembered her face, so in dreams, I would not see her face. But this was worse. She was like Grandma in the wheelchair, but all tangled in vines and branches. And she had no face. She moaned through doughy flesh as she writhed, tossing her head from side to side. I awoke panting at 2:00 AM. The patter and commotion in the hallway were insane. I was certain I heard a child laugh. Many children laughing. I imagined those damn neighbor kids had broken in to torment Grandma.

I finally got the courage to open the door as two naked children with wild hair, crazy eyes, and dirt-smeared head-to-toe screamed down the hallway. Three more were chasing each other up the stairs and turning for the other bedroom, where two more chased them back out again. Wild, dirty kids were everywhere. As they scurried, their hair flopped and waved in braids, dreads, or spikey shocks. I turned toward the end of the hall, where several were digging in the big pots by the arched windows. No, they were standing in the pots, up to their knees, pushing on the sides to wedge themselves out until they lifted feet covered in dirt like little zombies emerging from the grave.

A lump rose in my throat, and I stifled a scream at the destruction I was seeing. But my thoughts turned toward saving Grandma. She would have a heart attack if she were to hear them and see what they had done. I ran past three kids and yelled at them, "Get out! Get out of here! Where is your mother?"

They talked back, but it was in words that mocked Grandma's gibberish. What monsters these brats were. They were nothing like how I had remembered the neighbor kids. The neighbors were pudgy, mean kids, but these naked children were squat and muscled, their faces feral and twisted.

Like pistons, my feet pounded down the stairs. My jaw dropped in stunned silence. Where plants had been placed in the sitting room, and where they had lined the front hall, now stood revolting creatures. They could have been children dressed for—Halloween, a slasher flick, or a Druid ritual. They weaved and swayed in the pots, their long heads sprouting spikes or leaves, while their torsos—scaly, green, and twisted—smoothed into skin. Their waving limbs were turning to impossibly long, gesticulating fingers. They had narrow hands that pushed on the sides of the clay and porcelain vessels, extracting themselves from the dirt. Under plumes of greenery, strange faces rounded into turnip heads and formed gruesome, childlike features. Their expressions were long and sad like those of old men, until shedding their bark-like skin, they revealed savage lips and fierce eyes shadowed by heavy brows.

Even in nightmares, we act. I sped past the kitchen where one *child* had climbed onto the sink, its bare backside facing me as it gulped out of the faucet. It turned to stare at me, its maw dripping and dirty. These were not sprites or fairies—they were childlike horrors, evil trolls.

They had scarcely noticed I was there until suddenly, all changed. Silence. As if by some indecipherable cue, they became aware. Everywhere I looked, scores of naked, dirty children had stopped in silence, staring at me... yellow eyes, sharp baby teeth, their nostrils caked with snot and dirt.

I stepped backward out of the kitchen, never looking away from them. They followed, stepping carefully... dirty feet on stubby legs, fingers curling at their sides. Grandma's room was past the basement door along the hallway that led from the kitchen. She kept her door closed and locked when she slept. I did not want to go down the hall to her room, knock on her door, and draw attention to her.

Like with many other rooms in the house, I knew she kept the basement locked. But I also knew she kept a key above her bedroom door, *in case of fire*, she said. Somehow, she thought it was secure to hide a key above each of her outside doors, too.

I would try the basement door, hoping there would be a key above that door, too.

The plant children were ghoulishly silhouetted with the kitchen at their backs. My fingers scurried along the basement doorjamb but found no keys. At the corner of the trim, the wood had been pulled away, forming a crevice. With my fingertips, I pawed like a kitten until I extracted a ring of iron keys... three skeleton keys, and one freakishly ornate key like something from a fairy tale. I fumbled, trying each key in the lock. *The first one is never the right one.* The children crept closer, now mumbling in unison. The second key was too big. It nearly stuck in the hole until I shook it and pried at it. It jingled loose. The large, funky key could not be the right one. I tried the third skeleton key. I felt a cold hand on my leg. Each stubby, dirty finger was lined with sharp thorns that dug in, gripping my calf. With my other foot, I kicked it away, and the ugly child reeled back, tore loose from my flesh, and fell into the others with a solid, squishy thump like a shovel hitting a melon.

The third key turned. I rushed into the basement, slamming the door behind me, severing one mushy, thorny hand at the wrist. I covered my mouth but could not stifle the screams. The detached hand writhed and squirmed as it lay on the step, oozing a gooey aloe slime while it clutched about, searching.

My feet pounded down the tattered steps until my socks slipped on the damp floor. I looked desperately for a door to open or a wall to hide behind in the cavernous basement. I scrambled through a maze of stone and brick that was heavy with the damp odor of mold and coal. Scant streetlight filtered through horizontal windows hung with webs and covered in the haze of generations. I slapped at the walls until I groped an ancient, round light switch from a century past. I turned the knob on the switch.

Crack! Pop! I screamed again as lightning flashes blinded me, and I was showered with glass from exploding lightbulbs. Just missing my eye, a shard stuck in my cheek while others prickled my arms and legs. One dim bulb wavered on a cord.

I heard them.

The garbled, high-pitched, spitting speech of the plant kids was pouring through the ductwork. I heard the scrabbling and tinny scratching overhead. Through vent grates poked stubby, thorny fingers prying through, reaching outward like fat spider legs. Their scratchy voices grew louder, higher, blending like horrific mosquitoes thirsting for blood.

Behind me, a vent cover clattered to the brick floor, then another in the darkness on my left.

Running and flailing like a dropped firehose, my head swiveled, and my arms flapped. Every rough wooden door I tried was locked. The gray, sodden boxes and old trunks were not large enough to hide me. I dove toward a hallway leading into darkness, reaching for another rusty light switch. Another dim bulb lit in front of a low, green door that was secured with a large, black padlock that could have been from a pirate movie. I still held the ring of keys. I thrust the large rusty key, turning it with both hands. The shackle would not disengage, and I could not kick it with my wet socks. I grabbed the lock, turned it slightly, pounded it on the stone frame of the door, and turned the key again. It barely clicked. Grunting, I slowly pried the shackle open. I hefted the lock and kept it as a weapon. Wrenching open the heavy door, a sliver of dim light revealed yet another round light switch. The black knob on the switch resisted for a moment, then I was relieved when another hanging bulb lit up. I slammed the door shut as tiny hands thumped and scratched amid a thin, dreadful, chant-like revelry.

I was in a chamber lit by a single, hazy bulb. The stones pressed in, slimed with mold and bulging like toad skin. Ahead, shoulder high, was an arched door. Its surface was knotty and slivered, spattered with black and green moss. Behind me, the hideous plant children scratched at the big door. I still held the padlock. There was a simple gate latch on the inside of the big door. I rammed the shackle of the heavy padlock through it and secured the door behind me.

I was utterly trapped.

I worried, *Are the lights all on the same cord? What if they were to turn off all the lights? Could this small arched door be the only way out?* Then I had to consider... *On the other hand, what might be kept behind these ancient, locked doors?* Terror ahead and terror behind me.

Before I could catch my breath, something slithered in front of me from under the crusty, small door. Damp and slimy, slender as a frog's hand, fingers were grasping under the door. I cringed, stumbling backward.

A voice, raspy, yet wavering and gentle. "The key. The tiny key."

Could there be a horror worse than the plant children?

"The key. The tiny key," it said again.

There was a long pause as the moist hand grappled on the moldy floor.

"Kayl. We need the key," it said.

"W-who is that? What do you want?" I whispered.

"We can leave here if you give me the tiny key. The fifth one on the ring." I heard a ragged inhalation. "She does not know of the tiny key. Check the ring."

I waited, confused.

"Kayla, we know you are in there. Come out, and everything will be fine." Behind me, Grandma spoke with none of her garbled nonsense. Not spitting and slurring, but confident and loud. "Kayla, come out now. I was only trying to help you. Trust me, you do not want to end up in hell somewhere like your miserable mother."

My mother. That's right. No one called me Kayl but my mother.

"Kayla," Grandma said, "I was only trying to help you by giving you someone to care for and something to care about so you did not turn out like your junky mom."

"I—I don't know..." I clamped a hand over my mouth. I must not speak.

"Kayla, we know how to get in there. There is no way out. Open up." Grandma's voice grew stronger and trembled with anger. The door handle and padlock shook, and I could hear the plant children twitter.

The quavering voice came from under the small door again. The thin, frog-like hand, wet and dirty, waved as it spoke. "Kayl, ignore her. She is a witch; she will only hurt you. She wants to ensnare you the way she ensnared me."

"M-mother?" I took a deep breath, not convinced.

"Hand me the tiny key. We can escape," the little voice said more urgently.

Distracted, I fumbled with the key ring as I hesitated, turning it nervously. I felt along the iron ring until I noticed a piece of metal no larger than a pinky fingernail with a short stem protruding: a tiny key.

Behind me, "Kayla, I am your Grandma. My children know how to get around this door. Open it now, and we will let you go home. I would never hurt you."

She had lied about her stroke; she had never told me about anything. So, she had probably lied about my mother, too. I threaded the tiny key off the ring and held it a long while, weighing what Grandma was saying. *Why would my grandmother hurt me?* I have only tried to help her. She had never done anything bad to me during my entire life. *Sure, she is grumpy,* I imagined, *but even if she has been lying and did not have a bad stroke, she let me care for her.* I cannot imagine what may be on the other side of this door, pretending to be my mother.

But those hideous plant children!

"Don't listen to her, Kayl; she's a witch. She will put you in here with me and forget about you." The wet, filthy hand slapped the floor with each word. "Just. Like. She. Did. With. Me!" The voice was frightening as it changed... frantic and scolding. I toyed with the tiny key a moment longer.

"Kayla, I am going to count to three; then the children will find you," Grandma said.

"Kayl, I need the tiny key," the voice cooed.

"One..." Grandma said.

"Don't you remember me, Kayl?" came the thin voice.

What should I do? Whom should I trust? The wet, filthy hand scrabbled on the floor.

"Two! I am losing my patience, Kayla."

"Oh, Kayl, we can run away together. Just you and me." The tiny voice sounded so sincere. "Do you have a snack?" The voice grew desperate again. "Anything to eat? Anything at all? I am starving. I cannot live in the dark on sowbugs and slime anymore. I cannot!"

"Three! Now they will find you."

Only my mother called me Kayl.

POUND PULLER

Mary Beth Magee

"Just three tablets a day will melt away those unwanted pounds and inches," extolled the bikini-clad woman pushing the product on the screen. "Try a one-month supply of Pound Puller today for only $19.95 plus shipping and handling. If this product doesn't pull those extra pounds off, we'll double your money back!"

Her smile was over the top, and her figure looked like something from a graphic novel's cast list. If her voice was any indication, the chick was terminally happy. *Ugh!*

But if the reports I'd seen were accurate, her approach was selling Pound Puller in volume. My job was to investigate the product's claims for my health magazine. The DVD we were viewing contained three different versions of her commercial and an "interview" program where she chatted with satisfied consumers about the "miracle." I had lab analysis reports and a ton of data, but I was still unconvinced. The whole thing screamed, "Scam!"

"Is there anything else you need, Jennifer?" My editor, George Brooks, rose from his chair across the room. "I've seen about all of this that I can stomach for one day."

"I'm fine," I lied. "I'll keep you updated on my progress." I had a list of everyone who had ever ordered the product, provided by an informant in the company who was worried that something "weird" was going on.

My job was to find out what.

Pound Puller was adored by every one of its users, according to their hype. No hunger pangs, shakes, or noticeable side effects. Just nice, steady weight loss from the first day. I decided to start with past customers in our town, people who were no longer on the program.

I ran into a stone wall with the first client. Craig Jordan had moved, and he left no forwarding address. Same with Michelle Thompson and Bill Carter. After twenty-seven more people on the list were described as 'moved,' I headed back to my office and computer. An Internet search turned up nothing on any of them or the next 281. Finally, I got to a name that pulled up a social networking page. Allison Briggs showed up in the next town. Her page showed entries detailing her weight loss journey, but nothing more recent than six months ago.

I headed over to her address from the mailing list, hoping to find her there.

"Allison? No, she moved away a few months ago. Said she was going to Hawaii to make the most of her new bikini figure," said Allison's former neighbor. "I don't blame her."

"So, she had success with the diet plan she was on?"

"Oh, yeah. She loved it. Said it was worth a hundred times the price. She looked like a high fashion model when she left."

"A model?"

"Oh, yeah, slim and tan. I warned her about those tanning machines, though. She was starting to look a little leathery, if you know what I mean."

I followed up on a few more names. Same story at every stop. The person became slim and tanned and moved to a warmer climate to show off the new body. Hawaii must be ready to sink from all the new inhabitants, courtesy of Pound Puller.

I kept searching and finally struck pay dirt. Christy Stelling had just stopped ordering two months ago. Her last 30-day supply could only have been finished a few weeks ago. And miracle of miracles, she answered her phone! We made an appointment, and I hurried over to her home on the outskirts of town.

"So, you're well-satisfied with the results of Pound Puller?" I asked a few minutes into our conversation.

"See for yourself," she responded, spinning in front of me. "I never looked this good before in my life. It's like the pounds just melted off. I'm fit and slim and looking great. The company confirmed my weight loss and sent me my ticket to Hawaii. I'm leaving tomorrow."

I didn't tell her that she looked like garbage. She was too skinny, too tanned, and too desiccated for my idea of beauty. But this was the first I'd heard of the company providing tickets to Hawaii, and I didn't want to offend her.

"Pound Puller is paying your way to Hawaii?"

"Yep. I reached my goal, and now I'm headed to the islands. Isn't it great?" She pulled out a ticket and waved it in front of me. "A private plane to a private resort where I can celebrate my success with other successful Pound Puller users. Then, the company will fly me wherever I want to go. The world is mine!"

She let me photograph the details from her ticket before I congratulated her on her "success" and left.

When I sat down to give George the update, I built up the whole Hawaiian aspect. Then I hit him with a request for passage to Hawaii to follow up.

"Come on, Jenn," he whined. "We aren't springing for you to go on vacation."

"Look, these people fly off to Hawaii and are never heard from again. Something funny is going on. I want to check it out."

"Why don't you do some old-fashioned research from here? Check on the pilot, plane, and flight plans. Then maybe we'll talk about Hawaii."

George is a brick wall when he makes up his mind, so I started at the airport. The plane, a small executive jet, flew regular shuttles to San Francisco. From there, a larger private jet collected passengers brought in from all over the country and continued the journey. But here's the catch: the plane didn't go to Hawaii. It went south, headed to an island about 500 miles off the coast of Chile.

I called in a few favors from a friend in the weather service. He captured some satellite images of the island and shared them with me. A bare rock with a runway and four outbuildings showed up, nothing more, not even foliage. Hardly the paradise that Christy Stelling expected.

When I gave the information to George, he called some people in Washington. With Americans disappearing to a foreign island, an investigatory mission was ordered within a handful of days. I got permission to go along on the mission as a press liaison. A ship bearing commercial markings sailed us to the island. What we found once we docked was grim.

Three of the four outbuildings contained solar-powered cold storage facilities. In those giant refrigerators, we found more than 7,500 vacuum-packed "packages" of dehydrated tissue. Each was labeled with a code that looked more like drunken hieroglyphics than lettering.

The fourth building held a processing plant. A drying oven, a sealing machine, and an industrial-sized pulverizing machine took up most of the space with a large stainless-steel table in the center of the building. A rack of well-honed knives hung from one end of the table.

We only found one living thing on the island. The eight-foot-tall, scaled creature communicated with the team leader through some sort of a speaker device that translated his clicks and hisses into something that passed for English. After hours of questioning, the truth came out.

This thing was the equivalent of a cook for his "people." They had set up this island two years ago as a processing station. The food they processed was the poor deluded fools who used Pound Puller! The "cook" translated some of the labels for us. The symbols turned out to be a name, age, gender, and city of origin. One of the labels he decoded turned out to be for Christy Stelling. Poor girl, she didn't get the exotic world she expected.

"He" explained that the aircraft that brought the dieters to the island was specially constructed with an airtight passenger compartment. Once the plane left San Francisco, the passengers were rendered unconscious with an odorless gas. When the plane landed on the island, the victims were removed to the processing plant for, well, processing, as fresh meat. The finished product was transported to his home planet, where it was sold as a popular delicacy.

Someone once joked to me that human beings were only "food on the hoof" to mosquitoes. I thought that was gross at the time. How much more disgusting to realize that to these giant scaly beings, we are only not-quite-finished jerky, waiting to be sliced, seasoned, and dried for future consumption by some ugly but intelligent lizard on a distant planet?

The creature went crazy and jumped on one of the team members. It started choking him, and the mission leader dispatched it with a barrage of bullets through its scaly head. None of us expressed any sorrow, only disgust at the stinky yellow-green muck which oozed from its body.

The team hurried to collect all the intelligence they could. The labels were recorded for future deciphering and processing. We sailed out a safe distance. The team leader called for an airstrike to destroy the facilities on the island. The ensuing "light show" saddened me. I thought of the many victims incinerated in the strike, never to be returned to their loved ones.

I don't know if anyone will believe my story. I don't even know if George will print it. But if he does, please, read it carefully. Heed my warning. DON'T USE POUND PULLER! Who knows if those lizards will set up another plant somewhere? What's to stop them from doing it all again? They may try to reestablish their program if there is enough demand for the product. Beware of weight loss products that sound too good to be true.

REMEMBER! FOR YOUR OWN SAFETY, DON'T USE POUND PULLER!

Presences at the Table

Michael Simpson

"I'm not saying it's ghosts, but..."

"Come on, sis," Malcolm Cornwall complained from across the rather large dinner table. "You always say that, and you always come up with the same old story."

"I'll admit," his sister said. Her face flushed red, as much out of anger as embarrassment. "I've always believed it was ghosts, but..."

"But?" Malcolm laughed. "There you go again. But what?"

"I've always wanted to keep an open mind about such things," his sister huffed.

"Oh, I would say your mind was very open. It's quite drafty in there too."

"Go ahead, insult me. That's always been your way," she replied. "But your insults don't intimate me. I'm quite used to them. I'm not afraid of you."

No, Malcolm thought, *but you should be. If only he had killed you too, I'd have been spared all this chatter.* Out loud, he said, "I have to admit you're very courageous, continuing to accept my dinner invitations."

"It's what mother and father would have wanted. Tradition is very important; it keeps families together."

"That's true. But there's not much of our family left. Just you and me. I notice Virginia didn't come tonight."

"I could say she had another engagement," his sister declared, taking a rather brutal sip of her claret. "But to be frank, Ginny refuses to come to this house anymore."

"Does she?" Malcolm watched his sister drink with a certain smug attentiveness. "Is it a personal reaction to me? Or does she see ghosts too?"

"She feels the presences, like I do."

"Does she?"

"But she's also very up-front about no longer being able to tolerate you."

"I'm an acquired taste," Malcolm said as he abruptly jumped from his seat and started pacing back and forth in front of the large portraits of their parents on the dining room wall. Malcolm's sister was not shocked by this; her brother had always been restless ("fidgety," she called it) and unable to sit still for any length of time. His eyes also had the habit of darting around the room as if trying to take in all the obscure corners in quick succession.

"Presences? More than one?" he asked. His eyes settled on her as if she were the much sought-after calm in the middle of a storm. Yet there was a reluctance in his face too.

"Yes. More than one," she said, meeting his gaze.

"Did she specify a number?" he asked.

"I know you treat all of this like a joke," his sister responded. "But she was quite disturbed by it. And given our family's history…"

"History? Is that what you call it?"

"I know you suffered the most, more than the rest of us can imagine. The horror of it, to have lived through that night."

"It's been well over ten years now."

"I don't see how you can bear to stay in this house."

"I don't see how I can leave."

"You know my opinions about that, Malcolm. It's unhealthy, extremely unhealthy. And these dinners…"

"You continue to come."

"You should have stopped them after Robert died. You should have sold the house then and left."

"It's the family house. It's all we have."

"It's…" his sister struggled for words. "It's a house of death. Our parents. Those murders that night… out of nowhere… your best friend, your wife, and son. And then Robert. They all haunt this place."

Malcolm gave her a crooked smile. "I guess I've gone beyond just returning to the scene of the crime. I'm actually living in it."

"You're just being morbid," his sister urged. "That's not life." Now it was her turn to suddenly jump up. "And you're not a criminal. You didn't kill anyone."

"But I opened the door. I let him in."

"It was a random act. Anyone would have opened the door." Malcolm's sister seemed on the verge of saying more when she stood still for a moment and looked around as if she were confused about her surroundings.

"Malcolm," she said. Her voice was suddenly small. "Something's wrong. I see them. You need to call the doctor."

And before Malcolm could reach her, she grabbed the table and brought her plate and wine glass with her as she collapsed onto the floor.

****

Several months after his sister's death, Malcolm found himself once again sitting at the table opposite her. Only this time, she was silent. There was also a gray transparency about her, and her eyes had the stillness of the blind. Malcolm had been drinking heavily, and he waved his wine glass in her direction.

"At least you're not chattering anymore," he said with a weary smirk. "There's something to be said for that."

But his sister wasn't the only shape at the table. There were others, each equally silent and with the same blind eyes staring in his direction. The tablecloth was splotchy with spilled wine that had dried, and there were plates with half-eaten food arranged haphazardly around him. But mostly, there were wine bottles.

Malcolm looked at the ghosts and shook his head, a cracked smile on his lips.

"You know, you're all trespassing. I am now the sole owner and proprietor of this house. I could have you shot. I could shoot you myself, and I would be well within my rights. For all the good it would do."

His wife, son, and "best" friend sat at his left. All three were equally still, their unseeing faces turned toward him. To his right were his brother and his parents. The most distinctive thing about all of them were their faces with their empty, listless eyes; their bodies seemed like old, heavy drapes hanging from their heads.

Malcolm looked at the figures of his parents.

"I don't even know why you're here," he said. "You died of natural causes." Then he laughed. "You're not particularly frightening," he added. "Just very tedious and persistent. Let me offer you a toast in honor of your persistence."

He searched among the bottles to find one that still had wine in it and poured some into one of the glasses that also clustered around him. "Never drink from the bottle," he said, looking around sheepishly. "Especially in front of guests. It's impolite. But, a toast!"

He stood up somewhat unsteadily.

"I will recite from a poem in honor of the remnants of my most honorable family and..." (Here he attempted to bring into focus the image of man sitting next to his son.) "...and friend, my only and most foolish friend. Now for the poem...

> O Presences
> That passion, piety or affection knows,
> And that all heavenly glory symbolizes—
> O self-born mockers of man's enterprise;

Malcolm stopped abruptly. There was another figure in the room.

Leaning forward and placing his glass on the table, he gestured to the figure. "Come in, please. Let me see you. I don't recognize you, but you're welcome to the party."

The figure stepped forward and stood behind the chair Malcolm's sister occupied.

"Now I know you," Malcolm said. "You're not a ghost."

"Not yet, anyway," the man said. He resembled nothing so much as a thicker, shorter version of Malcolm himself. Only his eyes had a dull, heavy quality. The irises were the color of ball bearings, and the pupils were a black pinpoint that expanded and contracted with the steady rhythm of the man's breath.

"You can talk?" Malcolm said.

"Yes, when I need to."

Malcolm studied the man more closely and asked, "How did you get in?"

"The door was open," the man said. "I would have knocked, but it was already partially open. May I have a seat?"

Malcolm shuddered deeply and laughed. "No, unfortunately, they're all occupied."

The man looked at the dirty table and the empty seats.

"I see," he said. "That's fine. I wasn't planning to stay long."

"Why are you here?" Malcolm asked. He suddenly felt weak and ready to break down in sobs at any moment.

"I heard about your sister's death. I was sorry to hear about it."

Malcolm just looked at the man, unable to speak.

"Do you want to know why I was sorry?" the man asked.

Malcolm tried to get his lips to move, to utter some kind of sound, but his lips were trembling so much they were useless.

"I was sorry because there have been too many deaths in this house. And the police are beginning to wonder. They're beginning to think it's not the house but somebody in it. And they're looking into the past. That's not a good thing. They're looking for me. And you're the only connection…"

Malcolm stood, trembling and paralyzed. He watched helplessly as the pale figures around the table began to move as if drawn by the man who was slowly walking around the table.

"Leaving the door open. That was really careless, like that time, ten years ago, when you let a stranger into your house. Sure, you struggled with him and were wounded. But still. Four people against one. Even if one of them was still practically a child. But for it to have happened so quickly. The police are wondering."

"Why are you here?" Malcolm was finally able to get the words out.

"I guess I just don't trust you anymore."

Suddenly, Malcolm no longer saw the man but only the ghosts pulling at him and rushing into his body like a deadly cloak of ice.

Psychic Reading

Colleen Alles

She has me by the elbow. Even through the thick wool of my winter coat, her grip is ridiculously strong for someone so skinny.

But that's Miriam; Popeye in Olive Oyl's body.

She's pulling me recklessly now behind a rack of women's clothing. As she does, formal gowns in stiff, beaded material drag at my arm as though trying to get my attention.

Then, Miriam forces me up a small set of stairs.

This is where the saleswoman told us to go.

This is the Women's Lounge. The Women's Lounge is the anteroom to the women's restroom.

And it's huge. There's a long pink tufted couch and a matching loveseat. A gigantic mirror adorns one wall, and under it, a ledge that stretches for days.

And a man. A man is seated behind a card table in the corner of this lounge. On the table, half a dozen candles burn.

"This is *bananas*," Miriam says.

The man smiles. He's got shaggy brown hair and light blue eyes. He's wearing a brown corduroy shirt and dark jeans. He looks young.

"Welcome. Please have a seat." His voice is friendly. I don't know if I was expecting him to have a crystal ball and a turban, but he's just a normal-looking guy.

Miriam and I sit down in the two folding chairs. We take turns shaking his hand—first Miriam, then me. As I sit, smoothing my coat under my rear, I think, isn't this how all adventures with Miriam begin?

The night starts out normal enough... dinner at an Italian restaurant downtown, me stuffing my tired body with gnocchi. We order a bottle of red wine. Then another.

Then Miriam pitches an idea. She's spotted a poster in the restaurant's window advertising free psychic readings in the upscale women's boutique down the street.

"Powder?"

She nods. "Yeah. The old Jenkin's."

Jenkin's was a popular department store chain in the 1950s. The building, though, must have gone up in the 1800s. Stepping into this Women's Lounge was like stepping out of a time machine.

This room—it's from a time when women needed a private space in a public place. To take off their elaborate dresses to use the toilet. To rest on fainting couches. To take a break. This room is like a parlor for women out in public—a safe place to go when away from the safety of home. It's a wonder it's never been remodeled.

Evidently, to encourage holiday shopping, downtown retailers are having special store events... karaoke, photo booths, prize giveaways, gin tastings, and this one, a free psychic reading.

This is how I find myself buzzed in the middle of December in a Women's Lounge, smiling across from a man who has introduced himself as Dirk.

"Hi Dirk." Miriam's voice has a flirty edge. It'd come out for our waiter as well. She's taken off her scarf and laid it on the table.

"I'm Miriam, and this is Jamie. She just had a baby. This is our first night out."

"Wow," Dirk says, looking at me brightly. "Congratulations!"

"You can't tell, can you?"

She's complimenting my post-baby body, which she also did at the restaurant. But it feels silly since I'm still wearing my coat. Underneath, I don't look great. It will take time for the baby weight to melt off, I know. Next to my best friend and her sharp angles, though, I'm an amorphous blob of pale blubber.

"I've got dark circles under my eyes," I joke, setting my hobo bag on the floor.

"How old is your baby?"

I'm about to answer, two months, when Miriam cuts me off. "Aren't you supposed to tell us? You're the psychic!"

Dirk smiles. I wonder if he can tell how much wine we've had. "I'm not a mind reader, unfortunately."

I notice for the first time a mason jar near Dirk's left elbow. It contains a handful of bills; ones and fives. Not more than thirty bucks. Tips.

"Right. You won't tell us something we already know, huh?"

He smiles. "Have you ever had a reading before?"

"I've had my palm read; and I've had an astrological reading. Is that what this is like?"

Dirk shakes his head. I wonder if there are any women in the restroom—if, at any moment, a woman will come out into the Women's Lounge, wiping her hands, startled.

"I don't use astrological info, although I think it has merit. I just read people and go by feelings, you know—intuition, vibes, energy, all that kind of thing."

"So," Miriam says, "do you want to see my *aura*?" She's said *aura* like it's a dirty word.

I look at Dirk. He's chuckling. "Maybe. Who's going first?"

The room is silent for a moment, and I study Dirk's chin. It's a good one, I think. He doesn't have any facial hair, but a goatee would look good.

That's when I look over at Miriam and realize she's pointing at me.

"Okay, Jaimie. Ready?"

Although I don't hate new experiences, like having a psychic reading by a kid who looks barely old enough to order a beer, I feel for the second time since we got to Powder pressure beginning to well up in my breasts.

I didn't bring my normal pump. Rather, I'd stuffed the small manual one into my bag. I had not planned to use it, but I also hadn't realized we'd be out this late. I hadn't been out drinking with Miriam for a year. I was rusty. I should have known the night would take off on us.

"Actually, Miriam, can you go?"

I realize we may only have time for one reading before I will need to pump. Pumping is still a new trick, and I've only got one container to store the milk—*I should have brought two.* But I also remember that Miriam drove, and it would be rude to push her into driving before she was ready.

"Why?" Miriam's frowning.

"I want you to," I say, trying to give her a look that I hope she understands to mean, *please.*

Miriam says, "I'm ready for my close-up," as she puts both palms up for Dirk.

Dirk gives a smirk, then closes his eyes. He takes Miriam's hands into his, holding them and rubbing his fingers over her skin.

She asks how long he's been doing this, but he just smiles. It's her cue to be quiet. I'm aware of how creepy this would be if Miriam weren't here—alone in the anteroom to a bathroom in a building that's so old, there's a zero percent chance it isn't haunted.

"So," Dirk says. His eyes are still closed. "One way I like to get started is by you telling me what questions you have."

Miriam looks at me and winks. "The usual, I suppose. *Love.* Does everyone say, *love?*"

Dirk says nothing but smiles. He opens his eyes for a moment before closing them again. I bet he thinks Miriam is pretty. Everyone thinks Miriam is pretty. She is.

"Can you be more specific?"

Miriam gives Dirk a dramatic sigh. "I have this boyfriend. It's *very* off and on. *Very.*"

She's talking about Rich. Rich recently broke up with Lauren and immediately reached out to Miriam, which sent Miriam into a texting tizzy with me. I tried my best to keep up with our exchanges, though it was difficult between trying to breastfeed, trying to sleep, trying to shower, trying to eat, and above all, trying not to kill Mike, my sweet husband, who was trying his best but seemed helpless when it came to the laundry he couldn't finish, the meals he couldn't cook, the dishes he never put away.

Many of Miriam's texts had fallen through the cracks. Sometimes, though, I would answer at two in the morning as Ethan was happily sucking away, and we'd somehow found a position in the glider that seemed comfortable for both of us.

"Do what you want," I texted Miriam at one point; and then added, quickly, "You know I mean that in the most supportive way."

But still. We aren't in our twenties anymore. Rich has been playing with Miriam for years. We're supposed to be done with boys who don't know what they want. It felt strange to be texting about Rich Hooper as I was on maternity leave with my first baby.

"I'm wondering if Rich should get another chance," Miriam says, raising her eyebrows. "He doesn't *deserve* one, but since the universe has a grand sense of humor about the whole thing, I'd love your take."

Dirk is quiet. Miriam is still watching him. I'm not sure what he's divining from her hands, but he seems to be thinking.

My breasts are starting to speak up. My once-stoic body was now loud and bold, never afraid to speak up when it wanted food, water, sleep, or to sit down. The last month of my pregnancy, my body screamed for glazed donuts and to do nothing but lay in bed watching *The Sopranos*.

Now, my body yells, *you need to feed your baby.*

I wish Miriam could read my mind. We are usually so in tune. Couldn't she divine from just a look that I wasn't game for this for much longer?

****

"Interesting," Miriam says a minute later. With his eyes open, finally, Dirk released her hands. He told her that while the passion with Rich is real, there aren't many indications from the universe that a long-term relationship will work.

But Miriam keeps poking holes in what he's saying, making Dirk second guess himself.

I know I'd find this more amusing if my breasts didn't feel like softballs.

"Okay," Miriam says. She's fished a five-dollar bill from her wallet and sticks it into the tip jar, to which he effusively thanks her.

"Your turn."

"Oh," I start, looking between Dirk and Miriam. "You know, that's okay. I think—we should probably go."

Dirk looks hurt. I think he thinks I want to leave because he's done a bad job reading Miriam. He was counting on my five bucks, maybe.

"No, you *have* to."

"I'm sure Dirk has folks waiting," I add, although there wasn't exactly a line outside the Women's Lounge when we'd arrived. I don't add that my breasts hurt and that because my buzz is wearing off, I feel the discomfort more than I did when we first sat down.

"Come on, J." I know invoking my nickname is a sign she's serious. My breasts press against my bra. I fight the sudden urge to cry. Again.

Ethan spit up on the only "going out" top that matched my maternity pants, so just before Miriam pulled into my driveway, I'd tearfully grabbed a thin gray sweatshirt that had been Mike's at one point. I'd cried, kissing Ethan goodbye, too, handing him to Mike, who in turn had kissed me on the forehead and urged me to have fun.

"Okay. I just... I should get home soon," I say apologetically. Dirk smiles, but even in the candlelight, the hurt hasn't worn off his face. I feel terrible. "To my baby."

"I can be quick. Two minutes. Just ask me what's on your mind."

"Honestly. I can't think of anything."

"Ten words or less. Big life changes make for great questions."

He's hinting at becoming a mom, I think. I say okay, and Dirk brightens a bit.

"Will I be a good mom?"

Dirk smiles and gestures for me to give him my hands. I do. His fingers are long and slender. His hands are smaller than Mike's. I look at Miriam, and she's texting. Probably Rich. She's probably telling him that Dirk doomed their relationship. Despite my milk ducts, I smile.

The next few seconds are a bit of a blur. Dirk's eyes close, his face changes, looking more and more concerned. I'm telling myself not to worry if any milk leaks onto Mike's sweatshirt. No one can see it under my pea coat.

Finally, Dirk opens his eyes. The look on his face is concerning. I hold my breath. I look at Miriam, but she's still squinting at her phone.

"I'm sorry," Dirk mutters. "Jesus."

"What?"

"I don't know how to say this," he says, frowning. "I'm getting..."

"What?" Miriam presses. Her phone is still in her hand.

The smile is gone from Dirk's face. His voice is faulty when he speaks again. "I'm trying to understand what the universe is communicating through your energy, and I'm afraid it's not good. I see death in your future. A close family member. An accident. I'm seeing... it's your son. Yes. I see Ethan is dead. Jesus. I'm so fuckin' sorry."

I rip my hands from Dirk and push the cheap folding chair back from the card table. In an awkward motion, I grab my bag from the floor and rush into the restroom.

"Sorry—I need to go. Sorry." My voice breaks as I apologize.

I curse myself for caring about Dirk's feelings—Dirk, who is clearly horrible at this. He's doing it for free, after all.

I need to get away from him—this young man who has just told me my son is going to die. I know I'm just emotional—I'm tired, and I'm overwhelmed. I have to pee. I miss Ethan, his round cheeks, and my breasts hurt, and I can't take it anymore.

Inside the restroom, I'm confronted with a large space, six toilets in individual stalls. I grab one and lock the door, pulling down my maternity pants. This pair of underwear has been effectively ruined; I've stretched out the waistband and spotted blood countless times on the white cotton crotch. I don't care.

Peeing is a relief, and as soon as I am done, I step out of the stall to wash my hands. Then I'm back again, sitting on the toilet seat this time, although I think the plush couch in the Women's Lounge would be much more comfortable for this.

Women from the Victorian era had it right, I think. Privacy is everything.

I pull off my coat, Mike's sweatshirt, and then I yank down the cups of my bra. Milk is leaking from both nipples. I start crying again. I'm digging in my bag for my pump while milk leaks onto my flabby stomach when I hear the door to the bathroom close. I feel Miriam before she speaks.

"You okay, J?"

"I'm fine," I sniff. "I'm just uncomfortable. I need to pump."

"Do you want help?"

I chuckle. *Of course Miriam is offering to help. She would do that for me.*

I secure the manual pump on my left breast and begin pumping away like a madwoman. The relief is immediate. I close my eyes, pumping, and pumping. After thirty seconds, I switch and relieve the pressure in my right breast. I think about Mike giving Ethan a bottle, and I fight the urge to cry.

"I'll say this quietly so he can't hear," Miriam says. She's whisper-yelling at me as I pump milk into the plastic bottle. "But that kid doesn't know what the hell he's doing."

"You tipped him."

"He's *trying*. It's not easy. I have a cousin who does Tarot—Madeline. You remember her. She's good."

I listen to Miriam talk about Madeline until my breast feels soft again. Normal. I know she's just talking to fill the space and calm me down, and I love her for it.

The small plastic bottle is full. I feel sad. This should be for Ethan. I dump the milk into the toilet because it's full of wine and tears, and I have no idea when I'll be able to refrigerate it. I stick the pump back in my purse, not wanting to wash it in front of Miriam, even though over dinner, I told her I would show it to her.

I put Mike's sweatshirt back on, then my coat, stepping out of the stall. I find Miriam applying lipstick at the mirror. She doesn't look at me as I splash cold water on my face and take a long drink from the faucet.

"It's *shit*, okay?" Miriam says. She's still in a whisper as she throws her lipstick into her purse. "I'm sorry he said that. None of it's true. Ethan is gonna be fine. He *is* fine. You're a *great* mom. Let's get out of here. Let's get dessert."

I follow her into the Women's Lounge, where she says a loud but polite goodbye to Dirk. I try to echo it, but I feel like I can't speak, so I just hold up a hand dumbly. I see Dirk wave, but the look on his face is as grim as it was when he'd given my reading.

Walking out of the Women's Lounge, there's no line to see Dirk. Powder seems to be thinning out. It must be closing soon.

I can't shake the feeling that neither of us will forget the time we got a free psychic reading inside a Women's Lounge, and I cut the psychic off before he could finish because he told me my baby was going to die.

I can't shake the feeling that Dirk has cursed me somehow—or that this whole adventure was a mistake. I should have stayed home with Ethan, with Mike. I should have told Miriam I wanted to go home after we split the check at dinner. I shouldn't have let her drag me here.

I can't believe, as I recount the whole incident to Mike when I get home, how spine-tingly scared I get when I realize that at no point that evening had Miriam nor I told Dirk that my baby was a boy, or that I had named him Ethan, after my father's father.

SAMSON

Ariana Beemer

Everything felt gritty and cold. As the sun slipped into dawn, he stirred with a painful groan. Aches came into focus with the burgeoning sunlight, brown eyes wincing.

His head pounded. Why, he couldn't be sure. Tentatively he opened his eyes, fighting the immediate throb deep in his brain and a sharp pain in his hairline. Bringing his hand up, he drew it back to find it smeared crimson. Blood, still wet but not fresh.

The hair on his neck stands up, and adrenaline pushes him past pain to full alertness. Instinctually, he surveys his surroundings; the beach is barren but for himself and the few large rocks and dead trees making their graveyards here and there along the shoreline. At his feet is a knapsack, something he vaguely recalled being thrown his way by a barking man, head reflecting in clinical overhead lights.

Tossing it over his shoulder, he slips quickly and quietly off the open space of the beach and beyond the tree line. The air here is humid and still, heavy with the rotting decay of wayward fallen leaves and moss. Searching stealthily, he finds a group of trees with a thick, overgrown bush sitting at their roots. With expert precision, he cocoons himself and goes through the knapsack. A flare gun; unusual but useful. A gun would be better. He sighs inwardly, finding only a knife inside. A food ration with the smallest bottle of Tabasco sauce known to mankind. Crumpled up at the bottom is a piece of paper with two words written in shaky but vaguely familiar handwriting. *Kill Samson.* Shaking his head, he tosses the contents back into the knapsack and leans against the trunk of the tree.

Trying to calm his racing heart, all he can think is he knows what to do but not how to do it. *Kill Samson.* Easy. Some directive from a higher-up, naturally. Head pounding, he tried to remember who, but all he could recall was the vivid moment he'd been accepted into the Marines. It felt like a lifetime ago, but for all he knew, it was three weeks in the past.

His head hurt. Brain clouded, he tried to focus on his surroundings. Preparedness and acute awareness were two of the keys to survival. Even if he had no clue what he was supposed to be surviving, exactly.

The air felt thick with humidity, and the temperature was rising quickly. Beads of sweat ran down his face, dripping from his chin. *Think, think. Samson. Flare gun.* He only had one day's rations, which meant he was either expected to accomplish the mission in that time, or he had that much time left. Desperately, he tried to think of something, anything that he could trust himself to know, but nothing surfaced.

Closing his eyes, he tries desperately to hone in on his hearing, overlooking the sound of his own heartbeat. The waves crashed in the distance; leaves fluttered in the wind; a chirp from a bird.

Snap.

Brown eyes flew open. Then, again—

Snap.

Silently, he slipped to half-standing, back firmly against the trunk of the tree and careful to stay well below eye level. A hand slithered back into his knapsack, retrieving the knife. The sound had come from his right, less than fifty yards. *Close enough to kill a deer with a bow and arrow,* he thought, though how he knew that was a mystery.

Leaves rustled to his right, signaling someone—or something—getting closer. Whatever it was, it was careless, making far too much noise to go entirely unnoticed. His gain.

Pulse racing, his eyes search for movement. The trees have given enough barrier to prevent wind from stirring; the circle of sweat around his neckline is a protest of its absence, but his ears are grateful for the stillness. Surveying carefully, he searches for any sign of wayward movement. Ever so slightly, a branch sways, its leaves rustling like the beginnings of a crackling fire.

The hair on his neck stands up, breath catching in his throat. Heart beating fast, brown eyes hone in, alert for further movement. His fingers grip the knife tighter, slipping a singular finger up to ensure it is unsheathed. No point in stabbing with a covered knife. Finger meets metal as his eyes continue to watch.

Snap.

Sweat trails down his cheeks, dripping from his chin. Still as a statue, he pauses, waiting. The space between the two trees closest offers little space, but he knows how to move quickly. Silently, he drops the knapsack onto the moss at his feet, eyes laser-focused for movement. A leaf flutters slightly.

Snap.

The next moments happened in mere minutes but felt like a lifetime.

A branch breaks, falling with a loud thud, followed by a figure. In a fluid motion, he straightens, slipping between trees and back onto more open ground as the someone comes into dim sunlight.

Another man, of similar height and build. His skin is smeared with dirt, sweat, and likely dried blood. There are several large tears in his pants and shirt, exposing skin littered with scratches and gashes.

"Fuck you, Clark!" The voice is shrill, reaching a decibel and pitch unmatched by the body it spills from.

Face to face, crouching knees, brown eyes lock against blue ones. Rage coats the humid air, pulsating between them. This stranger is familiar, yet not. Shuffling feet to distract, he searches for any name in his memory that could match this familiar stranger but finds none.

"Samson?"

A queer moment of realization at the sound of his own voice. Tenor, with a tinge of bass. Some vague memory tugs at his brain, a woman with long hair and a bright smile, singing, "I love you concert choir, oh yes I do..."

"Samson? Samson?!" The shriek that greets him makes him wince; the rage is coated with anguish, and he knows this isn't Samson, but whoever they are, this stranger is now more dangerous.

"You killed Samson, Clark. Don't you remember? Don't you remember slicing his throat? Or did that pole to the head knock your memory out too?"

The last words are slick with taunting intention, unwittingly. But he doesn't. He doesn't remember.

"I had orders!" The words come out in military precision, the answer lacking only the precursory sir's and yes's he still somehow knew.

"From. Who." Spit hangs on his enemy's lips, the words coming in short, clipped fragments. The stranger's arm twitches, gripping the knife in his own hand. They are somehow mirror images holding different injuries, and it occurs to him that they may be comrades, or were once. Before Samson, whoever the hell he was.

"Why does it matter? Orders are orders. You know that."

"It matters. You killed our captain."

For a moment, time stops. His memory may be dismantled, but some instincts are drilled in with permanency, and this sounds like treason.

"Who's orders?" Words escape between gritted teeth. He feels his palms dampen with sweat, and he grips tighter.

"Fuck me if I know. I can't remember shit." His own words surprise him. It's the first time he's realized this aloud. "I got a note and a head wound; that's all I can offer."

His fingers grip the knife, adrenaline pumping through his veins. Heart racing, he breathes steadily, unwilling to so much as flinch without need. Knowing now that the wound at his hairline came from a pole also means a concussion. Reserving his energy is necessary; this he knows. The stranger flinches, anger rolling off him in waves. He notices fingers shaking, a sign of weakness to come.

In a flash, the stranger lunges with a scream echoing grief. He ducks easily, slipping around the stranger and behind, giving a precisely placed kick to the back of his knee. The stranger drops with a groan, flailing arms back, trying to make contact, unsuccessfully.

Deftly, he slips around again, placing a swift kick to the chest and then dropping onto the stranger, grabbing his arms as forcefully as possible. The stranger struggles, whipping his head with a scream, but this man doesn't faze him. Quickly, he gives a well-placed punch to the stranger's face, feeling cartilage crunch under knuckles and blood start to flow. His fist is slippery now, knife somewhere on the mossy ground. But his enemy has one.

Instinctively, he reaches for the man's right wrist, watching blood flow and blue eyes widen with wonder as he snatches it and bends back. The snap of bone sends screeches through the still air, and the knife is his.

Metal slips against skin, a slight surface scratch with a slow drag as brown and blue eyes meet.

"Tell me the truth." His words are heavy, cold. Crimson stains drab olive green, streaming from nose to neckline freely. He pushes a knee down, eliciting a wheeze and groan. "Who is Samson?"

The stranger smiles slowly, twin rows of stark white teeth against skin layered with sweat, blood, and grime. A short cackle bursts forth, so high-pitched it sends shivers deep down his spine.

"Samson went mad. Waited until lights out, then killed the crew." Another cackle, then silence as the smile slips away and the stranger's face turns stony. "It's a wonder what you can do with cleaning chemicals. But you... you and your buddy Dave had to become a problem. I will admit, he got me pretty good, but I think I got him better."

Somewhere in the recesses of his memory, a moment surfaces before fading; the flash of an oar in moonlight, his sleepy eyes watching a figure slump and then splash into the water.

"Samson is me."

The words trigger a reaction, blade slicing skin before another thought could have time to surface. Memories he couldn't trust, but madness? Men have known madness since the beginning of time, and where memory may falter, madness is true.

The words continue from Samson's lips as crimson rivers flow, an echo of protest or truth, but still mad all the same. Chest grows heavy, then still. No more cackles and echoes dissipate; the air grows heavy with humid silence once more.

In a daze, he leans back. Uncertainty settles for a moment, then flitters away. Somewhere, deep in his memory, he knows he's done the right thing. Feet heavy, he finds the abandoned knapsack and shoulders it, winding his way back to the beach.

He's thankful for the heavy silence. Slipping between trees and inhaling the heavy scent of decay and moss, he makes his way to the beach, following the faint scent of the ocean.

The sunlight burns his eyes, but despite the glare, he's thankful. Thankful to see it, even if this beach is a mystery from the depths of his memory. With a heavy sigh, he sinks into the sand, opening his knapsack and pulling out the flare gun. Four shots. Best try it and make sure it at least worked.

With a prayer, he aims upward and pulls. A wave of relief washes over him at the trail of smoke and burst of sparks. Pulling out the rations, he turns the package over to see what he got in the luck of the draw.

"Chicken and dumplings," he says with a smile. Too hungry to care, he rips it open and dumps the entire bottle of Tabasco inside, savoring the taste. They were already the best of the MRE's, even cold. It reminded him of home, wherever that memory was. With a sigh of relief, he sits on the barren beach, sweat rolling down, the taste of chicken and dumplings overtaking his senses. Eyes closed, he searches for the wind.

Instead, a shout. Distant, but there. Off in the distant waves, two figures in a boat. Familiarity and relief wash over him again.

"Clark! Clark!" A pause. Then again, closer. "I found him!"

Safety and warmth fill him. These are friends turned family, not friends turned foe; his memory knows this much to be true. Grabbing his knapsack, he stands, walking slowly towards welcoming waves.

SANCTUARY

Diana Kathryn Plopa

"Close your eyes to ponder, imagine, rest, meditate. In the dark you can think pleasant thoughts, pray on future plans, and remember happier days with pure devotion to the divine." His voice was low and even, nearly a whisper. She almost believed him.

She opened her eyes and blinked a few times. "I'm sorry," she said shaking her head. "I don't think this is going to work." The resentment in her voice was forced, but she didn't know how else to make him stop. "This was a mistake." She placed the pillow she was clutching on the couch next to her and stood. She hesitated for a moment staring at her shoes, and that, too, was a mistake.

"Please, Hannah," he said, resting a firm arm on her shoulder and easing her back to the couch. "Just a few more moments. I'm sure we can help you rearrange your thoughts long enough for the..."

"No," she interrupted, thrusting her body back to standing. She wasn't tall, nearly six inches shorter than him, and probably only half his weight. If he really wanted to, he could persuade her to stay. She refused to meet his gaze.

"Come now," he intoned, reeking of condescension. "You know your parents will be disappointed if I report to them that you were unwilling to..."

"No," she repeated. This time her eyes met his. Hannah could easily imagine becoming lost in those amber pools of infinite gentleness and... "No!" she repeated, nearly a full measure louder, and she hoped, stronger. This time, she took a step to the left... and then two more, heading for the door.

"If you would just..." he started.

"Look," she said, her hand firmly grasping the doorknob. "I appreciate what you're trying to do, but I can't do this today." Her head hung; eyes focused on the carpet where it met with the door. "I can't right now. It just doesn't feel right." *This is something I'm going to need to figure out on my own, parental disappointment be damned.* She pulled open the door and quickly walked through it, leaving him stunned in her wake. He was new to this post, and he'd never been rejected before. It took him a minute to process, and in that time, she made her escape.

Darting down the corridor and out into the day's beleaguered sunshine, she headed for home. She took more transfers on the bus route than usual. *Must reduce the chances of being followed.* Her paranoia was misplaced, of course. She knew, they knew, where she was going. *Where else would I go?*

Fifteen minutes after she walked in the door, her phone rang. They were nothing, if not predictable.

"Hannah, darling, we heard what happened with Brother Nathaniel today. Are you alright?" Her mother's voice sounded tinny, an affect of talking through the speaker. Her father was listening.

"Yes," she lied. "I'm fine. I just need a little bit of time to get my thoughts together before another session, that's all. It's not a big deal," she said. She forced a smile, hoping they would hear the truth of her facial muscles and miss the intention of her deflection. "Work has been a bit overwhelming this week, and I'm tired. I haven't been sleeping well."

"Well, you know," interjected her father, "that's exactly what these sessions are designed to support. Clearing those thoughts and frustrations through divinity is the best way to stay healthy." She knew he believed the rhetoric; they both did. But she didn't. Not anymore.

"I get it, Dad. But it was just more gas than I had in the tank today. I'll get back to it, I promise," she lied again.

There was a brief silence on the line; then her mother said, "Alright, dear. You sleep tonight, and we'll see you tomorrow, at the ceremony." Her mother's voice sounded hopeful. Hannah knew she was looking to her father, checking her verbiage, making sure she said the right thing, wondering if he had anything to add. It was the family's custom to defer to his interpretation of life. Her mother relied on that as much as she relied on breathing. But Hannah couldn't anymore. She was drowning in his sea of optimism with no real reward for her efforts. Nothing ever came of it, except the redundancy of nothing.

"Yes," her father finally said, an uneasy hesitation in his voice. "Things will look better to you tomorrow."

"I'm sure it will." Hannah expelled her own tormented sigh.

"I promise the ceremony will bring the solace you're seeking," reminded her father.

"We'll talk after breakfast," Hanna lied a third time.

"Good," said her mother. "Sleep well, dear."

Her father remained silent.

"Thank you, Mom. Goodnight." Hannah waited for the click on their end, and then disconnected the call.

****

After a fitful night's sleep, which was normal these days, Hannah indulged in a steaming hot shower and a decadent breakfast of waffles, bacon, orange juice, and hot chocolate. She knew these would be the last comforts she would see for quite some time, regardless of the vitality of her plan, so she took full advantage.

She paced the carpet's well-worn path from bedroom, to bathroom, to living room, and back to the bedroom as she gathered essentials to take with her. She'd obsessively practiced this ritual for nearly a year, preparing for the inevitable. The day had finally come. She hoped she was ready.

After cramming what was left of her life into her duffle and slinging the strap over her shoulder, she stopped at the window for a moment to watch the play of pink and yellow across a thin layer of clouds above the ocean. Within seconds, the show was over, and the sun rose on the day she'd been dreading for months. She would be twenty-five in just six short hours. Soon after that, she would be forced to lose her identity and absorb the role her parents expected. It was their legacy, and they were insinuating it onto her, just as their parents had done with them. It was supposed to be a gift, a treasure, but it was one of the greatest burdens she would ever carry. She didn't want it, didn't need it, and somehow, had to get rid of it. It wouldn't be easy. It was necessary... but only if she wanted to remain sane.

Sanity in her teenage years struck her as being overrated, after all, when you're young and have no responsibilities, sanity isn't a requirement. You can do, say, and follow almost anything or anyone—and get away with it—with no repercussions. She wished she'd prepared for the eventual shift.

Hannah dropped her keys in the dish by the apartment's front door. She pulled the cash out of her wallet and crammed it into the front pocket of her jeans. Then she dropped the wallet in the dish as well. She had no use of her identification and credit cards. *I won't be coming back here.* She picked up the picture from the hall table. A tumble of golden retriever puppies smiled back at her. Quickly, she turned the frame over and pulled out the backing. She removed the hidden photo and flipped it over. The soft grey eyes of her most devoted friend in the world looked back at her. She ran her fingers over his face for a moment, as if she were stroking his gentle beard. Then, blinking a tear away, she flipped it over and read the address and phone number written on the back. She put the frame with the generic puppy photo back on the table and tucked the photo of him into her coat pocket. She looked back for a moment, inhaled her courage, and walked out the door.

Vibrating with the fear of being caught, she walked four blocks to the drugstore. She bought a few protein bars, some water, and a pay-as-you-go phone. She couldn't bring her cell or her computer. *The probability that they installed tracking software? 100%.* Oppression works best when courted with control, and her family had a longstanding affair with both.

She took a bus to the train station and bought her ticket from the unmanned kiosk. Her face had been digitally captured with a time-stamp, she knew, but it would take a few hours for them to get the permissions necessary to find her. She hoped it would be enough of a head start.

After a train, two bus transfers, and a tenuous thirty-mile ride with a trucker she didn't completely trust, Hannah stood bone-weary at the foot of a two-mile long dirt road. Tenacity purred that safety was just a short hike away. She pulled out the photo and looked again at her salvation. She knew if she asked, he wouldn't turn her away. She tucked the photo back into her pocket and started walking.

The sun kissed the horizon through the canopy of trees in a precision of dark red and purple as she reached the doorway. She dropped her duffle to the slate porch floor and inhaled slowly, capturing whatever courage remained. With the focus of a cormorant fishing for its last meal, she pushed her finger against the smooth surface of the buzzer... one long, two short, one long. She held her breath as silence wrapped around her in a moment of pregnant urgency.

The slide of a deadbolt forced the air from her lungs as the door opened to reveal a man nearly twice her size, his eyes gently confident, a jet-black Tibetan Mastiff panting at his side.

"Sanctuary," Hannah whispered, as her five-foot, two-inch frame rattled with exhaustion.

"I knew this day would come," his voice thundered gently. He opened his arms, and she fell inside them, a deluge of tears finally feeling safe enough to show themselves.

"You're cutting it pretty close," he remarked. "When is your ceremony?"

"Three hours ago," she muttered.

"Then that doesn't leave us a lot of time," he said cautiously.

"Sorry."

"It'll be okay." He picked up her duffle and locked the deadbolt behind them.

****

"You shouldn't have come, David." Hannah hugged herself and took two steps back from the door.

David took a step inside the threshold, but no farther. The mastiff held him fast with a low growl. "But you missed your ceremony, our parents are frantic." His eyes were wide, and worry painted his face. "You can't just walk away like this... without a word..."

"I won't go back there... that place is dangerous. I won't be brainwashed like our parents... like you. I won't allow my children to suffer, always living in fear, like I did." Hannah crossed the room, putting distance and the large oak dining table between them.

"Don't be difficult, Hannah." David's voice shifted from sympathetic to harsh in the blink of an eye. "You can't stay here with this... monster."

"Watch yourself, David." She glanced over at Marcus. He returned her gaze with a warmth she'd only ever found in his eyes. "I've asked Marcus for sanctuary, and I refuse to disrespect his kindness. "You'd better leave before things become painful."

David took another tentative step forward. "Mom and Dad are on the way," he said with a flat edge. "I told them where to find you. I only came here first to try to stop you from doing something you'll regret."

"That was a mistake," she whispered, pulling a heavy chair from the table and dropping into it. "You've forced my options, David." Hannah nodded to Marcus. He trilled gently. The sound was almost imperceptible. At the signal, the dog slowly began to herd David into a corner. Hannah offered him a sorrowful smile. "Last chance, David. Leave."

"I'm not going without you," he howled, backing away from the mastiff. "I won't have you throw away everything that's good in this world for a moment of... what?" He shot a fierce stare at Marcus. "A flimsy excuse for devotion?" His voice cracked at the last comment, and he knew in that instant, he'd gone too far.

Hannah got up from the table and walked to stand behind the dog. She offered David a last, gentle smile. "I'm sorry, brother." Then, she turned away, taking the stairs to the basement.

Marcus trilled again, and the dog let loose a low growl, threatening just enough to get David to move. Marcus followed behind, his powerful silence reinforcing the animal's will.

David stumbled down the stairs, his words flinging through the air like obstinate arrows. None connected with their target. "Hannah! Wait! I thought you wanted peace. I thought you wanted a gentle life. You're not going to find that here. You need to come home, Hannah. Take the ceremony, things will be better, you'll see."

Hannah remained silent until they reached the bottom of the stairs. She stepped aside to allow David to pass, as Marcus and the mastiff ushered him into the next room. "I've never been a fan of repression disguised as peace. I'm sorry you fell for it." She drew the heavy door closed and removed the iron key from it's lock. "Now might be a good time to search your soul for repentance." She turned away from his muffled pleas and followed Marcus into an adjoining room. The mastiff remained on guard.

"Your parents will be here soon," said Marcus as he touched a torch hanging on the wall to the sunken firepit in the center of the room. "Most likely, they will have others with them. Now, it's up to you."

****

They sat opposite each other on the floor, the small fire burning between them. To Hannah's left sat a thick candle of myrrh, its flame releasing a healing warmth. To her right, a flat iron plate held a thin filet taken from just above David's third rib. It shimmered with a savage glow in the dim light. Marcus poured wine, drawn from David's blood, into a wooden chalice, a twisted claw carved into the stem. He set it to the side. The mastiff lounged nearby.

Hannah closed her eyes and collected her spirit. She could hear Marcus' heartbeat match its rhythm with her own. Their vibration hung in the air, modulating with each breath. Hannah opened her eyes and gazed at Marcus for a long moment, each enhancing the power of the other. She took a deep breath and began the incantation. As she recited the memorized, ancient Latin text, Marcus repeated each line in English.

I beseech you with these words

Untie the bonds of fate

I seek freedom without fear

Intelligence with the power of apathy

Protection from the counterfeit of others

Hannah heard them breach the front door. The sound of shattering glass and the panicked pleas from her mother mixed with her father's voice calling out the Holy Rite. Hannah did not waver but continued with the ritual.

I defend all who ask for sanctuary

I deny those who attempt to taint my resolve

I ignore the seduction of false prophesy

I reject all who manipulate the truth

The flock was growing closer now, she could hear them on the stairs. The dog rose to a protective posture, placing himself between the fire circle and the door, standing at the ready, just to Hannah's right side.

Beyond blood and bone, above heart and mind

By this sacrifice, I pledge myself to your service

Guiding those who come next

Defending you until my last breath of life

Hannah sprinkled the filet with a small measure of a copper dust and added it to the fire. A blaze of blue flame erupted from the offering with a sizzle that made the dog take notice. Marcus drank from the goblet and passed it to Hannah. She took a sip as well and spoke the vow again, ignoring the commotion just outside the door.

Beyond blood and bone, above heart and mind,

I pledge myself to your service.

In the next moment, Hannah's parents burst through the door with two others; Holy thugs on a faithful mission. Her mother held a large cast iron cross, fashioned from a blacksmith's nails, and held it toward her daughter's form. But the deed had been done.

Hannah was now consecrated. She stood to face them, her visage void of emotion.

"Hannah!" her mother cried, "What have you done?" She fell into her husband's arms, as he began to pray.

"Saint Michael the Archangel, defend us in battle. Be our protection against the wickedness and snares of the devil; May God rebuke him, we humbly pray; And do thou, O Prince of the Heavenly Host, by the power of God, thrust into hell Satan and all evil spirits who wander through the world for the ruin of souls. Amen."

"Your foolish prayers will do you no good," bellowed Marcus as he rose to stand before them. The mastiff circled around to his other side. "Hannah has been anointed and is now promised to the One True Path. You have no power here!"

In the distraction, Hannah tossed a generous handful of powder in the faces of her would-be liberators. That was closely followed by the torch none of them noticed in her hand. There was a bright flash that licked the ceiling, lightly scorching the timbers. The intruders spontaneously combusted, falling to ash in four tidy piles.

Hannah scruffed the dog's ears and spilled the small bucket of water, which sat next to the door, onto the firepit, dousing the flames completely. She shared a moment of silence with Marcus, their faces vacant of compassion for her foolish family.

Finally, he broke their connection with a gentle smile. "I'll check on supper."

Hannah gathered a broom from the hallway and swept the ashes of her tyrants and their companions into the firepit. She gazed at the pile of grey for quite some time, and imagined how soundly she would sleep tonight, knowing that she eliminated her life's greatest threat. At last, she closed the door behind her, and snuffed the torch on the wall.

****

At the top of the stairs, she was greeted by the mastiff's exuberance. He knew he was getting spare ribs for supper.

SANITIZED

Ken MacGregor

"It's not enough to clean, Jimmy," I told him. "You have to *sanitize*. You have to kill the germs. Then, the job is done, and done right."

I swept the cloth across the counter, spraying ahead with the disinfectant.

Jimmy watched me, but seemed distracted.

I waited.

His cheeks reddened.

"What?"

"This is not just a job, Jimmy. People are counting on us. Especially here, in this room, but the whole building, too. Some of the germs in here can kill a person. You understand?"

Jimmy nodded. He was paying attention now.

I walked him through the rest of the routine. We'd do it again tomorrow. It's not hard work, but there's a lot to remember.

"The other thing you need to know, Jimmy," I went on, "is to stay out of the way. Some people here work late, so you might see them sometimes. They have important jobs, and they don't need any distractions. *Capiche*?"

"You Italian?"

"Nope. Polish/Irish. I just like the word."

****

I pulled the steaming Stouffer's French bread pizza from the oven. It sat on a steel fish-shaped platter; my hand wore a yellow oven mitt. Both things had been Veronica's. I made a point, now, of using the things she had loved.

While the pizza cooled, I surfed the TV: Sitcoms; reality show; country music concert; news. I didn't much care for country, nor did I have much use for what passed for entertainment these days. I watched the news.

A high school girl, fourteen, was beaten and stabbed; terrorists had blown up a market full of people; a man shot seventeen children inside their classroom. They wrapped it up with a puff piece about a dog show.

I should have watched a sitcom.

I cleaned up, drank a large glass of water, and brushed my teeth. I still had all my teeth; taking care of them was important to me.

****

I let Jimmy work while I supervised. We learn by doing, my mother always said.

Jimmy mopped the floor, looking down.

I unlocked the cooler where they kept the bad things. Keeping an eye on Jimmy, I slid a glass vial into my pocket. If anyone noticed it was missing, I had a convenient scapegoat in the room.

At the end of the day, Jimmy had a good grasp of what to do. I walked him out and clapped him on the back.

"Been nice working with you, Jimmy."

"You're working with me tomorrow, aren't you?"

I smiled enigmatically. "Depends," I said.

Jimmy walked away into the predawn haze.

When I was alone, I pulled out the glass vial and opened it. I couldn't see anything, but I knew invisible, airborne, rampant death was in that tube. I coughed, once.

"It's not enough to clean this world," I said aloud, my throat already sore and scratchy. "It's too sick for that. You've got to *sanitize* it."

I fell to my knees. Blood leaked from my nose. As my vision was going dark, I heard someone else cough.

SEND IN THE CLOWNS

Gabriel Mero

The beat-up black Lincoln Continental cruised down the dark country road, bright headlights barely illuminating the way ahead. In the small town of Pinconning, Michigan, the roads outside of the main drag didn't have streetlights, so one had to rely on their headlights or people leaving their yard lights on to see. Tonight, all the lights were off.

Killian Nichols sat behind the wheel of the car, one hand on the steering wheel, the other holding his cell phone to his ear. Although his mouth was moving a million miles a minute, his blueberry blue eyes were fixed intently on the road, wary of deer or anything else that might hinder his journey home.

"Oh! I forgot to tell you!" he exclaimed, smacking his hand on the varnished wood of the steering wheel. "Margot had her babies."

"She did?"

Killian was on the phone with his mother, Jenna. They had always had a fantastic relationship, but when her husband had accepted a job in Indiana, Killian opted not to move with them. He had been nineteen at the time and wanted some independence. They had only seen each other a few times in the eight years since then but stayed in touch as best they could. They hadn't seen each other since January, and it was now October.

"Yeah. I guess she had them a few hours ago; I don't know. When I turned airplane mode off my phone,

I got a text from Nicki saying that the babies were here."

Nicki was Killian's cousin and Margot's oldest sister. She was a registered nurse with three children of her own.

"Well... good for her. Everyone's okay, right?" Jenna asked.

"Nicki said everything went well. I'm assuming they did a C-section."

"I would think so. They had to last time with Anna, right?"

"Yeah."

"That's what I thought."

Killian turned his blinker on and slowed down to make the turn into his grandmother's driveway.

The house was nothing too impressive. A three bedroom, two bath little number. However, the fourteen acres that Killian's grandmother, Martha, owned was what made the property special. Martha had been born and raised on the property and lived there her whole life. The original house burned down back in 1984 when Jenna was about thirteen.

Killian pulled off the cracked paved road onto the gravel-covered dirt driveway. His eyes instinctively went to the yard to see if any of his cats had heard his car and were waiting to greet him at the door.

He didn't want to live with his grandmother forever and tried to keep his cats inside, but being a country girl born and bred, his grandma was constantly leaving the doors ajar, letting his cats out. It wasn't that he didn't want the cats to be happy, but he knew that once he moved out into an apartment, he wouldn't be able to let them out. There was a difference between living in the country and living in town. If any of his cats wandered off or got hit by a car, he'd be devastated.

Killian pulled up to the garage and then backed into a parking spot beside the rock garden. He turned the key in the ignition to kill the engine and then unhooked his seatbelt, sighing. It had been a long week at the bakery where he worked, and all he wanted to do was get cleaned up, have a meal, and relax. It was late by a normal person's standards, but Killian was a night owl, so anything before 2:00 AM was early for him.

"Did you hear about those clowns that are showing up in people's yards in the middle of the night and scaring the shit out of them?" Killian asked.

Jenna had raised him on horror movies. They bonded over watching any and every horror movie they could find. It wasn't that either of them wanted to kill someone; they just both found the psychology of it fascinating. They both suffered from depression, so a little mindless killing was like a mental and emotional vacation for them.

"No!" Jenna burst out into laughter. "What the hell?"

"Isn't that crazy!?" Killian barked. "I can't imagine what I would do if I got up in the middle of the night to get a drink, looked out the window, and saw a fucking clown in the yard!"

"You'd probably shit yourself!"

"Probably!"

"Do they do anything else?"

"Not from what I saw. It was an article I saw on Facebook the other day. One of my coworkers shared it. I didn't actually read it, but I thought that was so bizarre."

"It certainly is!" Jenna agreed.

Killian got out of the car and made his way up to the garage. He flipped the lid on the keypad mounted on the side of the wall and punched in the four-digit code. The door rumbled and started to rise; way too loud for this late at night.

As the door continued to rise, he noticed that his grandma's car was not in the garage.

"That's weird..." he muttered, chewing his lip.

"What?" Jenna asked.

"Grandma's car isn't here."

"It's not?"

"No. And it's not like her to be out this late."

It was eleven o'clock at night. Martha was usually tucked into bed, passed out, snoring with the TV blaring next to her bed.

"No, it isn't. Maybe she went to see the babies?"

"That's possible," Killian conceded. "I just find it odd."

"I'm sure it's nothing to get worried about..."

"I'm not worried. However, my curiosity is piqued. Maybe she's getting some dick from someone."

"Killian!" Jenna chastised, barely containing her laughter.

"What? Seventy-nine-year-olds need love, too."

"I don't want to think about my mother getting dick."

"Now you know how I feel when you tell me your sexscapades."

For the past four years, Jenna had been having an affair. Her husband was gone a lot and barely paid attention to her while he was home. She hadn't married him for his money, but it certainly made for a nice life not have to worry for once about paying the bills. Killian wasn't overly fond of his stepfather, so he stayed out of it.

"I tell you that as a friend."

"Not my mother, I know." Killian shook his head.

He closed the garage door behind him and went through the entryway to the kitchen. The house was completely black. Utterly quiet. *Yes!*

Locking the door behind him, Killian opened the fridge and pulled out a bottle of Pink Moscato wine. He grabbed a wine glass from the cupboard and filled it before putting the wine bottle away. He took a deep gulp of the fruity goodness.

"I should let you go; I was too lazy to work out today, and if I don't do it now, it won't happen. I don't want to start getting fat."

"Yeah, we don't want that to happen."

Jenna was obsessed with staying fit and looking her best. They say vanity is a sin, but to Jenna, the real sin was letting yourself go. How could you possibly feel good about yourself if you were overweight and wearing ratty clothes?

"Enjoy your night."

"Oh, I will. Grandma's gone, so I have the house to myself!"

"Perfect."

"Right? Maybe I can finally get to sleep in tomorrow instead of being woken up at 8:00 AM by her slamming the vacuum into my door."

"That would be nice."

"Yeah," Killian replied dreamily. "All right. I'll let you go. Talk to you later."

"Okay. Later."

"Bye."

Killian hung up the phone and took another swallow of wine before heading through the small dining room and down the hallway to his room. Fishing the keys out of his pocket, he unlocked the door, quickly stepped in, and flicked on the light.

Lying side by side on his bed were Killian's two favorite cats. Alistair and Romana. They were twin orange cats. Their mother was his tortoise shell, Clara.

The previous summer, Clara had started going into heat. To keep her safe, Killian took to locking her in his bedroom until he could get her into the vet to get fixed. His cousin Mason, being the sneaky little bastard that he was, had used a butter knife to peel the molding away and force the door to open. Clara had gotten out and snuck outside. The rest was history.

Alistair and Romana were kept in his bedroom so they wouldn't get outside and end up splattered across the road or torn to shreds by coyotes. Plus, there was a clowder of stray cats that lived in the backyard carrying who knows what kind of diseases. Before getting Clara, he'd had an adorable Russian Blue he named Channing. The cat followed him everywhere and was his best friend, until he'd been diagnosed with Feline Leukemia and had to be put down.

"Hi, babies," Killian cooed, smiling. "How is Daddy's Baba and Baby Bop?"

The two orange cats looked at their master with excitement and stood, tails twitching excitedly. As he did every night when he got home, Killian bent and kissed each cat on top of the head. Alistair rubbed his head against Killian's face. Romana purred loudly before vocalizing.

Killian turned and stripped down to his boxers. No matter what the weather was like, he had to take a shower when he got home from work. He worked at a bakery, and it was mostly hot as hell in the kitchen, except in the wintertime. He grabbed a pair of sweat pants and a sweater out of the dresser and then went out into the hall again.

He slammed the door shut behind him and walked into the room across the hall, Martha's room. He crossed the room and went into the tiny bathroom. Reaching into the shower, he turned it all the way to the left – hot – and stepped out of his boxers.

He checked his face in the mirror for acne, grateful that he'd been blessed with good skin post-puberty. Still, an occasional blemish did pop up. The steam started to fog the mirror, and Killian jumped in the shower, letting the piping hot water cleanse the dirt, flour, and sweat off him and soothe the sore muscles in his neck, back, and shoulders.

When he was suitably calm, Killian turned the handle all the way to the right and waited for the water to go cold. His pen pal from India told him that if he wanted a blemish-free complexion, he needed to rinse his face with cold water after a shower to close all his pores back up before dirt and grime could get into them.

Killian dipped his head under the icy cold water for as long as he could stand it – about five seconds – and then jumped out of the way of the stream of water and shut it off.

He hurriedly dried off, threw on his clothes, and padded back into his bedroom. Alistair and Romana had moved from the bed to the chair by the dresser, which faced the window. Killian smiled at them.

Suddenly, he heard a faint yowling through the window and knew immediately that it was Valerie, his oldest.

He rolled his eyes and hurried into the living room to open the door. Valerie rushed inside in a blur of gray. She immediately buried her face in the food dish. "Hello to you, too, Princess," Killian teased, scratching her head. Valerie arched her back and continued eating. She didn't like the other cats, so she spent most of her time outside, coming in only to eat and drink before heading back out again.

Killian swallowed the last of the wine and went into the kitchen to fill his glass again. He was off the following day, so if he got a little tipsy, it wouldn't matter. It might even help him sleep. If the wine wouldn't, his marijuana would.

He quickly ducked back into the bedroom and threw on a light jean jacket and some combat boots before shutting the door and heading back to the kitchen. As he opened the door, Valerie came running up.

"Seriously, Val?" he asked.

"Ow," Valerie replied.

"You just got in. Why do you need to go back outside already?"

"Ow."

Sighing, Killian threw his hands up. "All right. You can walk with me."

The garage door opened, and Killian and Valerie ducked out before he shut it again. With no one home, he wasn't going to leave it open like he normally did.

He crossed to his car and reached into the visor for a little checkered bag. He opened it up and withdrew his one-hitter and the plastic baggie of marijuana he got from his friend, Elizabeth. He grabbed a pinch of the green leaves and tapped it into the cigarette-looking pipe. When he was satisfied that it was packed in well enough, he lit it and inhaled deeply.

The foul, noxious smoke filled his mouth, and he could immediately feel himself relaxing – really relaxing. He wasn't big on smoking pot, but he occasionally bought some for when he was extremely stressed. It was the only thing that calmed him down without an after-effect the next day.

He took a couple more hits, his mind clouded, and then he cast a nervous glance toward the house. Pot always made him paranoid. As he scanned the house, he could see that no one was there to bust him – certainly not Martha. She was avidly against marijuana, and he didn't think he could bear the disappointment she'd feel if she knew he imbibed, however sporadically.

His heart leapt into his throat as he looked toward the road and saw a dark figure standing there. He dropped the one-hitter and whipped his cell phone out, opening the flashlight app. *What the fuck is that? WHAT THE FUCK IS THAT?*

The light illuminated the figure, and he immediately heaved a sigh of relief. *Calm down, drama queen,* he berated himself.

What the light showed him was a figure in a colorful costume of red, blue, and yellow. It had a white grease-painted face with big red lips and a circular red nose. A red curly wig topped it off. A clown. It was a fucking clown.

"Nice one, man," he called out. "You scared the shit out of me!"

The clown stared at him, the painted-on smile leering at him. He didn't say anything, didn't move. Just stood there.

"I've heard that this is a thing now. So cool! You guys are doing such a good job."

The clown turned and walked away, disappearing into the gloom.

Killian stared after him for a few moments, shaking his head. "That was fucking awesome!" he exclaimed, chuckling.

He pulled his phone out and dialed his mom's number, waiting for the call to connect. He picked up the one-hitter as he waited.

"Hello?" Jenna answered, sounding sleepy.

"Oh, my God! You will not believe what just happened."

"What?"

"I went outside to smoke a little pot, and I looked out toward the road, and there was one of those fucking clowns in the driveway."

"What!?"

"Yeah!"

"That's creepy."

"Yeah. I almost had a heart attack at first."

"Those people better be careful. They're going to scare the wrong person and end up with a face full of buckshot or something."

"It's a possibility," Killian agreed. "He just turned and walked away when I tried talking to him."

"Apparently, he takes his clown job seriously," Jenna teased.

"Guess so."

"Did you see where he went?"

"No. It's so fucking dark out here. I can barely see in front of me."

"The joys of living in the country."

"Yeah." Killian chuckled. "Anyway, sorry to wake you. I just wanted to share my experience."

"I wasn't asleep. I was watching the ID channel. You know how much I love those murder cases."

"Oh, yeah."

"I'm about ready to step out for a cigarette anyway."

"Okay, I'll let you go. I'm going to take a walk out to the woods."

"At this time of night!?"

"Yeah, why not?"

"You're going to fall and break an ankle, and my mom can't carry you, even if she was home."

"I'm good. I've got my cell phone with me."

"What good is that going to do?"

"I downloaded that flashlight app."

"Oh."

"Yeah. It's bright as fuck, so I'll be fine."

"Okay, if you say so. Just watch out for deer and shit."

"I will. Haha."

"Okay. Bye."

"Bye."

Killian put his phone back into the pocket of his sweatpants and started off toward the woods.

He had to traverse through tall grass and weeds, past the old barn, and his uncle's old broken-down van.

Valerie trailed along beside him silently. As he walked, he took hits off the one-hitter, his mind growing cloudier by the puff.

At the edge of the field, the grass turned to dirt, and rows of corn rose taller than Killian. He walked this path every day on his four-mile walk. He almost knew it by heart.

Sticking to the far-left path, he stumbled here and there over uneven ground. It was half a mile back to the woods, but it always passed quickly. Before he knew it, Killian was flicking on his flashlight so he could find the opening to the woods. There were several, but only one had a real path. Even though the woods weren't too big, he was geographically challenged and could get lost just about anywhere.

By this point, the wine and marijuana had a strong enough effect on him that he wasn't walking straight anymore. He was swaying and giggling, and time had slowed down. He could feel his heart beating in his chest, though it seemed so loud that surely everyone in the world could hear it now.

Killian stumbled along the path, the flashlight lighting the way. He tripped over fallen limbs, caught his feet on rocks, and grabbed trees for balance.

He continued this way for what felt like ages but, in all actuality, was only about five minutes. He came to the end of the path and sat down on a fallen birch tree, its white bark shining in the glow of the flashlight.

Valerie leapt up onto the tree and sat down beside him, her eyes in constant motion as she took in their surroundings.

They sat like this for quite a while, Killian enjoying the quiet and Valerie enjoying the proximity to her master.

Their peace was decimated by a loud rustling of leaves as something moved behind them. Killian flew to his feet, his heart beating faster than the speed of light.

What was it? A deer? A wild boar? A possum? A raccoon? A cat? A stray dog? Killian's mind rambled on and on with possibilities.

His breath came in ragged gasps as he switched the flashlight back on and shone it on the path. The movement was getting closer. Killian swallowed past the lump in his throat. He knelt and picked up a branch. It wasn't the best weapon in the world, but it was the best he could do under the circumstances.

The sound stopped, and Killian shuddered, his muscles coiled like a snake about to strike. His fingers tightened on the branch. He bit his lip to keep from making a sound.

The thing stepped out into plain sight, and he threw the branch to the ground. It was a deer. A doe. The doe looked at him with cobalt eyes, sizing him up.

"Hey, girl. You really scared me!" he sighed. "I probably scared you just as badly, huh?"

The doe turned and tore off into the woods, a crashing sound following its quick escape.

Killian watched it run for a few seconds and turned around and screamed.

Standing three feet away was a clown. It wasn't the same one as before. This one's costume was blue and white. It had face makeup similar to the last one, but the wig was purple.

Killian's hand flew to his heart. *This is the last time I come out here after dark,* he decided. *Especially after drinking and smoking pot!*

"How many of you are there?" he asked, no longer amused.

The clown just stared at him as if he didn't comprehend the question.

"You can cut the shit now, dude. You got me; good for you. Why don't you go scare the piss out of someone else?"

The clown continued to watch him like a scientist observing a specimen in a cage.

Killian shook his head. "I'm not sober enough for this. Go fuck with someone else. I'm just out here trying to relax."

The clown started walking toward him, reaching into his pocket.

"What? More fun? What part of 'fuck off' did you not get?" Killian continued, balling his hands into fists.

The clown pulled out a knife, the moonlight shining off the long steel blade.

Killian felt his heart catch in his chest. This clown wasn't like the other one. This one had cold, malicious eyes, dead on the inside. This one wanted to kill him.

As the clown drew nearer, Killian waited until the last second and then quickly snatched up the branch and swung it at the clown. His aim was off due to his inebriation, so instead of hitting the clown in the head, as he'd intended, he caught the clown in the shoulder.

A cry of pain escaped the clown's mouth, and he dropped to his knees. Killian took the opportunity to start running away. He stopped when he realized that he couldn't find Valerie.

A deep growl emanated from the darkness, and then a gray flash flew toward the clown.

The clown cried out again as Valerie dug her sharp claws into the clown's fleshy hand.

Killian watched in shock as the clown grabbed Valerie by the back of the neck and whipped her toward the tree. Her body slammed into the trunk with a resounding *crack!* She lay still on the ground. Dead.

"Valerie!" Killian cried, his heart shattering into a million pieces. Anger flooded his system, but he kept it in check as the clown turned his attention back to him and flashed the knife again.

Killian took off at a sprint, not even feeling the branches and leaves scratching his face and catching in his hair. He risked a glance over his shoulder and saw the clown running behind him. Obviously, this guy had trained in running with clown shoes on.

Killian followed the path, paying attention to what lay ahead of him so he wouldn't be surprised if another clown appeared. He kept looking left and right, checking for a white grease-painted face. *So far, so good.*

He was so busy checking his surroundings that he missed the fallen tree halfway through the path. He caught his foot on it and went crashing to the ground. The air rushed out of his lungs, and he lay there for a few seconds, dazed.

He lifted his head and saw that his phone had landed a few feet in front of him. Adrenaline coursed through his veins, and he pushed himself to his feet, snatching up the phone. He turned and shone it behind him.

The clown that had been pursuing him was nowhere to be seen.

"What the fuck?" he whispered, his breath coming in quick spurts. He was not used to running. He'd also smoked on and off for four years, so his lung capacity was not what it should have been.

He looked around him, heart hammering against his rib cage. *Where is that son of a bitch? How did he just disappear?*

"Fuck it." Killian turned off his flashlight app and continued on the path. The clown didn't have a flashlight, so it would be harder to find him in the pitch-black woods. Killian was at least semi-familiar with the playing field.

As he got closer to the opening in the woods, Killian sped up, pushing himself harder and harder.

He burst out into the grass and continued on through the cornfield. The corn leaves sliced at his face and hands as he propelled through them, but he didn't care. All he focused on was running. He had to get back to the house. Had to get safe. Had to call 911.

Killian's journey through the corn was loud and messy. He fell several times, his sweatpants covered in mud, his boots untied at this point. Still, the clown had yet to descend upon him.

After what felt like a year, he was at the end of the field. The house was within reach!

Hope started to fill his body at the familiar sight. He was almost there. *Almost safe!*

His lungs seared like they were on fire as he pumped his legs faster and faster. *I'm so glad I gave up smoking,* he thought, struggling for breath.

Finally, he reached the garage. He punched in the code, his hand shaking. *Wrong.*

"Fuck!" he cried, trying again. *Still wrong.*" God damn it!"

He tried again, and the door started to rise.

"Yes!"

He dropped and rolled under the barely open door, bouncing to his feet and hitting the garage door opener on the wall. The door descended and crashed to a stop.

Not taking a break, Killian opened the screen door dividing the garage from the entryway and locked it behind himself. It wouldn't be hard to cut through, but it was at least a deterrent. He glanced over at the side door and saw it was also locked.

He locked the door to the kitchen as he closed it and went through into the dining room. The sliding glass door was locked but was easy enough to break through. As was the door in the living room.

Killian whipped his phone out and dialed 911. It took forever to connect.

"911 dispatch. What is your emergency?" the operator asked.

"Please. You must send someone out here. They're trying to kill me."

"Sir, you need to calm down," the operator said calmly. "Who's trying to kill you?"

"The fucking clowns!" Killian exclaimed.

"The clowns?"

"Yes, the fucking clowns! Just hurry!"

"Where are you?"

"My house. 1810 Seven Mile Road."

"Okay. We'll have an officer out there right away. Are you tucked away somewhere safe?"

"I-I think so. I got back in the house."

"Are the doors and windows locked?"

"Yes, I think so."

"Okay. Just stay calm. Won't be long now."

"Thanks."

Killian hung up the phone and dialed Jenna.

"Hello?" she answered, definitely groggy. Definitely asleep.

"He killed her," Killian gasped.

"What?" Jenna sounded wide awake now.

"He killed her."

"What are you talking about?" Her voice was panic ridden.

"The clown. He killed Val. Oh, God." A sob squeaked out.

"What are you talking about, Killian?"

Killian sniffled, tears streaming down his cheeks. "I went out to the woods with Val. There was another clown. He pulled a knife on me."

"What!?"

"I knocked him down, and then Val... she... she tried to protect me. She jumped on him. He threw her against a tree and snapped her neck."

"Oh, my God!"

"I got away."

"Are you safe? Where...?"

"I'm in the house. I locked all the doors. The cops are on their way."

"Where's my mom?"

"She's... she's still not here," Killian said slowly. Realization was just now sinking in. He hadn't seen her car in the garage. There weren't any close neighbors, either. He was alone in this battle.

"Did you call her?"

"No."

"You're sure everything is locked up?"

"Pretty sure." Killian's mouth dropped open. The Bilco doors. He hadn't checked them. "I forgot the Bilco doors..."

"Stay on the line!" Jenna commanded.

"I will."

Killian went into the kitchen, grabbed a butcher knife from the drawer, and then opened the basement door. It creaked slowly open, and he looked down into the cold darkness below.

Swallowing nervously, he flipped on the light and started his descent into the basement. With each step, his heart seemed to beat louder and louder, his breath shaky.

He got to the bottom of the steps and peered through them to the door that led to the Bilco doors. He couldn't tell if it was locked or not. *Fuck!*

He went around the steps and then behind, reaching out for the cold metal of the handle. "Here goes," he said into the phone.

He tugged, and the door didn't move.

"Well?" Jenna pressed.

"It's locked," Killian said with a sigh of relief.

"Maybe you should get out of there. Lock yourself in your car until the police arrive."

"I can't leave the cats!" Killian protested.

"Seriously? Fuck those cats! You're my son, and I am worried about your safety."

Killian groaned. "My keys are in my bedroom. I put them in the bowl when I got home."

"Hurry up and go get them."

He ascended the stairs and looked out the sliding glass door. There were three clowns standing in the backyard staring at him. The two he'd seen before, and one fat one, in a yellow and white suit.

"They're right outside," Killian whimpered.

"The clowns?"

"Yes."

Killian held the phone up and took a picture of the clowns, illuminated by the lights on the back deck. He sent it to Jenna.

"Get out of there!" Jenna cried.

Before Killian could move, the sliding glass door shattered into a million pieces.

"What was that!?" Jenna shrieked.

"They broke the sliding glass door," Killian informed her as he bolted down the hall to his room. He ducked in and slammed the door, locking it. He tugged it once, and it came open. *Fuck! When Mason had fucked with it, he'd buggered up the latch.*

Killian tried again, and once more, the door came open.

"Christ!" he groaned.

"Killian? What's happening!?"

He slammed the door a third time and then threw all of his weight against it. This time when he tugged on the handle, the door stayed firm. He hurriedly pocketed his car keys. He could hear his mother's voice coming through the phone but ignored it. He threw the phone into his pocket.

Alistair and Romana looked up at him from their place on the chair, their yellow eyes wide with wonder. Killian swatted at them, and they both went and hid under the dresser.

Killian dove onto his bed and rummaged around on the side. *It has to be here somewhere. It has to!*

His hand touched cold metal, and he pulled up his katana. He'd bought it from a coworker a few years ago. He didn't know if it would work in combat, but it was all he had. There was a gun squirreled away somewhere in the house, but he didn't know where, and he'd never used anything other than a BB gun anyway.

He pulled the sword out of its sheath and held it before him, slowly backing away from the door.

Outside the bedroom, footsteps crunched on the broken glass in the kitchen and then shuffled down the hall. Suddenly, silence fell over the house.

Killian exhaled sharply, his eyes wide with panic. *How much longer is this going to go on?*

A loud thundering shook the door as one of the clowns on the other side smashed into it with something heavy. Splinters flew in all directions.

Before Killian could react, arms broke through the window behind him and pulled him outside.

Both Killian and his assailant crashed five feet to the ground. The wind was knocked out of his lungs again, but this time it was harder to recover. His vision swam, and he wanted more than anything to just close his eyes and let sleep take him.

The arms grabbed him again, and he shook away.

"Get off me!" he shrieked, kicking out.

The person threw him back to the ground. He turned and saw that it was another clown. This one was obviously African American under the grease-painted face. The nostrils were wide and flared, the eyes a dark chocolate brown. This clown was wearing a rainbow costume.

"Who are you!?" Killian bellowed, reaching around for his lost katana. "Who are you?"

Before he got an answer, something struck him in the back of the head, and darkness embraced him.

****

The first thing that came back to him was his sense of smell. He could smell sweat, shit, and body odor. Something else, too, something he'd never smelled before.

Slowly, he opened his eyes, and his vision started to clear. He was in a barn or something. A big, wide space. *A factory, maybe?*

He looked down and saw that he was chained to a wooden chair. He tried to move, but the chains held him firmly in place. *What the fuck is going on?*

"Where am I?" he croaked, his throat dry.

Someone passed in front of him and put a straw up to his mouth. It was the African American clown.

Normally Killian wouldn't drink something offered to him by a stranger, but his throat was so dry, drier than he'd ever felt it before. Greedily, he sucked on the straw. Cold water soothed his dry, hot throat.

"Thanks," he said, nodding.

The clown ignored him.

"Who are you?"

Again, no answer. *Are they deaf?*

The clown disappeared behind him, and Killian tried to gather his surroundings. Wherever he was, he had not been there before, but that wasn't saying much. He wasn't one to get out of the house unless he absolutely had to.

The clown walked back in front of him and looked at him. Killian looked back. There was something different about this one. The darkness that the others had in their eyes was not present in this one's eyes. His orange clown suit was splattered with what looked like blood stains.

"Help me?" Killian whispered. "Please?"

The clown looked around warily as if afraid of being seen.

"I won't tell, I promise," Killian pressured. "No one has to know."

The clown tilted his head as if considering and then walked away again.

"Fuck!" Killian bellowed, pulling on the chains, which rattled resoundingly.

Time tiptoed by, dragging on endlessly. Killian wasn't sure if minutes passed, or hours, or days. *Weeks?*

Finally, he felt his chains go slack, and he stood up, whirling around. The four clowns stood behind the chair he'd been chained to. They leered at him menacingly, their dead eyes chilling him to the bone.

The yellow clown was hefting a chainsaw, which he started, and it whirred loudly. The red one had a pickaxe. The blue clown brandished the knife he'd used before. The rainbow one had a pair of garden shears. The orange clown had a pickaxe in his hand.

The clowns continued to stand in place as if waiting for him to make a move. Killian slowly shifted his stance, eyes glued to the five clowns, ready to spring if any of them so much as moved a muscle. Chances were that he was no match for them, but he at least had to try.

His boot slid slightly, and he cast a quick glance down at the floor. A trail of blood stopped just under his feet. He followed the trail with his eyes and cried out when he saw the source of the blood. Nailed to the wall of the building, wrinkled body pale and stiff, was his grandmother. Her eyes and teeth had been removed, her face frozen in a wail of pain.

"What's going on!?" Killian demanded, blinking back tears. "Why the fuck are you doing this!?"

The yellow one stepped forward. "Why not?" he growled. His answer chilled the blood in Killian's veins.

Without another word, the four clowns started moving.

Killian spun on his heel and started running. He didn't know where, he didn't know why; all he knew was that he had to survive.

As he followed the twisting building, he started to realize that he did, in fact, know where he was. This was the old garage. He hadn't been inside since he was a kid. *But that is the old lawn mower.* The old rotor tiller was next to it. *What the fuck was going on?*

He burst through the broken door and welcomed the fresh air outside. He saw that it was still dark out. *How long was I unconscious?*

He pedaled toward the house again, stopping when he realized that he wouldn't be able to get in because he'd locked all the doors. Sure, he could go through the broken sliding glass door, but the clowns would just follow. He needed to get somewhere they couldn't.

An idea struck him, and he went around to the front of the house. He stopped outside his window and grabbed his dropped katana and his phone from where they lay in the grass.

He checked the time. It was two o'clock. He'd been out for a half hour, at most. *So where are the police?*

Deciding to worry about it later, he ran back to his car and got inside, locking all the doors. He managed to work his keys out, and he started it. The car rumbled to life just as the yellow clown's chainsaw tore into the bumper.

Killian threw the car into drive and sped down the driveway. He cranked the wheel around and punched the gas. The car moved toward the yellow clown, catching him full-on. The clown flew backward, his body crashing through the brush and rolling away.

Killian went to throw the car into reverse when he heard the hiss of a flat tire. Smacking his palm against the dash, he got out again.

The other three clowns descended on him. Killian took a knife to the shoulder, and the pickaxe skewered his foot.

As the blood flowed from him, he started to feel woozy. But he wasn't going down without a fight. With all his might, he brought the katana down in an arc.

The red clown's head flew and tumbled off into the grass. His body crumbled to the ground, spewing blood like a fountain.

Killian faced the other two. The blue and rainbow clowns stared back, wielding their knife and gardening shears menacingly.

They moved as one, and Killian blocked the shears with his katana. The knife bit into the back of his shoulder blade, and he cried out, jabbing his elbow back. It connected with the red clown's nose, and he felt something give. There was a wet, sickening *crunch!* The red clown dropped to his knees as blood gushed from his broken nose.

The rainbow clown dropped his shears and stepped back. This one was obviously the newbie of the group.

Anger setting in, Killian pounced on him like a jaguar and drove the katana blade through the back of his head. The clown kicked, and he pulled the blade out and stabbed it in, again and again, blood spraying all over his face.

When the clown finally stopped moving, Killian stood to face the red clown, who looked up at him in fear.

"Mercy?" he begged.

"Fuck off," Killian replied coldly. He stabbed the katana right through the clown's throat. The clown's legs thrashed wildly, and his eyes bugged out of his head, but his life quickly drained out of him with his blood.

Killian pulled the katana out and dropped to his knees, his wounds getting to him.

He could hear a car pulling into the driveway and craned his neck to see who it was. He saw the familiar colors of the Pinconning Police Department and tried to stand.

The cop got out of the car, gun raised. "Stay where you are!" the cop ordered.

Killian dropped the katana and instinctively raised his hands above his head. "I'm Killian Nichols. I'm the one who called you."

"What seems to be the problem?"

"Nothing now. You took your sweet ass time getting here. I handled it."

The cop holstered his pistol and walked over to Killian. "What do you mean?" the cop asked.

Killian pointed to the bodies scattered out of the cop's line of sight. "I took care of them."

"Took care of who?"

"The grease-painted motherfuckers who tried to kill me."

"Clowns?"

"Yeah. Five of them."

Suddenly, the yellow clown came bursting out of the field, running straight for Killian.

Killian yanked the gun out of the officer's holster and switched the safety off. Walking forward, he squeezed the trigger.

The first bullet caught the clown in the shoulder. Killian continued to squeeze the trigger long after the clown fell to the ground, a bullet hole dead center in the forehead.

The officer had to gently take the gun from him and usher him back to the car.

****

About an hour later, several officers were going over the property. The four bodies had been bagged up and carried into the back of the ambulances.

Killian was being attended to by a paramedic.

"The wounds are mostly flesh wounds. I think you're good to go," the paramedic said with a warm smile.

"Thanks," Killian said, not really listening.

The cop took Killian off to the side and looked at his notepad. "Do you recognize any of the guys who attacked you?" the officer asked.

"No, why would I?"

The cop chewed his lip for a moment, not wanting to be the one to have to tell him. "It appears that the four men were living in the old building. We found piles of human feces and the remains of cats, coons, and such. They've been there for at least a year now."

"So, they were here the whole time?"

"Yes."

"Watching us?"

"One can assume."

"That is so fucked."

"We've checked the property as best we can, and we don't see any signs of more of them."

"Thank God for that."

"You should go inside and get some rest. One of my deputies will stay with you until your family comes home."

"Thanks."

Killian was escorted inside the house, and he stopped at the trashed skeleton of his door. Taking a deep breath, he opened it and let the wreckage hit him. His assailants had knocked everything over. All of his autographed photos were slashed, and the frames were broken. The bed was a mess of shredded mattress, blankets, and pillows.

Alistair crawled out from under the dresser, cautiously making his way to Killian. Killian picked the orange cat up and kissed the top of his head. Romana followed her brother and clawed at the bottom of Killian's pants.

How nice it must be, Killian thought, stroking his cats, *to be unaffected by what had happened here just a few hours earlier.*

He stood there for a long time holding the cats, grateful.

SUNSET

Andrew Allen Smith

Amanda walked into her bedroom to see John sitting on his side of the bed in his pajamas, staring out their window at the slowly setting sun.

"How did you get home?" Amanda set down her purse and walked over to look at her husband's face. "Did the doctors let you go home?"

"They said there was nothing they could do for me." John didn't look up but instead stared and brushed his blue satin pajamas until they were straight. "I didn't see the point of staying there if there was nothing they could do for me."

"There might be something," Amanda pleaded for a moment. "Come on, let's get in the car, and I'll take you back."

"I just wanted to watch the sunset from home. Our view has always been so beautiful."

"Well, I want to save you." Amanda was flushing as she usually did when she got nervous, "You don't understand. You have to get better."

John looked up at Amanda. "I understand perfectly. I'm sorry you never understood."

"I've always done everything for us." Amanda was adamant. "I never wanted this day to come. I never wanted you to be sick."

John lowered his head for a moment. "No," it was nearly a whisper, "you just wanted to be comfortable."

"I wanted us both to be comfortable." Amanda was standing above John. "I wanted to spend retirement together. Let's get you back to the hospital."

John looked up at Amanda. "They said there was nothing they could do for me. I tried to call you before I came here, and I think they tried to call you as well, but we didn't get an answer."

"My phone is completely dead. I put it on the charger."

"I'm sure it is dead. It's the most important thing in your life. You spend every waking moment revolving around what is on that phone. You have Tik Tok videos, Facebook posts, LinkedIn, Snapchat, and dozens and dozens of people to text, and I was always right here. You lost the passion for me somewhere in our life, but I still have it for you. Every single day I tried to show you how much I cared about you, and every single day something was more important than us. You found a way every day to avoid affection, to skip by those passionate moments we used to share and to definitely avoid being physical with me."

"You know that I couldn't." Suddenly there was emotion in Amanda's voice. It just wasn't the same.

"I know," John lowered his head again, "I know all of your statements and excuses better than you do. I was stupid enough to think you were having an affair for a while. Then I found out you weren't. I was at one of the bars you went to watching while you had a drink with Zach. I was so surprised that it was just business because I thought someone with your passion had to be with someone else and just fell out of love with me. I blamed myself for a while but then realized it had nothing to do with me. It sounds old-fashioned, but it would have been nice to be together daily. I don't think you ever understood that I love you. I don't think you know what that means. Instead, you had excuses and reasons for avoiding me. It didn't matter what I did or how many times I asked."

"It wasn't just me. You said so," Amanda's tears were rolling.

"I lied to you because I love you." John looked out at the sunset in the fiery sky. "I thought that somewhere inside you knew the truth and that someday I would become important. I wish that had been true."

"Watch the sunset with me for a second," John said as the sky became a fantastic series of colors.

On the charger in the other room, Amanda's phone began to buzz. "Hang on, let me grab that."

Amanda walked into the other room and picked up her phone. A dry voice answered, "Is this Amanda Story?"

"This is Amanda." Amanda walked back into the bedroom and saw the colors of the sunset start to fade.

"Amanda, this is Doctor Phelps. I'm sorry to say that your husband has passed away. There was nothing we could do for him. I'm very sorry."

Amanda looked down at the phone and then at the sunset. She pressed the red button and hung up while dropping the phone on the floor. She fell to her knees and watched the sunset through blurry, tearful eyes in her bedroom alone.

TEMPTATION

Chelsea Gouin

I've always loved the color red. It represented everything I wanted, everything that I didn't have. Red was the color of the apple that Eve bit and forced her out of Paradise. Red was the color of power.

I was a nobody, just a mousey girl who couldn't get through a gym class without collapsing. That was the only time I ever saw red. The color would consume me, along with my loathing for my weakness. I was cursed with epileptic seizures that kept me hiding in the background.

Despite my medical condition, I decided to overcome my adversary. This week, that adversary just happened to be the rock wall. With each determined stretch, I convinced myself this was my opportunity to re-make myself. At the top of this rock wall was the new Erica. I could almost see the looks of my classmates when I reached the top. Their looks of judgment and, worse, pity, would melt into looks of approval. All I had to do was reach and...

Where am I? The air around me was icy, and the walls were an unfamiliar white. *Am I dead?*

"Been a while since we've seen you here," came a female voice. As the room came into focus, I saw a familiar head of wild brown curls. *Damn.* I'd landed in the hospital again. After a few gentle reprimands and an affectionate pat on the head, I was left to my own contemplations once more.

My peace and quiet didn't last long, however. Suddenly, the gurney started to roll, and a firm hand and male voice forced me to be still. My heart raced with fear as we rolled into the hospital's morgue. *Who was this mysterious man? An angel guiding me to the afterworld?*

No, one look at those cold eyes, and I knew he was no angel. "Who are you?" my words trembled with both fear and awe at the man before me.

His dark lips quirked into a sensual smirk. He asked me questions about my seizures, his tone faintly amused. Finally, he reached the end of my bed and locked his gaze on mine. His fingers lightly traced my exposed calves, sending electric sparks through my body. No, he wasn't an angel, but a demon, of that I was now sure.

What if all those things went away, and everything else..." His hand caressed my cheek, brushing away a lock of my frizzy blonde hair, "...got better?"

"How?" I asked, mesmerized by the sheer power of his voice.

"Let me show you," His eyes morphed into the deepest color of red. Here was the serpent offering me a juicy apple of temptation, and I was all too willing to take a bite.

THE ARTIST

Chelsea Gouin

He would spend hours in the dark room, perfecting his craft. The tips of his fingers would grow numb from the long toil for perfection, his wrists would ache, his arms longed for rest, and his eyes strained in the dim moonlight streaming from the window. But for *her,* it was worth it, his one true love; and of course, she loved roses.

He was used to working at night. The peace of nature's natural symphony in lieu of the noisiness of daily life suited his needs. Long ago, he'd been scorned by others for his outward appearance, but not *her*... she saw the artist within, and ever since her act of kindness, he repaid her with roses.

The Artist was no botanist, however. He often relied on the gardens of others to fashion the perfect bouquet. He twined the stems together in a gorgeous display to be left at her door for a morning surprise, with only a small calling card with his well-wishes attached to let her know her midnight admirer was still near. She may have chosen another to give her hand, but his heart would always belong to her.

But tonight, tonight, he was fashioning the *perfect* bouquet; his magnum opus. With the rising cost of just about everything, the Artist had to get creative. For tonight's masterpiece he had to use a bit of improvisation to complete it to perfection.

Red roses were out. A fabricated story of how chic white roses were was the popular tale spread across the papers, hiding the inflation of seed prices. But his love preferred *red* and white just would not do.

Carefully, the artist continued to craft, peeling back each layer carefully so as to not disturb his dye. Truly this Artist was a crafty one, sneaking into the mansion without being detected, detaining any that might discover him at work in the almost black bedroom. By now, his fingers were stained red as he dipped the rose into the hollowed basin, making sure each petal got just a drop to run over its velvety skin, watching as white absorbed red and its petals transformed before him. *Beautiful.* The flowers were the most vibrant and as lush as if they'd been freshly plucked.

When each flower had been painted, he wasted no time twisting their stems to their unique shape, creating a brand new bouquet that would surely dazzle his love. When his task was complete, the Artist slipped the ring off the dead man's finger; an easier task to complete than his first attempt when he tied the man to the bedpost. The ring was the perfect addition to this bouquet to be left on his love's doorstep. The Artist's flowers straight from the heart.

THE BLOODBATH OF THE BLUE FLAME

Danielle Ice

Ledvig could hear it, the wind screaming and kicking at the door of the dim tavern where he sat with a lukewarm tankard of what he had been told was mead. He had a scarred hand wrapped loosely around the handle, and his other arm was lamely lounging against the bar. No one was next to him or within a friendly distance. Even the local thugs drunk on piss-poor mead and their displays of manhood wouldn't so much as glance in his direction. He didn't know the men, nor did he care, but they were all the same in every town he visited as he would bide his time.

He would only be here long enough for it to happen. He didn't know when it would happen, only that it would. And that he would be there to end it.

"Bad business, that. Isn't it, Kvaldr?" said one man in a wheedling tone to his burly companion.

Ledvig could see the person who just spoke by their reflection from his tankard. This man had dark, beady eyes and a gangly build with long arms. The way his head twitched this way and that, waiting for an answer, was also much like a crow waiting for its prey to die before digging in.

"Yeah, yeah," Kavalr garbled back, his voice thick with drink and phlegm.

He presently hawked up the bile in his throat and spit it onto the floor. His hand was the size of a bear's paw, and he used it to clean off whatever had stuck to his chapped lips.

"I mean, shouldn't we try and find her? The reward would be substantial. We can follow the lead that people saw her go into the mountains," said the first man again, his wheedling morphing into childish whining.

"No bitch in this town is worth going into that cursed place, especially one that's been gone as long as she has. The last man who went up there died like a mangy dog. We were only barely able to patch the bastard's face together for the funeral rites."

"But that was simply an attack by a wild animal," the first man said, lowering his voice and clasping his hands.

"It's not worth it for a request that's been on the board for nearly three winters," Kvaldr said sternly, "Let it go, Preshik."

Ledvig dared to take a swig of his drink, and he shuddered after it slid into his gut. He thought about the prospect of traveling into the mountains, which surrounded this snowy town like a granite cage. There would be wolves and bears, certainly, but that wouldn't be too much of a bother. It was the beasts of the blue flame that the second man had been afraid of, and with good reason.

No one knew where the harbingers of carnage came from. They descended from a range of mountains called the Ebony Fingers one day twenty years ago. One would usually find its way to a town or village every few years. Soldiers from the king's seat, Eferjald, would be sent to deal with the problem. They would either find the beast eviscerating its second or third town, or join the heaps of bloodied bodies.

Every man, woman, and child had a right to fear these nightmares turned into flesh and alight with azure fire. There was no hiding from them. There was no bargaining. There would only be prayers to their gods that the death would be swift and that they would not see their insides on the claws of whatever form the beast had taken before they closed their eyes forever.

Ledvig himself had seen plenty of these beasts, and they all had the one telltale sign that they had been tainted by some evil in the mountains. The razor of icy blue flame that sliced down their hides to the tips of their tails. The look in these creatures' eyes would be a nauseating mixture of joy at the gore they wrought, the horror that they would not eat what they killed, and confusion about why they were slaughtering everything in their path. The poor souls of the creatures were trapped inside a prison that, no matter how much blood and tears they spilled, would never let them free unless someone ended their agony.

He was the angel of death and mercy, and it had been three years since one had barreled down the mountains. Now he just had to wait for the sign.

"Hey, old man," one of the aforementioned thugs bellowed.

Ledvig did not turn his head, and he took another swig of his drink. It seemed there was one far enough gone to overcome their initial fear of the newcomer. Ledvig never thought himself a threat, being old enough for young men to leave alone, but not old enough to escape some other mens' notion of using him to beat out their frustrations.

He chuckled to himself at the thought of anyone else being able to add to the tapestry of scars that littered every scrap of his world-worn body. He knew what new scars on top of old ones looked like since he had plenty of proof, and he knew no one could make him look any more grizzled and patched together.

"I'm talking to you, asshole!"

"Might need to determine which asshole in this place you mean, Jerolt," said one barmaid serving the men in a playful tone.

Jerolt's friends laughed, but Ledvig knew what was going to happen next.

The woman's scream was drowned out as the men laughed even louder, and Ledvig's spine suddenly felt like knives stabbed into every inch of it. His groan was hidden by the raucous laughter, but he knew the pain would go away as soon.

"What did you say, you whore?" shrieked the worm named Jerolt.

Ledvig took a long, heaving breath before getting out of his chair and finally looking the man in the face.

The face was different on each man who dwindled their days in dingy taverns and brothels, but the look in their eyes was always the same—cold, unfeeling, but still searching for someone to tell them it was all going to be fine. They were still little boys, no matter how old they got.

"I thought it was a fun jest," Ledvig said.

His voice was quiet, but the severity in it could cut the balls off a braggart, so he'd been told by one bartender years and years ago.

He saw the child in Jerolt's eyes shrink into the bowels of his black soul as anger tried to suffocate it, squeeze it, do anything to make it die, and disappear.

"Then you have a fucking bad sense of humor. Doesn't he?" Jerolt said to the barmaid on the floor, one side of her face swollen.

She nodded quickly to him. He smiled a crooked grin and moved to step over her, but not before trying to stomp on her face. The wench had wits and speed enough to get out of the way before his foot made contact, but this made the fool even angrier.

Ledvig only had one weapon, a sword given to him by his late wife, but he couldn't risk having it out of the sheath yet. It was coated in a particular concoction of his own design, and it wouldn't be worth using it on some pathetic wretch in a tavern.

He needed to save it.

He decided to laugh to get Jerolt's attention. It was quite a stupid display, after all.

The drunkard stopped chasing the barmaid long enough to swivel a face twisted with rage at Ledvig, but this face did not frighten him. Ledvig had seen the wrath of unholy things that no man could ever dream of in their most sickening nightmares.

"So what's this I hear about a woman going missing? Want to share the bounty with me?" Ledvig said, easing his posture and sitting back down into the chair, his spine barely allowing him to stand anymore from the pain.

Jerolt abruptly halted and tilted his head like a dog that heard a new noise.

"Well? Do you desire some coin or not?"

"Kavash is her name," he said. "But where could you know where she is?"

"I don't; that's why I need help."

The pain in Ledvig's spine tried to force him to hunch over, but he knew it wouldn't be too long now. Likely, only a few more minutes. Nothing he could do now could save them, except his own wits and skill.

"I believe she may be in the mountains. Do you know why she would go there?" Ledvig pressed.

Jerolt shrugged, "To hell if I know, sir."

Ledvig smirked. How polite young, poor men became at the prospect of some measly coin to fill their appetites with whatever they desired.

"You're not getting that bounty before we do!"

The crow-like Preshik had decided this was the time for bravery as he leaped out of his chair, jabbing a long finger at Ledvig. Money could make knights out of cowards if there was enough to tempt them, and it seemed there was enough bait to make a crow go for the throat.

"Then, by all means, please," Ledvig said, motioning to the door. "You have a head start."

The young man was stunned to the spot, and it wasn't long before his drunk friend, Kvaldr, patted the table, ordering him to sit back down. It was clear that Kvaldr had learned enough about the mountains to stay from going farther than the view of the village.

If only we had known about the danger before that day, Revitska, my jewel.

"Kavash is long gone," said Kvaldr, some sobriety making his tone more sturdy. "There will be no finding her."

Jerolt, slowly comprehending what this meant for him, was standing stupidly, assessing what to do next. From how his gaze ambled back and forth between Ledvig and the barmaid, Ledvig assumed he was deciding who he would bruise and batter to compensate for him not receiving funds for more drink.

Ledvig was patient, waiting for the man to make his decision, mostly because his spine was now trying its best to lurch out from his back. He knew it would be mere moments before complete bedlam would ensue. He rested one hand on the hilt of his weapon, readying himself.

"Can we not gather a search party and find her?" Preshik asked Kvaldr.

"She may be your mother, but no one will go into the mountains with you," Kvaldr said, one hand fondling his beard and not meeting Preshik's eye.

"Then I will go myself!" Preshik declared to the tavern, silencing most's casual conversation.

"You will not need to go," Ledvig said.

"Of course I do, or are you as heartless as you look?" Preshik said, his chest puffed out in boyish indignation.

"I mean that she will come to you," Ledvig said.

"What the fuck does that mean?" said the barmaid, who had hidden in a corner and was nursing the cheek now turning purple.

The sound of something that didn't belong followed the wind as it tore at the door, as if the wind itself was trying to escape the calamity.

The tavern was silent as the grave, all having heard that unnatural, primal sound of rage and loss. It was a haunting, low roar that was intriguing at first, but the longer one listened, the more something was not right. There was another low growling groan, louder this time, and it called to the deepest instinct in one's soul to flee, lest one would see the horror in its face and see terror incarnate.

The first roar was an announcement, the second one a warning, and the third one was a death knell as a scream rang out into the dusk and was cut short.

Everyone in the tavern yelled and screamed and headed for the front door. Some that took a moment to think scrambled over the bar and tried to escape through the back door. Ledvig knew better. He knew that no matter where they might run or hide, they would all meet the same grisly fate if he did not act.

From the sound of others screaming and another howl, the beast announced its intention to rip into its first kill.

Ledvig was the last to leave the tavern, and he knew exactly where to go. He followed the walls of the oak and plaster shacks so as not to be trampled by the stampede of horrified people. He could tell which ones had seen the beast and which ones hadn't by the white on their faces.

He turned a corner and was greeted by the creature as it was pulling and yanking the insides of its first victim open. There were no screams, Ledvig was grateful for that, at least, and the fire in his spine was put out now that he had seen the creature.

This beast's lips were pulled back as its teeth were stained red by the spurting lifeblood of the person at its mercy. The blue flame along its back was like a snake, writhing this way and that and occasionally rearing upward to try and put its fangs into the shack behind it. This particular beast had chosen the form of an impossibly large gray wolf that walked on two legs, but its form was skeletally thin, where ribs tried to puncture the skin of its chest. Its amber eyes were focused both joyously and joylessly on its prey.

It had torn open the person's chest cavity, and its claws rooted inside and heaved out whatever it could grab. Flesh and viscera were flung out as blood leaked from the open wound. The creature continued to dig and claw, discarding everything inside until it would claw a hole through the spine and into the ground below.

This was common for the first victim of these monstrosities in every village. They would be so enraptured by the rose red insides and would pull and tear at everything red until there was no more red to be found, but this was the moment to strike. Otherwise, he would become the one to next lose their organs.

He drew his sword, and the whooshing noise from the unsheathing weapon had an unexpected reaction from the creature. It turned its head to Levig.

Normally nothing could distract the creature from its plaything, so this alarmed Ledvig, but the next thing the creature did startled him even more.

It laughed, and the laugh chilled every fiber of his muscles. It was wet, gurgling, like someone choking on their own blood, trying to not breathe their last. The eyes of the creature did not blink or show emotion of any sort.

They were focused intently on him as the blood-red snout of the creature remained slightly agape.

Ledvig readied himself into an attack position, as he had been taught as a boy. He was prepared to give his all, as he had for the past seven of these horrid animals. The first had broken his heart, but the others were a duty. Slaying them was his burden, and he knew it would be until he was the one with his eyes open and frozen in fear as his life was ripped mercilessly from his body.

The creature stopped laughing suddenly and launched itself at its new prey, only to receive a smart cut on its snout as a reward. It recoiled, and the creature's snout began to boil and bubble, now bleeding its own light, yellow-bile color. The poison on his blade was doing its work, and he had an advantage, but he could find no joy in his success.

He seethed through gritted teeth, "Not so cocksure now, are you?"

The creature screeched, this time sounding like a dying eagle. It shook itself, spilling yellow and red blood on the shacks around them. Ledvig examined the work of the poison. It had eaten through fur and skin, eaten through muscle, and now what remained was bone. What was left were two openings for the nostrils where hot air came out in billowing clouds.

He had hoped the poison was strong enough to break through bone, but it was clearly not enough. He would have to apply more when the next one scourged its way through helpless villagers.

Acid pain fueled the creature's labored breathing through its open jaws, every inhale making the creature inflate in size. It was calculating how to strike next, and

Ledvig didn't move fast enough when it eyed a wooden cart right next to it.

The cart flew through the air and smashed into Ledvig's chest, knocking all the air out of his lungs as he was hurled onto his back with the cart on top. He thought a sharpened part of the cart had impaled him at first when he felt something stab through him, only to realize some of his ribs had cracked. He tried to gasp for air, only to have the cart and his broken ribs stop him from catching any of the frigid air in his lungs.

He heard a low, guttural snarl and knew the creature was just on the other side, deciding whether to crush him or tear his legs off first to ensure its prey couldn't escape.

Ledvig started to see void blackness rim his eyesight. The cart was so heavy, and he wasn't sure he knew he was doomed, but if he had to die, this death would be preferred over what the poor person not far away had to endure.

He thought one more time about Revitska, her long hair the color of the mountain peaks under the snow, her eyes the color of a frozen lake. The last time he had seen her, her eyes were at least still the same. He fell into the memory of her eyes as the blackness around his own forced his to shut and embrace what would come next.

Then suddenly, the creature shrieked, and the weight off of him was lifted. His eyes snapped open, and he saw Jerolt and Preshik heave the cart off of him and one other man wielding the sword he had dropped, which he realized was Kvaldr when his eyes readjusted. The beast's left forearm was now bubbling, and when the creature tried to stifle it with its other paw, the poison and yellowed blood began to eat at its paw. It writhed and screamed in agony, not sure how to make the pain stop.

The man brandished the sword, making another cut at the creature while it was distracted as Ledvig forced himself to his feet. Ledvig could tell this man had decades of knowledge in hunting and battle, and he knew this creature was already nearing its end. Kvaldr landed another hit, this time across its chest, and Ledvig knew it was over.

The poison could not force itself through bone, but it would feast on the organs between the cracks in its ribcage. Ledvig had seen this same fate claim only one other beast, and he promised himself that he may have been an executioner, but he was no torturer. But this warrior could not have known what he had done.

Ledvig had to believe they were monsters that needed to be put out of their rabid misery, but it wouldn't be long before he and the other men would see the beast for what it truly was. When the flame on its back went out, then they would all see, and they would all turn against him.

No matter how much it clutched at its chest, rammed itself into shacks, or beat its head on anything hard it could find, the process of being eaten alive was now its gruesome fate. Ledvig knew it would begin to lose its vigor when the poison eroded the heart or lungs, and by the sound of the gurgling, the venom had found its way to the lungs first.

Ledvig looked to the other men, and they looked satisfied at the animal's agony. They had every right. But he knew all too well that the satisfaction would melt into horror when the creature finally fell down and breathed its last.

He remembered when he had slain his first beast, he was proud, discovering that using poison was the only way to kill these creatures. It had raked its mountain lioness claws against his back, but he had still won. He had watched it die, and then he had wept.

The large wolf fell to its side, the remnants of what was in its chest beginning to leak out as a mixture of liquified organs and blood into the mud underneath it.

Not much longer now.

"Why didn't you warn us that that thing was going to be coming?" Preshik said as he had decided he was done watching the life of the creature fall into the muck and slush.

"If I had warned you to evacuate, it would have either followed you, or it would have attacked another village," Ledvig said, though it was a herculean task with his cracked ribs.

"You decided we would be pigs for slaughter, then!" he replied.

He could deny it and say the creature had chosen its path, but no amount of correction or reasoning could break through the skull of a man that was scared to death and was about to weep just as he had done.

Ledvig looked to the creature and watched as the flame on its spine sputtered and then slowly faded to where not even the smallest flicker of embers could be found.

That's when the creature morphed, its bones reshaping and cracking, its fur sloughing off like the skin off a carcass that had been in water too long, and hair growing from the top of its head. The hair was growing long, too long.

Ledvig stepped over to the devolving creature and took off his cloak, and rested it over the torso; a poor man's burial shroud. He could at least offer the decency of this soul in death if he could not in life. Even if he had created the only concoction that could defeat them and make them suffer as they left the world, he could do as any decent man would.

The snout shrunk, as did its whole body, into a small, petite form. He prayed to whatever god was listening that Preshik's pain would be fleeting as the men around him began to realize what was happening.

The wolf was no longer a wolf, but a woman, eyes open in angry horror, hair tangled and matted, the bones in the middle of her face open to the cold, and soaking in her own insides.

Jerolt vomited, and Preshik joined him. Kvaldr, still holding the sword, dropped it on the ground, and his shoulders shuddered.

"What is this?" Kvaldr said, staring at the remains of what looked to have been a woman in her early forties, who was likely the missing woman they had spoken of in the tavern. She had been a family's matron, a friend, a woman who would have had a vastly different life had she not ventured so far into the mountains one fateful day.

"You were not wrong when you said the mountains were cursed," Ledvig said.

Kvaldr finally turned to Ledvig, and his eyes were red and swollen. Ledvig looked over to the corpse and found Preshik leaning down to close her eyes, as an unmistakable sob escaped his throat.

"What did this to her?" Kvaldr asked, regaining himself as he cleared his throat.

"I wish I could say I knew. The same fate befell my late wife," Ledvig replied.

"Fuck..." Jerolt said as he joined them.

Preshik screamed. The sound was like it had traveled from twenty years before, Ledvig's own scream ringing in his ears. Tears trailed down his reddened cheeks, and he pounded at the ground, splashing guts and muck onto himself.

"He killed her!" Preshik said suddenly, raging to his feet.

Preshik stood toe-to-toe with Ledvig, and he felt the remorse radiating from his eyes.

"Nonsense! He saved our lives!" said Kvaldr.

Ledvig dropped his eyes to examine the muck pooling around his boots.

"You did know," Preshik said in a deadly whisper.

"I come to villages often and see if there are any people who went into the mountains. Any who have been gone for years have been condemned to a cruel fate."

"And how do you know that?" he sneered.

"Because of Revitska."

Her frozen blue eyes were seared into his memory like frostbite. He didn't think about the scars she had left on his body or how sick he felt when he realized he had killed her. He could only punish himself. She had gone into the mountains since game was scarce that winter.

She was determined to go at night, where she was certain wolves would be most abundant. She would be alive if he hadn't allowed her to go. He would still have a beloved wife whose knowledge of potions was unmatched. He would have never left home on this quest for penance for his mistake.

Understanding traced the wizened lines on Kvaldr's visage.

"She had killed so many in our village, and of course, we all thought she was some creature sent from someplace to punish us for any unknown wrongdoing. She took arrows to the back, spears to the stomach, and cuts everywhere on her body, but nothing stopped her except for her strongest poison," Ledvig explained.

To administer the poison, he swept it along the blade Revitska had given them as a wedding gift and plunged it into her heart, but not without suffering a life-altering slice along his spine. After Revitska changed back into his wife and not a lithe mountain lioness, he was cast out of the village. The chief thought the blight of the blue flame was because he had abandoned his wife to the mountains, and her ghost had come back to haunt them, even though Ledvig had led the charge to find her two years prior, and had nearly died.

"How did you know it was coming?" Jerolt asked, awe unmistakable.

After Ledvig had healed and had been banished, he wandered to find answers. In a village surrounded by a range of mountains years later, his spine felt like it had been lit on fire, until he saw the second beast—a black bear with blue flames along its back. When he saw it, the pain subsided.

"Gods alive," Kvaldr said after Ledvig answered his question.

Ledvig made it his mission to destroy the people who had been afflicted with the curse of the blue flame, and his wife had given him a gruesome gift and reminder of his purpose in life. After killing the second beast, which had revealed itself to be a young man, he had been sent away, thinking he had brought the beast with him. His curse was to live a lonely life by snuffing out others. He felt no remorse or satisfaction, only that the job had to be done.

Ledvig turned on his heel to leave the scene behind when Kvaldr asked one last question. "How did you know it would come *here*, I mean?"

Ledvig swallowed a lump in his throat as he thought about how many people would fall prey to the mountains from an unknown but vicious predator, but he had a realization. His spine tingled, but not in a warning this time.

"Pick up the sword, Preshik," Ledvig said.

"I'm not going to—"

"DO IT!" Ledvig said, the order coming from the depths of his being.

Preshik started like a child being scolded and brought the sword to him meekly, his eyes wide.

"I have a way for you to make it so that your mother's death isn't in vain," Ledvig said. "But this path is not for the weak."

Preshik looked down at the sword which was spattered red and light yellow, and then looked back to the mangled corpse of his mother. Ledvig watched as the pieces of the puzzle connected in Preshik's mind. He looked at Ledvig with eyes that glowed with a determined fire.

"Take me with you to destroy these creatures. I can't let anyone else feel the way I do at this moment."

Rage and despair moved these creatures to kill everything in their path, but rage and despair could also present drastically different results in those who wanted to do good; in those who wanted to make things right. Ledvig had been spurred the day Revitska died to devote himself to ending others suffering, but how had he been so selfish to think he had been the only one with that desire?

"Good man," Ledvig said, a smile cracking across his face for the first time in twenty years.

The poor man may have had the look of a crow, but his heart was swelling into one of a mountain lion. Ledvig put an arm around him, and Kvaldr opened his arms expectantly, still waiting for his answer.

"First lesson, my boy," Ledvig said, "these creatures are creatures of habit. What was the first thing your poor mother did? After turning into the beast of the blue flame, what did she do?"

Preshik thought to himself, a finger on his chin as a sad realization dawned on him.

"She came home."

"Yes, they always come home," Ledvig said, something sparking in his chest that he hadn't felt in a long time.

Was it hope?

THE DEAL

H.G. Evans

"You think I'm being paranoid, but the truth is, I'm worth a lot more to her dead than alive."

"No, you're not paranoid at all. She wants you dead."

John stared at his brother-in-law. "And you're just now thinking to fill me in on this?"

Mark shrugged. "It's not like Samantha's going to do anything about it, bro."

It was like John hadn't heard. "I *knew it.* Sam's been acting different lately. Distant and irritable about stupid stuff that never bothered her before."

"Bro. Really. She's not going to act on it. It's one of those phase things. You know how often I wished Laura dead? Did I actually kill her? No."

"*Laura* doesn't have a million-dollar insurance policy."

"It doesn't have anything to do with the money."

John paused, momentarily stunned. "Of course it does. She's always hounding me about buying the latest and greatest designer thing and then is pissed when I say we don't have the money for it. She's never happy."

A sly grin twisted Mark's lips. "Ever think she might have found out about that Borneo tryst?"

John felt a chill wash over him. "No way. There's no way she could know about that." His eyes narrowed. "Unless you told her. You're the only one who knows about it."

Heaving a sigh, Mark finally put down his phone and angled his body toward John, leaning both arms on the table. "You and I, we've got our understanding, man. You don't tell Laura when I step out on her, and I don't tell my little sis when you decide to have a little fun."

"You make it sound like I do it all the time. It was *once*."

"Don't get your boxers in a bunch. Nothing's changed. Bro code. I don't rat on you, you don't rat on me."

"Then how would she know about Borneo? She wasn't there, and she sure as hell doesn't know anyone from there."

"Hell if I know. That's your problem, not mine." Mark swiped his phone off the table and leaned back in his seat.

"Dude." John leaned forward and snatched the phone from Mark's hand. "Sam's always said that if I cheat on her, she'll kill me. Literally *kill* me."

Mark was beginning to look annoyed. "Everyone says stuff like that. They don't actually *do* it." He snorted. "Though Sam *does* have one hell of a temper."

"Exactly. When she told me that, she had a *plan*, bro. A step-by-step plan as to how she would do it."

"And you believed her?" Mark crossed his arms across his chest and laughed.

"You didn't see her face, man. I've never seen her so pissed—and I hadn't even *done* anything yet."

Mark shook his head, but the certainty in his expression had slipped. Barely imperceptible, but there. John pounced.

"See? You know she would. Sam would literally kill me if she knew about Borneo."

Mark didn't deny it that time but still shook his head. "Like you said. How would she know?"

John lightly tapped the edge of Mark's phone on the table as he thought. "I don't know. But I bet that's it. She hasn't let me touch her since—"

"I do *not* need to know about that," Mark said, hands rising, palms out in a halting gesture. "Bro. She's my *sister*."

John ignored him. "I've got to figure out how to stop her."

"You do that." Mark leaned across the table and grabbed his phone, kicking his feet up onto the seat of the chair next to him. "I've got boats to research. Laura finally caved on getting one."

Again, John didn't bother replying, deep in thought as he tried to figure out how to thwart his wife's plan to kill him.

****

By the time John headed home from the bar, he had decided two things. One, Samantha had messed up by telling him how she would kill him if he ever cheated on her—John already had the upper hand. Two... he needed to kill Sam before she carried through with her plot to kill him.

John wasn't naïve. Sure, he could just leave Samantha. They didn't have kids, even though Sam had been hounding him about that too. But John knew his wife.

As her brother said, Samantha had a hell of a temper. To cheat on her was unforgivable; she wouldn't forget it, and she wouldn't rest until she had revenge. Sam would call it justice, but John knew it was revenge that his wife craved when wronged. And she had made it clear that revenge would involve his death.

Pulling into the driveway, John sat for several minutes, staring at the house he and Samantha had bought just before their wedding three years ago, watching the shadow of his wife move behind the thin curtains covering the windows. An ache spread through John's chest, intensifying as the seconds ticked past.

He loved his wife.

****

John and Mark were college roommates, inseparable after the first week of freshman year. When Mark invited John to come to the family lake house over the summer, John immediately accepted. They were going to raise hell, like all young men in their twenties did. Beer and women. That was the extent of their plans for the summer.

Then John walked into the lake house and saw Samantha. Only a year and a half younger than her brother, Samantha was beautiful, funny, and possessed a confidence John found sexy and appealing. From that moment on, there were no other women. Samantha was the one he wanted, and the one he got.

John regretted his indiscretion in Borneo as soon as it happened. When John and Mark had left for Borneo, John had been pissed with Sam for freezing him out when he told her he didn't want to try for a baby right then. She hadn't let her touch him for weeks after. John shuddered to think what she would do if he ever told her the truth—that he didn't want children at all.

The other catalyst for his one-night stand was that he was drunk. Very, very drunk. So, when the hot waitress at the bar suggested they meet up after her shift, John was waiting at the door when she walked out.

Mark hadn't seemed to care; he had taken a scantily clad brunette back to their hotel and seemed relieved that John wouldn't be there. *What happens in Borneo, stays in Borneo,* Mark said, lifting his hand for a fist bump before walking off with the brunette.

John had no idea if Mark had betrayed him or not to his sister, but he doubted it. Mark knew that if he betrayed John, John could simply turn around and tell Laura about the far more multitudinous indiscretions of her husband. Mark didn't want to lose the hefty inheritance that would befall Laura when her father died, and John didn't want to lose Sam—whom he still loved. They held a mutual understanding.

Having racked his brain for how Sam could have known about the waitress in Borneo, John was at a loss. He had thrown all his clothes from the trip in the wash as soon as he got home, not letting Samantha touch them. It guaranteed his wife didn't come across any lipstick on his collar or any clinging perfume odors. Receipts didn't matter; she knew he was going to Borneo, and the waitress took John back to her place for the hookup, so there weren't any questionable hotel charges on his card. There wasn't anything that would indicate he had been unfaithful to Samantha.

So how the hell did she find out?

After several minutes passed, John realized it didn't matter how Sam had found out about the waitress. She was planning to kill him, and she wouldn't stop until she succeeded. Which meant John only had one option.

His heart heavy, John finally opened the door to his truck and stepped into the night. This wasn't what he wanted, what he had planned when he said his vows three years ago. If Samantha was different, this wouldn't be necessary. She was too focused on herself, on what *she* wanted, and to hell with everyone else. Not getting what she wanted meant ruin for anyone in her path.

Resentment pulsed underneath the distress that had consumed his mind only moments before. John recognized it in an abstract manner, then, as it became a persistent nudge, fixed that aggravation in his mind and clung to it, fanned it into a flame of fury that would propel him forward into the task now at hand as he walked into the kitchen.

Samantha turned from her place in front of the oven, offering a smile. It was a detached upturn of the lips; however, no warmth behind the action. It was simply an action borne from habit.

"Your favorite for dinner," she said, leaning down and pulling a pan of pork from the broiler. "Cherry pork over angel hair pasta. We haven't done it in a while, and I know you're stressed because of work." The pan was set carefully on a set of trivets lined up on the counter. "Thought you could use a pick-me-up."

I'm not stressed because of work, John thought, watching his wife with an aloofness that matched the reserved air coming off her in waves. *I'm stressed because you want to kill me.* John knew the urge to make his favorite meal wasn't a desire to "pick up" his mood. No, it was Sam's way of putting him six feet *under.*

John knew the food that looked and smelled so delicious was laced with deadly poison. He even knew *which* poison. His wife had, after all, outlined her plan to him years ago. Did she remember that conversation? Did she remember that she had given up her one means of gaining the upper hand?

She must not. Then again, Samantha was counting on John's ignorance about her knowledge of Borneo. He wasn't supposed to have any idea that she was aware of his worst sin. His worst sin until this evening, anyway.

"Grab the salad, would you? I thought we'd eat in the dining room for once." Sam used tongs to fluff the pasta and cherry glaze before carefully placing each piece of pork just so along the top.

John didn't speak; he just walked over to the counter and picked up the crystal salad bowl Mark's wife, Laura, had given them as an engagement gift. It was supposedly imported from Venice, but John couldn't tell the difference between the bowl in his hands and the glass vessels lining the shelves of the local home goods store.

"How is Mark?" Samantha brushed past where John stood beside the dark wood of the dining room table, salad bowl forgotten in his hands as he tried thinking of the best way to carry out what needed to be done. "Laura called about destinations for the summer trip. You know, the one we planned for June?"

John nodded absently, still cradling the bowl of salad and standing motionless. Sam didn't seem to notice as she placed the bowl of pasta and cherry pork in the center of the table.

"She thought we should all go to Borneo, you know, because of how much you and Mark enjoyed your guy's weekend there."

The crystal bowl from Venice slipped from John's fingers. It landed on the hardwood floor, shattering into hundreds of pieces and spraying salad and cherry vinaigrette over the wide planks.

Samantha gasped. "John! Are you okay?"

No, John thought, amazed that his wife could bring up the place of his indiscretion so casually, that she could believe he wouldn't know she was deliberately prodding at the wound already gaping wide. *No, I'm not all right. But you know that, don't you?*

"Don't move; you'll cut yourself. I'll get the broom."

John watched his wife run from the room, his emotions oddly disconnected as he bent at the waist, unfolding back to his full height as Samantha raced back into the dining room, broom and garbage can in hand.

"I mean it, John, don't move. You'll cut yourself." Sam began sweeping the salad and crystal into a pile.

Her pretense of concern was almost laughable. It was also infuriating. John felt rage build to a crescendo in his chest.

"Borneo?" he said quietly. "Really?"

"What?" Samantha glanced up, then back down at the mess on the floor. "Oh, the trip. Sure. I mean, if you guys had such a great time, why not all four of us go together?"

Something inside John snapped at her nonchalant tone. "Stop the act, Sam."

There was a hitch in Samantha's movements, a quick glance in his direction before she resumed her charade. "What are you talking about?"

"Borneo?" John sneered. "You want to go to Borneo. Really?"

Samantha paused, her forehead creased in a facsimile of confusion. "Yes," she said slowly. "I just said–"

"I'm not an idiot, Sam. I know that you found out about Borneo."

Samantha's hand tightened on the broom, a flash of… something indefinable sparking in her eyes. Her voice, when she spoke, was measured. "What about Borneo, John?"

But he wasn't about to play her games. He had no patience for them tonight.

"Playing dumb doesn't suit you, Sam. I know what this whole thing, this whole meal," John swept his arm toward the table, "really is."

Samantha's expression darkened, her words clipped and impatient. "Look, I was just trying to do something nice for you, okay? Because you've seemed really withdrawn lately. But once again, you have to ruin it with one of your tantrums. Seriously, what are you even talking about?"

"*Stop playing dumb,*" John roared, his arm sweeping out again, but that time connecting with the bowl of pasta and meat and sending it to the floor to mix with the remnants of salad and Venetian crystal.

"What the–" Samantha gasped. "John, what is *wrong* with you?"

"With me? What's wrong with *me*?" John reached out and wrapped a hand around Sam's wrist, yanking her toward him. The broom fell from her grip and landed among the detritus with a clatter. "I'm not the one who started this whole spouse-killing venture."

"Spouse-killing... John, what is going on?"

He had to admit, she was a great actress. Better than he realized. John would have believed Sam had no idea what he was talking about—if he didn't already know better.

"I may not have started your little game, Samantha," John said quietly, "but I sure as hell am going to finish it."

The wide shard of crystal he had picked up from among the debris pressed against the soft, thin flesh of Samantha's neck. He waited, just long enough for his wife's eyes to register what was happening, then drew the sharp crystal across the skin.

****

"John? John, what's going on, bro? I was finally on the verge of getting Laura to give me some action. Needless to say, your call ruined the mood..."

Mark inhaled sharply as he rounded the corner and stepped into the dining room. John tried to see the tableau from his friend's eyes.

Food and glass littered the floor, dark red blood from the gaping wound in Samantha's neck mixing with the wreckage. The woman herself, John's wife and his best friend's sister, lay amidst it all, body contorted and empty eyes wide and fixed. John sat at the dining room table, still holding the crimson-stained crystal shard.

"What the hell..." Mark breathed.

His expression was appropriately horrified, John thought, though more surprised than he thought his friend would be. What did he truly think would happen after their discussion at the bar? This was the only way for John to survive.

"I need your help, Mark. I can't make this go away on my own. Bro code, right?"

"What the *hell*?" Mark's face was turning as red as the blood pooled around his sister's body. "What the actual *hell*, John?"

"You said..." John couldn't seem to connect with any emotion. He was numb as he stared up at his friend. His wife's brother. "You said she wanted me dead. She would have killed me. You know she would have."

Mark's hands trembled as he knelt beside his sister, as he pressed fingers to her neck in a vain attempt at feeling life there. "John... it was a joke, man."

"What?" Mark's words floated through the air, disjointed and bouncing off John's deadened mind before fading away into nothingness.

"You... you were so ramped up. So paranoid. It was ridiculous, thinking Sam would... I just went along with it, figuring... I'd tell Sam later... we'd laugh about it... it was a *joke*, bro."

John stared dumbly at his friend, his wife's lifeless body... and felt the world fall out from beneath him.

THE DRIFTER

Andrew Allen Smith

Why can't people understand?

I have tried for a long time to keep my distance from people and instead pay close attention to myself and the inner peace that seems to be the smallest part of my very being. Many see this inner peace that I seek so sincerely as who I am, but they often find that that is not who I am, and that is when I have to move on.

As I walk down the gravel of another forgotten side road, I consider the past several days and all of the actions and interactions that have led me to another long walk to another forgotten town. The brisk wind blows across my face, but I barely feel it. My hands hold my jacket, not for comfort but for the shame of the past few days.

I arrived in Ansel only a few weeks ago. It was a beautiful little town with white picket fences in the downtown… one of the downtowns where modern yuppies rush to chatter about the overpriced boutiques and the excessive cuteness of the restaurants. I was wearing what I'm wearing now and walked into the town, hoping for silence and peace. Jobs were easy, and I found a job cleaning in a few minutes in a small warehouse right off the main street.

The warehouse owner was in a bad way as the post-COVID landscape had made workers tough to get and workers with good ethics even more challenging. I told him I could start immediately, and he gave me an extra day to find a place to stay. I filled out paperwork with him with a valid ID and the Social Security number that would allow me to work indefinitely. I was now Derek Griffin.

I had enough money to last for a while. It was easy to find a small over-the-garage apartment less than a block away from my new job. I didn't usually even carry a bag. The furnished apartment was perfect. It even had towels and one roll of toilet paper. This was something people took for granted until COVID happened.

I signed a month-to-month lease. Mrs. Abigail, a little old lady of unknown age and a sharp mind, had several questions but seemed to like me and was hoping for a year's lease. I told her I often had to move on for work but would pay her one month ahead, which seemed to end her nervousness.

There was a drug store in the downtown area and a small second-hand store where I purchased some clothes and got some everyday sundries, including soap to wash the dust of my latest long walk away from my body. It was harder to clean away the memories. Much harder to hide the scars.

The warehouse job was good work. It didn't take long for me to be completely immersed in cleaning, stacking, and loading. My size made it easy for me to carry almost everything, but I knew how to use the forklift and pallet jacks as necessary. My new boss was Mr. Johnson. He was ex-military and, for an ex-Marine, was very calm. I worked extra on the first several days as he was behind and only had two other warehouse workers that were young, inexperienced, and full of themselves. I gave them distance, ate alone, then went home to my new place and sat awake thinking of the past.

After my first week, I met Caroline. she was the daughter of Mr. Johnson and did some of the books for him. I guessed she was probably twenty-five but had no real clue and didn't want to get involved. She had other ideas. Each day she would try to talk to me, and I would nod and do my work. As the sweat-soaked my long sleeve shirt and my hands glistened, she would come up and comment about how I needed to slow down and not strain myself. I would nod politely and continue my work, oblivious to the suggestion. I did not need to slow down. All I needed was to find my peace.

In the second week, Caroline stood in front of me with her palm out to my chest and said, "Did I do something to make you dislike me?"

I was a little taken aback. It was infrequent that people noticed me until that time that I had to leave. It was even rarer that someone paid attention to what was happening with me or even cared if I existed. I found my voice and said, "No, ma'am. I'm just trying to be a good worker."

"Well, you're probably the most exceptional worker my father has ever found, or so he says, but all you ever do is work. You stop and eat for a few minutes and keep working. I don't think I've ever seen you take a break, and I don't think I've ever seen you talk to anyone. You look like you need a friend."

"I don't have many friends," I lied. I actually had no friends. Once upon a time, I had a friend, and it did not end well in that story. "I just want to get my work done."

"I don't have many friends either," Caroline was looking at the wall. "The world seems to look down on a single mom who's only twenty-four."

"I don't judge," I was trying to make conversation, but since I rarely made conversation, I wasn't very good at it. I was good at other things I didn't want to be good at.

"You just try to get your work done." Caroline was still looking at the wall and not at me. "It would be nice if you could talk to me for a few minutes because the other workers and everybody else just stare at me or act like I'm an awful person. You don't have to, but it would be nice to have someone to talk to."

I considered for a moment, this was a bad idea, and I had been here before. There were 1,000 reasons I should not talk to this woman and only one reason I should.

"I will take my lunch at 12:30 if you would like to talk," I picked up the vast crates and walked away, leaving Caroline staring at the wall.

I tried to set things aside and find my peace, but I knew Caroline would again be why I would leave. It seemed there was a Caroline, Johnny, or Mary Ellen in every town. Someone who needed something that they thought I could give. I had faced this before and not walked away. Now here I was again. Perhaps this time would be different.

12:30 came, and I sat down on a crate. Caroline joined me with a small lunch box, and we ate relatively quietly for the first few minutes.

"I suppose you have some questions," Caroline was staring out at the open sky through the warehouse doors.

"No, I have no questions," I looked at the sky as well, trying to find some peace in this now repetitive conversation.

"Well, I'll answer the ones that you won't ask. I dated a man in high school that got me pregnant. I have a daughter named Anna. She is the light of my life and makes my father smile all the time. With my mother gone, it is just him, me, and Anna. Anna's father lives in the area, and I had to convince my dad not to kill him. You know how Marines are, always ready to solve the situation."

Of course, I knew how Marines were. I had learned a long time ago that Marines were tenacious and to give them distance if possible. I had no desire to tell Caroline this, so I just listened.

"I'm a small-town girl and don't want to be in a big town. I would be happy with just me, my dad, and Anna. I'm not dating, and I'm not looking to date, so don't worry, I'm not trying to date you. I don't have any friends because Anna's father has pretty much poisoned that well. I'm just me."

"It is good to be you," I kept staring out at the sky and saw the pickup truck pull up.

Caroline saw the pickup too. She stood up and put her lunch away. She walked to the warehouse door as a tall, well-built blonde man approached her. I couldn't initially hear what they were saying and honestly didn't care. I suppose I could have listened, and it would have been easier. Instead, there were suddenly finger points at me, and the man pushed past her towards me. It only took a few moments for him to be in front of the crate I was sitting on, asking questions about who I was and what I thought I was doing with Caroline.

I had faced his kind before. I put away my lunch, picked up my lunch box, stood up, and walked away.

"Don't you walk away from me," the man said as he walked back in front of me. "I want some answers right now."

"I don't want trouble, and it would be best for you to walk away," I turned to walk away and felt his arm grab my shoulder and try to spin me around. I stopped, but he could not move me. I turned and looked at him, and he realized somewhere in his mind that he was well overmatched. He was probably 6'5", but I was taller. He was probably 240 pounds, but I was heavier.

There was a look on his face I had seen too many times. He pushed his finger into my chest and said, "If you don't want trouble, stay away from my girl."

Caroline was indignant, "I am not your girl. Except for Anna, you are the biggest mistake I ever made."

Behind her, Caroline's father walked up, "I 100% agree with that. You do know that you are trespassing right now."

"I'm leaving, old man," the younger man said. "Remember to stay away from my girl. You're not so big that I can't take care of you."

Inside I was saddened. It was likely I would soon lose my small apartment where I felt comfortable, my extra set of clothes, my new toothbrush, and a place that I found peaceful. Why were people always so quick to distrust? Why did people want to test me to my extreme? Why did the people who thought they were monsters not realize there were real monsters in the world?

Caroline looked at me, "Are you okay?"

"I am fine," I looked back at the sky and watched the pickup truck leave. "I try to avoid conflict."

"That was Sam," Caroline was obviously angry, "Sam is Anna's father, but there is nothing between us. I wish he would go away, but he never does. I'm sorry that he is such a pain in the ass, and I'm sorry if he bothered you or made you feel bad."

"I know his type," I stared at the blue sky and noticed a cloud that looked a little bit like an elephant slide past the open warehouse door, "I'm not concerned."

Mr. Johnson shook my hand and said, "Thank you for not running away. That boy has run off good help before. People get afraid of him, and they just leave, or something else happens. If he bothers you, let me know. I'll get the Sheriff on him."

"He won't bother me," the elephant had moved on, and now there was an earthworm-shaped cloud sliding across the sky. I looked down at Caroline and her father. "I'm not afraid."

My voice rang with such conviction. I'm not sure they knew how to take it. They looked at me with an uncomfortable silence that closed in around us.

"Well, that's good. Just remember what I said," Mr. Johnson told me, breaking the moment as he walked back up to his office.

"Sorry about our lunch," Caroline said. "I really wanted to know more about you."

"There's not much to say," I looked down at Caroline, away from the clouds and my peace. "I am just me."

I went back to work. The two younger guys started following me around. As I stacked crates and unloaded trucks, they began to help more where usually they were nowhere to be found. Normally the trucks would take most of the day to unload and stack, but with the two extra workers, it went quick, and I began sweeping out the warehouse. The two boys quietly joined. Not a word was said, but when I looked up, they would nod at me with some type of respect.

"Thanks for standing up to Sam," one of the boys said, "this place is hard to work at with him showing up all the time."

I nodded but said nothing and kept working. The last truck of the day came in, and we unloaded it rapidly. It took no time to stack and reload, and the warehouse was in near-perfect condition. It was Friday, and Mr. Johnson handed each of us envelopes. As the two younger men left, Mr. Johnson looked at me, "You sure have made a difference with them. I put a little extra in your envelope just for that."

"Thank you," I said, gathered my lunch box, and walked the short distance to my tiny apartment.

The weekend was uneventful. I made it uneventful by staying in. I helped Mrs. Abigail on Sunday for a few hours with her garage and cleaned it up. Mrs. Abigail told me about her husband, her life, and her children. Her husband died last year. Her children were long since gone, living in California, and she never heard from them. She asked me no questions and just allowed me to listen. I listened and was amazed and how few breaths this woman took as she explained her life history to me.

Monday morning came, and I was at work bright and early again. Sam was waiting in his pickup truck, and as I walked to the closed doors, he got out of his truck and walked up to me. Out of the corner of my eye, I saw two other men walking toward me from different angles. "Not even two weeks," I thought to myself. I hadn't done anything and would have to move on again.

"I wanted to do a little follow-up to our discussion," Sam was looking at me dead in the eyes, thinking that I was unaware of all that was happening around me. Sometimes I thought humanity was stupid as they ignored their senses. Behind me, a man was carrying a baseball bat. I saw it as clearly as if I was looking at it, a wooden Louisville Slugger. The other man brought a split 2" x 4". Sam was looking at me dead in the eye.

I looked down at him and saw all the fear in his eyes that he was trying to hide. I whispered to him, "You don't want to do this. I am the monster you fear at night. You will lose."

He paused for a moment. He was unnerved but then suddenly shook himself back into reality, thinking what he saw was what was real. Humanity again.

The baseball bat came across the back of my head and shattered. I'm sure the man that swung it was feeling his hands in new ways as his hands and fingers were not built of the same thing I was. He backed off, holding a shattered piece of a bat. The second man had swung the 2" x 4" across my back, and it too split but did not shatter. I never stopped looking at Sam, but Sam looked at the two men, and his eyes widened.

"It would be good to leave me alone," I started to move forward, and Sam put out his arm.

"You stay away from Caroline," he put his palm on my chest.

I looked down, calmly reached up, and took his hand from my chest. As I moved it away from my body, I put more and more pressure on his arm. Sam began to sweat, and his eyes pleaded until I let go and said again, "It would be good to leave me alone."

I walked into the employee entrance of the warehouse and realized how stupid I was. Perhaps humanity was not as stupid as I was. I could have just walked away and done nothing. I could have stepped away from the men and avoided showing them even a portion of what I was capable of. Instead, I brought attention to myself.

Caroline walked up to me, oblivious of everything that had just happened.

"Hey, big guy," she said. "I brought you a donut."

She handed me a small bag, and I opened it to see a long john and a napkin. "Thank you."

"There are about twenty minutes before anybody else gets here. Why don't we sit down and talk for a few?"

This was a bad idea. I knew this was a bad idea, yet I sat down with her and started eating the long john.

"It was pretty awesome, you standing up for me," Caroline was smiling at me. Why weren't people afraid of me? I was easily twice her size; by that alone, she should have given me a wide berth. Instead, people always thought I was good and calm and that person they could trust. Caroline turned around momentarily and motioned, and a small blonde girl wandered up. "This is Anna. Anna, this is my friend Derek. Derek works for Grandpa."

I smiled and looked down at the child. I knew what to do and how to try to make people comfortable, but kids were more intelligent than adults, and Anna looked at me as though I had escaped her nightmare last night.

I put out my massive hand and said, "Nice to meet you, Anna."

The tiny girl took my hand and shook it. Her eyes were always on mine.

"Mama, can I go color?" Anna asked in a voice that was so sweet it would cause normal humans diabetes.

"You go ahead," Caroline leaned over to me. "I have to take her to school this morning and just wanted you to meet her."

"I should tell you that Sam met me at the door. He and two other gentlemen attempted to scare me away."

"Are you okay?" Caroline sounded concerned. I wasn't used to people being concerned about me. I stopped for a moment and thought about it.

"I'm fine," I finally noted, "they couldn't hurt me, and I think they left a little wiser to that."

"Don't be so sure," Caroline said, "Sam is about the stupidest person I know."

I laughed inside. It was the same story again. Someone always didn't want to pay attention to the signs everywhere I went. Everywhere I went, someone wanted to take on the bigger person just to show they could do it. If only I could work without my shirt, and they could see they might feel differently. Even if I rolled up my sleeves, they might start to understand.

Caroline stood, and I stood as well and put out my hand. Caroline deftly slid my hand aside, moved in, and hugged me. I felt her warmth even through my long sleeve shirt and T-shirt. She held me, and for just a moment, I awkwardly put my arm around her and patted her softly on the back.

Anna walked up as Caroline stepped away from me, "Mama are we going to school?"

Caroline was flushed, and I felt terrible that I had that effect for a moment. It would not be suitable for either of us to spend more time together. I knew I would have to leave anyway, but the hug felt nice.

"Yes, honey, let's clean up so we can get in the car and leave Mr. Derek alone so he can work."

I watched the two of them walk away as I had watched so many in the past. I had to let go of the past, but it seemed it continuously repeated itself. In every town, there was someone nice who only wanted to be friendly; in every town, there was someone ignorant of the world who wanted to be evil. I thought about how long it had been since I had a hug and how good it felt. I set that aside opened the warehouse doors, and began to work.

Fifteen minutes later, I was interrupted while stacking a pallet. Mr. Johnson walked up and grabbed a box next to me, and helped me stack a new shipment.

"I saw Caroline was down here with you," he picked up another box, "and I saw those boys outside this morning. It looked like they hit you pretty hard, but it didn't bother you, did it?"

All I needed was one of the good people against me, "No sir. It didn't bother me."

"I've seen a lot of shit in my life, and I've never seen someone take a baseball bat to the back and shatter it. I'm guessing you've got a titanium plate back there, but I really don't want to know. I just need to ensure you don't hurt my girl." He looked down for a moment, "I think I've hurt her enough for both of us by not killing that sorry little pissant."

"If you killed him, he would win. It sucks how the bad guys win if the good guys do what they need to do to make it right."

"You got that right," Mr. Johnson looked out the open warehouse doors. "If I hurt him, I go to jail, and she loses her father. If I kill him, she loses me forever, or he kills me, and she has to put up with him forever. I've been playing a losing hand for too long, and I can tell you that it's obvious that you can protect her better than I can."

"No sir, I can't," I hung my head for a moment, not knowing how to say it. "I will do all I can, but eventually, I will have to move on. I've traveled the whole world moving on because people can't understand what it's like to be me. My," I paused, "my father set me on a challenging journey. I traveled the Arctic Circle, I have been spurned by many and applauded by more, but always I have to move on in the end."

"That's about the most cryptic shit I've ever heard." Mr. Johnson picked up another box almost as big as the one I was stacking. "I would say you're a mercenary, but there's something more to all this, and I'm not going to ask again. You're doing a great job, and those boys working with you respect you and are working more than they ever have here. As long as you're good to my Caroline, you are welcome here, and I'm sorry I didn't come out and stand next to you this morning."

"I'm not a mercenary." I placed the giant box on a new palette. "I'm just me."

"Well, you keep being you," Mr. Johnson said as he wiped his hands and brushed off his pants. "I appreciate you letting me help you."

I looked at him and smiled. I often wondered what my smile looked like, but he smiled back, turned, and walked to his office.

I didn't see Caroline until the end of the day. She was back with Anna and came into the warehouse on her way home. She walked over to me and handed me a small bag, "I got you some food."

"You didn't have to do that." I could smell the food and knew it would taste good.

"If you haven't figured it out yet, I don't need anybody telling me what I can or can't do. If I wanna get you food, I will get you food," Anna looked up as her mom talked to me. "Now you eat that and have a good night. I have some work to do, and Anna will keep me company."

I thanked Caroline, took the bag, got my lunch box, and took the slow walk home only a few blocks away.

When I reached my tiny apartment, Mrs. Abigail was standing in the driveway, wearing a lovely pink moo moo with curlers in her hair. "Are you having a good day, Mr. Griffin?"

"Yes, ma'am." I started to walk up the stairs to my little apartment.

"Do you smell smoke, Mr. Griffin?" Mrs. Abigail turned and looked towards the area I had just left.

I looked up and saw the trailing smoke go into the air. It has always amazed me how smoke and fire were almost as alive as I was. I heard the sirens in the distance and left my pack and dinner on the stairs rushing back the way I had come.

As I got closer, I could hear the flames, and turning the corner, I saw the warehouse I had just left engulfed in flames. My walk became a run as I made it to the front. Mr. Johnson was lying on the ground, face bloodied, covered in soot, trying to sit up.

"They took Anna," he looked at me with the pleading eyes of a father. "Caroline is still in there. The fire is too hot, and I couldn't get to her."

I saw the flames rising in the warehouse, and it reminded me of so many years ago when I was the target and people tried to set me on fire. I survived and have respected fire ever since. Some people thought I was afraid, but I was not. I knew fire was a primal force that could barely be stopped. I knew what that was like.

I grabbed a hose from outside the warehouse, sprayed myself with water, and then rushed inside as firefighters ran to try to stop me.

The inside of the warehouse was a scene from hell. Flames attacked cardboard and wood, and the heat would have instantly caused an ordinary man to collapse. I looked at the office and saw the door was open. At the bottom of the stairs, Caroline was there. Her body was crumpled to the ground, and I ran and picked her up. She felt limp in my arms. I did not even want to consider the possibility that she was gone. The door was still open, and I ran to it. I curled her as small as possible, so my body shielded her from most of the heat. I grabbed her hair with my arm when it started to spark and realized my shirt was also on fire. I ran faster, and as I entered the air in front of the warehouse, I felt the hose spray down on me from Mr. Johnson.

Paramedics rushed to Caroline, but they all looked at me as well. I stood quietly for a moment until I realized that what was once a shirt was now ashes, and the water spray had revealed the terrible scars all over my body. My wrists bound together by suture now grown together as one. My neck, arms, shoulders, and legs all bore the scars of my creation. I saw one of the people watching gasp as another simply mouthed the letters, "WTF."

Mr. Johnson looked at me as Caroline coughed. "Are you okay?"

"I'm fine," I looked around and saw the truck, then I saw Sam holding Anna in the back of his truck.

I began walking towards them, and Sam saw me. Anna was screaming. Sam's two friends jumped into the back of the pickup as Sam pushed Anna into the front seat and started the truck. I started running towards them, but the truck started spraying gravel as they drove away. I was frustrated until a large F350 pulled up next to me. Mr. Johnson was sitting inside. "Get in."

I got in the truck, and before the door was closed, the giant engine roared to life after Sam and Anna.

"I'm not gonna ask what happened to you," Mr. Johnson was purely focused on the road ahead but spoke as he drove, "I just need to save my granddaughter. Can you help me?"

"Yes sir," I said as he took a corner in a full slide.

"They're heading out to the quarry. The boy is an idiot, and I'm worried about what he may do. Caroline told him to stay away and that she was getting a protective order to keep him away from Anna. He said something idiotic and started beating up Caroline. I knocked him down, and if it weren't for those two idiots he has with him, I would have ended the situation. Instead, he set my place on fire and left Caroline to die. He would have killed me too if all the people hadn't come up."

"I know his kind. They are cowards, and we will get Anna back," I watched the road slide past. Soon we were on the tail of Sam's pick-up.

Sam took a sharp curve on a gravel road, and suddenly we were parallel to a deep quarry. Without warning, he slammed on the brakes, and the two men in the back struggled to hold on, not to be thrown from the vehicle. Sam jumped out of the front and closed the door trapping Anna inside. He was carrying a tire iron, and the two men jumped out next to him.

I got out of the truck as Mr. Johnson slowed and jumped to the ground while the truck came to a stop. I landed with a solid thump and was steady. I walked to Sam and his friends with careful determination. For the first time in a long time, I felt I had a reason for being in the situation I was about to be in.

"You seem to have a wardrobe problem," Sam slapped the tire iron on his hand as he walked toward me.

"Look at his skin," one of his friends said. "He looks like he's been ripped to pieces and put back together again."

"That sounds like a good idea," Sam slapped the tire iron against his hand and winced a little when it struck.

The three men widened out around me. I saw Mr. Johnson over to the side. He pulled a baseball bat out from behind his seat and started walking over as well. This changed things a little for Sam but not for me. I looked over at Mr. Johnson, then glanced at the cab of their truck, and he understood. Anna was the priority.

"We're going to try this again, and this time it's not going to go as good for you." Sam moved forward and swung at me. I grabbed the tire iron as it swung and held it tight. It vibrated in my hand from the impact, and I know that Sam felt it far worse than I ever could. I pulled the tire iron away from him and threw it into the quarry.

"All I wanted was to finally be left alone, and there is always someone like you." My eyes narrowed on Sam. "I'm going to ask you nicely to leave me alone. If all of you leave town, this will go easier."

"Sure, we'll do that." Sam was wearing a nasty smirk even though it was apparent that his hand still hurt as he held it. "So we can avoid the murder charge from killing your ass."

"Just remember," I looked at all three of them, "I gave you a chance."

The two men swung at me from different sides. I let them hit me. Sam swung immediately after, and I wondered if he broke his hand. One of the men ripped the rest of my shirt off, exposing the numerous scars from where limbs had been attached, nerves stretched, and a circulatory system built from scratch. To an outsider, I was nothing but a patchwork man, but I was a miracle born of a man's dream and the living power of the storm. I saw Mr. Johnson get Anna into his truck, and I swung sideways, knocking both men twenty feet into the air. They crashed onto the ground and rolled in pain.

Sam was indignant even in the face of impossible odds against him. He pulled the pistol from his pocket and aimed it at me. I smashed it in my hand, and the pistol exploded as my fingers crushed the cartridges to the point where the bullets went off. Unfortunately, Sam's hand was there too. The bloody fingers he pulled away were dark with powder burns as blood ran down his arm.

"You just couldn't leave me alone, could you?" My voice was rising, and I felt pure anger. I liked Caroline, Anna, and Mr. Johnson. I liked Mrs. Abigail. I was furious, and there was a tear in my eye as I dropped Sam to the ground crying like a child. "Let's set the record straight on what you're up against."

I walked the twenty feet to his truck and knelt. I slammed my fingers through the side of the door and around the truck's frame right at the door. I screamed. It echoed in the quarry and through the woods surrounding the quarry. It was a primal scream born out of the storm that gave me life. I stood, and the truck tilted up as I pulled that side off the ground. The truck was now at a forty-degree angle with the tires nearest me dangling off the ground, but I wasn't done. I pulled the truck back towards me in one motion and pushed up. The snap was like lifting a piece of paper, and the truck was now above my head, held by the frame in my hand. My fury knew no bounds as I looked over at Sam and his friends, watching me in disbelief.

"Do we have a problem?" I said in a voice louder than one hundred thunderclaps. I let the truck slide towards me just a little, then pushed it. Muscles never meant to see life again flexed with the power they should never have had as the truck went airborne and landed somewhere in the middle of the quarry. There was a crash, then a splash as the truck sank to the bottom of the water in the quarry.

I brushed my hands off and walked to Sam. The two men who had backed him up were now huddled together, looking at me in disbelief and terror. I reached down, and Sam cringed as I lifted him by his shirt and felt the threads strain. "Should you join your truck?"

Sam lowered his head. "No." He looked at his hand. "I'll leave town."

"Only to come back later for me? Or for Caroline or Anna?"

"I might be less than perfect, but I'm not that stupid," Sam was sullen and obviously in pain.

"Gonna tell the world and have them come for me?"

"Who would believe me?" Sam was crying. "I'm such an idiot."

I dropped Sam and walked over to Mr. Johnson's truck. He too was looking at me in disbelief. Anna was snuggled into his arms, having seen nothing.

"Should I walk home?"

"No," he said, "Get in. I think I owe you a lot."

The drive back to town was quiet. Anna held my hand. The warehouse was damaged horribly, but the insurance adjuster was already there. Caroline was at the hospital, and I asked Mr. Johnson to drop me off at my apartment.

"I am going to see you tomorrow?" Mr. Johnson asked.

"It might be better if I move on," I put my hands in my pockets, "I'm not sure if I should stay. Once people learn a little about me, they don't want me around."

"I thought you just wanted to be left alone." Anna was now asleep on the front seat.

"I just want peace." I lowered my eyes for a moment.

"I can't always promise peace, but I can promise a good paycheck. It looks like we have a lot to rebuild. See you in the morning?"

I looked up at the sky. It was the first time someone had seen even a little of what I was, and they still wanted me around.

"Yes sir." I felt the breeze flow against my skin and knew I needed to change clothes, "I'll be there early so we can get started."

"I'll tell Caroline, and I'll let you know how she is in the morning." Mr. Johnson drove away. I walked to my little apartment, hoping that tomorrow would finally be a peaceful day.

THE EAVESDROPPER

H.G. Evans

Eavesdropping became a habit that winter.

It's their own fault, really. If they didn't want to be overheard, they should have taken better precautions before starting their conversations.

I simply cannot be blamed for what occurred due to their lack of care in establishing safeguards. I mean, really. To say I am at fault is truly ridiculous.

The first time was merely happenstance. And, I might add, I was firmly situated long before those two came along.

It was not my fault that the two seating areas were separated by only a bookcase. Granted, one that reached from floor to ceiling and ten feet in length, but the chairs in both areas were positioned right up against the wall of books. Back-to-back, you could say. And a shelf of books does not a good sound barrier make, in my humble opinion.

Who chooses a bookstore to plan a murder, anyway?

And if you do happen to be so inclined, it would seem only logical to choose a place that would ensure privacy. To this end, I will reiterate—I cannot be blamed for what happened next.

It wasn't the whispered words themselves that distracted me from the mediocre plot my second favorite author had contrived—really, I expected so much more from her, but everyone has a mishap now and then, I suppose—it was the urgency that floated between the books to my unsuspecting ears that seized my attention.

As the words on the page before me faltered under suddenly shaky vision, my mother's voice rang between the walls of my mind. *Matilda, how many times must I tell you that eavesdropping is rude? One day, young lady, you will listen in on the wrong conversation and then...*

Mother never did finish that particular sentence, not that I found that to be a distressing thing. I rarely listened to Mother, for various reasons. Not the least being her penchant for exaggeration.

But I digress. We were discussing the fate of one unknown victim whose life it was now my responsibility to save. After all, one cannot sit by and simply let another human being be murdered. That would be uncivilized in the worst way.

Unless it was a pedophile whose demise was being decided. Yes, then I could stand by. Return to the middling plot between the covers of the book clenched tightly in my fingers. Or an abuser. Yes, then too. Really, there was nothing more abhorrent than a human being who was willing to hurt another for no reason other than power or pleasure. Sometimes both, if one was honest with herself while overhearing—not eavesdropping, mind you. I could not help that these ruffians chose to sit so close while scheming—the expiration date of the unsuspecting prey. The two men must be quite foolish if they allowed such a mishap to occur. Much easier to stop them, then.

Or help, possibly? If their quarry truly was a bane upon the virtue of the human race, well, it wouldn't be a sin to help their agenda along, would it?

Unfortunately, the conspirators ended their conversation before I could learn the identity of their victim. It seemed that the daily grind impeded upon those who assisted Death as well as those of us featuring more mundane existences; Plotter One's lunch break was over.

They would be back, then, tomorrow, same time? It worked for Plotter Two, the deeper voice of the connivers. It was quite pleasant to listen to, actually, melodic and smooth. But again, I have strayed from the hub of their dialogue.

Tomorrow.

They were meeting again tomorrow, to finalize plans.

Well.

It meant rearranging my weekly excursion to the grocery store, but I was able to sort it out and regain my position from the day before, though it did require a few harrowing and nail-biting moments when I found the chair occupied by a young man in ripped jeans and headphones that covered half his head—the poor dear, he really should invest in some earbuds, they were much more economical, and shouldn't he be in school anyway?—but only four minutes passed before he lifted lanky limbs from the cushions and wandered off. It was a wonder he didn't trip, scrolling through his phone while walking. It was a feat undertaken by all young people nowadays, and one I will never understand. Look up, see the world, that's what I say.

Admittedly, I had peeked into the alcove on the other side of my reading spot as I navigated the shelves of books, but Plotters One and Two had not yet arrived. Just as well, what with the delay Mr. Headphones generated.

I know what you're thinking; *Matilda is now eavesdropping. There can be no question, this time.* But I assure you, that is not the case. I was saving a life—a notably honorable thing to do, unlike a common spy's snooping. Or was I planning to assist in the demise of the unsuspecting target? It was impossible to know, as I did not yet have all the information needed at my disposal.

So, it happened that the second instance of listening in on Plotters One and Two did occur in a premeditated manner, but it was not eavesdropping. This was life or death. I would receive a medal, an article in the paper, no doubt, when it was all said and done.

I settled into the cushions but could not relax, nor concentrate on the words before me. I admit to simply staring at the pages as a means of continuing the ruse of reading, though the inked lines bounced off my mind and right out of my skull before any could truly penetrate.

It was indeed irritating to have my daily peaceful interlude interrupted, though I could not pretend there wasn't a fission of excitement as well. While routines were preferable, they could also grow tedious.

So deep was I in my musings that I almost missed the arrival of Plotters One and Two. It was Two's velvety baritone that pulled me from all other thoughts, landing squarely on their resumed conspiracy.

It wasn't long before I realized their plans were to be set in motion tonight. Their quarry would be at

Seaman's Wharf at nine o'clock that very evening.

My pulse accelerated toward sprint speed, galloping along as I realized the imminence of the affair.

Tonight.

I still did not know if I should be hindering or helping the plotters on the other side of the bookcase, but if I were to show up at Seaman's Wharf and see the man— for they continually referred to their prey as *he*—then I would know. I was certain a man with unsavory aptitudes would be obvious at first glance.

So excited was I for the evening's event that I almost missed the departure of the plotters. That would not do at all. I needed to see their faces, know who it was I would be impeding or assisting in a few hours' time.

I scurried from the depths of the cushions, cursing my lack of foresight. I should have been prepared for every occurrence, yet my coat and purse had been haphazardly discarded upon arrival. It was to my detriment, as I leaped from the chair only to trip over both objects and crash to the floor, novel flopping from my fingers and skidding across the polished wood slats.

By the time I regained my footing and disentangled myself from the well-meaning, though entirely unwanted, intentions of the man who believed chivalry to be all well and good and dashed across the alcove to assist me... the plotters were gone. The *harrumph* that blew past my pursed lips was unladylike, to be sure, and enough to cause Mr. Chivalry to retreat to his own chair. After straightening my shirt and smoothing my hair, I gathered my things and rushed home.

Preparations must be made before the trek to Seaman's Wharf.

It wasn't as difficult to hide as I expected. The newly purchased black clothing—dull and lifeless in color and appeal (precisely why I never wore the horrid color)—did its job quite well at blending my form into the night. Concealed by shadows and a dumpster that gave new definition to the words repulsive and stench, I crouched. And waited.

Like any good sleuth, I had scouted the area during daylight and arrived an hour early to maneuver into place without being seen. Because of my prowess, I had an excellent view of the boardwalk (virtually deserted during the frigid winter months), the entrance to Seaman's Pub (never lacking for patronage, no matter the season), and the pier itself. I was quite satisfied with my efforts, though my limbs were stiff with cold by the appointed meeting time.

Adrenaline spiked as the time on my watch drew closer to the nine o'clock hour, flushing my cold skin and dancing along every nerve ending. My gaze swept the boardwalk, the pub, the pier, repeatedly as the minutes ticked by. Each shadowed form sent my heart racing, only to stall with disappointment as the patrons swept the pub door wide and disappeared inside.

At five minutes past, concern dulled the edges of adrenaline. Perhaps I had misheard the time? The place? But no, my hearing was excellent; I had just completed my yearly physical with my doctor who had checked all boxes on the form with enthusiasm. No, my information was unerringly correct, of that I had no doubt.

Most likely, the victim was running late. People these days had no true concept of time. Or of manners.

They unfailingly showed up several minutes past the appointed time with no apology on their lips to ease their disgruntled host. Truly heinous conduct.

Though, in this case, it could prove to be in favor of the prey; perhaps Plotters One and Two would grow bored and leave without completing their task. I had yet to see anyone who would match their descriptions either. Admittedly, their likenesses were due to my imaginative mind, having never seen their faces, but I was confident I would recognize the plotters upon first sight.

At ten minutes past, annoyance had edged out all excitement and adrenaline, allowing room for the cold to numb each extremity. This was all very disappointing, to say the least. Something had gone awry, there could be no other explanation. Unforeseen circumstances had delayed the inevitable.

Fifteen minutes past the hour, I had had quite enough, thank you, and was ready to abandon this charade and partake in the pricey merlot I had purchased to celebrate the conclusion of events—whatever that might entail—and erase the chill from my body. I supposed it could also be used in commiseration as well.

As I rose from my crouched position, stiff muscles protesting all the while, I was startled by a velvety smooth voice behind me.

"There you are! We have been waiting for you, darling. Come. We don't want to miss the show!"

I suddenly found my arm tucked into the elbow of a tall man, his gloved hand folded over mine where it lay on his arm. Stunned, I could do nothing but keep in step as he propelled me to the pier and down the worn planks.

"I must tell you, we were beginning to think you had abandoned us."

"Oh?" I answered in a daze, an insistent nudging to the back of my mind creating as much of a distraction as the warmth of this stranger's hand on mine, his body strong and lithe beside me.

"But I told them both, 'She will come. We must have patience.'"

I glanced up at the chiseled profile of my unexpected companion just as his head turned and his gaze bore down into mine. It was then that it all clicked into place in my mind, the affectionate words a direct contrast to the coldness in his eyes, the voice—familiar, yet previously unplaced—pressing against the memories of bookstore conversations hidden behind a wall of books.

I stared up into the face of Plotter Two, suddenly very cold indeed.

And that was how I found myself trussed up like a turkey, ropes digging painfully into the skin at my wrists and ankles as Plotter One finally cut the cabin cruiser's engine, the abrupt lack of sound from the boat's motor almost as jarring as the circumstances in which I now found myself.

It appeared that I had made several gross miscalculations, though many were still not quite clear. And by "many," I mean "all."

I was at a complete loss as to why I had been bundled onto the boat parked at the end of the pier— one shrouded in darkness that I had missed entirely in my perusal, aka stakeout—and why I seemed to be the only bound occupant. Surely Plotters One and Two had not abandoned their original mission just to confiscate little old me.

"If you are thinking I am a witness and therefore must dispose of me, then I assure you I have nothing to tell." It was the only reason I could think of as to why I found myself in this predicament.

Plotter Two lounged on the padded seat across from my constrained form. Though the night was dark, no moonlight to speak of, there was sufficient lighting on the boat to see the mirth on my captor's face.

"Really, you are remarkably slow," Plotter Two drawled, leaning forward.

Well, that wouldn't do. Not at all. I refused to be spoken of in such derogatory terms.

"I beg your—"

"She said this one wasn't too bright," Plotter One interrupted as he climbed down from the wheel.

"I will have you know—"

Plotter Two's fingers snapped loudly an inch from my nose, effectively startling me into silence. "You still aren't getting it, darling." His melodic voice was tinged with annoyance. "*You're* the mark."

"The what?"

What mark? Was there a stain on my clothing? Perhaps I had rubbed up against that foul dumpster? Though, wearing black and being the dead of night, I found it hard to believe these two would see any imperfection on the material. Maybe there was a smudge of something on my cheek?

"The *mark*, love. The one we were after."

Well, that didn't sound right at all.

"No, you were talking about a man. You kept referring to your quarry as 'he.'"

Plotters One and Two exchanged a look that fanned the flame of my own irritation.

"Untie me, you imbeciles. I was simply there to help you." No need to mention the inverse option and that I hadn't decided yet as to which I would choose. It would not be helpful at this time.

Plotter Two sighed. "I need you to focus for a moment, love. Ever hear of *staging*?"

What was this idiot prattling on about? I glanced out over the water, but it was too dark to see anything. I settled for listening to the waves lapping gently against the hull of the boat.

"Hey." Plotter One's finger snapped in front of my face much as his partner's had; someone should really tell them it was unconscionably rude. "We're tellin' ya that the conversation you eavesdropped on in the bookstore was all for your benefit, sweetheart. We weren't after anyone but you."

I shook my head to dispel the confusion clouding my thoughts, but everything remained muddled. "That doesn't make any sense."

Plotter One sighed and turned toward the shadowed maw of the cabin. "You wanna come out here and set her straight?"

It was more with interest than fear that I watched a slim form mount the cabin steps onto the deck. After all, there was no real danger; this was all a simple misunderstanding.

"I warned you, didn't I, Matilda darling?"

It took a moment for my mother's voice and the apparition before me to merge and make any kind of sense.

"Mother?"

She tilted her glass of wine in my direction, almost as if in a toast. "You really must learn to be quicker on the draw, my dear." Mother tapped a manicured finger against her temple.

"Really, Mother? A bit overdramatic, don't you think?" I turned my gaze pointedly to the ropes holding me hostage.

"Not in the slightest, Matilda. You see, your eavesdropping habit has gotten you into a bit more trouble than you realize."

"Mother, I don't eavesdrop." The words were exasperated, a repeat of a thirty-year-old conversation. "This is ridiculous."

Mother ignored my irritation, strolling a few paces closer as she sipped her wine. "You weren't too far off, sweetheart. You were witness to a confidential conversation never meant for your ears. Just not the one you think."

I sniffed. "I'm sure I don't know what you mean."

Mother sighed. "No, I don't suppose you do."

"Then untie me and let me get on with my evening, won't you?" The wine waiting on my counter beckoned.

"I'm afraid that won't be possible, darling. You see, while the exchange you overheard in the bookstore was meant for you, the one you chose to listen in on last week outside my office door…" She shook her head sadly. "I always warned you about your penchant for nosiness. That it would get you in trouble one day."

"I have no idea what conversation you are referring to," I said, though there was something tickling the edges of memory… phrases that had seemed mundane at the time taking on a fresh and… sinister meaning. I looked at my mother with a new understanding; had she been involved in nefarious deeds my entire life? Or only more recently?

Mother bent at the waist to look me in the eye. I found myself unable to look away.

"Don't lie, darling; it's not becoming of a lady."

"Neither is tying up your own daughter," I sniffed, though the words lacked heat. Unease had seeped into my bones, a suspicion that this banter might be more significant than I first believed.

"Your nasty little habit is no fault of mine." Mother straightened. "You must take responsibility for your actions, Matilda."

"I carry no fault here," I snapped, writhing against the bindings around my wrists and ankles. "If people do not want their discussions overheard, then they should take better precautions."

It was no use; the knots were expertly made and refused to give even the slightest bit. I halted my struggles, panting from exertion. How much further would Mother take this before releasing me? I had never known her to go to such extremes to make a point before.

Mother sighed. "I see we are at an impasse."

I glared up her, wondering just how far she would take this new persona—though she wore it so easily, I had to wonder how new it might truly be.

"I'm sorry, darling. I truly am." Mother rested her palm against my cheek for the briefest moment before turning back toward the cabin stairs. "Don't say I didn't warn you."

I was still staring at the place where Mother had disappeared when Plotters One and Two each grabbed an arm and hauled me to my feet. I wobbled precariously, my tightly bound ankles unable to provide stability.

"To the edge now," Plotter One said, gesturing toward the silver railing that circled the cruiser.

His voice was pitched much higher than Plotter Two, and quite nasal in quality. It was not pleasant to listen to at all. I gave Plotter One my best haughty stare. "And how do you suggest I get there when you have me trussed up like a common barn animal?"

"Hop, sweetheart, I don't care."

Hop? How undignified. I most certainly would *not* be hopping anywhere. "I don't think so," I stated primly.

And what did they think would happen once I reached the rail? If they expected me to swim to shore as punishment for the imagined deeds Mother had laid at my feet, I would not be doing it while bound by rope. They might as well release me now.

Plotter One sighed and looked at his partner. "No hope for it, then. Let's get this over with."

It was as firm hands once again grasped my arms, lifting and moving my body toward the railing, that the unease felt before returned full force. Perhaps they didn't mean to untie me at all. *Perhaps they...*

One last appeal certainly couldn't hurt.

"Mother is prone to exaggeration, you know," I said as the cold silver barrier pressed into my stomach. Frigid winter wind tugged at the repulsive black clothing, causing a shiver to move through my body. "I do not eavesdrop."

"Sure, sweetheart." Plotter One's voice was distracted as he peered over the rail and into the dark water below.

"I cannot be held accountable for other people's lack of caution."

"Uh-huh."

Really, Plotter One could be more engaged in the conversation. It was insulting to have him so preoccupied while I spoke. I turned my attention to Plotter Two.

"Surely you can see how this conjured fault cannot be laid at my feet."

"Yup. Sure do," Plotter Two said, the words belying his unfocused tone and gaze.

Rough hands lifted my body, the railing no longer a hindrance, with both men taking part in the effort. The drop to the water below was quick, the frigid waves shocking my system into immobility. I sank quickly, the blurred forms of Plotters One and Two receding as the water claimed me.

Surely, they would see the error of Mother's claims and retrieve me from the icy bonds that held me as absolutely as the rope affixed to my wrists and ankles.

Surely, I would not be held responsible for the fallibility of others.

Surely, I would not be punished for something that was no fault of mine.

Surely—

THE EVIL WITHIN...

Marianne Wieland

I am here. With you. In you. Behind you. Everywhere and nowhere. Can you feel me? I'll never leave you. Ever. You know me. You always have. I see you look to the right. That's it. I know you feel me. I see it in the way you walk. In the way you look behind as you try to pretend you don't know I am there. I back off to give you enough space to think I might have left you, but in your mind, you know I am still there. Watching.

My power over you grows every day, but the time when I am strongest is at night. As the light dwindles from the day, I see your steps grow faster, and in your haste to reach safety, you trip and almost fall down the embankment. My intention was that you would. But because of me, you have developed a bit of caution in the things you do. The places you go. But no matter how hard you try, I will be with you, just out of your reach.

The light from the day is almost gone. Snuffed out one more time. Will you see another day? I hope so, for I am not finished with you. I will never be finished with you. I see you stop and pull your sweater tight around you as if that might help keep me at bay. You rub your forehead and look behind you once again. There. I am a living thing, and I am growing as the night grows. And I know you know it too.

Your goal is in sight now. I see you quicken your steps in your haste to outrun me, but I will be there when you arrive. And you know that. The house is dark. You hesitate to enter. Did you leave a light on? I know you think so. But you are not sure. I see you look behind once more before you enter. You think you can close the door and keep me out, but that is impossible, and we both know that.

I watch as you enter the house and quickly lock the door. You lean your back to it and close your eyes for a moment. But I am with you. I own you. You will never escape from me. Not in this lifetime.

I hear you gasp. I see your eyes fly open. You are paralyzed by your mind. Good... good. I know what you are thinking. I see it in your face. You wonder if you might have locked it inside with you. You still cannot move. I see sweat forming on your forehead as you contemplate how you will get out of this. But I am still there, watching and waiting as you empower me.

The light illuminates the room. You found the light switch, and for a moment, I feel you push me away. I feel how hard it is for you to take a step, but you manage to do it. I see you searching around the room with your eyes for something in which to protect yourself. There is no protection from me. And I know you know that.

You slowly make your way into the kitchen and turn the light on. You grab a kitchen knife like that will have any effect on me. I see the hairs are raised on your arms. Just as I planned. I follow you as you move from room to room, turning on the lights as you go. There is no hope. I will win. I know this even though my power over you has grown less and less with every light that comes my way. You did this, and you will pay.

I back off for now. I let you feel safe for a short time. But I am not finished with you. I am never finished with you. I sink into the shadows as I watch you pick up your phone and punch in 911, but you do not hit send. I see what you are doing. You think you can beat me at this game, and that help will come to save you from me, but that will never happen. We have been playing this game for too long for you to let me go now. I have become part of you.

The weather is turning. Good… good. This will work in my favor. You hear something fall in another room, and instantly I am there. Back with full force as your finger hovers over the 'send' button. You grab the knife and the phone as you slowly make your way behind the couch. I grow. You feel me in every nerve of your body. In every breath you take. You know I will win. I always do.

You hit 'send' like I knew you eventually would. I hear your frightened voice as it talks to the dispatcher. You say you think someone is in your house. They will send an officer to check it out and tell you to remain calm. They will not be in any hurry as this is a call they get from you almost every day. I rule you. I have destroyed your credibility. You have lost your friends and most of your family because of me. Soon you will have no one, and it will just be you and me. Here. Together. Forever. I will never leave you, and that is your greatest fear.

The knock on the door sounds, and you jump, grasping the knife tighter. Will you use it on someone? I know you think so if you have to defend yourself. But I will be there twisting your thoughts until your fear is two-fold. I prey on that in you. You don't know which danger is worse. The physical threat or the threat of the law. Consequences. I will make sure you don't forget either. I will keep these thoughts alive long after the officer has gone.

You sit on the couch as the officer searches the house. He says it is clear. No one is there, just like no one is ever there after you place the call. He rolls his eyes as you beg him to check in the attic and the basement. He tells you the open window has been closed and that the wind probably made the noise you heard. I see the panic in your eyes as he gets ready to leave. You are thinking of the open window. Someone could have come in that way. You know the search was not thorough. It never is.

You know you cannot sit there forever. It is late, and you are tired. You are afraid to sleep. I am still with you. Beside you. I will give you no peace. No rest. You feel my power growing inside you. You think you see a shadow in the hall. I see your panic rise. I tickle the back of your neck, and it feels like the finger of death is upon you. Good... good. I have you where I want you.

There. Right there. I know you see another shadow. Is it me, or is it real? I have twisted your thoughts, and you can no longer separate reality from imagination. I see your fingers clutch the handle of the knife once again. I want more. This is not nearly enough for me. No... not nearly enough. I want blind terror from you, and I can make it happen. I move through your mind invading your senses. I make you hear music, and you frantically look around. Bach's *Tocatta and Fugue in D Minor*. Yes... you were frightened by that one early in life, just as many have been, and you have never forgotten it. I have made sure of that. Run, little mouse. You won't escape.

Here I am. Waiting for you to let me overtake you. I am your master now. I make the music continue, getting louder and louder. I see you drop the knife and put your hands over your ears, trying to shut me out. You back into a closed door, and you feel me on the other side. You feel me shake the door trying to get to you. I see the fright on your face. You can almost see me now.

I have overtaken your senses. All of them. I have never overtaken them all at once. What will you do? I grow as you feed me. You can hear me in the music. You can feel me at your back. Can you smell it? The smell of death. Of blood. Do you remember? I will make sure that you do. I increase the intensity of the music. Wait! You stop. Your hands are still over your ears. Is that someone coming up the basement stairs? You see the door start to open. I grip you with everything I have now. Your scream seems like it will never end. Over and over, you scream. I feel you gasp for breath. You can't take much more. Good... good. You have given yourself over to me. At last.

They are coming, like they have before. You can't hear the sirens because the music is too loud, and your screaming doesn't stop like it has before. You are remembering that day, aren't you? I meant it to be this way. This has been my goal. I knew I would break you. You know you deserve it after what you did. Yes... remember? I know you do. I was born out of your unspeakable act.

Your screams have cut into your vocal cords, but you know they are still coming for you. You knew they would eventually. You knew you would never escape. I make sure you see blood on your hands and clothes just like that other time. You retch from the smell, but your stomach is empty. You begin to cough, and you don't know whether to cover your ears or your nose. I see you moving quickly from room to room, looking for a place to hide, but you won't find any solace.

They are at the door now. Shouting your name. Trying to break in. People have gathered on your lawn. Some look worried. Others just say they aren't surprised at anything that goes on in your house. The door is broken now. Kicked in by those you called for help. I have you backed into a corner. Nowhere to go now. You have picked up the knife. Good... good. I know the moment that you realize what you must do.

Hurry! You must be quick. They are almost upon you! I see you grab the knife and hold it in front of you like you held it in front of him. He begged for mercy, but you gave him none. There will be no mercy for you now. You plunge the knife into your gut like you did to him. Yes. You have done this before. You know how it ends. Your mouth is open in a silent scream. Your bloodshot eyes are bulging. You fall to the side.

Many are there now. But they are too late. I have won like I knew I would. I played the game through to the end. Your end. You got the ending you deserved. I made it so. You always knew I would. I back away. I have done my job.

They have gone. All that remains now is the blood you spilled. I am but a memory. Someone is coming. Who would be here? Yes... curiosity seekers. Young people. I wait. They come in looking for a good scare. Little do they know the horror that I can create. They squeal at the sight of the blood. They run, laughing out the door. They got what they came for. All except for... one.

She is riveted to the spot. Equally drawn and abhorred by the sight of the blood and knowing that death ruled this house a short time ago. She gasps when a branch hits the window. She backs away and almost falls over in her haste to get away. I grow quickly. I move over her.

She looks behind her. Good, good... you know me too...

THE EX

Anonymous

"Andy wants to go to the beach one more time," Rachel said to her new husband as her young son tugged on her leg. "His dad is supposed to be driving up to get him today, but I have no idea when he'll be here. Do you mind hanging out to wait? Just send me a text when he arrives, okay?"

"Of course," James replied, keeping the rest of his thoughts to himself. It was the first time that Rachel's ex-husband, Frank, had agreed to drive all the way to her place to pick up their son. Generally, he forced her to drive halfway—usually over half way—to meet him. Rachel was surprised when he offered to drive the whole distance this time. But James wasn't surprised. He knew how men like Frank thought, and he knew this was not done as an act of kindness. He had agreed to drive the six hours for one reason and one reason only: he wanted to check out their new property. Specifically, he wanted the chance to figure out what was wrong with their property so that he could bring that up to Rachel every chance he got in order to make her feel bad about her purchase and make himself feel a bit better about his own miserable life.

Yes, James knew how Frank thought.

Looking around at their new land, James acknowledged that there were things that Frank could find to criticize. They had bought a fixer-up, and there was a lot of fixing-up to do. But James could see beyond that work to the potential that was there, and in his mind, the place was perfect. Twenty acres of tall trees—maples and ash and what the locals called "ironwood" trees. The house was solidly built and mostly just needed a bit of "prettying up." There was a nice, new, deep well and a decent septic system. And there was a large garage—large enough for him to keep half a dozen tractors inside: one with a mower deck for the grass, one with a tiller attachment for when they were ready to plant their garden, one with a back-hoe attachment, one all decked out with a snow blower and cab for when winter came, and of course the one or two that he was currently tinkering on. *Yes,* he thought, looking around at their new homestead. *It really is just perfect for us.*

His thoughts were interrupted by the sound of a car coming down their remote dirt road. He turned to look, thinking again how wonderful it was that their peace was seldom disturbed even by the sound of a passing car. This car, though, didn't pass. It turned and pulled into the driveway. *So here he is,* James thought to himself. *He has braved the "wilderness" in order to try to bash another one of Rachel's dreams. But he's not going to get away with it this time.*

James should have sent a message to Rachel right away, letting her know that Frank was here. The beach they were at was only five minutes away. They could be back in no time, and Frank and Tommy could be on their way once more. James didn't text Rachel. He wanted a chance to talk with Frank first. Alone.

"Where's Andy?" Frank asked as he stepped out of the car.

"Rachel took him down to the beach," James told him. "They should be back anytime," he added, knowing it was a lie. They would probably be gone for hours.

"So, this is your new place," Frank replied, scanning the house with obvious contempt in his eyes. "It looks like you've got a lot of work to do."

"Perhaps," James acknowledged, "but it's all things I can do, things I've done before. I've done a lot of construction in my day. You?"

"Oh, I've done a bit," Frank replied, the lie rolling easily off his tongue. James knew it was a lie—Rachel had told him enough stories of her past life for James to know exactly what Frank was capable of and what he wasn't. Building of any kind was not something that Frank was capable of doing—he was much better, it seemed, at tearing things down. Things and people.

"The house needs some work," James repeated, preparing his trap. "But we really bought this place for the land. You up for a walk?" he asked, knowing full well that Frank was not the walking type. "I want to show you the best part."

Frank looked at him skeptically, clearly trying to decide if the effort of a walk was worth it.

"I have a small hunting cabin in the woods," James told Frank. "About a quarter of a mile in. The perfect man cave. You just have to come see it." There was a shack in the woods, and James did have plans to hunt from it come fall. That much was true. He hadn't had a chance yet, to do much more than store a few of his hunting things in there—it wasn't really ready to show off to anyone yet. But no matter. It would serve its purpose.

He started walking towards the forest, knowing that Frank would have no choice but to follow him. Before long, he heard Frank's panting behind him. He didn't bother to turn around until they reached the shack.

Then he heard Frank snicker. "*This* is your ultimate man cave?" Frank asked, incredulous. "*This* is what you brought me all the way out here to see?"

"It might not look like much from out here," James acknowledged, "but there are a few things inside that might impress you. Come on," he added, motioning for Frank to step through the sagging doorway. He stepped in after and closed—and locked—the door.

Perhaps it was the sound of the lock that suddenly set Frank on edge. Perhaps it was the fact that the windows were all boarded up, and only a faint hint of light shone through a small crack in the ceiling. James could feel Frank's tension rise, but he was still trying to play it cool. "So," Frank asked as he scanned around the small building, trying to accustom his eyes to the darkness inside. "Where are these things that might impress me?" He turned around then, and came face to face with one of "these things"—a shotgun held by James and pointed directly at him.

"I don't do a lot of hunting, really," James admitted. He could admit anything now; what did it matter? "Mostly just getting rid of unwanted vermin from the property."

Frank, realizing he was trapped, let down his friendly facade. He would fight back with the only weapon he had—his words. "I should have known not to trust you," he spat at James. "You're just like that bitch, Rachel. All she's ever done is try to ruin my life."

"That woman gave you everything she had," James replied, working hard to keep his temper in check. "She gave you all she had to try to make you a better man. It's just too bad it took her so long to realize that was impossible."

"What the fuck do you know?" Frank replied. "I'm a better man than you'll ever be! Better than that cunt, Rachel!"

James took in a deep breath before replying. There was no need to let Frank get him riled up—that's what he wanted. But James was in control now, and he was going to stay in control. "You don't even realize what you had. Rachel is the best thing that happened in either of our lives. As far as I can tell, she only has one fault: she is too nice to you."

"Nice? You call her nice? Why, she..."

But James wasn't even listening to Frank. He didn't need to now. He had confirmed exactly what he needed to know. "Luckily for me, I don't share Rachel's weakness," was all he said. And he cocked the trigger.

Frank stopped talking in mid-sentence, suddenly realizing the full truth of his situation. This man was not threatening him. This was not just some manly power-play. This man was 100% capable of actually killing him.

"No, wait," he said, instead, changing tactics. "Don't hurt me. I... I have a son!" he cried out in desperation.

"A son that would be better off without you in his life," was James' calm reply.

"Have mercy!" Frank cried. "Please..."

"You want mercy?" James asked. "Okay. I'll tell you what. I will give you the same chance I would give any other pest. Start running," he said, and he unlocked and opened the door.

Frank ran, or at least made his best attempt at running. He hadn't gone more than fifty yards before the bullet hit him in the back, traveling through his heart on the way out the other side.

James left the body where it lay. He would take care of it later, but he had a few other things to deal with first.

As soon as he got back to the house—and back into cell phone range—his phone beeped, telling him that he got a text.

It was from Rachel. "Has Frank shown up yet?" it said. "Andy is having so much fun. Doesn't want to leave. Okay if we stay a bit longer?"

James smiled as he typed his reply. "No sign of Frank. Take as long as you want. Have fun!"

Then he made a call to one of his buddies. "I've got a car for you to scrap, if you want it," he told his friend. "But you have to come get it now." *It pays to have connections,* he thought to himself as he hung up the phone.

Then he went to his garage and fired up the tractor with the back-hoe. "We've been talking about digging up the ground to plant a garden," he said aloud to himself. "I think today is the perfect day to begin."

****

A few weeks later, James sat on his tractor—the one with a tiller this time—with Andy sitting on his lap, preparing the ground for the garden. "I know you're sad that your dad never came to get you," he told the young boy, "but I think you're going to like living up here with us. I will teach you how to drive a tractor. And how to build a fire. And how to hunt."

"Can I drive the tractor now?" Andy asked eagerly.

James looked at the small child on his lap and laughed. "Soon," he told him. "But first, you have to understand: a tractor is not a toy. It's a tool, just like a gun is a tool. And it's good to have tools around when you need them. Tools are there to help you take care of the people you love."

THE EXCHANGE

H.G. Evans

Later that evening, they sat alone in their apartment, wondering if they had made the right decision.

Samantha's hands were ice cold and trembled violently as she tried to fully comprehend the ramifications of what they had done. Thomas wrapped his warm, strong hands around hers, bending his head in an effort to catch her eye.

"It was the right thing to do."

Samantha bit back a harsh laugh at her husband's choice of words. "How could doing... *that* ever be the right thing to do?" she asked coldly.

Her brittle tone did not cause Thomas to falter for even one second. His own voice was strong and sure. "We saved our daughter."

At the mention of Emmalee, Samantha's heart slowed, her mind calmed. Emmalee. Everything they had done was for Emmalee. Their wonderful little girl, only five years old, who was at that moment blissfully unaware of what her parents had done as she slept, cocooned in the unicorn-themed room at Thomas's parent's house.

Samantha forced herself to think only of her daughter. Emmalee had barely begun her life and deserved to have the world laid at her feet. Even while in the throes of fighting for her life against the cancer ravaging her small body, Emmalee smiled and laughed, her little heart refusing to be trodden down by something as mundane as sickness.

"What we have done—*everything* we have done—is to save our little girl."

Samantha inhaled slowly and deeply, absorbing Thomas' words. He was right. Of course, he was. The personal cost did not matter as long as Emmalee lived.

"I want her here. With me," Samantha whispered, feeling her hands still inside her husband's confident grip.

"We should wait until morning; let her sleep."

"No." Samantha's head shook from side to side. "No. I need her here. I need to be able to see her, to hear her breathing." *To remember why I just sold my soul to the devil.*

Samantha forced her gaze to remain steady as Thomas looked deep into her eyes. Finally, her husband nodded.

"Okay. Let's go get her."

Exhaling with relief, Samantha rose to her feet, unwilling to wait a second longer. "Thank you," she whispered.

Thomas pulled her to him, holding her tight against his chest. "We'll get through this, Sam. We did the right thing."

Samantha could only pray he was right.

As the next few days passed, Samantha kept Emmalee close, drawing strength from her daughter's pale features and joyful smile. It was that smile; however, that was a double-edged sword. It simultaneously reminded Samantha of why she had done the unthinkable, yet reminded her of how Emmalee was too young to truly understand what had been taken from her. What would her daughter think if she knew what her mother had done? Samantha shuddered; she could only hope Emmalee would never know the truth.

****

The day Samantha dreaded finally arrived, time unwilling to be leashed and held back, a force to be reckoned with. Her fingers trembled against the pearls at her throat, the black dress that once hugged her curves now hanging limply from her frame. She had lost weight, unable to consume any sort of food as her heart and mind continued to rage with turmoil.

Thomas came up behind her, resting his hands on her shoulders as he met her eyes in the mirror. "My parents are here to watch Emmalee. It's time to go."

Samantha merely nodded, not trusting herself to speak, as she slid out from beneath her husband's grasp and picked up her purse. *Just get it over with,* she chanted internally. *Just get it done, and you never have to see them again.*

The ride to the funeral home was quiet. Both Thomas and Samantha were lost in their own thoughts. Samantha's fingers dug into her small clutch to keep them from shaking, though she couldn't help but notice her husband's grip on the steering wheel was firm. Disgust rose in the form of bile in the back of Samantha's throat, but she forced it back. Turning on each other, blaming each other, would do nothing. They had made this decision together. They had *acted* together.

Samantha's legs felt weighted, bogged down by guilt and grief as Thomas led her toward the tall glass doors. She wanted nothing more than to turn and run but could not escape the truth that this must be done.

An older gentleman in a crisp black suit opened the door for them, his demeanor somber and gentle. Samantha idly wondered if those working at funeral homes took a specific class on just the right way to act. She wondered if there was a class on how *she* was supposed to act. Were there rules for this type of thing? What did one do, exactly, when faced with the loved ones of someone you had—

The door closed with a swish of air, and they were inside; Samantha's lungs constricted as she suddenly felt trapped. As if reading her mind, Thomas' hand tightened around hers, reassuring and calm, as always. She alternated between being thankful for his composure and hating him for it.

"Samantha."

Brianna's arms surrounded Samantha, pulling Thomas's hand from hers. She felt the loss keenly, suddenly frantic as she became unmoored from her lifeline.

"Thank you so much for coming," Brianna whispered against Samantha's hair.

"Of course." The words were strangled, hoarse.

"How is Emmalee?" Brianna finally stepped back, and Samantha took a ragged breath.

"Okay. She doesn't really... understand."

Brianna nodded sympathetically, her already red eyes filling with tears. "She was such a good friend to my Roselyn. I'm so glad they had each other."

Samantha's heart hurt. Physically hurt, even as she nodded. "I'm so sorry..." *For more than you could possibly know.*

Swiping a finger under each eye, Brianna managed a shaky smile. "We knew she was weakening. Her cancer was just too..."

But she might have lived. She might have recovered if only—

"Sam, listen."

Startled by the hand that suddenly clamped down on her arm, Samantha stared at Brianna with trepidation.

"I told them to harvest Roselyn's bone marrow. For Emmalee."

Samantha felt her knees weaken with relief. All of this hadn't been for nothing after all.

"I know Rose was too weak to undergo the procedure before, but now that she's... gone–" Brianna's voice hitched slightly, but she plowed on "–Grant and I both agree that Emmalee needs the transplant. Rose was a match. One of our daughters should live–"

Samantha stepped forward, wrapping her arms around Brianna as the grieving mother fought to control the sobs wracking her thin form. "Thank you," she whispered, her heart suddenly lighter and heavier all at the same time.

"Roselyn would have wanted to help Emmalee." Brianna sniffed, snatching a tissue from the box a funeral worker had discreetly placed on a nearby table as they talked.

"She was such a sweet girl," Samantha murmured, trying to shove aside the image of Roselyn's wide, trusting eyes as Samantha held the young girl's hand. She was the distraction while Thomas injected the solution that would stop Roselyn's heart into the IV line. Roselyn had no idea that the parents of her friend were there for more than a routine visit.

"Your family has been such a blessing the last few years," Brianna said as her husband appeared by her side, murmuring that they needed to begin the service. Grant offered a ghost of a smile toward Samantha, his eyes haunted by pain as he led his wife away.

Such a blessing...

Brianna's words echoed inside Samantha's head, chipping away at her sanity. She had to make sure Brianna never found out. Brianna and Grant could never know that...

I exchanged your daughter's life for mine.

Thomas's arm was around her shoulders as he led Samantha to a seat near the back of the room. She was thankful for that small gesture; she did not want to see the small, still face of the girl in the casket positioned at the front of the room.

As the service began, Samantha drew strength from the man beside her. He was a man, a *father*, who would do anything to protect his family. Hadn't she, as a mother, proved the same? Every decision they made was for Emmalee.

Samantha inhaled slowly, straightening her shoulders. They had made the right decision. Their daughter would live, and that was all that mattered. Samantha nodded decisively, though there was no one to convince but herself.

They had made the right decision...

THE IMAGINARY PARTNER

Michael Simpson

Late in the morning on a dank October day, the woman who came weekly to clean Harvey Oglethorpe's apartment found his body slumped on the floor of the room he used as an office next to the desk that had his computer. When the police accessed his files (Harvey's passwords were scribbled in a small white notebook conveniently located in the desk drawer), the screen displayed a Word document that had been automatically saved but never closed. It was assumed Oglethorpe was working on it when he died. The document was totally blank except for the following lines:

As he looked into the room; he couldn't believe what he saw. There it stood. The thing of ghost stories that his grandpa told him when he misbehaved.

Private Detective Oscar Manning and his imaginary assistant, Claude, stared at the screen while a police detail worked through the room, dusting and taking pictures.

"Obviously, the start of a first draft," Oscar said.

"Obviously," Claude agreed. "I wish he'd had time to write a little more."

"So we'd have more clues?" Oscar asked.

"Yes," Claude said.

They were soon approached by homicide detective Franklin Pitchmen who said, "We're finishing up here, Manning. Glad you could visit, and I hope you are disappointed. The medics say it was a heart attack. Open, shut, if you know what I mean."

"No doubt," Oscar said and gave Claude a look. "But that raises the question," he asked the police detective, "of why you were called."

"It's a rough neighborhood, Manning. There's always the possibility of someone having broken in. But everything is in ship shape. Carpet he fell on was a little messy, but that's about it. So, like I said, open and shut."

Detective Pitchmen was a large man who was chronically irascible. If he had smoked, he would have gone around constantly chewing the stub of a cigar. As it was, he chewed gum, his mouth vigorously working the rubbery nugget until a police wit described him as a hippopotamus masticating a rubber ball. From then on, his nickname was Frank "Hippo" Pitchmen. But no one ever said it to his face.

"What do you make of what Oglethorpe was working on when he died?" Oscar asked while Claude carefully scrutinized Pitchmen's face.

"I'd say he barely got started. Nothing like a heart attack to blow your concentration. I suppose you have some kind of pet theory about this."

"Oh, I agree he died of a heart attack," the sagacious private dick declared. "But I believe it was brought on by a sudden and terrible shock. Whether the person who delivered that shock should be charged with murder, I'll leave up to the lawyers."

"Oh, come on, Manning. It was a heart attack. My men are leaving. Open, shut. You're trying to make something out of nothing."

"That may be. But that 'nothing' was in this room with him when he died."

"Next thing you'll be telling me, it was a ghost."

"In a way, it was something more terrible than a ghost."

"And what is that?"

"A relative!"

At that point, Pitchmen was so incensed his furious gasp resulted in his pathetic piece of gum being sucked down his throat. He got into Oscar's face, his eyes frantic like the lights signaling an oncoming train and snarled. "Is that imaginary sidekick you're always talking to still with you?"

"Yes," Oscar said.

"Well, I want you and him out of here in the next few seconds, or I'm throwing you both out. He might not feel it, but you sure will."

****

As Oscar got into his battered Volkswagen Beetle, circa 1969, Claude asked, "Where to now?"

"Where do you think?" Oscar asked back.

"Given the few clues we have, I assume we're going to try to locate Oglethorpe's grandfather."

"False lead. His grandfather is dead. We're going to talk to his grandmother."

"You know where she lives?" Claude said, somewhat taken aback.

"Everyone knows where she lives," Oscar said.

"I don't."

"Well, you're the exception that proves the rule."

"Where are we going then?"

"To the Oglethorpe estate."

They had been driving for several minutes, when Claude asked, rather hesitantly, "Why did Pitchmen say I was your 'imaginary side kick'?"

"Because he can't see you."

"Why can't he see me?"

"To be completely honest, no one really sees you. At least, I haven't met anyone yet who could see you." Oscar gave his partner a quick sidelong glance. "I know it may take you a while to process that."

After they drove another three or four miles, Claude asked, "Why can't anyone see me?"

"Because you're a trans-dimensional being." Oscar winched as he said it. "I know that doesn't really explain anything. It's just words. But it's a start. It means you don't exist in the dimensions that Pitchmen can deal with."

"I don't understand."

"Neither do I, but that's the only way I can talk about it. I don't want to call you a 'ghost' because you aren't. I could say you were a spirit, but that wouldn't be right either. What it comes down to is that you're a being whose primary existence happens to be in dimensions most people don't connect with. You'll just have to settle for that."

"Well, as long as you can see me, it's all right, I guess. I'm not imaginary to you, am I?"

"No, you're very, very real. As real as I am."

"Good," Claude said. But then another thought occurred to him. "Is that why you never introduced me to anyone? And exactly how long have we been partners?"

"Hold on, my friend. Right now, we need to concentrate on this case. We can talk about the other stuff later. Besides, we've arrived at the estate.

As he spoke, Oscar drove through a large stone archway that opened up to display a large field, consisting mainly of dusty furrows and the occasional bit of stubble. In the distance there was a tall wooden water tower with a rusty metal windmill, and next to it was a long low building that could only be described as an extended shack.

"That's the Oglethorpe estate?" Claude said.

"Most of it is underground," Oscar explained. "They don't want to be overrun by tourists."

****

When Mabel Oglethorpe opened the door and let them inside, It was Oscar's turn to be confronted with something to process. "I've heard of you, Mr. Manning," she said, "but who is your handsome friend?"

"You can see him?" Oscar stammered.

"Well," Mabel declared, smiling broadly, "he seems a trifle modest but that don't make him invisible. What are you called, son?" she said, addressing Claude.

"Claude, ma'am."

"And your last name?"

Claude looked to Oscar, but Oscar just shrugged. The old woman caught the exchange and quickly said, "Well, I guess it don't matter. What do we need last names for anyway? We're all friends here. Never did like my husband's family name much anyway. Kids used to tease him when he was a boy, called him Ogre Throwup. I almost didn't marry him because of that name, but I've gotten used to it. Please sit."

She sat on a large stuffed chair and had them sit on a couch that had seen better days, its age disguised somewhat by the colorful Navajo blanket that covered it.

"I can offer you clear spring water, but that's about it," she said, and when Oscar declined, she looked at Claude before she continued. "I gather you're here to talk about my grandson's death?"

"Yes," Oscar said. "We wanted to ask you about the writing..." Here he hesitated. "The writing Harvey was doing when he died."

"Harvey was always writing. Never could get anyone interested. He just wasn't much good at telling stories. Now, my husband, his grandpa, he could tell stories."

"Your grandson had started a story when he..." Oscar began.

"When he had his heart attack, you mean?" Even though she spoke softly, Oscar felt uneasy around the old woman. There was something about her eyes; there was a brightness and animation in them that clashed with her heavily wrinkled face. It was almost as if the old face were a mask and there was a youthful actress behind it. Oscar looked to see if Claude shared that unease, but his partner seemed quite relaxed and delighted with the situation. *Of course,* Oscar said to himself, *it's because she can see him.* But she not only saw him, she talked to him.

"You're awfully quiet, young man. Why don't you tell me what you two are getting at."

"Well, we have a theory, Oscar and me, that your grandson was scared into having a heart attack. And we think the story he started to write is a clue because he mentioned being scared by ghost stories his grandfather told him when he behaved badly. And we were wondering if you remembered any of those stories and what kind of effect that had on Harvey when he was a boy."

Oscar had never heard Claude say so much all at once and talk so breathlessly.

The old woman laughed. "Well, well, that's quite a mouthful. It seems outlandish to me—hard to believe people can really be scared to death—but I know what kind of stories my husband was capable of telling, and he used to tell real scary ones. Made them up on the spot. And, of course, they'd be sitting around the campfire and it'd be dark and he'd talk about all the creatures that were out there only waiting to grab boys who'd been bad. The dark made a lot of difference. People's imaginations can go kinda wild when there's not enough light around to see clearly. Are you sure you wouldn't like some water? I've got some chips in the pantry, store-bought, and not much to talk about."

"That's fine," Oscar said, but Claude suddenly chimed in, "I'd like some."

"Fine," the old woman said and disappeared into the kitchen.

While she was gone, Oscar whispered to Claude, "Don't you think there's something strange about her?"

"No, I really like her. She saw me, Oscar, I mean she really saw me."

"I don't like it," Oscar said. "And I think we should leave as soon as possible. It's already getting dark."

Oscar seemed almost giddy. "What's the matter, partner, you afraid of ghosts?

****

When Mabel Oglethorpe returned she brought a bottle of wine along with the chips. She poured herself some and offered it to the two men. Deferring to Oscar, Claude declined.

The old woman settled in her chair and, after a few sips, also settled in a long talk about her husband. "He was a strange one, all right. Even though he was a scientist, he was fascinated with ghost stories. He would talk about how quantum physics... What did he say...? He said that it supplied 'a theoretical basis for the existence of ghosts.' Me, I have my own theories. But he took an almost perverse delight in tormenting little Harvey. I remember one night out camping... after that night, I told him he had to stop. It was just supposed to be him and Harvey out there, but he told me to come out after it was dark and he thought it would be funny to give him a real scare, make him think there was a real ghost out there. When he got to a certain point in the story I was supposed to jump out of the darkness wearing one of those Japanese masks he picked up when he was in Japan. When I look back on it, it was a terrible thing to do to poor Harvey. But considering what he grew up to become, maybe..."

Since she had settled into a silence, Oscar was surprised to hear Claude ask a question.

"You said you had your own theories about ghosts, Mrs. Oglethorpe?"

"Call me Mabel."

"So you have your own theories... Mabel? Can you let me know what they are?"

"Not really mine, but it's what the Japanese people think. I first heard it from my husband, but he didn't set much stock about it. But I studied it some, and it seems to explain things as well as anything does. At least to my tastes. You see, the Japanese believe that any strong emotion, and we're always talking about jealousy here, if it was strong enough it generated a spirit that had to act on that emotion. That's what ghosts were. Sort of super-charged emotions. But they believed ghosts weren't necessarily dead people. A living person could generate a ghost if the emotion was strong enough." Here she laughed. "Of course, it was always jealous women who created these ghosts. They could go anywhere and attack the person they were jealous of—even kill them.

****

The overcast day had turned into a deep, dark starless night by the time Oscar and Claude drove back to the city.

"Well, what do you think, Claude?" Oscar finally asked.

"About what?"

"About Harvey Oglethorpe's death. I think his grandmother was somehow responsible. Remember all her talk about strong emotions and ghost spirits from the living people being able to travel great distances to kill people."

"I wasn't thinking about that."

"What were you thinking about?"

"I was thinking that I was a ghost." There was a tense resignation in Claude's voice.

"Why? Because people can't see you?

"Mabel saw me. She knew I was a ghost, but she saw me. And..."

"What?" Oscar asked impatiently.

"I just need to figure out where I came from. And why... what strong emotion..."

"Now's not the time to go into that."

"You said you would explain."

"Not now, Claude."

For a long time, the only sound was the churn of the car engine and the wind buffeting the car as it sped down the road.

"Oscar," Claude finally asked. "What happened to the partner you had before me?"

"That was a long time ago," Oscar said.

"I don't think so. What was his name?"

"What does it matter?"

"I guess it doesn't matter, but I think I know. How did he die?"

"It was an accident."

"I know better. You betrayed him. I can feel it now."

There was another long silence. The headlights from approaching cars flickered sporadically, revealing the inside of the small Volkswagen. There was only one person visible in the car. He had a grotesque expression on his face and the car suddenly swerved erratically and ran off the road.

When the driver of the approaching car was questioned by the police he said it was almost as if the man was having a stroke of some kind or a heart attack. The coroner later confirmed that Oscar Manning had died of a heart attack.

The Night's Mare

Chelsea Gouin

The clink of the hooves,
The scratch of claws,
The choking darkness.

The time has come
I cannot escape
Drowning in the midnight air.

Writhing in the sweat-soaked sheets,
Trying to hide from my mind's cage.
Trapped in the terror.

Minions of the night crawl from below
The servants from the abyss follow.
Creeping, Crawling, Crying

A scream sticks in my throat,
Eyes wide in captivated fear
Helpless to escape.

And the Night's Mare
Swoops in...
Carrying His victim

...away.

THE ROOM

H.G. Evans

Bought by a street vendor and weightless with the carefree abandon only youth and copious amounts of alcohol can bring, the dress now hung heavily on her slight frame.

All buoyancy was gone, the cheerful airiness of its folds now hanging limp with damp and sand. Her mind scrambled to remember, to understand the dread weighing forcefully on her shoulders.

What had brought her here, to this moment? On the beach, wet, dawn breaking over the horizon. Alone.

She wasn't supposed to be alone.

She staggered through the sand, granules clinging to her feet, collecting and weighing down the hem of her dress. Her legs trembled with fatigue, but her mind could not recognize the reason for the exhaustion permeating her body.

Failing to lift her foot high enough to clear the sand, her ankle twisted, her leg folding beneath her until she fell to one knee. She stayed there, motionless, panting from the exertion and wondering if it would be the worst thing if she simply lay down on the beach and allowed the breeze to carry sand over her body, rendering her invisible.

For some reason she couldn't comprehend, the thought of disappearing didn't alarm her. Rather, it felt... comforting.

"Miss? Miss, are you okay?"

Her head swiveled as if in slow motion and stared blankly at the man coming toward her. He was only a few years older than her twenty-five, his face handsome, body muscular under his t-shirt and board shorts but not overly so. His feet were bare of shoes or sandals and cut effortlessly through the sand. Her gaze shifted to her own feet peeking out from beneath the hem of her water-logged dress and declared them traitorous.

"Miss? What's your name?"

He was beside her now, one warm hand beneath her elbow, supporting her. She gazed up at him without comprehension. Name? He wanted to know her name? She grappled for purchase within her mind, the area that should hold the information she looked for oddly blank. Then, suddenly, it was there.

"Sadie."

That warm, strong hand now propelled her forward, through the loose and shifting sand and up to the boardwalk.

"Sadie, I'm Patrick. Are you okay? Are you alone?"

A stool suddenly materialized beneath Sadie, a smooth and worn wood bar top beside her. She didn't remember Patrick leading her there, didn't remember him supporting her as she clambered up onto the round seat.

Was she okay? Was she alone? Sadie didn't know how to answer that. She was very much alone, obviously, but despite the oddly blank slate of her mind, she knew she shouldn't be. Was she okay? Physically, it appeared as if she was. Emotionally, Sadie was a wreck.

"I... I should be with someone," she finally stammered, looking around as if she would find them hiding behind the worn wood of the bar or the tables and chairs extending over the small patio. "With... people," Sadie amended carefully.

She had come to Cancun with more than one person, she was sure of it. Three others? Possibly. Sadie vaguely remembered feeling part of a couple... a couples' trip? It had a ring of truth to it.

"Do you know where they are?" Patrick was looking at her closely, concern marring his tanned features. A lock of dark hair fell over his brow in a way that felt oddly familiar.

Sadie thought about Patrick's question. She felt as if she *did* know where the other people... friends?... in her group were, but the answer would not come forth in her mind. Finally, Sadie shook her head, not sure what else to do.

"Do you know where we are?" The lines of Patrick's face had deepened.

"Cancun," Sadie whispered; that answer, at least, came easily.

Relief relaxed Patrick's expression slightly. "Yes. Good." He looked over the bar, then slid from his perch. "Look, I'm going to get you a shot of whiskey, okay? It's supposed to be good for shock."

Sadie didn't argue, her gaze really taking in their surroundings for the first time. "Should we be here?" she asked, noting the vacant beach, the sun still hovering just over the horizon. The small bars and huts along the boardwalk stood empty, many shuttered as they waited for the sun, for a more acceptable time to be consuming alcohol than dawn.

"Don't worry, I know the owner," Patrick said, winking across the bar before flicking his gaze upward.

Sadie's eyes followed, resting on a wooden sign that read *Flannigan's Bar*. That wasn't helpful.

Patrick laughed suddenly, and Sadie flushed as she realized she had said the words aloud.

"My last name is Flannigan," Patrick said, sliding the aforementioned shot of whiskey across the bar toward Sadie. "My great-grandparents started this bar, if you can believe it."

"Right now, I can believe just about anything," Sadie muttered. *Where had that thought come from?* Sadie tossed the shot back, relishing the burn as it traveled from her throat to her stomach and settled there.

One of Patrick's eyebrows rose in question, but he didn't comment. For which Sadie was extremely thankful.

"So. Since we're confident we aren't going to get arrested—"

Glad you're *confident,* Sadie thought.

"—why don't you tell me about these other... people... you mentioned?"

I wish I could, Sadie thought ruefully. Unfortunately, that portion of her memory was alarmingly blank.

Patrick seemed to read her mind, sliding another shot of whiskey across the bar, followed by a glass of water. "Take it slow. Relax, let the whiskey do its thing. It will all come back in time."

Sadie tossed back the second shot like it was water sitting in a glass a few inches from her hand. As it burned a path down her throat, Sadie was accosted by flashes of memory.

A blonde-haired girl laughing as they clung to each other, drunk. Kisses in moonlight, feet flirting with ocean waves with a wavy-haired, muscular man beside her. The blonde with her arm slung around a man with impish green eyes as he chanted for Sadie to chug the drink in her hand, then providing another like magic once she complied.

My friends, Sadie thought, relief mixed with unease washing through her. "Lauren," Sadie said quietly, more to herself than to Patrick. "Her boyfriend Marcus. And... my boyfriend. Jeff."

Patrick leaned his forearms on the bar, nodding encouragement. "Good. That's good. Do you remember where you were with them last?"

Sadie pinched the bridge of her nose, head pounding as she tried to recall more. "We were at a bar... farther inland." Flashes of light, a pulsing beat, Lauren's laughing face, Jeff's hands on her waist... "Jo... Jojo's?" Sadie asked it like a question, still not able to latch firmly onto any one memory before it slipped through her mind and disappeared.

Patrick's brow furrowed. "Jolynn's Tavern?"

Slapping the bar in triumph, though the victory wasn't hers, Sadie jabbed her finger in Patrick's direction. "Yes! Yes, that's it. Jolynn's."

Patrick grinned. "Now we're getting somewhere." He shoved another shot in Sadie's direction, but she shook her head and nudged it a few inches to the side.

"I need some water."

Now that she was remembering things, she didn't want alcohol to dampen or distort the memories. Patrick obliged, pulling a bottled water from a fridge under the bar and pouring it into a glass before sliding it toward Sadie. She took a huge gulp, the coolness of the water pushing aside the humidity and heat of a morning barely begun and energizing her brain.

Another image slithered across Sadie's consciousness, this one shadowed, incomplete. She frowned down into her glass as she tried to pull it forward, wipe it clear in her mind, but then it was gone again; except for one small piece of knowledge that lingered.

"Hey, why the long face? You're doing great. At this rate, we'll find your friends before breakfast."

Sadie barely heard, her thoughts spinning that one piece of new information over and over in her mind. "Marcus. He... introduced us to someone."

Patrick's brow furrowed to match Sadie's own frown. "At Jolynn's? Another vacationer?"

Sadie shook her head. "No. An islander." She wasn't sure how she knew that, but she did. Another gulp finished off her water, and Sadie gestured for a refill.

Pulling another water from beneath the bar, Patrick's expression was thoughtful. "How did Marcus know him then?"

"He must have met him at the bar." No, that didn't sound right. Sadie lifted the glass to her cheek and pressed it there, relishing the cool condensation against her skin. "No. No, Marcus and Lauren met him during their snorkeling excursion."

"Another snorkeler?" Patrick's voice sounded skeptical.

Sadie shook her head. "The guide. He was the guide."

Patrick nodded slowly. "Okay. Okay, then we should be able to look up the company and who was working that day, find out who this guy is." He looked closely at Sadie. "And he showed up at the bar you guys were at last night?"

One shoulder lifted and fell. "Showed up or was already there. Marcus saw him when he went to the bar to get more drinks, brought him over to me and Lauren."

"What happened then?"

Sadie frowned, scouring her mind for that elusive detail. It was frustrating how some details came back so easily and clearly while others had to be pulled from her consciousness.

"Take your time, Sadie. It will come."

Patrick took a large gold coin out of his pocket and spun it on the smooth bar top. Sadie stared at it, mesmerized, as the coin flashed in the rising sun. It was the size of an American half dollar, and something about that flashing orb nudged at Sadie's mind. But it was gone before she could grab hold. One thought, however, lodged into place and wouldn't budge.

"We don't, though."

Patrick leaned his arms on the bar, ignoring the still-spinning coin and focusing on Sadie instead. "Don't what?"

"Have time." Sadie's eyes lifted to meet Patrick's gaze, dread rising suddenly in her chest. "We don't have time. I need to figure this out. Now."

Somehow, she knew this with certainty. She needed to find Jeff, Lauren, and Marcus *soon*, or something horrible was going to happen.

Patrick didn't question Sadie, just nodded in acceptance and grew even more serious. "Okay, then, let's think this through. Marcus brought this guy over to you and Lauren. Do you know his name?"

Sadie shook her head in frustration. "No. I don't remember." Maybe that shot wasn't such a bad idea after all. She grabbed it and slung it back, following it with a swallow of water.

"Do you remember what you guys all talked about?"

"Um..." Sadie bit her lower lip, eyes squinting closed as she tried to reach past the haze clouding her mind. It struck her then that, though she could picture the faces of Jeff, Lauren, and Marcus, the man Marcus introduced them too remained faceless, a dark void where his head should be. Why couldn't she remember *his* face?

Sadie's head began to throb as she tried to push out images and words that wanted to remain hidden. She wished she could just turn back the clock to before they went to Jolynn's Tavern, before Marcus brought over that faceless man. Sadie's instincts told her that he had everything to do with this situation and the dread rising inside her. If they could go back... if they could escape to before they met him—

"That's it!" Sadie straightened on the stool, adrenaline shooting through her veins.

Patrick's hand closed around the spinning coin, stopping its motion with an almost violent clench of his fingers. "You remembered something? What is it?" His eyes sparked, and Sadie could see the same adrenaline flooding her body take hold of him as well.

"Escape." Sadie's palm slapped down on the bar. "An *escape room*."

Patrick's brow furrowed in confusion. "Come again? I don't get it."

Sadie was so excited she could barely get the words out. "This guy, the guy Marcus brought over at Jolynn's. He was manager or owner or something of one of those escape rooms."

At Patrick's unchanging look of bewilderment, Sadie sighed. "One of those rooms where you get 'locked in,'" she curled the first two fingers of each hand in air quotes around *locked in*—everyone knew you weren't really *locked in*. Lawyers would have a field day with *that*. "You have to complete a series of puzzles to unlock the door and get out. But it's timed, usually an hour or so." She wasn't sure why that was important, but she threw it in anyway for good measure.

Sadie was ecstatic; she had remembered something that, like the escape room, would be the key to this whole mystery. She was sure of it. Yet Patrick's perplexed expression didn't change.

"Sadie..." His voice trailed off hesitantly, and Sadie felt her stomach drop somewhere down toward her bare, sandy toes. Still clutching the coin in one hand, Patrick reached out with the other and laid it overtop

Sadie's hand, now clenched into a defensive fist. "There aren't any escape rooms, or puzzle rooms, or whatever they are, here on the island."

Head shaking in denial, Sadie pulled her hand out from under Patrick's. "Maybe we went to the mainland then. I mean, Cancun is always up on the latest trends. The mainland would have one." A sudden thought had her eyes widening in satisfaction. "That's why I'm wet. I must have fallen off the ferry or something and managed to swim to shore."

Even as the words left her mouth, Sadie realized how flawed that logic was. If she had fallen off the ferry, there would have been search parties, boats out looking for her, people swarming the shores to help find the missing woman who was dumb enough to fall off a boat.

But the water remained quiet, the waves gently lapping the shore in uninterrupted rhythm. The shore remained undisturbed by shuffling, frantic feet, the morning air clear of shouting voices or worried murmurs. Sadie's shoulders fell.

She hadn't fallen off a boat.

"Are you..." Patrick hesitated, his eyes searching Sadie's face. "Are you sure it was an escape room this guy was talking about? Maybe he owns a store that sells puzzles of some kind?" A phone appeared in Patrick's free hand, the other discarding the gold coin on the bar top. He looked at Sadie expectantly, ready to start an internet search on whatever she revealed next.

A flash of irritation spiked through her. Her memory might not be completely reliable at the moment, but she was *sure* about the escape room. Images were flashing through her mind at an increased rate that made her heart pound.

"It was an escape room," Sadie ground out through gritted teeth. "I know because I was *there*, inside that room, with my friends."

Patrick's phone slowly lowered to the bar. "You remembered more."

Hell yeah, she remembered more. Sadie's eyes closed as Lauren's laughing face materialized in her mind, the feel of Jeff's hand wrapped around hers so real that Sadie's fingers actually flinched on the bar as if to return her boyfriend's grip. Marcus in the front seat of a Jeep... the stranger's Jeep, as they blazed through the island of Cancun with the wind in their hair.

Sadie's entire body trembled as her mind spilled out visions of a small cottage on the shore, set apart and standing alone, without another building in sight. Unease settled over Sadie in the present, though she had no recollection of that same disquiet then. Alcohol had dulled her inhibitions, and those of her friends, the exhilaration of being free from daily obligations and on *vacation* in *Cancun*...

There had not been one spark of apprehension about the secluded cottage or about the owner—a stranger to them all, no matter how friendly and likable he seemed. A stranger whose face still would not come into focus despite Sadie's efforts.

"Sadie?"

She jerked in surprise as Patrick's warm hand touched hers tentatively. Her eyes flew open, her chest heaved with the revelations laid before her. Yet there was still so much more to remember.

"He took us to his cottage. Out in the middle of nowhere. But it was on the beach." Sadie looked at

Patrick expectantly, but his expression didn't light up with excitement at her revelation like she had hoped it would.

"There are a lot of secluded cottages on the island, Sadie."

"Of course there are," she muttered, then took another swig of water. The coolness of the liquid was refreshing, sweat beading on her forehead as the rising sun warmed the beach to borderline uncomfortable levels.

"Don't get discouraged," Patrick said quickly. "You're doing great. Every detail is important."

Sadie didn't bother to answer. Was she imagining the condescension in his tone, or was it truly there? Either way, it was sufficient to create agitation in Sadie that propelled her mind to strive even harder for the truth.

"What else do you remember?" Patrick picked up his gold coin, absently sending it spinning on the bar again.

Sadie closed her eyes against the flashing orb and forced it back to that cottage on the beach. Though something inside her resisted, as if cautioning her that she really did not want to know the truth...

Pushing the premonition aside, Sadie bore down with her mind.

"...design escape rooms for a company on the mainland. They all come to fruition right here in this cottage, tested and endorsed by islanders such as yourselves before being given the final seal of approval by the company."

Sadie felt more than saw the stranger's smile, his face still shrouded in mystery.

"This one is still in the testing phase. You guys want to give it a shot?"

"This is so awesome," Lauren squealed in Sadie's ear, tequila lacing each word and fanning across Sadie's profile even as Jeff and Marcus whooped and hollered their consent.

Sadie was horrible at puzzles and wouldn't normally choose an escape room as a mode of entertainment, but four margaritas had softened her aversion, blunted her dread at being outed a fool as she tried to piece together puzzles that she had no hope of solving.

The four friends crowded into the small room filled with gadgets and paraphernalia meant to portray a medieval dungeon. Marcus and Jeff were immediately engrossed in examining the rusted torture devices lining the walls. Sadie and Lauren glanced at each other, rolling their eyes as the guys spouted theories about what each tool was used for, each idea more gruesome than the last.

Sadie turned toward the shadowed stranger. "So, what's the story?"

"Story?" The faceless man's head cocked to the side.

"Ooo, yeah!" Lauren said, stumbling in her wedge heels as she spun away from the guys and toward the door. She fell into Sadie's side, then righted herself with a giggle. "These always have a story! Is the executioner coming and the prisoners have to solve the riddles in order to escape before he arrives? Oh!" Lauren's index finger shot into the air, manicured nail stabbing toward the ceiling. "I know! The king's most trusted advisor is planning to assassinate the king and the queen uncovered his plot! The advisor lured her to the dungeon and locked her in and she has to escape in order save the love of her life before he's killed!"

A snicker dimmed Lauren's triumphant grin, and both girls turned to glare at Jeff. Sadie's boyfriend threw his hands in the air and turned back to testing the shackles mounted to the wall. Marcus, however, laughed again. "What is it with girls and needing a romance in every story? Why can't there just be good ol' torture and death?"

Lauren's mouth opened to refute her boyfriend's claim, but a smooth voice at the door had both women turning toward Marcus's new friend.

"Why not, indeed?"

Something about the way the stranger said it made the hair at the back of Sadie's neck stand on end. Before either woman could say anything, the door was already closing.

"Patience, my subjects. The plot is revealed once the door is locked and everything is in place."

Sadie's eyes popped open as the thud of the door closing and the clank of a lock sliding into place reverberated through her memories.

"He locked the door," she said breathlessly, eyes wide as she stared across the bar at Patrick. "He actually locked the door. You aren't supposed to do that."

Patrick's eyes narrowed. "So you knew something was wrong right away?"

Sadie shook her head. "No. I mean, yes, because—no, not at that exact second." The words fell over themselves, tangling together in her rush to explain.

"I mean, I didn't remember hearing the lock slide into place then, in the moment. I just remembered that now."

"Okay..." Patrick's eyebrows drew together skeptically.

"I'd had a lot to drink, all right?" Sadie snapped, her face flushing at the admission. Or maybe it was the heat. Once that sun popped over the horizon, the temperature skyrocketed. Sadie snatched a handful of bar napkins out of a nearby holder and pressed them to her forehead, then her chest, soaking up the sweat.

"No judgment here." Patrick's hands went up in surrender, so similar to Jeff's movement in the escape room that Sadie felt a lurch in her chest.

She shoved the thought aside and watched that damn coin rotate. It was still spinning, defying gravity and logic as time continued to tick by and the gold coin continued to circle around and around and...

"What happened next?"

Sadie's gaze shot up to Patrick's, instantly pulled back into the escape room and the horrors there. Though her mind valiantly tried to shield her mind by keeping the final moments hidden, Sadie knew she would inevitably be led there, to the terror that caused her to wake up on the beach. Alone.

Bile burned the back of her throat, but Sadie pushed it away. She had to face it. She had to know what happened in that room, no matter how much it might hurt.

"Sadie?"

Was that impatience in Patrick's voice? Sadie didn't allow herself time to analyze it, plunging instead back into the memories that were slowly inching into the light.

"He... um, he... after he left, we just kind of looked around the room, trying to see if we could figure out anything or find some of the clues before he told us the storyline." Sadie took a deep breath. "When he finally came over the room's speaker, we... we thought he was joking."

"Joking?" Patrick's spine straightened slightly, his expression curious.

"Yeah." Sadie breathed the word, her eyes once again sliding closed as she desperately wished for that to be true, even now. A chill raised the hair on her arms, and Sadie shivered.

"All right, my subjects—are you ready to play?"

They whooped and hollered in response, Jeff and Marcus even doing a testosterone-riddled chest bump. Lauren had clamped down on Sadie's arm, her eyes shining with excitement. Sadie, however, suddenly wished she hadn't had so much to drink.

"Listen closely, then, as the rules will only be explained once."

"Ooo, he sounds so serious," Lauren giggled in Sadie's ear, keeping her voice pitched low.

Sadie found she couldn't laugh along with her friend; a wriggle of foreboding had wormed its way into her stomach, making it clench painfully.

"This is a test of your humanity."

"Well, that disqualifies me," Marcus bellowed with a sly wink at the rest of the group.

Lauren swatted his arm, grinning mischievously.

The disembodied voice continued as if Marcus hadn't spoken.

"There are four of you in this room. Only one of you will walk out."

The small chamber quieted as the occupants tried to sort through the declaration, make sense of the words despite their alcohol-laden minds.

"That's right," the stranger continued smoothly. "Only one of you will live through this experience. The one strong enough to take their fate into their own hands. Survival of the fittest."

"What is he talking about?" Lauren hissed, her excitement dampened by the humorless tone and grim words.

"Let me spell it out for you," the voice said, having obviously heard Lauren and becoming impatient with their lack of insight. "One of you must kill the other three in order to leave. Only then will the door be unlocked, and the survivor allowed to walk out of here, free to live their life knowing they were the strongest of all the rest."

Sadie shivered, thankful for the warmth of Jeff's arm as he moved closer and pulled her to him. She wanted to leave. She didn't want to play this game anymore. It was no longer fun, no longer felt adventurous.

"Who, out of all of you, is willing to kill in order to survive?"

The question fell over the room, landing with the weight only terror could bring.

Then there was only silence, the four friends staring at each other in disbelief. It was Lauren who broke through the hush first.

"This is stupid. I'm getting out of here. The bar was a lot more fun."

"Come on, guys, he's just joking," Marcus said, though the words carried a heaviness that drowned out the carefree statement, making it fall flat.

"I'm with Lauren. I'd rather go back to the bar," Sadie said, pulling away from Jeff and following Lauren to the door.

The metal handle was cool to the touch, hard beneath the softness of her palm. After a quick glance at Lauren and her friend's nod of approval, Sadie pulled.

"What happened?"

Sadie was jolted back to the present, Patrick's words shattering the reverie. Suddenly cold, she wrapped her arms around her stomach and rocked back and forth on the bar stool, a low moan vibrating in her throat.

"Sadie, what happened?"

It was Patrick's sharp tone, rather than the words, that brought Sadie back to herself.

"It was locked," she whispered, noticing that the gold coin now lay flat on the worn wood of the bar. Motionless.

Patrick fell silent and Sadie glanced up to see his handsome features smoothed into a bland mask. It was more frightening than if he had looked confused or irate on her behalf. The lack of emotion was... unsettling.

"What happened then?" Patrick's question rang with the same banality as his expression.

What happened then?

Sadie shivered, refusing to let her eyes slide closed, unwilling to relive the next part. The part that had abruptly become crystal clear in her memory, the veil pulled back to reveal the true natures of everyone trapped in that escape room. Instead, she spoke as if reciting facts, latching on to Patrick's affected apathy and claiming it as her own so she would have a shield. A shield against the truth.

"We tried to break the door down, tear through the walls… it was like a fortress. A… prison." The word sat like a huge lump in the back of Sadie's throat, but she swallowed it down and forced herself to continue.

"Hours passed. We screamed, we threatened, we begged…" Then they fell silent.

"Did he respond? Say anything else?" Patrick's gaze had sharpened, his throat moving up and down as he swallowed convulsively.

"Nothing," Sadie said flatly. "The room was stifling, the air stale. Hot. We sat against the walls and…"

And, nothing. They had nothing to offer the man who had locked them in that tiny room, their own private torture chamber. And they had nothing left to offer each other, the fight having been drained out of them, hopelessness and despair moving in to take the place of hope. The horror of their situation, that they had truly been kidnapped by a madman and left to their own devices, began to wear on their minds. On their sanity.

It was then that the shift occurred.

Sadie realized Jeff was no longer sitting with his arm brushing against hers. Instead, he leaned against the wall with several feet separating them. Lauren and Marcus were also divided, sitting across from each other instead of huddled together, Lauren's tears soaking Marcus's shirt as they had during the first hours.

Glances skimmed over and past each other, never quite landing and taking hold. Suspicion darkened those gazes, muscles tensed almost imperceptibly as minutes continued marching past. It was when Sadie began to see the other three stare at the violent weapons and devices hanging from the walls, decorating the tables, that she knew.

"We were being driven insane," Sadie whispered.

Patrick had picked up his coin, set it spinning again. The motion soothed her and set her on edge at the same time. The clash of emotions was disconcerting.

"He was wearing you down, getting the four of you to reach the point where paranoia would take over. Make you act and react in ways you normally wouldn't."

"But is that really true?" The question shocked Sadie as much as it seemed to surprise Patrick.

"What do you mean?" He leaned away from the bar, arms crossing over his broad chest.

What *did* she mean? "Do extreme circumstances really cause us to act differently? Or do they simply bring out what has been buried inside us all along?"

Patrick's head cocked to the side as he studied her. Sadie felt her eyes slide from his, unable to hold his gaze for reasons even she didn't understand. Perhaps because he had a way of making her feel stripped bare with one glance. Exposed.

Finally, he spoke quietly. "Tell me what happened next."

She didn't want to, yet felt compelled to unveil the truth.

"What happened next was that I realized if I didn't act first, I'd be dead."

"You really think your friends would have killed you? Each other?"

Was that awe in Patrick's voice? Disbelief? It was hard to discern fact from fiction, the paranoia that had crept into her mind while sitting in that escape room now threatening to take hold of her mind.

"Yes." The admission stung. Hurt. But she had seen it in their eyes, had seen the drive for survival take hold of each of them. She recognized it in them because she felt it within herself.

The weapons were too much. Too messy, too… direct. Sadie's stomach rolled at the thought. She tried to ignore the fact that her friends—her best friend, her boyfriend—were scanning the walls, the contents of each corner, with the same intent Sadie now harbored in her heart.

Her gaze passed over the bottle three times before it sank in. The skull and crossbones, the brown medicinal glass. Poison.

"I got up and walked around the room, pretending to look for a way out even though we had exhausted all possibilities," Sadie said quietly. "A last-ditch effort, Jeff would say." His name on her tongue sent a shaft of pain through her chest.

"How?" Patrick's voice remained void of emotion, dangerously so, but Sadie couldn't think about what that meant. Couldn't think that he would have no choice but to call the authorities once she had purged her sin and laid it bare. "How did you get them to take it?"

"There... there were four bottles of water and four glasses near the door where we came in." Sadie's mouth was dry, and not from remembering the dehydration of that moment. "We just hadn't noticed them before because we were so focused on finding a way *out*."

A muscle jumped in Patrick's jaw. The gold coin lost its momentum and began to wobble on the bar.

"I swiped the poison when they weren't looking. Poured water into four glasses and..."

"And handed three of them to your friends."

The coin stilled on the bar with a soft clink.

Sadie didn't answer. She didn't tell Patrick that, as she distributed the glasses of water under the guise of caring for her friends, Lauren's gaze had softened, the paranoia and steel that had infused them fading under Sadie's gesture of humanity. That moment would haunt her forever.

Would having given water—*only* water—to her friends been enough to help them band together? To forget the madman's "game" and stand strong against him? Would that small action of compassion have been enough to break the bonds holding them captive?

She would never know.

Sadie's vision blurred and she blinked rapidly, trying to dispel the tears. Only... no liquid dampened her eyes. A flush of heat washed through her, closing off her throat and making it hard to breathe. Her earlier premonition that something horrible would happen to her friends if she didn't remember... that they were running out of time... it was all wrong.

Something horrible had *already* happened. Something so terrifying that Sadie's mind had closed over itself, over the truth of what she had done. Over the truth of *who she was.*

"You killed your friends. To survive."

Patrick's voice was hard. Cold. Splintering into slivers that sliced Sadie's heart into a million pieces. And yet...

"I was the strongest." Her blurred gaze rose to meet his. "Survival of the fittest."

"And how does that feel?" Patrick's arms leaned on the bar, his eyes penetrating the fog that seemed to cloud her eyes, the heat that encased her body.

The truth slipped past Sadie's lips before her brain could process what it meant. Before she could filter it into something less... horrifying.

"It feels damn good."

"Your friends don't agree."

Sadie's gaze sharpened before blurring again. The sun warmed her back, drying her dress and making it stiff with salt and sand. It felt as if it was already a hundred degrees. "What?"

Patrick picked up the gold coin and flipped it through the air. Sadie snatched it mid-flight, instinct overriding confusion and inflamed physical senses. As the metal touched her palm, things she had missed all slid into place.

"I never told you it was a man who Marcus brought over to meet us." Her hazy gaze shifted from the fingers curled over the coin and over to Patrick. "I said he had met someone. But you knew it was a man. You said it was a man before I ever did."

Patrick's lips pulled back into a terrifying smirk. And suddenly the faceless man, the "friend" Marcus had introduced them to, became clear.

"It was you," Sadie whispered. Pain seized her chest, causing her to double over the bar, the coin sliding from her hand and falling onto the wood. It settled there, and flashes of that coin dancing through the air and across another bar—Jolynn's bar—bombarded Sadie's mind.

Patrick's palms came together in a slow clap, then another, the sound deafening to Sadie's overwrought senses.

"Gold star, Survivor," Patrick drawled.

He leaned forward, forearms resting on the bar, head tilted so he could look into her face. It was only then that Sadie realized her head lay on the wood, heavy and immovable. Why did her body feel so weighted? And why was it so damn hot?

"Spoiler alert." His voice lowered to a whisper. "You are not the survivor in this story."

Sadie struggled to piece it all together, to understand how she could have forgotten the face of the man who forced her to kill.

"Once I unlocked the door, you walked out of that room without a backward glance. Do you remember *that?*" Patrick's upper lip curled back in a sneer. "Pathetic, really, all this sniveling and upset over people you murdered to save yourself, then walked away from without looking back."

Sadie's chest constricted, her lungs fighting for air. If she blinked fast enough, her vision would clear for a millisecond, then resort to blurred imagery. She didn't understand. She had done what was required of her to live. *She had killed her friends.*

"If you *had* looked back, Sadie darling, you might have realized your friends were only sleeping. That bottle full of *poison*," his voice conveyed contempt, "was nothing more than a sedative."

No. No, that couldn't be right. Sadie tried shaking her head in denial, but her body would not obey.

"After I shot you with an amnesiac—temporary, of course; what would be the point of all this if you didn't eventually remember what you'd done—and dumped you a few yards off the shore for your triumphant swim back to the beach, I returned to the escape room."

Movement diverted Sadie's attention from the man looming over her inert form, a mirage moving closer, then splitting into three separate images. Not a mirage, then. She blinked rapidly. Three... people.

"Yes, you really *are* seeing them, Sadie," Patrick whispered next to her ear. "You aren't hallucinating. You see, once I woke them from their slumber, I let them know what you had done. And gave them a choice."

Patrick trailed a finger down Sadie's hot cheek, but she felt nothing but heat and pain. And panic. Terror unlike any she had ever felt before.

"I gave them the option of turning me in to the local authorities. I even offered them a ride there, which was quite magnanimous of me, if you think about it."

Arrogant prick, Sadie thought, striving to make her thoughts audible and failing miserably.

"Your friends seemed quite interested in that option," Patrick continued, oblivious to her inner musings. "Until I mentioned a second choice."

Sadie felt a tear roll from the corner of her eye and over the bridge of her nose. The three blurred images did not move any closer, but Sadie felt their hatred as clearly as if they were a mere millimeter away.

"That option," Patrick said, gently pushing a damp strand of hair off Sadie's neck, "was to kill you in retaliation for what you were willing to do to them. In return, they would leave my country and never tell a soul about me or my little... game."

Sadie's breath whistled through a tightening throat, her lungs refusing to draw in oxygen, her heart stuttering sluggishly in her chest. Yet the terror remained, sharp and constant regardless of her failing body.

"Guess which option they chose, Sadie?" Patrick whispered, his breath fanning over her cheek as he once again leaned close.

Sadie didn't have to guess but knew he would tell her anyway.

"You see, that bottled water you've been drinking was injected with something especially for you, Sadie."

Her vision darkened, the remaining air in her lungs leaking out between parted lips as Patrick delivered his final shot.

"Now, *that*, Sadie. *That* was *real* poison."

THE SHADOW MAN

Veronica Sanchez

Lilah is sitting alone on her bed, reading a book, when she hears a strange whisper in her room. Lilah glances up from her book but the whisper had gone quiet. She dismisses it as her imagination and goes back to reading. After a few minutes she hears a whisper again, louder this time, but incomprehensible.
Lilah feels the hairs on her arm rise up and stays entirely still, not moving a muscle.

"Hello? Is someone there?" Lilah asks, but the room remains silent. Hands shaking, she picks up her book and begins to read again.

"Lilaaah," a voice whispers quietly.

Lilah feels a cold prickle at the back of her neck and feels her heart begin to race. It's as if someone is breathing down her neck. She glances around fearfully and slowly gets out of bed. As she sets her feet down on the floor, she feels something cold grab onto her ankle. Lilah feels the blood drain out of her face as she screams and jerks her ankle free. She runs for the door and works to turn the handle, but it's as if someone is holding onto it on the other side. She turns from the door and looks at the bottom of her bed but sees nothing. Lilah presses against the door and looks around rapidly but there doesn't seem to be anyone there but her! Lilah stands at the door for half an hour, but nothing else happens. She had already tried to open her door multiple times, but just as before, the door wouldn't budge. She slowly makes her way back to her bed, her heart beating rapidly.

"I'm just going to sleep," Lilah murmurs to herself and lies down shakily. She closes her eyes fearfully, and when nothing happens, she begins to relax.

As Lilah falls asleep, she again feels a deep chill settle over her, as if she's standing in a freezer. Lilah feels something begin to wrap around her chest, she struggles against it, but it only pulls tighter. Desperately, Lilah tries to open her eyes but finds that she can no longer move. As she struggles against the darkness pressing her down, she hears a man's booming laugh ring in her ears, practically stopping her heart. Lilah's mind is hazy and filled with panic as she screams, but no sound comes from her lips. Just as she begins to feel hopeless, she feels the weight lift and, with a scream, bolts up in bed, looking around wildly.

"Lilah? Lilah, are you okay?" Lilah's roommate, Lexi, looks at her worriedly. Lilah glances around once more, her heart racing with adrenaline.

"Yeah, yeah, I'm okay. I just had a really terrifying dream, is all." Lilah looks over at her roommate and notices her tears.

"Lexi! what's wrong? Why are you crying?" Lilah gets out of bed, and rush's over to Lexi. She rubs and pats Lexi's back in comfort, trying to calm her friend down.

"Lilah, I... I was asleep and... and I woke up because I got really cold and I thought the air was on, but it wasn't, and then I looked at you and.... and there was a shadow standing over you, Lilah. It was so scary!" Lexi covers her face and cries as Lilah glances around the room, her hands shaking slightly as she continues to comfort her friend.

"It's okay Lexi, it was a dream. It was ONLY a dream."

THE ÜBEL-NACHT

Christian Collison

Will sat on the edge of the lake, looking out across the calm water. Every so often, there would be a ripple as a fish would eat one of the water bugs that skimmed the top of the lake. Other than this, the body appeared as smooth as glass. The sun was going down, carrying the humid heat of the day with it, and now a blanket of cooler air was being laid by darkened storm clouds in the sky. The humidity still enveloped him, though, and he could feel sweat running down the sides of his face. The sweat from his hands gripping the handle on his pellet gun made a wet mark when he wiped them on his green cargo shorts.

As he had walked along the trail that led from his family's house down through the woods to the beach, he had pumped his gun so he would be ready. Many of his schoolmates had newer BB guns that used CO_2, so they were already pressurized and needed no pumping. Will's dad had handed down his own Michigan-made, Daisy 1894. This was the BB rifle that resembled the Winchester rifles of the old west, complete with lever-action pump for providing the air pressure. Sometimes, while shooting at targets his father had nailed on the tree, Will would imagine himself as Chuck Connors in the TV show *The Rifleman*. When visiting his Grandma, they had enjoyed watching this show together when it came on one of the local stations. Conner's character, Lucas McCain, had this way of shooting his 1892 Winchester .44-40 that reeked of cool, even if, most of the time, he never even wounded any of the bad guys with his shots.

He adjusted his legs beneath him, trying to remain silent. He realized that he was not as fast as Lucas McCain, and because of this, he would probably only get one shot. It would have to be perfect. The sun had completely retreated behind the horizon and left the world in darkness. The nighttime bloodsuckers were coming out, and he could feel them hovering around him as the moisture of his sweat called all the mosquitos within a four-mile radius for a buffet of blood. Their bites were irritating and itchy, and he knew they would feel even worse tomorrow, and yet he still made no movement.

From his self-made blind in the woods, he could survey a huge section of the lake and the beach that surrounded it. His parents had built some wooden steps that led from the beach and through the wooded path back to their house so that they could get down to the lake easily from their sliding-glass back door. Not wanting to give away his position, Will had chosen to avoid the steps and instead walk down through the woods. He had to remain silent and hidden if he was going to shoot it.

They would all stop making fun of him then. Mike, Dan, and all the other boys from *John the Baptist Academy* would finally stop making fun of him. Maybe then they would stop stealing his personal books from his backpack and ripping pages out of them. Maybe then they would stop chasing him down during recess, as a group of three to five boys, tackling him just out of sight of the teachers and punching him in the back and ribs until he cried. That had been one of the worst. His mom had noticed the bruises on him when he had been walking from the bathroom to his bedroom after his shower. As punishment for his fighting and "sinful behavior" at school, she had taken away all of his comic books for two weeks. He had cried himself to sleep that night. Those heroes in his books and comic books, they were his only true friends, and once gone, he felt truly alone.

A soft rustling came from somewhere off to his right. Will held his breath as he lifted the BB gun to his shoulder. More rustling, and his heart was jumping out of his chest. A small rabbit burst out of the woods and quickly hopped across the beach. It frantically zigzagged back and forth as though it knew someone with a BB gun was watching it and may shoot at any second. After a moment, it jumped back into the woods on the other side of the wooden stairs.

His muscles relaxed again as he chuckled to himself. Will let out a small sigh of relief. The night was really sticky, and the moon clearly reflected the sun's light from the other side of the earth, which was then grabbed and reflected by the rippling water of the lake. Will was reminded of something he had read once about a hall full of gold and mirrors. The story explained how the mirrors were all aimed at each other in order to properly fill the room with light from the sun. Now, using this light, the beach was quite visible. Maybe tonight wouldn't be the night; maybe tonight he would not even get to see the Übel-Nacht.

His Gram had been the one who told him the story. She had told him many things through the years, many stories, most of which he had never seen evidence of. He had always passed them off as stories she told to get him to stay in his bed at night, just as her grandma had probably told Gram the same stories to get her to stay in bed as a child. You had to knock on wood while saying something unfavorable, or the tree people would hear you and make the bad thing happen. Cats were never allowed around children in front of her. She feared they would "suck the breath" of the child. Children that snuck out past their bedtime to play at the water's edge would be found by the Übel-Nacht.

Will was a big boy; of course, he had not believed her when she had told him the story. He understood that it had probably been made up by his Great Gram to keep a young Gram, and all the other children from sneaking out for a midnight swim. She had laughed when he had told her so, replying that once as a little girl, she had caught a glimpse of the horrid creature.

"I was not much younger than you," she had said, sitting in the dark, knitting in her old chair as the light of the TV reflected across her face. "My mother and father had left me to watch my younger siblings while they went into the town for the monthly dance. I had finally gotten all the children into bed and asleep. Our dog was outside and wouldn't come in for the night; he just kept barking and growling in the yard where my father's land ended into the lake. From where I was at the kitchen window, it looked like he was barking at the water itself. Hoping to bring him into the house and quiet him before he woke the babies, I walked out into the backyard calling his name. As I called out and the dumb dog still didn't return, I became furious that I had to leave the light of the back porch of the house to get him when I saw it.

"Our dog wasn't barking at the water but rather some type of animal. I had never seen anything like it before, it was about the size of an infant, and it lay on the shore of the lake. As soon as I saw it, I remembered the story my grandmother had told me of the Übel-Nacht and how it eats children that were up past their bedtime. I raced across the backyard toward the house, leaving the dog there, quickly locking the door behind me as I ran through the backdoor. I hid in the bedroom, lying with my brothers and sisters, until my parents came home later that night. I told them everything. My father thought I was being foolish and was angry with me until the next morning.

"When we awoke the next morning, we found our dog floating by the shore of the lake. He had drowned in the night. That dog had spent its entire life in that house by the lake; he had swam with all of us kids since he was a puppy. My father said that its skin had grown soft and dark, unlike any other drowning he had seen before. I knew what had really happened. You promise your Gram to always mind the Übel-Nacht and never sneak out to go by the water... you understand?"

The story had creeped Will out. As a God-fearing woman, his Gram had always made a point not to lie, not to him or his Grandpa or anyone else. There was no one that he knew that was as thoroughly honest as Gram, sometimes almost to a fault. He knew she had seen something and that she had believed it to be the Übel-Nacht.

A light clicking sound came from his left. He realized that he had been nodding in and out of sleep at his post. The sound seemed to emanate from the direction of the Wheyton's house. Mr. Wheyton was their neighbor on the east side. He had been an old charter fisherman and had retired on the lake so he could take his boat out on the water and fish at his leisure as he wished. He had always been a gruff old man, kind of rude. Will had always attributed his gruff attitude to his choice of a life alone with no wife or kids.

ntik ntik ntik   ntik nitk ntik   ntik ntik ntik

It was a weird sound; being the young night just after dusk, maybe Mr. Wheyton was securing his boat to the dock. That would explain it. Or maybe it was some type of summer bug or frog sending out its mating call. It grew a little bit louder yet remained at the same speed.

Ntik ntik ntik ntik nitk ntik   ntik ntik ntik

A ripple crossed the top of the lake; it became a wave as something in the water moved from the center of the lake to the beach in his yard. His hands tightened their already painful grip on his BB gun. He was going to see it; he was really going to see the Übel-Nacht. He would show it to Mike Voleski and would make him cry and pee his pants in front of all the other kids. Mike had asked Will if he was scared right before he had hit him in the stomach. Will had admitted his fear and still gotten hit, then Mike had said that there was nothing he was afraid of. That was when Will got the idea to prove him wrong, prove him wrong in front of all the other students, and make him cry. Now all he had to do was to wait for the Übel-Nacht. He would shoot it in the leg with his pellet gun, which would incapacitate it long enough for him to put the dog leash he had bought from the dollar store on it. Then he would have one of these creatures as his pet.

The ripple got larger as it came closer to the shore. Then he saw… it… whatever it was. It was about the size of his Aunt's Pomeranian, Bitsy. It had appendages like human arms that it used to anchor itself to the ground as it pulled its dark, black, oily body out of the water. There was no head or eyes that Will could see, yet it knew where it was going as it continued to shimmy itself out of the water and onto dry land. In the rear of the creature was a small flattened hind flipper not unlike those seen on sea lions.

Another appeared out of the water, and another, and another. The creatures flapped their appendages and used them to gain ground as they emerged from the night water, all crawling halfway up the beach before stopping as if waiting for something. Will hadn't planned on there being so many. If he was quick enough, he could maybe wound one or two of them, and then he would have a couple of these creatures to keep. Their skin looked almost rubbery in the light of the moon, so he had a good feeling that a BB would be able to demobilize them. He pulled the stock of his BB gun up to his shoulder, closed his left eye, and gazed down the barrel with his right.

Ntikntikntik ntik nitk ntik ntikntikntik

He laid his right index finger gently on the trigger as he brought one of the creature's appendages in line with the sight at the end of the barrel. A bead of sweat ran down his forehead in the humid summer night. Then he pulled the stock off of his shoulder. The creatures had all climbed together into a circle and were now shaking. The vibrations of their body against each other created an indescribable sound, some type of hum, low and almost inaudible.

NTIKNTIKNTIK NTIK NTIK NTIK NTIKNTIKNTIK

The clicking he had heard before was now layered on top of the low hum. The ticking seemed to hold some type of phrase, and now there were no rests between each "phrase;" it just rattled louder and louder. Twigs began to snap, break, and pop behind him. Will brought his gun around and aimed it toward the noise behind him, but there was nothing there. Nothing stood behind him, even though he was almost positive he had felt something watching him. His heart began to pound in his chest as he looked toward the house. Should he leave now and hide in the safety of his home? How could he? The creatures were right there in front of him, they would make him famous at school, and everyone would want to be his friend. There would be no more bullies for him. Now he just had to wound one of these... things.

Still holding his BB rifle with both hands and lowered to his chest, he swiveled around to face the lake again. It was now he noticed it. Silence. There was no sound of a low hum, no ticking. The frogs and insects had even stopped their mating calls; there was nothing but the light sound of rippling waves hitting the shore. His stomach dropped, and his hands felt cold. They were now gone. All of the little black creatures, they had silenced themselves and left; to where, Will had no idea. The gun dropped as he unintentionally released the BB rifle from his hands, and it fell to the ground in a muted thud, the barrel hitting the soft sandy ground. *What am I going to do?*

There was no way that anyone at school would believe him now, especially Mike Voleski. Will's eyes began to well with tears thinking of all the embarrassment he would feel as the stomach punches and other forms of elementary school playground bullying continued. The tears began to stream down his face as he realized that this would probably continue through his school years. There was no hope of...

NTIKNTIKNTIK   NTIK   NTIK   NTIK   NTIKNTIKNTIK

The tapping returned loudly now behind him, sounding as if someone was tapping two sturdy branches together. There was something familiar in the pattern of the sound now. Will couldn't quite put his finger on it, but he had heard this rhythm repeated before. But where? Drying his eyes with his sleeve, he turned around to face the origin point of the sound. He stopped abruptly and held ever so still in the darkness; even his breath refused to leave his body out of fear.

About twenty feet in front of him stood something nearly incomprehensible to his young mind.

The skin was dark and gelatinous, almost see-through, yet with a dark sheen-like oil. Its shape was of a human figure standing nearly six feet tall. As it slowly walked through the woods with silent steps, its head twitched back and forth. The twitching reminded Will of the horse flies he had seen on Gram's farm, heads twitching back and forth as they rubbed their eyes with their legs. This creature had no eyes that Will could see, and as he watched, he noticed the black-boned pincers protruding from where a human jaw should be. The pinchers snapped open and closed, emitting a clean snapping sound that rang through the woods.

NTIKNTIKNTIK NTIK NTIK NTIK   NTIKNTIKNTIK

Will felt the area just below his waist grow warm and wet as terror made him begin to shake. Some of the urine ran down his leg and made a light *pat pat pat* noise on the leaves at his feet.

The creature snapped its head in his direction and bent down as if smelling the air. As it did this, Will could make out the five or six dark creatures that moved around on its back. They were the things he had watched come out of the lake. They now hung suspended from its back, attached to the goo of its skin. It took a silent step closer. The creatures on its back began to move in a frenzied fashion. He could stifle it no longer. A cry came out as his breathing began to speed. In one burst, he turned and ran in the direction opposite of the creature, which took him toward the beach and the stairs that would lead to his house.

He pushed aside low branches, hurdled some growth, and jumped out into the clearing of the stairs. He could hear the ticking following him into the clearing.

NTIKNTIKNTIK   NTIK   NTIK   NTIK   NTIKNTIKNTIK

Without even a look back, he ran up to the back door of the house and started banging on it. The overhead light enveloped him, and he knew that he would be making himself completely visible to the creature, but he had no idea what else to do. He normally would have been afraid of his father's wrath for sneaking out and waking the family. Right now, his father's wrath was the least of his worries. After a moment, the door opened. His father stood there, shirtless in a pair of striped sleep pants, his long blond hair wild, unkempt, and full of interrupted dreams.

"Will, what the hell are you doing outside? I thought you were already in bed. Aww, look, you pissed yourself." His father's tone was stern, almost angry at first, and then he looked into his son's eyes and saw terror. He stepped aside, allowing the boy entry into the house.

"What is it, Will?" Outside, the night was silent; not even a breeze caused a rustle in the woods that surrounded the house. Will could see the water on the lake as it reflected the moonlight like a mirror. The boy tried to open his mouth but could not force any sound out. His dad took him upstairs and helped him change his underwear, and get him into his pajamas. He opted to sleep with his bedroom ceiling light on. His father decided to sleep in the room with him that night after Will began to uncontrollably shake and sob when Dad turned to leave.

The next morning Will came down from upstairs and plopped down at the kitchen table. The events from last night now seemed just like a bad dream. Will's dad, all dressed in dirty jeans, work boots, and a plaid shirt, sipped his morning coffee as he read the paper before work. Will's mom looked angelic as she prepared eggs and bacon for their breakfast. He sat silently watching her.

"Honey, will you look at that?" Will's dad said, pointing at a story in the paper, "I guess they fished Mr. Wheyton's body out of the lake this morning." He began to read aloud.

"'My son Mike is terrified,'" said Mrs. Voleski a neighbor of Wheyton's. He said when he found the body that you could see through his skin and that he was covered in some kind of bug bites on his back.'" On the beach, in the sand, the letters S.O.S were scratched, presumably by Mr. Wheyton. For now, the police are investigating it as a possible suicide."

"I can tell you what happened," said Will's dad folding the paper up and laying it on the table next to his heaping plate of scrambled eggs, bacon, and hash browns. "The old bastard probably got drunk as he usually does while fishing and passed out in the lake."

Will's body stiffened. He could feel a tremble begin as recognition came over him.

NTIKNTIKNTIK   NTIK   NTIK   NTIK   NTIKNTIKNTIK

Three dits. Three dots. Three dits.

    · · ·   ▬ ▬ ▬   · · ·

S. O. S.

THE WITCHY WOLVES OF THE OMER PLAINS

Lindsey Russell

Omer, Michigan isn't known for much, aside from being Michigan's smallest city and sucker fishing every April. However, one unique legend dating back hundreds of years stands out: *The Witchy Wolves of the Omer Plains*. Harking back to at least the Civil War, *The Witchy Wolves* is an old Chippewa legend that has been passed down for generations. According to legend, there is a spirit animal – half dog and half wolf – that protects the souls and graves of Native American warriors. It will attack anyone that disturbs the final resting place of Chippewa warriors. Somewhere along the line, the legend became well-known in the mid-Michigan area and became associated with the Omer Plains.

I grew up right on the edge of the Omer Plains, which is the only place I've ever heard *The Witchy Wolves* legend referenced. It's an area of dense forest and dirt roads near the Rifle River in Arenac County, Michigan. I first heard this legend from my dad when I was around six or eight years old. While it did scare me, I chalked it up to something my dad had just made up to scare me. He loves to tease and is an outdoor lover. I first remember him telling me the story when we took a walk in the woods right in the middle of the plains.

I never put much stock into it until I experienced something unusual myself, and then several years later, so did my boyfriend. The legend is that the Omer plains are haunted by the Witchy Wolves, dog/wolf spirits that are said to protect the spirits of Chippewa warriors. It is a fact that there are Native American burial grounds in the area. This isn't unusual as I've been told that the Chippewa tended to bury their dead near water, and the Plains are cut in half by the Rifle River. There is a newer cemetery in the area as well.

In the 60s and 70s, this legend was spread by high school kids in the area who partied in the Plains. Even when I was in high school in the late 90s, it was still common to party out there in the woods. Well, back in the 60s and 70s, this legend took the form of teenage girls getting scared by these "wolf spirits." Kids from out of town were scared to get out of their cars according to first-hand accounts of this written online, which can still be found today. Knowing when my dad grew up, this just reinforced the idea that it was completely made up... at least until I had my own unexplained experience.

When I was in elementary school, fall meant gathering apples that had fallen from the old apple trees that were in our front yard. It was one of my chores. My dad fed the deer in our backyard every fall and winter and used the apples for deer feed. The entire chore took about twenty minutes. Well, one day I was picking up apples and saw what I thought was a pack of dogs cross the road on the top of the hill. While it was quite far away, the "dogs" looked large and appeared to be just shadows. It scared me horribly, especially after remembering the legend of the Witchy Wolves from years before. The dog's shadows crossed right in front of the heart of the Plains, home of the Witchy Wolf legend.

Fast forward several years. I had chalked the childhood experience up to an active imagination and had pretty much forgotten about it. My boyfriend and I were home for Christmas after having moved to Texas after college. He was driving from my parent's house back to Bay City when he swears he saw the same type of shadows that I saw as a child and in almost the exact same area. He did know of the legend when he supposedly saw something, but he also had his doubts about its veracity.

To this day, I can't say for sure what we saw, but it just made me think that there might be something to this old Native American legend. Today, people in the Omer area embrace the legend and the Omer plains retains its spooky reputation. The legend is very much alive and well. While I'm not exactly sure what I saw, I do think that legends such as that of *The Witchy Wolf* should be preserved. They were created to teach lessons and are a connection to our past.

THE WOMAN WITH THE VELVET RIBBON

Amy Klco

Have you heard the old ghost story about the woman with the black ribbon around her neck? I know, I know, it's an old classic, right? Probably told a million times before. But have you ever wondered *why* it is told so often?

All I know for sure is what happened to me—and, to be honest, I don't even know if it really happened. I'd like to pretend that it didn't—that it was all a figment of my overactive imagination.

What I do know is that it *was* my overactive imagination that started it all in the first place. That and the slumber party.

I was seven years old—or was it eight? It was the first time I'd been invited to a slumber party—the first time I'd been invited to any kind of party. It was, if I am to be truthful here, the first time I really had any friends.

I was excited. I was nervous. I was scared. Scared of spending the night away from home for the first time. Scared about what the other girls would think of me. I was determined, though, to not let the other girls know just how scared I was.

Once we all climbed into our sleeping bags and the lights were turned off, I thought the party was over and it was time to go to sleep. I soon realized, though, that there would be very little "slumber" involved in this party. In fact, I would end up getting very little sleep that night, or for many, many nights to come.

It was the first time I had ever heard a ghost story—
I had been a bit sheltered until then—and I heard a lot of
them that night. They didn't scare me, though. I was, I
thought to myself, much braver than I'd ever realized.

The rest of the stories are long gone now, from my
memory. But the woman with the black ribbon—I was
not able to forget about her. She wouldn't let me forget.

"Once upon a time," the story went, "there was a
beautiful woman with long black hair and dark eyes. She
always wore a long, black, lacy dress and a black velvet
ribbon around her neck."

"One day," the story continued, "a man fell in love
with her and asked her to marry him. She agreed, on one
condition: 'You must never ask me to take off this
ribbon,' she told her future husband, 'and you can't ask
me why I wear it.'"

Do I really need to tell you the rest of the story? The
man's curiosity got the best of him. He waited until she
was asleep, untied the ribbon, and took it off—and her
head fell off, too!

Okay, okay, you can laugh now. I know, it's a
pretty goofy story. I thought so, at the time, too. Not only
that, but it didn't even make sense—how could she stay
alive if the ribbon was the only thing keeping her head
attached to her body? I mean, really? That's just silly!

Or it should have been "just silly." Why then, did
the image haunt me so?

One by one, as the night wore on, the other girls
fell asleep, until there was no one else left awake—
except me and my "overactive imagination." And the
image of her, burned into the back on my eyelids.

As I said, I didn't sleep that night.

And it wasn't just that night. For several nights after that, every time I closed my eyes, I saw her. Staring at me. I couldn't sleep. And I couldn't tell anyone why. How could I admit that I had been scared by a foolish ghost story?

It was the third night after the slumber party when things got strange. That night, when I closed my eyes to sleep, her image was gone. All was black.

"Finally," I thought.

Perhaps, if I had kept me eyes closed, everything would have been fine. It was when I opened my eyes again that the trouble really began. It was when I opened them that I saw her, standing next to my bed.

She was dressed in a long, black, lacy dress, just like they said she would be. And just like in the story, she wore the black, velvet ribbon around her neck.

She opened her mouth to speak, but no sound came out. She made a face, grabbed for her neck, then yanked at the ribbon to pull it off.

I'll admit it—I freaked out. I screamed.

Almost instantly, my bedroom door flew open, and my mother rushed in. Just as quickly, the woman disappeared.

"I... I saw... there was this... and she had... ribbon... neck... and then..." I tried to tell my mom, but the words were all a jumble.

"It's okay, dear," she replied in a soothing voice. "It was just a dream. Just a bad dream. It's all over now. You're safe."

"But I... and she... and the ribbon... and..."

"Everything is fine," she repeated. "It was just a bad dream.

"Would you... could you... stay with me? Just for a while?" I asked my mom. I didn't want to be alone. I was afraid to close my eyes, even more afraid of what I would see when I opened them up again.

My mom stayed with me that night, singing me lullabies like I was still a small child. I don't remember falling asleep, but when I woke up the next morning, I was alone. Mom was gone, but that was okay—in the light of day, I knew that the woman wasn't real.

I knew she was in my head, just something I had made up. Nothing to worry about.

And so, I didn't worry about her again—until I went to bed the next night. Until I was alone in the dark. Until she came back again.

Once more, she stood by my bed. She tried to speak, but nothing came out. She reached for her throat to yank her ribbon away.

This time, though, I stopped her. I reached out to halt her hand, but my own slipped through hers as if it wasn't even there.

It was enough, though, to make her pause. She looked at me. Tried again to speak. Still no sound came out. And yet, I understood what she was saying.

Did I read her lips? Could I tell what she was trying to say by her body language? By the look in her eyes? Could I read her mind?

Maybe it was a bit of all of the above.

"Help me," she said without a sound. "Save me. Free me."

She reached again for the ribbon, but not to try to rip it off, this time. Instead, she simply pointed at it. And I knew, without her saying anything, that this was not a ribbon: it was a collar, a noose, a cage. It was not *her* ribbon: it belonged, instead, to every woman, throughout history, who had hidden her voice from the world, every woman who had traded her own soul for a pretty dress, a velvet ribbon, and a man to fall in love with her and to never, ever ask her what she had hidden underneath.

As I said at the beginning, this happened when I was eight years old. How, then, you might wonder, did I understand all this? What does a girl of eight know about the sacrifices women make to be accepted, to feel loved? The answer, of course, is that I knew nothing. And so I did the only thing I could do at that age—I repressed the memory.

For a long, long time, I didn't think about what happened at all. Like many childhood experiences, the events just faded away from my mind, faded from my thoughts, faded from my memories altogether.

What brought the memory back to me after all this time? It was another "slumber party" of sorts. A camp, this time. A chance for young writers to learn from us "veteran" authors.

I created this activity, a way to think about your life, to explore who you are, and to write about a moment in your past. Like all good teachers, I did the activity with the kids, little knowing what I was getting myself into. I was just writing a story from my childhood, a story about when I was frightened by what was nothing more than a silly ghost story.

Or was it?

What I realize now is that the woman with the black ribbon never really left me.

I may not have understood, when I was eight, who—or what—she was. And yet, when I look back now, I realize that I have spent the last forty years of my life doing what she asked: doing my best to free her, over and over again.

Every time I meet a new woman, I try to look beyond the surface. Has she, like so many women, put on the ribbon—the ribbon that is really a tourniquet?

It starts out simple enough, I know. It's just a pretty piece of cloth to catch a man's eye. Then a word held back, to keep him interested. Then a sentence. Then a thought. Then a feeling. And then your soul. Until, at last, there is nothing left to hold your head to your body—to hold yourself together—except that pretty velvet noose around your neck.

Now, every time I see that ribbon, every time I see a woman who tries to share her soul but can't, I cry inside, silently hoping that it is not too late. Then, I reach out to her. To help her. To save her. To teach her how to untie the ribbon—and set herself free.

Turn Away

Craig A. Brockman

"Turn away, don't look at me," his voice whispered. "Turn away. Please turn away. Don't look. Please."

He covered his eyes, avoiding the mirror, then let his hand slide down his unshaven cheek. Why had he come in here? Oh, yes. To scrape off the stubble of salt and pepper growth from his cheeks. *Take a shower? No, I don't think so. Not today.*

"For God's sake, you smell like an old man," he muttered. *I'm not an old man. Middle-aged,* he thought to himself. "Yes, middle-aged." He paused. "Right?"

He turned toward the toilet but changed his mind and shuffled out of the bathroom, pausing in the hall. Gray light filtered through lace curtains on the landing. Below the window, the cracked and heaving sidewalk edged the overgrown yard. A woman trudged along, an old woman—or was she middle-aged? Waddling, balanced by a bag in each hand. *Such a heavy coat for a warm day,* he thought. Her legs were bloated, spilling over sturdy brown shoes that shuffled on the concrete. She stopped, turning her head, like a blind person, searching, searching until her milky eyes rose to meet him in the window, her gray mottled face, cheeks sagging with a trace of dark secretion at the corner of her mouth.

"Turn away," she croaked. "Turn away, don't look at me, you bastard!"

He jolted back from the window, laying a hand over his chest to feel for a racing heart.

An old song whined on the stereo downstairs. Though he had streamed music for years, the melody crackled and ticked on vinyl. The song snaked upstairs, heavy on vibrato and reverb in the empty house. A woman's voice lacking tone or substance sang some tune that he remembered from somewhere. *Where was that? Where were we when we heard that?* It wavered as the singer's voice grew to a higher pitch. *What is that song? Where was that?* The words were at the edge of recognition as he started down the steps until, finally, the song wafted more clearly from the living room.

"Turn away, don't look at me. Don't look at me, my dear..."

What is that song? I never heard that... did I?

"Don't look at me. Don't look at me. Turn away, don't look at me, my dear," the song repeated. He was drawn into its haunting tune, on the verge of recall. The needle scraped across the record, and a banshee voice rasped, "Don't look at me, damn you!"

He staggered into the living room where the stereo LED infernally flashed 12:00. It was silent. Nothing played.

He snapped his head around, hearing the boring two-tone doorbell. He pulled back the curtain but saw no one. *Ding-dong. Ding-dong.*

"What the hell...?" he said.

Swinging the door open, he was met by a boy wearing a striped tee shirt and blue jeans. The child stood on bare feet, his spiky hair matted and specked with leaves and dirt.

"Trick or Treat," the boy said flatly, his lips turned up in a grin, at the center the vague scar of cleft palate repair. The boy's eyes were dry and lifeless. "Trick or Treat," he said with more urgency, through his teeth.

"Oh, um, it's Halloween? Isn't it September? Or is it October already? No. It's, it's September, son. Good one. Good joke."

"Trick or treat," the boy whispered, no longer smiling.

"Okay, sure, sure. Let me get something for you." *Was this kid mental or what? What the hell? Just get him something, so he gets out of here. Ha. Reminds me of something I would've done.* He smiled vaguely and fingered his own cleft palate repair. Rustling through a cupboard, he returned with two chocolate and vanilla sandwich cookies. They were stale, and he did not have time to drop them in a bag, but the weird kid would have to deal with it.

The kid was no longer at the door.

"Little asshole."

He returned to the kitchen, where he noticed that the basement door was open. *That's why it smells like moldy basement in here.* Since her death, he had avoided that dark place. She hated it down there and had begged him to move the washer and dryer upstairs. But he loved to sneak up to her in that damp and smelly cellar. She would giggle as his hands slid under her dress, around her waist, and…

At the top of the stairs, he inched his fingers along the wall, reaching in the dark to the light switch. Just as he touched the switch, a scrabbling blob dropped on his wrist. A bulbous black spider, its short hairy legs flailing while it lingered on his hand. "Ah!" He swatted it away. It made a liquid thump and slid down the wall, legs waggling.

From below, he heard a whisper, "Turn away. Turn away, William." Only she called him William. She stood in the dark at the bottom of the steps. Like the woman outside, her eyes milky, her mottled cheeks sagging. Her face alone was visible until she floated forward, her heavy knees slowly pumping as though climbing steps. Years of fluid accumulation had left her body bloated and flaccid as though thrown together in clay.

"Turn away, William. Don't look at me. Turn away. Please."

He slammed the door.

Ding-dong. Ding-dong.

"Oh, God. Now what?" he shouted. "Now what?" His hand trembled as he wiped his brow.

The striped t-shirt moved in front of the porch window then the shadow moved back to the door. "If this little bastard tries to…"

He swung the door open. "What the hell do…"

The boy's face had mutated, flat and ugly like those pug dogs. His dead animal eyes were wide-set, and his drooling mouth flinging spit as it barked. The boy fell to his knees and attacked, tearing with underbite teeth through the man's sweatpants into his shins. The man felt ribbons of skin ripped from muscle and ligaments torn from bone until the boy pulled back and howled deep in his throat, sounding like both dog and boy as it quavered. It licked blood from a cleft lip.

The man fled to the stairway, throwing himself against the rail, kicking at the boy, and gasping for air. He had gained several steps before he looked back. The boy was gone, the door was closed, and his pants were not torn or bloodied. No ribbons of skin hung from his shins.

Clinging to the rail, he pulled himself upward. Up to the landing again, back to the bathroom, he splashed his face and rubbed his stubbled chin. *Don't look in the mirror. Turn away.*

He shuffled into the hallway, down to the bedroom. *I need to lie down. Rest. Sleep. I'm dreaming, of course, I'm dreaming. When you fall asleep in a dream, you awaken in real life. You awaken.*

But what is this? Who are these lying on my bed?

A thick, bloated ankle and gray foot protruded from under the sheets leaking dark fluid onto the floor. Two gray bodies, bellies straining stained sheets dotted with flies. A black wave of stench poured from the door, pressing him backward.

"Turn away." His voice whispered from the bed. "Turn away. Don't look. Please." Hoarse and nearly silent. "Turn away. Please don't look."

"Don't look. Don't look at your death."

UNTITLED

Taysia Lucas

Late nights, only to wake with the luminous burning of the sun at six in the morning. Eyes used to the dark suddenly flashed with light. The sound of alarms going off over and over. Don't want to move, for what's to come is too much to handle. The screaming of an angry voice echoes through the hall.

Get up. Get ready. Fight through it. A life of fighting, but this is a challenge. Loud unrecognizable sounds come from a distance.

Only, I'm still at home. It was just pans falling out of the cabinet. My mom is getting my sister breakfast before her bus gets to the house. When brushing my teeth, I drop my toothbrush. When I go to pick it up, my brother appears behind me, scaring me. I slide on my shoes, put on my coat, sling my backpack over my shoulder, and go outside.

The bus is loud, irritating, and bumpy. People surrounding me, and a stranger occupying the rest of my seat. I want to get off. My ears vibrating with every pitch of the million voices. My head screaming, hurting, wanting the noise to stop.

When I get off, we're at school. We wait outside until the clock strikes seven thirty-five. The door with automatic locks opens, and students rush in, pushing me out of the way.

A long walk to class, skipping breakfast since I'll eat when I get home. My teacher surprised, I'm on time, and I rarely am. Only a few hours, I keep telling myself, then I go home.

Boring classes. Multiple tests. Only when I get to my fourth class, I'm happy. It was English, a class I like. The students begin reading.

Suddenly interrupted with blaring alarms with an announcement stating we're on lockdown, but it's not a drill. The students rush to the hiding place in the class after pushing their backpacks under the desks. I cower under the table, my neck cramped, my back curled, my mind rushing, wanting everything to stop. The teacher was panicking. He locked the door. He forgot.

The sounds of heavy footsteps approaching became audible. An angry voice screaming, echoing through the halls. Through the glass window by a door came a bright light into the dark room, reaching our eyes. Pounding on the door, a loud recognizable sound. The door handle started to jiggle, petrifying me.

Sweating, crying, shaking, I tremulously texted my mom, "I love you." I can't move, for what's to come is too much to handle. I can't fight through this. I am not impervious.

We have two doors.

The second door opened, followed by a pair of shoes sauntering into the room. Screams are heard, then silence.

WEDNESDAY NIGHT

E.M. Reed

Isabella Foyer decided that she would be going to the bathroom alone. Isabella, who preferred to be called Izzy, was the lightest sleeper in her yurt.

It was Wednesday, halfway through the week and camp.

Izzy searched for a flashlight; her mother had packed her bag for her without permission.

After many minutes of searching, Izzy came to the conclusion that her mother had forgotten to pack her a flashlight. A flashlight was something on the camp's DO BRING list. In all caps at the beginning of the page were the words BRING A FLASHLIGHT.

The yurt was held up by cement blocks around the perimeter of the structure. There was a wooden path and a wooden deck that led down to the sidewalk. Izzy's bathing suit and towel were on the deck, drying. Izzy put them there so that if she needed to change quickly, she could run and grab the towel and bathing suit, spiders and all.

The path to the bathroom was easy to memorize. A wide semicircle would lead you to the boys' door to the bathroom. If you turned right and walked about five steps, you would be at the girls' door.

In Izzy's opinion, everything was more eerie when it was dark out. Everything was illuminated at odd angles or black from clouds covering the sky, hiding the stars and moonlight.

Izzy's socks and flip-flops were the only choice Izzy was able to change into in the dark yurt. The flip-flops made sucking noises as Izzy walked down the wooden pathway to the cement path. Izzy inhaled deeply, filling her nose with the scent of wet leaves.

The sucking got louder when Izzy started walking on the cement pathway; she started walking the semicircle.

Izzy was a normally clumsy person. Of course, Izzy's flip-flops got caught on the even pavement squares. Izzy knew the path to the bathroom well—being woken up every night for someone to go to the bathroom with a "treadie" will do that to you—so it was odd when Izzy walked into something.

Izzy was knocked onto her butt; the pain in her butt bone was the same as when Izzy had ridden her bike for the first time all summer right before she came to camp. The day after, Izzy was unable to sit on anything because of the pain.

When most of the pain was gone—and the shock—Izzy crawled over to see what she had run into. The pavement under her hands as she crawled told her she hadn't strayed from the path.

The feeling of a man's pants under Izzy's fingers made her freeze. She began to back up, hoping the man didn't notice her touch his pants.

"Where do you think you're going, sweetheart?" The voice of the man was familiar to Izzy.

The night before Izzy had left for camp, Izzy had been watching the news with her dad.

Bob Jenkins was a serial killer. He had been on the news for weeks, twenty-one murders in the span of two months. There was something similar each target had with the person after them, then the next person, then the next...

All the murders were of girls, their ages spanning from ten to seventeen. No adults. There was a pattern with the girl's skin. The color started at pale white, steadily growing darker as more people were murdered. When it reached the point where the skin was almost black, it would start going back, going through the same colors as before until it went back to pale white. It went back and forth multiple times. My skin was a very pale white, the start of a new pattern.

Each victim's hair was either brown or bleached blonde. There was the occasional black hair throughout each pattern.

A scream started building up in Izzy's throat. The scream was about to escape her lips, warning the counselors that she needed help. Izzy wasn't alive long enough to have the scream escape her lips.

On the news the next morning, Izzy's body comes up. Her body was found Thursday morning.

A small but bright flashlight is under the pillow in Izzy's bunk where Bob Jenkins put it.

Bob Jenkins lives on.

PAGES PROMOTIONS PROJECTS SERVE COMMUNITY WITH THE WRITTEN WORD

Discover more about past and future Pages Promotions Community Service writing projects by visiting our website at

https://www.pagespromotions.com/community-service-anthologies.html#/

- Simple Things

- Monster Hunter Intern and Other Tales

- The Portrait of Herbert Losh and Other Stories

- The Gift and Other Stories

- By The Seat of Our Pants: Madness

- By The Seat of Our Pants: Chaos

Made in the USA
Columbia, SC
08 February 2023

11984653R00287